BODILY HARM

A Novel

Deborah Sheldon

Undertaker Books

Undertaker Books
www.undertakerbooks.com

BODILY HARM

For Roomie.

How I wish I could put this book in your hands.

Thank you for being my friend.

NOTES & WARNINGS

The police departments in this novel are fictitious, and do not reflect the structure, operations or philosophy of any actual police department in Victoria or Australia.

Reader Advisory: This novel contains graphic scenes of violence and sexual assault; it depicts stalking behavior, derogatory language, and alcohol abuse; it contains references to child abuse and neglect.

ONE

The windscreen wipers on Cara Haynes's company sedan kept a steady beat against the drizzle. Peak hour on Toorak Road was such a bitch. An hour to get back from work every single night, with her rented house less than ten kilometres away. Ridiculous. The last place she called home, a country town up north, had offered a commute of a few minutes. Too bad the printing company she worked for had gone out of business. Melbourne, with its hundreds of printing firms to choose from, had seemed a good idea at the time.

The music on the radio cut out as her mobile phone rang. It was her boss at Premiere Press, Don Reinecke.

"Hi Don, what's up?"

"Good news," he said. "What do you know about Blackbird Books?"

"Blackbird Books? Never heard of them."

"They're a boutique publishing company that's been wasting time with chapbooks, small print runs, authors kicking in half the expense, that sort of thing."

"A vanity publisher." Cara bristled. "I think I can aim a little higher than that."

"Wait, listen. They bought a lit mag a few months ago and a good one too."

"What happened? A government grant?"

"Apparently a benefactor of some kind, somebody's dead uncle, who knows," he said, "and who cares? Because here's the cherry: I have it on good authority that Blackbird has signed an author who's already auctioned the story rights to a television production company." Don started gasping like he always did when anticipating a business windfall. "The novel will have to come out the same time as the mini-series, assuming the mini-series goes ahead, of course."

Cara's blood quickened. If she secured the book printing contract for Blackbird, the sales commission alone might be enough to cover the deposit on a one-bedroom apartment. After a lifetime of nomadic renting, she felt ready for a mortgage. Not because of any nesting instinct—she was happily single and didn't care that her thirtieth birthday was coming up fast—but from a desire to never again have to deal with landlords.

"Blackbird Books is with a competitor," Don said, "which means you'll have to poach them for me. Do you think you can manage that?"

"I've been a sales rep for a long time. Ten years. I know what I'm doing."

He paused. "I could have given this gig to Martin, you know."

"Yes, I know."

"Or Trish. Both of them are first-class reps."

"And either one would do a great job." Cara sighed. *Just indulge him, for God's sake.* She continued, "Look, I'm grateful for this opportunity, Don. I'm only five weeks with your company, and that's not long, and you're backing me on a big client anyway, so thank you."

He gave a hearty laugh. "All right, that's my girl. We'll talk about Blackbird tomorrow morning. Say, eight o'clock, my office?"

"I'm looking forward to it."

The call ended. The last rays of sunlight gave the evening a chalky cast. A flurry of wind threw hail across the windscreen, kicking the automatic wipers up a notch. In the next day or two, Cara mused, she might ring a few real estate agents. Perhaps an apartment somewhere warmer might be the go, like far north Queensland or Western Australia.

The traffic crept forward, again and again, until vehicles peeled off left and right for the Monash Freeway. The road ahead emptied out, a shining wet ribbon. Cara could finally gun the sedan above walking speed. Not long now until home: a takeaway pizza on the coffee table next to a glass of chardonnay, the space heater turned up full bore, Handel on the CD player, and after that, a hot bath to soak the chill from her bones.

In the street before her turn-off was a shopping centre; a strip comprising perhaps thirty stores, mostly takeaway outlets. Cara found a parking space right out front of the pizzeria. The gale snatched the car door as she opened it, flinging it wide and pelting her with rain, gusting at her stockinged legs and slipping beneath her jacket collar as she ran into the shop.

A brass bell jangled. The door closed behind her on its pneumatic hinge. A damp heat, muggy with garlic, hung in the air. Rain droplets began to steam off her skin and clothes. There were no other customers. Summoned by the doorbell, the short and wiry old man who presumably owned the place appeared behind the counter via a rear door, flapping aside the curtain of clear PVC strips with both hands as if ducking through water. This man had taken her order at least twice per week for the past month, yet he didn't show a flicker of recognition. That's life in the big city, Cara thought. She approached and rested her forearms on the high counter.

"Yes please, miss," the owner said, taking a notebook and pencil from his apron pocket.

"I'll have a small supreme this time."

"Small supreme. Sure, okay."

"Are there prawns on that?"

"I can give you prawns, sure, no worries."

"And I don't want olives."

"No olives, okay. Garlic bread?"

The doorbell clattered. The owner glanced up past Cara's shoulder. Instantly, as if stung, he dropped the notebook and pencil. His bored expression became a look of terror. Fear telegraphed itself to Cara's nervous system in less than a heartbeat. Her teeth clicked shut as the first wave of adrenaline hit. Footsteps ran behind her. The owner's petrified grimace had her immobilised; she couldn't look around.

"Get down!" yelled a deep voice. "Get down on the fucking ground."

Into her line of sight came a skinny male body dressed in black, vaulting the counter as if it were nothing more than a knee-high country stile. The male didn't have a face. Cara's heart gave a lurch. Where was his face? Featureless apart from crazed eyes, he wore a mask, Cara realised, with holes at the eyes and mouth. No, not a mask. A woollen balaclava.

Which meant he was a robber.

This was a hold-up.

And there were two of them: one behind the counter, one at her back.

Something jabbed into her spine, something that felt like a piece of pipe. It had to be a gun. Panic ran in hot needles through her legs, destabilising her knees, even as a slice of her consciousness broke away, fleeing, to marvel that no more than three seconds had passed since the doorbell had sounded. Three seconds ago, in the opposite world to this one, she'd been tossing up whether to buy a side order of garlic bread, and thinking about how nice it would be to get home, take off these high heels and put on her new slippers, the ones with the sheep's wool lining. Three seconds.

The owner began gibbering words that Cara couldn't understand: rapid-fire sounds that wailed and begged. The gun barrel hit her spine again, hard this time, making her eyes water.

"No," she said to the person behind her. "Don't do that."

"He told you to get on the ground, didn't he? Get on the ground, okay? Right now."

"Give us the money!" the other robber screamed at the owner. "Where's the money?"

Then he shoved at the cowering owner with a large firearm, perhaps a shotgun. Could it be a shotgun? The only firearm she'd ever seen was a .22 rifle. That was years ago, back in foster home number two or three, crystallised in her memory as somewhere rural, the meat on the table more often than not wild rabbit shot on the plains. *Eat your tea,* that particular foster mother had always demanded. *You shut up and chew.*

"Where's the fucking money?"

Cara blinked. Her fingernails were breaking against the countertop, her legs trembling. The second robber, the one who had been standing behind her, clambered awkwardly over the counter. The owner was bleeding from a cut on his eyebrow. What had happened to his eyebrow? Things were occurring, but she wasn't taking them in, wasn't processing them. How had a small pizza supreme, no olives, come to this?

"Don't make me ask you again. Where's the fucking money, prick?"

"In the till," the owner said. He punched buttons on the till. The drawer slid open with a cheerful beep.

The second robber shoved his pistol into the waistband of his jeans and approached the drawer. He was fat and round-shouldered, with dark stringy hair poking out from the edges of his balaclava, tattoos of blue stars over his knuckles. He grabbed the cash in both hands, stuffing it into a double-handled airline bag that was now sitting on the counter. How did that bag get there? Once again, things were happening right in front of her but staccato, as if her brain was stuttering like a neon sign: on, off, on.

The skinny robber yelled, "Where's the safe?"

"Don't hurt me," the owner said. "I've got children."

"Open the safe."

"I swear on my daughter's head, I have no safe."

"Bullshit. Where's the money?"

The robber hit the owner across the face with an open hand, staggering him.

"All right," the owner said, "here, in this cupboard. You see? This cupboard here, that box for a pasta roller, you see the box? There's cash in it, lots of cash."

"Grab it, Sammy."

Dutifully, the fat robber bent down, then stood up again with a cardboard box in his hands. He slammed the box on the countertop, opened the lid, ran his fingers through a sheaf of loose hundred-dollar notes, and started laughing—*heh, heh, heh*—in a slow, happy wheeze.

The skinny robber said to the owner, "Okay, where's the safe?"

Chin quivering, the owner shook his head, and gestured helplessly at the box.

On the side of the box in gold lettering were the words: *includes ravioloni attachment.* Cara stared at this for a time, mystified. Ravioloni? Jesus, what was that? She'd never heard of it. A type of ravioli? She focused with great concentration on the gold letters, waiting for the meaning of it to jump out, to become clear to her.

"Last chance, you dumb bastard."

"I swear to you, I swear on my—"

The robber swung the butt of his shotgun. The skin across the owner's cheek popped and moved aside, slipping as easily as a wet rag, to reveal a sliver of milk-white bone. Then blood spurted. The robber hit again, this time across the owner's jaw. It sounded like the snap of a tree branch. The owner slumped across the countertop, bounced off again with the next blow, dropped out of Cara's sight behind the counter.

"Hurry up," the fat robber said, zipping the airline bag. "Come on, George."

"Where's the fucking safe?" the skinny robber said, swinging the shotgun over and over. There was no answer. Each hit sounded like an axe chunking into wood.

"Stop it," she said. "You're killing him."

"Come on, forget it, let's go," the fat one said, struggling over the counter, dragging the airline bag. Then he noticed Cara, still clinging to the countertop, and said, "I thought I told you to get on the ground."

"I'm sorry," she said. "I'll do it now."

She bent a knee. Too late. The skinny robber was somehow already at her side. He raised the butt of the shotgun. She put up her hands. Despite the camouflage of his balaclava, she could see his mouth twisting into a smile. Before he could strike, the world faded to black, and she fainted.

Night had fallen. There was no moon. In front of the pizza restaurant sat two marked police cars parked haphazardly alongside an ambulance, the emergency beacons flashing on each vehicle. The dark green BMW had to pull in two doors away outside a milk bar. Detectives Mick Thompson and Alec Castellano got out of the BMW.

Mick paused for a moment, surveying the scene. As usual, the commotion had brought out the gawkers: up and down the strip, peeking from doors held ajar, scores of faces showed the typical range of curiosity, excitement, distress, horror, fear. To get a better look, some gawkers were out on the footpath despite the cold and wind. Mick stepped onto the kerb. Alec did the same.

"Want anything while we're here?" Mick said, jabbing a thumb towards the milk bar.

Alec offered a doubtful smile, as if unsure whether Mick was joking.

Mick strode towards the ambulance, Alec in his wake. The two detectives, both tall and wide-shouldered, dressed in two-piece suits and trench coats, compelled the gawkers who lined the footpath to goggle and move aside. Mick noted the reactions from his peripheral vision.

The ambulance had its tail door open. The two paramedics were in the deck, fussing over a patient on the stretcher. Blood-sodden dressings obscured the patient's head.

"Excuse me, fellas," Mick said. "Armed Offence Squad."

"How are you, Mick?" one paramedic said. "We've got to stop meeting like this."

"G'day, Phil, I didn't recognise you without a beer in your hand. This is Alec Castellano; new to the squad from uniform."

Alec said, "Nice to meet you. Although, you know, it would've been better to have met under different—"

"Fuck the chitchat," the other paramedic said. "We're trying to take care of this bloke."

"Sure," Mick said. "Quick question: is he going to die or what?"

Phil shrugged. "He got done pretty hard."

"Okay. I hear there's another victim?"

"Yeah, a woman. Shaken up but unhurt. She's inside the pizza joint."

"Thanks. See you later."

Mick walked from the ambulance towards the pizza restaurant. Alec followed. With a nod from Mick, the constable on guard opened the door. The detectives stepped inside.

The pizza restaurant had the standard layout: about a dozen tables at the front of the shop, a clear walkway between tables to the counter, a rear door behind the counter leading to the kitchen, a chalkboard menu on the wall. Non-standard for a pizza restaurant was the blood spatter. About a cup's worth decorated many of the surfaces at one end of the counter, including the cash register. That was just the blood Mick could see from the entrance. There'd be more behind the counter: over the floor, the cupboards, flicked across the nests of plastic takeaway containers.

"See that mess?" he said to Alec.

"Yeah."

"Keep your fingers crossed. The last thing we need is Homicide involved."

Mick glanced around. In the corner table by the window, hunched over as if she had stomach pains, sat a woman. From professional habit, Mick took a mental note of her details: Caucasian; short brown-black hair, blue eyes, probably Scottish or Irish in ancestry; a dancer's body, lean and small-chested; late-twenties; woollen skirt-suit, high heels with matching bag indicative of white-collar status. He lingered for a moment over her dark eyelashes, her cherry-red mouth.

A uniformed officer standing over her was saying, "Did you see any cars?"

"No," she said. "I was on the floor."

"Did they leave by this door here, or through the kitchen?"

"I already told you, I don't know."

Irritably, Mick turned to Alec and said, "What's the connie talking to her for?"

Alec lifted a shoulder.

Mick approached and pushed aside the constable with a gentle hand to the chest, saying, "Excuse me, mate. Armed Offence Squad."

The constable frowned but said nothing; moved away.

Mick pulled out a chair and sat down opposite the woman. He waited in respectful silence. Alec remained standing a few feet away. After a moment, the woman lifted her eyes to Mick's gaze. Actually, her irises were not so much blue, but a soft greyish-blue, the colour of steel. Her lashes were very long.

"Are you okay?" Mick said.

"I think so."

"Can I get you anything? A drink of water?" When she didn't answer, he went on, "I'm Detective Senior Constable Mick Thompson. This is my colleague, Detective Constable Alec Castellano."

She nodded feebly.

"Don't worry about remembering our names," Mick said. "If you forget, I'm happy to remind you. Can you tell me your name?"

"Cara Haynes."

"Okay, Cara. You saw what happened here?"

"Yes."

"Did anyone hurt you?"

"One of them went to hit me, but before he could, I fell down. Is the owner all right?"

Mick smiled. "Yeah, he'll be fine."

"I thought they were going to kill him."

"He'll be home in a day or two. Don't worry about it."

"They wouldn't stop hitting him." She brought the back of one hand to her mouth. "They kept smashing him with the end of the shotgun for no reason, over and over, for absolutely no reason, just over and over."

Mick glanced around to check that Alec was paying attention. Alec, however, gave a tiny shake of his head as if suggesting that Cara was a dead loss. What a joke. How would a greenhorn like Alec know whether or not a witness would prove to be golden? Right now, while at the scene of the robbery, with the other victim's blood still fresh on the walls, Cara Haynes was emotionally overloaded, shut down from shock. That could change. In the safety of the Armed Offence Squad, her powers of recall might improve dramatically. Alec Castellano had a lot to learn, that was for sure.

Mick put a reassuring hand on Cara's shoulder. "Can you come with us, please? We need to talk to you some more."

TWO

It was 8 p.m. on a Tuesday night, and St Kilda Road hummed with pedestrians while trams and vehicles streamed in and out of the city. Cara observed the hubbub, without any particular interest, from the back seat of the unmarked police BMW. A rock ballad murmured from the radio. The detective named Alec was driving. The other one, Mick, who occupied the front passenger seat, had a silvery scar running from his temple to his jaw, and she kept looking at it, wondering how he'd got it. Perhaps she would ask him. But later; right now, she was too busy trying to stop herself from trembling.

Alec turned the car into a service lane and then into a driveway, where an automatic gate opened up. On the way past, Cara glanced at the bronze lettering fixed over the building's entrance: *Melbourne City Police Complex.*

Although she had driven along here many times—the Premiere Press office was in nearby South Melbourne—she had never before noticed this particular building.

After parking the car, they took her inside the complex to a short corridor lined on both sides with elevators. The detectives were very tall. She doubted if the top of her head would reach their chins, and she was wearing stiletto heels. Feeling small made her afraid. During the ride in the elevator, she kept her gaze on the floor. The carpeting had a short nap, worn shiny by countless feet.

"You okay, Cara?" Mick said.

"Yes."

"Nearly there. Just a few more floors."

Then the elevator stopped. The doors opened. People got in. A man laughed and started to say something to Mick, but suddenly fell quiet. Cara, eyes still downcast, imagined that Mick had given the man a warning look, had perhaps inclined his head at Cara as if to say, *Can't you see I've got a victim here?* She felt both grateful and ashamed. The doors closed. The elevator lurched upwards again.

At the ninth floor, Mick and Alec led her into the Armed Offence Squad, an open-plan office with islands of desks all the way to the far windows, the walls on either side broken up with the occasional closed door. The outside darkness had turned the floor-to-ceiling windows into a mirror. Cara could make out her own reflection: a ghostly, white-faced little girl. The cavernous room was deserted except for one island of desks where two men were lounging.

"Hey," Mick called out.

The two men looked around and stood up. They were large. Both wore suit pants, shirts and ties. The man with a paunch straining at his shirt and his tie pulled askew gave a low whistle and muttered, in a voice deep enough to carry, "Here comes some talent."

"Shut up, Bull, you dickhead," the other man hissed, smacking Bull across the chest with a quick backhander. "That'll be one of the victims."

"Yeah, fuck off, how was I to know?"

Cara wished she were at home, doors locked, curtains drawn.

Mick shouted to the men, "This is Cara Haynes, our witness to the Benny Pizza robbery. Get busy and make her a coffee." He turned to her. "How do you have it?"

"Black, one sugar."

He repeated that in a loud voice. Then he said to Alec, "Go help Bull and Stevo."

With a polite nod in her general direction, Alec went off to join the others.

As Mick took her to a door marked Interview Room, he said, "Sorry about that. They can be rude sometimes. It comes from dealing with scumbags. Right, take a seat in here."

He opened the door. The tiny room had a meagre collection of furniture: a square laminate table and two plastic chairs. There were no windows. The effect was claustrophobic. Cara took a step inside. A stippling of small brown stains ranged across one of the walls in a narrow spray, as if flicked from a paintbrush. Her heart gave a squeeze.

"What are those marks?" she said, pointing.

After a moment, he said, "Spilt coffee. Our interview subjects can get boisterous. Why don't we go into one of the offices?"

Most of the doors were locked. Mick found one that was open, and ushered her into a plush office chair. He took a seat on the other side of the desk. On top of the filing cabinet was a potted plant with green sword-shaped leaves. She stared at the plant while Mick rifled through the desk drawers and found a notepad and pen.

"Ready?" he said.

She nodded, and took a steadying breath.

Rather than firing questions, however, he stared at her with a calm, gentle smile. Somehow, the combination of his features—the square face, wide mouth, the nose that looked broken across its bridge—gave the impression that he was trustworthy, or maybe the effect wasn't from his strong features, but from his clear and open gaze. In any case, whatever the reason, Cara had a fleeting desire to rest her head on his shoulder.

Mick said finally, "How are you feeling?"

"I don't know. Kind of numb."

"That's normal. If you were feeling okay, I'd be worried about you."

She gave a faint chuckle. "Well, there's definitely no need for you to worry."

"Listen, you'll get over this. One day, I promise, it'll be a distant memory."

She closed her eyes against a sudden pricking of tears.

He said, "I can put you in touch with trauma counsellors."

"What for? Does talking about it ever do any good?"

"On occasion, yeah. Why not see if the counsellors can help?"

In a flash, the image flooded her mind of that ruined face, split down to the bone. She could hear again the chunking of the shotgun butt. For a giddy, nauseating moment, she thought she might be sick.

"Are you going to catch those men?" she whispered.

He didn't answer. Cara opened her eyes. The detective wore a grin that was broad enough to show both rows of his even, white teeth. Taken aback, she actually laughed.

"What's so funny?" she said.

"You. Are we going to catch them?" He spread his hands wide. "Shit, of course we are. We're the Armed Offence Squad."

They laughed together. The knock at the door startled her. The door opened. Alec came in with a mug of coffee, which he put on the desk in front of her.

"Thank you," she said. "I really appreciate it."

"No worries."

"Where's the sarge?" Mick said.

"On his way." Retreating, Alec closed the door quietly behind him.

Mick said, "Okay, Cara. Do you think you can start telling me what happened?"

Mick approached his crew, who were hanging around their desks.

Bull, standing up and propping his hands on his hips, said in falsetto, "Two men wearing black. I didn't see anything, didn't hear anything, don't know anything."

Bull and Stevo guffawed. Alec, meanwhile, leaned back in his seat and regarded his colleagues with the kind of cool, non-committal stare that made Mick feel uneasy. A man who resisted being a team player was a man to watch.

"You're oh-so-fucking wrong, my friend," Mick said to Bull. "Our witness was very forthcoming."

Bull pulled a lewd face. Before the joking could go any further, Detective Sergeant Frank Ward entered the squad room. Bald as an egg, Ward had a stocky build that was running to fat in his middle age.

"Sorry I'm late," he said, pulling up a chair. "You've spoken to the female witness?"

"Yeah," Mick said.

"Good stuff?"

"Not bad."

Ward nodded. "Where is she?"

"Making a few calls," Mick said. "I've got her in Ray's office. She saw the blood in the interview room and it spooked her."

"You tell her it was coffee?" Ward said.

Mick nodded.

"Righto, I'll get the cleaning company onto that first thing tomorrow." Ward slapped his hands together and looked about at his crew expectantly. "Okay, what've we got?"

Mick said, "It's our pizza bandits, no doubt. Two offenders: one with a shotty, one with a pistol. They had the same airline bag as last time."

Stevo referred to his notebook. "Nothing concrete yet, but it looks like the getaway car could have been a dark-coloured Commodore, maybe a model from the '90s."

"Yep, it's them, by Christ," Ward said.

"That makes two in one week," Bull said. "Cheeky bastards."

Mick said, "She gave us names. The little one is George. The big one is Sammy."

"Excellent." Then Ward said, "Alec, what's the story with the proprietor of the pizza shop?"

"They're still operating on him. They'll let me know."

Ward's mouth tightened into a line. "Seventeen hold-ups in eight months and not one bloody arrest. Let's hope he survives."

"Look," Bull said, wrenching off his tie and cramming it into his trouser pocket, "I'm warning you boys: if Homicide steals this case from us, it'd better not be Nye's crew. They'll fuck it up like they fucked our Kazemi case, the stupid bastards."

Mick jolted a little at the Kazemi name, tightened his expression into a scowl.

"Have you seen that turd Nye's got on his crew now, that shithead from Arson?" Bull continued.

"Yeah, the one with the bum-fluff on his chin," Stevo said, chortling.

"Oh, fuck that. I'm not working with him. No way, no how."

The men laughed.

Stevo, abruptly poker-faced, whispered, "Heads up, Mick. Here's your patient."

Mick looked around. Cara stood in the open doorway of the office, staring at them with wide eyes, hugging her handbag as if clutching a life preserver. Mick walked over.

"All done?" he said.

"Yes. I told my boss I wouldn't be going in tomorrow."

"I'd take off the rest of the week, if I were you."

Glancing past him at the crew, she recoiled, just a little, the barest flinch. The crew was probably ogling her. Bull in particular, the dirty bugger. Casually, Mick shifted his weight to one side, enough to block their view. She relaxed.

"That's it for now," he said. "I might have a few more questions later on, if that's okay."

"Of course, I understand." She gave him a business card from her handbag. "Here are my numbers for work and mobile. Would you mind ringing me a taxi? I'm new to Melbourne; I don't have many numbers in my phone yet."

"I can drive you home if you like. Save you the money."

She smiled. "That'd be great. I'm a bit shaky."

"No, you're doing fantastic. Wait here a minute." He wandered over to the crew, and said, voice low, "I'm giving her a lift in a squad car."

With a snigger, Bull muttered, "Keep it clean."

"Piss off, dickhead," Mick said, which got some laughs.

"How come he gets the good jobs?" Bull said. "I wouldn't mind having a go at her."

Alec shook his head. "You're a sick bastard."

"Aw, shut up, Mario," Bull said.

"Hey! Don't call me Mario, all right?"

"Give it a rest, for God's sake," Ward said, taking off his suit jacket and draping it on the back of his chair. "I don't want to be here as it is, without having to listen to you two bickering like a couple of schoolkids."

Mick grabbed his briefcase. "Who needs a ride home when I get back?"

Stevo, gazing fixedly at a computer screen, raised his hand.

Mick went over to Cara, still standing in the office doorway, paralysed.

"Let's go," he said, taking her elbow.

Obediently, she began walking alongside him. Her behaviour told him she was in shock. A few days ago, at the last job pulled by the same pizza bandits, Mick had attended the scene and found the eighteen-year-old delivery boy standing motionless and unseeing by the coffee machine. Mick had steered the boy towards a chair and, resting both hands on the boy's shoulders, had gently helped him be seated. The poor fucker didn't seem to realise that Mick was even there. The Armed Offence Squad had its own term for this characteristic type of dissociation: the zombie zone. And for a crime spree that had already put dozens of civilians into the zombie zone, Mick would personally beat the living shit out of both pizza bandits the minute he got his hands on them. The thought of how good that would feel sometimes kept him awake at night.

Mick and Cara took an elevator to the basement. When they reached the squad car, he held open the front passenger door for her. She got in like a lady: sitting down first, swinging both legs in together. He drove the car out of the underground parking bay. The rain had stopped.

Braking at the crossover, Mick said, "What's your address?"

She told him.

"I know the street," he said. "Along Toorak Road past the pizza joint, right?"

"Yes, that's right."

He steered the car onto St Kilda Road. Traffic had thinned. The radio played softly. At the next red light, he glanced over at her. The woollen skirt, hitched up across her thighs, showed plenty of sheer, tan-coloured nylons. He looked back at the red light. Pantyhose or stockings, he wondered. She had no visible tattoos, had unpainted fingernails and wore only light makeup, which meant, he decided, pantyhose. The light turned green.

"So, you're not from Melbourne," he said, accelerating the car.

"No."

"How long have you been here?"

"Not long. About seven weeks, give or take."

"Like it?"

"At first, but now I'm not sure."

"Aw, don't let tonight give you the wrong idea. Melbourne's a safe city. You were in the wrong place at the wrong time. It's not likely to happen again."

She didn't say anything.

Mick said, "Where are you from originally?"

"Oh, lots of different places."

He laughed. "Any place in particular?"

"Not really."

"Okay, fair enough. I don't like talking about myself either."

After a while, she said, "Does that mean if I asked you about the scar on your face, you wouldn't tell me?"

Reflexively, Mick lifted a hand and touched his jaw. He could trace with his fingertips the exact course of the scar by the numbness of the skin around it. After nearly four years, the feeling still hadn't come back and he supposed it never would. Similarly, the matching scars on his shoulder, chest and back were numb too.

"I got stabbed," he said.

"Oh my God. With a knife?"

"A box cutter."

He remembered the hotel car park from that day. The suspect had punched him with what Mick had assumed, at first, was nothing more than a closed fist. Fresh to the Armed Offence Squad, Mick had made the typical new-recruit error of assuming that the criminals he'd encounter would be like those he'd dealt with while in uniform: people with a veneer of civilisation and common sense, open to reason; people who knew to give up when caught. That assumption had almost got him killed. The suspect had stabbed him while Mick had been politely introducing himself, holding out his identification badge, calling the suspect 'sir'. If Sergeant Frank Ward hadn't exited the hotel's rear door when he did, and if he hadn't reacted as fast and come running across the car park, bellowing, pulling his gun... Anyway, ever since the stabbing, Mick understood that armed robbers, especially the professional kind, were a different breed of human altogether. You had to treat them like pit bulls.

"Was it someone you were trying to arrest?" Cara said.

"Along those lines, yeah." Mick looked around, and had to grin at her shocked expression. "Hey, no big deal. It's not like I died."

She gave him a wan smile.

They drove in silence for a time. Mick took them over the entry ramps to the Monash Freeway, past Cara's local shopping centre with Benny's Pizzeria—still with police cars out front, the forensic team would probably be there by now—and then he sneaked a look at her. Ashen-faced, panting a little, she had her gaze fixed front and centre, straight through the windscreen. His thoughts turned darkly towards the pizza bandits. Just for Cara Haynes, for her alone, he would make sure to break every tooth in their heads.

He turned into the street she had named. Cara pointed. They pulled up outside a compact, single-storey brick house with a modest lawn out front, and a handful of shrubs lining a side fence.

She tightened her grip on her handbag, knuckles showing white. "Thanks for the lift."

"Any time. Let me see you to the door."

They got out of the car and walked along the driveway, side by side.

"Not a bad place," he said. "You live here by yourself?"

"Uh-huh. I might have to get a flatmate though. The rent's pretty steep."

On the porch, he said, "Do you want me to come in and have a look around? Would that make you feel better?"

"Don't trouble yourself. I'll be fine."

"Are you sure?"

"No," she said at last. "Not really."

She let them both in with her key, and groped for the light. The lounge room sprang into view: two couches arranged around a coffee table; a cheap television set propped, forgotten, in one corner; an expensive CD player against the wall next to the heater. So, she was a music lover.

"No bad guys in here," he said.

She managed a crooked smile.

"You want me to look in the cupboards too?" he said. When she blushed, he continued, "I've driven home plenty of robbery victims over the years, and I've checked a lot of cupboards, believe me."

"I feel stupid."

"Don't. I do this all the time."

While she stayed behind at the front door, he walked across the lounge room and past the table, chairs and bookshelves in the dining area, and then into the kitchen. Once there, he began to whistle, so that she could hear his passage through her house and not get alarmed.

He took his time, searching thoroughly to satisfy a little of his curiosity about her. There was nothing unusual inside the pantry or fridge. The freezer was stocked with low-calorie microwave meals, typical of a young, career-minded woman who lived alone and probably ate out most of the time. Through the kitchen was the laundry. On the top layer of dirty clothes inside the hamper were a crumpled business shirt, a bra with a floral green print, and apricot-coloured underwear. He went through the laundry into the bathroom. Next to the sink lay a hairbrush, toothpaste, toothbrush, plastic cup, towels hanging on a rack, a dressing gown on a door hook, a hair dryer plugged into one of the electrical sockets; once again, what you'd expect for a single, childless, middle-class woman without a drug habit or criminal connections.

Exiting the bathroom, Mick ended up again in the lounge. Cara hadn't moved from the front door. He pointed into the hall at his left, and said, "You want me to check down here too?"

She nodded.

The spare bedroom held a desk and cardboard boxes. The wardrobe contained summer dresses, items of luggage, a tennis racquet, more boxes.

The other room, Cara's bedroom, featured a double bed, neatly made. Upon the dresser were perfume bottles, a saucer with dress rings, and a jewellery box containing necklaces, a few brooches. Two-piece business suits filled most of the wardrobe space. He wondered what Cara Haynes did for fun. On the bedside table sat a lamp; digital alarm clock; a stick of lip balm; foam ear plugs, probably for noisy neighbours; a paperback novel. Just like the bathroom, no sign of any man. Oddly, there were no family photographs anywhere on display. Come to think of it, he hadn't noticed any photo albums in the bookcases either.

Mick went down the hall and ended up in the lounge room again. Cara was still by the front door. He stopped whistling and shrugged.

"Everything's fine," he said.

She seemed to wilt for a moment, and then recovered quickly. "Thank you. Would you like a drink? Tea? Coffee?"

"Water, if you don't mind."

She went through to the kitchen. Her handbag, unzipped, sat on the console table by the front door. The bag contained nothing out of the ordinary. Apparently, what you saw of Cara Haynes was what you got, which, in his experience, was pretty rare.

A few seconds later, she came out with a glass of water. As he took it, he accidentally touched her hand. She watched him with her grey-blue eyes. Over the rim of the glass, he watched her too. Her lips were small but full. He imagined kissing them, licking them. Stop it, he thought. If he made a move on her, there would be a misconduct charge, and hell to pay. Sergeant Ward took a dim view of what he termed 'taking advantage' of crime victims. Mick did too. A traumatised woman was in no fit state to make informed decisions about anything.

Cara took the empty glass from him, and said, "I appreciate the lift home."

"No worries. Here," he said, getting a business card from his jacket pocket. "This has my mobile number. If you need me, night or day, give me a call."

Accepting the card, her look was sassy; probably an echo of her usual self, the one he hadn't met. She said, teasing, "And you'll ride up on a white horse?"

"We work around the clock. We're always on call. Okay?"

"Okay." She appeared sombre again. "Thanks."

He opened the front door and backed out of it. "Keep smiling."

"I'll try. Thanks again."

He shut the door. The latch of the deadlock clicked behind him. As he walked to the squad car, the cold night air biting at his ears, he thought about Cara Haynes and how she might like to get ready for bed. He imagined her doffing those high heels, undressing, combing out her hair.

THREE

Cara twisted her head on the pillow to check the digital clock: 2.47 a.m. The rain had come and gone in torrents all night so far. The rattling on the roof tiles made it difficult to hear any unfamiliar noises within the house, like the rasp of a window getting levered open, or the creak of a floorboard. Oh, quit being such an idiot, she thought. No one is breaking in. She switched on the lamp and got out of bed. Normally, she slept nude; tonight, she wore a t-shirt and tracksuit pants. And now she was going to check the doors and windows again.

As she made her way through the house, she switched on every light. The folds and bulges of the curtains made her heart jangle against her ribs. Even while berating herself for acting crazy, she poked at curtains with a broom handle, half-expecting to find someone lurking there, someone wearing a balaclava.

Where's the fucking safe?

No, enough of that. She forced her thoughts along a different track.

First thing tomorrow, she would contact the real estate agent to arrange for a locksmith. Every window needed a keyed latch. If she offered to pay for that herself, surely the landlord wouldn't object. Then she would contact her insurance company. The extra security might get her a discount on her contents insurance. Yes, that course of action sounded very sensible. And after making those calls, she would walk to the shopping centre and retrieve her car.

She closed her eyes against a sudden vision of white bone.

Goddamn it.

She put down the broom, went to the CD player, and put on her favourite Bach album, a compilation of chorale preludes. The volume needed cranking to lift the music above the sound of rain, which meant she had no chance whatsoever of detecting strange noises, but that was good because at some point she had to stop indulging this panic attack.

Shit.

Exhausted, she dropped onto one of the couches.

If only she had someone to call.

There was no one, of course. Moving around so much growing up, shuttled by welfare agencies and government departments from one foster home to another, meant she didn't have any school friends. The last family she'd lived with were the Lysaghts, and she hadn't spoken to them since they'd kicked her out on her eighteenth birthday; the same day that the government had kicked her out of the foster-care system. Her address book contained only business acquaintances. Over the years, the occasional colleague had tried to befriend her and without fail, whether male or female, had wanted to share personal details and secrets. But if friendship required laying herself bare, Cara just couldn't do it. Obviously, she lacked something critical in her makeup, that special whatever-it-was quality that would have enabled her to connect with others in a meaningful way. She thought of Neil, her most recent boyfriend. During their final argument, he had accused her of playing mind games, convinced that her standoffishness was a calculated ploy to make him needy, insecure.

Cara put her face in her hands. God, if only she had someone to call.

Maybe she could ring Neil anyway. It had been a few months. He might not be angry now. Or maybe she could ring that detective, Mick Thompson.

She went over to the console table by the front door and picked up his business card. It had a straightforward design: plain white with navy lettering, the flipside blank. She tapped the edge of the card against her chin, considering. While he'd been standing right here a few hours ago, drinking that glass of water, a moment had passed between them. She had felt it in the tide of her blood, in the singing current that had run through the nerves in her belly. He wanted her. She thought about that, and about the width of his shoulders, the largeness of his hands; those blue and unblinking eyes.

Should she call Mick?

Bach surged from the speakers, the chords swelling and dropping, rolling on invisible waves. Mick's mobile phone number stood out in raised type on the white card, the print smooth beneath her fingertip. She checked the time: nearly 3 a.m. If she called Mick, what would she say? *Hello, sorry to wake you at this ungodly hour, but I'm scared?* She gave a little snort of contempt. No way. Besides, she thought, putting the business card back onto the console table, if you ask someone for help, they never forget. They always hold it over you.

Mick glanced out the window of the squad room. Sunrise already, with the clouds tinted pink and yellow. He checked his watch. They'd been back on call for a couple of hours, getting nowhere.

The crew was sitting around the desks and slurping the takeaway coffees that Sergeant Frank Ward had just brought in; Bull chain smoking; each man looking grouchy and puffy eyed. Ward was eating his customary sausage roll for breakfast. No wonder he was getting fat. In contrast to the crew, the detective inspector of the Armed Offence Squad, Brian Vaughan, looked fresh. Mick sipped coffee and tried to pay attention to the round-table discussion. After only four hours of sleep, however, his mind was tending to wander. Shit, Vaughan had the hairiest eyebrows that Mick had ever seen, like two pads of brushed-out steel wool. If Mick had eyebrows like that, he'd trim the damn things.

Alec was saying, "The owner is going to be okay. He's off the critical list."

"Thank Christ," Ward said around a mouthful of sausage roll. "At least that gets Homicide off our backs. Stevo, give them a bell, would you? Let them know to give it a rest."

Stevo picked up a handset on one of the landlines.

"And tell them to go nab another wife-killer while they're at it," Bull said, "so they can put their feet up for the rest of the day, the fucking pansies."

Ward smiled. "I want to transfer you across to Homicide just to see what happens."

Bull cut his eyes at him. The others laughed. Mick didn't join in. He was busy thinking about Cara Haynes, wondering if she were out of bed yet, whether he could come up with a reason to visit her. Then he yawned, took another gulp of coffee.

Detective Inspector Vaughan said, "We didn't get a rego? Aren't there CCTV cameras in this shopping centre?"

"Yeah, two," Mick said. "One at each end of the strip, but they're not infrared. We've got footage of a car leaving at high speed, but it's too dark and grainy to make out any plates. It's probably a different car anyway."

Vaughan shook his head. "No, the bandits always drive an old Commodore."

"But it's a different one every time," Mick said. "Listen, those '90s models are easy to pinch. If you've got a key to one, you've pretty much got the key to them all. And you can start a few of the models with any flat piece of metal, like a dipstick. These blokes are familiar with stealing these kinds of Commodore. They probably sell them off to a chop shop after every job."

"Fair enough," Vaughan said. "I'm only trying to look for something, anything."

Bull said, "Yeah, these blokes are fucking ghosts."

Mick got up and approached the corkboard on wheels. On it, a copy of every photograph they had of the pizza bandits. While the men talked behind him, Mick studied the shots again, carefully, scrupulously, one snap at a time, pausing over every feature. Occasionally, you could get lucky that way. Occasionally, a clue jumped out, a detail that you hadn't spotted before, even after looking at a particular photo a hundred times. Like the case of the robbery of a convenience store last year, when Mick had finally noticed in one of the blown-up CCTV stills that the masked robber appeared to be wall-eyed. Since one of the witnesses Mick had interviewed had been wall-eyed, a bit of pressure, correctly applied, had led to the man's rapid confession.

Mick leant close to the corkboard, his nose almost touching it. Come on, you bastards, he thought as he scanned images of the pizza bandits. *Tell me who you are.* The skinny one, George, had a habit of jutting his head that suggested a hunchback. Mick focused on that and allowed his mind to drift, hoping for the Eureka moment.

Ward was saying, "They might be bikies. Obviously not the old guard, not the ones with the beards and long hair, but the new blokes. Those names we've got, George and Sammy, sound Middle Eastern to me. Greek, Turkish?"

"Or Anglo-Saxon," Alec said. "Didn't England have about half a dozen kings named George?"

"Did they, Mr Fucking Dictionary?" Bull said.

"You mean 'Encyclopaedia', not 'Dictionary'."

"Aw, fuck off, Mario."

"Enough," Ward broke in. "All right, we can't establish shit from their names. Greek, Turkish, English, whatever. Let's move on."

Stevo said, "It's not bikies, Sarge, I'm telling you now. The new breed is into drugs, not armed robbery. Our pizza bandits are nicking chump change. One night's cook-up of meth would sell for twice what our bandits have made from their seventeen jobs put together."

Mick turned from the corkboard. Other detectives were straggling into the squad room by now. A few of them looked his way and gave him a nod. A couple of men from Harlan's crew walked in together. Mick watched their progress to an island of desks by the window. So far this year, Harlan's crew had a clean-up rate of seventy-six per cent. Mick's crew—or rather, Sergeant Ward's crew—had only seventy-one.

Detective Inspector Vaughan said, "Nobody's heard anything about these bastards? Not even a whisper? Somebody must have the mail, surely."

Mick said, "That Brownie bloke from Ballarat, the career robber who did time for a couple of pubs he knocked over in the western suburbs. He could be one of them."

"You mean Rodney Brown?" Ward said. "That rings a bell. Didn't we like him for that supermarket job a while back? The Kazemi job?"

"Yeah, that's him."

Stevo nodded. "You think he's the one with the shotty?"

"Could be."

"But he likes them sawn-off, as I recall," Ward said.

"Yeah, but he's a fan of pistol whipping. Not many robbers use a firearm like a club."

"Very true," Ward said. "Okay, what about the other bloke?"

Mick shrugged. "I don't know. Someone he met in the bin. He only got out a year ago."

Ward said, "We could have the Dogs check him out for a day or two, see what's up."

"Go ahead," Vaughan said, exiting his chair. "And make it quick. You wouldn't believe the pressure I'm getting from Upstairs."

The crew watched the detective inspector as he crossed the squad room and disappeared inside his office, shutting the door behind him.

"Prick," Bull said.

Ward clapped his hands. "Let's get on it, chop chop. And look, we've got to push for help here, understand? Start calling in favours."

"Will do." Mick took the keys to the squad car from his pocket, and turned to Alec. "You coming or not?"

The TAB agency had a typical layout: multi-coloured carpet; vinyl stools clustered about tables and benches; a dozen or more TV screens showing horse races, sporting matches, dog races, you name it; a fully stocked bar; cashier's cage; and finally, an ATM for when the clients ran out of gambling money. At 8.34 a.m., the place had a few customers already, exclusively male, scattered singly throughout the premises, each man keeping his own counsel. Most watched the televisions. Others read newspapers or leaned over betting forms.

Mick and Alec approached a man named Dave, who was sitting by the bar, sucking on a beer stubby and messing about with a mobile phone. They stood behind him for a time. Mick glanced at Alec and winked.

"G'day, mate," Mick said. "It's been a while."

Dave looked around and jumped. Fumbling, he switched off his phone and stuffed it in his pocket. "G'day, yourself. You're looking well."

"Too bad I can't say the same for you. This is my colleague, Detective Constable Alec Castellano."

"So, what can I do you for?"

"The pizza jobs," Mick said.

"Sorry. Don't know nothing about them."

Alec said, "Sir, would you come outside with us, please?"

"What for? I told youse I don't know nothing."

Mick stepped closer. "Watch yourself."

"No worries," Dave said. "Don't get your knickers in a twist."

Getting up, he swung one leg from the bar stool as if dismounting from a bicycle. He turned to Mick with a bravado grin. Mick grabbed him by the scruff of the chequered flannelette shirt, manhandling him towards the glass exit doors. Other patrons looked over, alarmed.

"Take it easy," Alec said. "What are you doing?"

Mick frogmarched Dave out of the TAB and around the corner to a laneway. Once they passed a line of overflowing dumpsters, Mick shoved him against the brick wall with enough force to bounce him off again. The man's eyes were bulging, his face grey with fearful resignation. Mick felt the customary thrill. It never got old, even after all these years.

Then he felt a hand on his shoulder: Alec's hand. He shrugged it away.

Dave said, "What's with the unfriendly attitude, mate? I don't want any trouble."

"You've got it anyway." Mick took a step closer. "Are you going to tell me what I want to know or am I going to make your life shit?"

"Come on," Alec said. "Ease down."

Dave, quailing, showed Mick his empty palms. "Aw fuck, I told you, I don't know."

The breeze rose, carrying on it the stink of rot from the dumpsters, the acrid odour of urine from the laneway's cobblestones. Mick squared up. Dave cringed against the brick wall.

Alec said, "Mick, can I talk to you over here for a second?"

Dave managed a wobbling smile, and a laugh that carried a derisive sting. "You've got nothing on these boys, have ya? Not even a sniff."

"Shut up. Who are the shitmen doing the jobs?"

"If I could have a quick word with you, please. Just for a second."

With a roll of the shoulders, Mick feinted a move. Dave, yelping, shielded his face with both hands, his fingers curled into loose, shaking fists.

"You see?" Mick said, turning to Alec. "Now I have to defend myself."

Putting the strength of his back into it, he punched Dave in the side, doubling him up. Dave sagged to the cobblestones, wheezing and retching.

"I'm coming back tomorrow," Mick said. "You'd better be here and you'd better tell me what I need to know."

He was fastening his seatbelt by the time Alec ran over and jumped into the car's passenger side. Another five seconds, Mick thought, fuming, and the bastard would've been catching a taxi back to the squad. Like a shocked little kid, Alec was goggling at him, wide-eyed and breathless. Christ, if the dumb shit didn't toughen up, the routine of the Armed Offence Squad would break him in half. Or get him stabbed.

"What the fuck was that?" Alec said.

"I could ask you the same question. The only thing you didn't do was suck his dick."

"For God's sake, you were threatening him when he hadn't even—"

"He knows who they are."

"Maybe he does, but did you see how many witnesses he had inside the TAB? That was really stupid. What's the matter with you?"

Mick clamped both hands on the steering wheel in order to keep them there. "I've been working my arse off for eight months trying to catch these shitbags. Don't you tell me how to go about it, okay?"

"But there were dozens of witnesses to how you—"

"When you've been in the squad for as long I have, you can tell me what to do, okay?"

"Okay," Alec said, sitting back in the seat. "Whatever. Shit, forget it."

Mick started the engine. On the drive to the Melbourne City Police Complex, they didn't speak. In his peripheral vision, Mick could see Alec looking at him every so often, in a way that seemed thoughtful, wary.

Mick would have to watch out for him. That much was clear.

The landlord had agreed, thank God. Now, every curtain in the lounge room was pulled back on its railing. The afternoon sunshine, magnified through clouds, ground itself like a knuckle into Cara's eyes. With her legs tucked beneath her on one of the couches, she watched the workman as he fixed the lock on the last window. His faded denim overalls, a shapeless sack, made him look a mile wide.

"Almost done," he said.

Good, she thought; then she could have a nap. She'd hardly slept the night before.

He gave a final twist of his screwdriver, and offered Cara two keys on a ring.

"It's the same key," he said. "They'll open every one of these window locks. The work's guaranteed for six months. Give me a buzz if anything goes wrong."

"Okay."

"Not that it will. These locks are high-grade stainless steel. Nothing but the best."

Cara looked at the keys lying in her palm. This is what happens when you overreact, she thought. This is what happens when you give in to that particular kind of fear that only strikes in the middle of the night.

"Contact your insurance," the workman went on, returning the screwdriver to a hard-shell plastic case lying open on the dining table. "You could get a rebate."

"Thanks. Let me get my wallet. Is cash okay?"

"The best kind of okay you can get."

She went to her handbag sitting on the console table by the front door. What a waste. The money she was paying the workman, including his emergency surcharge, would have cleared this month's debt on her credit card. She reached inside the main body of the handbag.

It did not contain her wallet.

Her fingers scrabbled around, increasingly desperate. She emptied the contents of the bag over the console table. There was definitely no wallet. Panic struck her in the ribs. She opened the handbag's zippered compartments, hauling out chewing gum, travel-pack tissues, a couple of kicked-around tampons in plastic wrap. No wallet. She could feel herself hyperventilating, her head spinning down towards a grey-white void.

"Miss, are you feeling all right?"

Cara spun around. The workman's lined and puckered face was full of concern. She set her teeth. To lose control in front of this complete stranger would be humiliating.

"It's nothing," she said. "I can't find my wallet."

He gave an uncertain smile. "Do you want me to write an invoice?"

Cara took a breath. "No, I'll give you a cheque. Is that okay?"

"Sure, why not? Money is money, according to my dear old mother, anyway."

Cara wrote the cheque with a shaking hand. As soon as the workman had gone, she snatched up Mick's business card from the console table and called the number at the squad room. The phone rang twice.

"Armed Offence Squad."

She recognised his voice straight away. The wave of relief took the strength from her body. She groped for the couch, sitting heavily.

"Mick, it's me, Cara Haynes."

"Cara? What's wrong?"

"You told me I could call any time."

"Are you at home?"

"Yes."

"Hold on, I'll be right there."

Within ten minutes, he was knocking. She fell upon the door, flinging it wide, and smiled despite the prickle of tears. There he was, filling the doorway with his big shoulders and his dark trench coat, looking down at her with a dopey grin. She had an urge to kiss him, hard, to grab at the back of his neck so he couldn't pull away.

"Come in," she said.

And he did.

"They've taken my wallet," she continued, and couldn't say any more.

She put her face in her hands. Next, unexpectedly, she felt his arms about her. Weakly, she dropped her forehead to his chest, smelling the heat from his skin, the faint musk of sweat through his business shirt.

"Don't worry," he murmured. "It's okay. Everything is okay."

She turned from him and wiped at her eyes. "Can I get you a drink? Wine? Beer? Oh, but you're on call. What about a coffee?"

"Actually, a beer would be great."

She hurried to the kitchen, feeling strange, light-headed, as if gliding through a dream. She returned with two stubbies. He opened both of them, handing one back to her. She sat down on one of the couches.

"You can't find your wallet?" he said.

"Not since the robbery. Please tell me I'm overreacting."

"Okay. You're overreacting."

She laughed. He did too. Then he put the stubby on the coffee table while he took off his trench coat, shrugging his shoulders out of it. Briefly, she imagined him removing his jacket and tie, unbuttoning his shirt.

"Forget about it," he was saying, "those bastards wouldn't steal a customer's wallet."

"How do you know that?"

"Because these blokes have done a lot of jobs. They only ever go for the till."

After folding the coat, he slung it over the armrest of the other couch and took a seat.

"They wouldn't come after me?" she said.

"What for? They want cash from pizza parlours. They're not interested in aggravated burglary. Relax. You probably left your wallet at work." He took a long swallow of beer, watching her. "I'm glad you've had the day off. Did you take my advice and have the whole week?"

"No. I can't. There's this account I've got to chase. An outfit called Blackbird Books."

"And it can't wait?"

"Apparently not."

"Doesn't your boss know what happened to you last night?"

"I told him." She sipped her beer. "He asked if it'd interfere with my work performance."

"Nice bloke."

"That's sales for you."

Mick put the stubby on the coffee table, stood up, and began to amble around the room, looking about with a critical eye like a prospective tenant deciding whether or not to move in. At a bookcase, his head tipped to one side to better view the titles on the spines.

"You've done pretty well," he said. "Upmarket sales job with a company car."

"I fluked it, to be honest."

"Yeah? How so?"

"Ten years ago, I went for the position of receptionist. They offered me a shot at sales with full training. It turns out I was good at it."

"No surprise there." He gave her a grin. "I bet you'd be good at a lot of things."

She felt herself blush. He wandered back over to take a seat on the couch next to her. If she shifted her leg, she would touch against his knee.

He said, "Why did they offer you a sales job when you didn't have any experience?"

"I don't know."

"Must've been your good looks."

"Ha. Good looks won't save me if I screw up this account. The trouble is I don't know if I can do my job at the minute. My head feels all over the place."

"That'll pass."

"Yes, but I don't have time to wait. I need to deal with things now."

Mick put a gentle hand on her wrist. "Then I'll help you, okay? We'll be a team."

She said, "That might not work. Sorry, I'm not comfortable accepting help."

"Perfect. I'm not comfortable giving it, either."

And that made her laugh. They held each other's gaze. A few seconds slipped by. If she continued to say nothing, do nothing, he would lean over and kiss her, and she would let him.

She stood up. "Well, there's one thing you can do for me."

"Name it."

"Could you drive me to Benny's Pizzeria? I need to pick up my car."

FOUR

Early Thursday morning, the rain was gusting across South Melbourne in sheets. Cara turned her sedan from the lane into the undercover car park at the rear of the Premiere Press building. She manoeuvred into her space, killed the engine, and waited for her breathing to slow down. Ridiculous, she thought. There wasn't any reason to feel anxious. This was her workplace. She'd been coming here for weeks. *Get out of the car.* She closed her eyes while her stomach turned over.

As soon as Cara walked through the back door into reception, Lucy stood up with a gasping mouth and bugging eyes.

"Morning," Cara said, trying to smile.

Lucy dropped the phone headset to the reception counter. "Oh my God, I couldn't believe it. When I heard, I thought to myself, oh my God, is this for real?"

"No, it's okay, honestly. I'm fine."

Cara headed towards the stairs. Moving with surprising speed despite her teetering high heels, Lucy got there first and clutched at Cara's arm. To keep from shaking her off, Cara focused intently on the girl's clumped mascara, liquid eyeliner, blue iridescent eyeshadow.

"It must have been really awful," Lucy whispered.

"Yes. It was."

"You poor thing. I want to hear all about it."

"Maybe later."

"Promise?" Lucy said. "You know, I had a cousin who worked at a service station. After he was held up, he had a nervous breakdown and wasn't ever the same."

"Is that right?"

"Uh-huh. And he lost his wife, his children, his job, everything."

The reception phone began to ring. Lucy gave Cara's arm a final squeeze, tottered back to the desk and picked up the headset.

"Premiere Press, how can I help you?" she said, and then blew Cara a kiss.

Cara nodded in reply and took the stairs. Mick was right. She shouldn't be here.

Her office was less than twenty feet down the hall on the second floor. Coming the other way from the kitchen, however, were the other sales reps: Trish and Martin.

"Damn," Trish said, hurrying over. "Are you okay? What are you doing at work?"

Martin said, "I saw the robbery on the news. How come you didn't get an interview?"

There was, as usual, a glint of amusement in his eyes. Cara seethed. Martin liked to think of himself as worldly, which meant his every comment had to be arch, droll. In reality, he was an irritating little shit who assumed his private school education made him superior to everyone else in the office. She had hated him from day one. His first words to her, delivered with a smirk and a raised eyebrow, had been: *Welcome to the jungle.*

Cara said, "Thanks for the moral support."

Throwing his head back, Martin chortled as if they were bantering together.

Trish slapped him on the arm. "What the frick is wrong with you?"

"Oh, come on. Can't you tell I'm joking?"

Ignoring him, Trish said, "How are you feeling, Cara? And don't lie."

Cara shrugged. She wanted to go into her office and close the door. No, more than that; she wanted to climb back into bed, pull the doona over her head and cocoon herself in the darkness, in the quiet.

"What an incredible experience," Martin was saying. "Were you scared?"

"Of course, I was scared. What do you think?"

"But how invigorating to be flung out of the banal and into life's viscera. I mean, it's not the kind of thing that happens every day. Now you have something remarkable to tell the grandkids."

"Martin," Trish said through her teeth.

Cara turned on her heel and made it to her office. Within seconds of slamming the door, there came a knock.

"Piss off," she called.

"It's me: Trish."

Cara opened the door and headed around the desk to her chair. Sitting down, she made a show of adjusting her pens on the blotter and straightening her diary, grabbing at her folder of colour samples.

"What do you want?" Cara said. "I'm busy."

"You should go home."

Cara looked up. Trish had curly red hair, a plain honest face and a straightforward, almost country way of speaking her mind. If Cara ever wanted a friend, Trish would be it, no contest. But Cara didn't want a friend.

"I can't go home. Don wants me to get started on Blackbird Books."

"That's nuts. Why don't I cover for you?"

"Because I'm only five weeks in, not even past my probation, and I need a big score on the board. What'll I do if he sacks me? I've got two months' rent and a security bond down on my house. I'm stretched thin already." Cara put her forehead into the palm of one hand. "Shit."

The phone rang. Cara picked it up.

Lucy said in a sing-song voice, "Hi there, are you taking calls this morning? I've got a Mick Thompson on line one."

"Put him through." Cara glanced at Trish. "Sorry, I've got to take this."

Trish smiled, backed out of the office, and closed the door.

A click sounded over the phone.

"Cara Haynes," she said.

"Mick Thompson, Armed Offence Squad. How's it going?"

She sighed. Pinned to the corkboard on her office wall were postcards featuring Van Gogh paintings, a few of her favourites.

"Truthfully?" she said.

"Please."

"In a word: shithouse."

"That's two words, isn't it?"

Despite herself, she giggled. "I'm not sure. It might be hyphenated."

"You're too clever for me. Let's have lunch."

"Lunch?" Her heart rate accelerated. "Well, I don't know. I've got a lot to do today."

"Yeah, me too. There's a good pub near your office. I'll pick you up at twelve-thirty. My shout."

"Hang on a minute, I haven't—"

"Wait on the footpath. I don't want to stop. The parking officers in your street are bastards."

"They'd ticket you? I'd have thought your badge would make a difference."

"Nope. Parking officers are cockheads, not fellow law enforcement."

She laughed. "See you at twelve-thirty."

Mick hung up the phone from Cara, exited the empty office, went back to join Bull and Alec at the desks. He picked up a newspaper and turned to the sports section.

Minutes later, Bull said, "Ah, fuck no."

Mick looked up. Bull was staring across the squad room at Stevo, who was striding over from the elevator hall, approaching with his arms wide and his shoulders shrugged up around his ears.

"Bullshit," Mick said. "So, nothing?"

"Nothing," Stevo said, dropping into a chair.

Mick threw the newspaper, scattering it across the desks. "It's been a day and a half. What the fuck are the Dogs even doing?"

"They reckon they've got other surveillance to do first."

Bull snorted. "Yeah, for what? A piss-ant dope pusher."

Mick shook his head. "We should have done it ourselves."

"Huh?" Bull said. "Who wants to do a sit-off on a house all bloody day and night?"

"Do you want to catch these bastards or not?"

Alec started gathering up the sheets of newspaper. "The Dogs will come up with something soon."

"And in the meantime," Mick said, "Brownie and his mate rob another pizza joint."

Stevo leaned back in his chair, stretched, and put his hands behind his head. "What can I tell you? I spoke to Chambers himself, even offered a couple of slabs, but it didn't wash. They'll get around to Brownie when they get around to Brownie, and if we don't like it, we can shove it up our collective arses. Quote, unquote."

Mick checked his watch, grabbed his jacket from the back of his chair, and started walking away. "This doing nothing is giving me the shits. I'm gone."

"Where?" Alec said.

"To check out a line of enquiry," Mick called over his shoulder.

The Little Penguin Hotel featured polished wooden floorboards, white linen tablecloths, and wait-staff that actually behaved like graduates from hospitality school. Mick topped up Cara's glass of sauvignon blanc. He had ordered the most expensive bottle, the one from Margaret River, and yes, Cara was impressed with that too; it showed on her face, in the glint of her eyes. Everything was going smoothly, including the conversation.

"How's work?" he continued. "Are you managing?"

"Not really. I seem to be just pushing paper around my desk."

His mobile phone rang. According to the display, it was Bull. Mick hesitated, until he reminded himself that the pizza bandits only worked after dark. He switched off the phone and pocketed it again.

"Not important?" she said.

"Nope. Tell me about the gig that's worrying you."

"Blackbird Books?" She took a sip of wine. "My boss was making noises about it this morning. He seems to think that if I don't do something immediately, today, the world will come to an end. I've got an appointment next week with one of the owners. Granted, she might not want to hear my sales pitch, so it's no guarantee, but at least it's a start." She put down her glass. "And what about you?"

"What about me?"

"Your work in the Armed Offence Squad must be interesting."

He lifted and dropped one side of his mouth. "Crims rob establishments. I catch the crims."

"And that's it?"

"That's it."

She smiled. "Okay. What do you do when you're not working?"

"Nothing much."

She sat back in her chair. "We can lapse into silence if you want."

And he didn't want that. Leaning forward across the table, he said, "All right: fishing."

"Deep sea or river?"

"River. I've got a tinny I take out along the Murray up in Echuca. I usually fish near Torrumbarry, or upstream towards Barmah and the red gum forests they have there."

"It sounds beautiful."

"Yeah, it is. And peaceful. When you go out at sunrise, there's nothing but parrots calling overhead, clean air and blue sky, sunlight off the water." He felt himself slipping, the gentle memories of rest unbalancing him. He shook it off. Picking up his wine glass, he winked at her. "If you've never eaten a fish caught fresh off the line, you've never eaten fish."

"I bet. What sort do you catch up there?"

"Yellow belly, cod, silver perch. Sometimes redfin."

"Do you use yabbies for bait?"

"When I can catch them, yeah."

"And I bet you barbecue the fish whole, right? At your camp next to the river."

"That's right," he said, and laughed in surprise.

"It sounds like you're a country boy."

"Good guess. Yeah, I'm from Wangaratta."

"Wangaratta," she said, drawing out the word. Then she added, "Good old Wang, hey? I've been there once, it's a nice place. Have you still got family out that way?"

He wondered, but only for a second, about his father and older brothers; where they might be, and whether his old man was alive at, shit, seventy years of age? Eighty?

Then he said, "Yep. Everyone's back on the homestead."

The waiter approached their table and, with a flourish, placed their meals in front of them. Cara had ordered duck breast, Mick the beef fillet. Each plate was artfully arranged.

"The food looks wonderful," she said.

"It should. This is one of the best pubs around." He touched his fingertip to the gravy and tasted it. "I know a few other restaurants you might like. How do you feel about Italian food?"

She gave a wry smile. "As long as it's not pizza."

"Agreed. Then I'll pick you up at your place tomorrow night about seven."

"Oh?" she said at last. "You're very sure of yourself."

"I'll take that as a yes."

Cara, sombre-faced, didn't answer. Somehow, he'd taken a misstep. He kept his mouth shut and waited, returning her gaze as if he didn't care what happened either way.

"Mick, what's this about? I mean this lunch and everything."

"Nothing. It's just lunch."

"Are you married?"

He chuckled. "Do I look like I am?"

"I don't know. Married men are found in different shapes and sizes."

"You're obviously single."

"Obviously."

"With no family or friends in Melbourne."

She picked up her napkin, fussed with it, laid it on her lap. "That's right."

"I reckon you're a bit of a loner."

"Actually, I'd describe myself as self-sufficient. Maybe like you." She fixed him with her grey-blue eyes. "You didn't answer my question. Do you have a wife tucked away?"

"No."

She relaxed, smiled apologetically. "You're very secretive."

"It comes with the job."

She propped her jaw in the palm of one hand and looked him over. "I'd like to know what you're hiding."

"I might show you one day," he said, grinning, and picked up his knife and fork.

After lunch, he took her back to Premiere Press. The drive lasted about ten minutes. The closer they got to the building, the more distracted she seemed. When he pulled up outside the glass-fronted reception area, which gleamed under fluorescent lights and featured a blonde on the desk, Cara stiffened. He'd seen this kind of reaction a hundred times, and it always bothered him. And because it was Cara, it bothered him a lot.

He engaged the handbrake, left the motor running, and waited. She didn't make a move to exit. Instead, she kept staring into reception.

"Don't worry about what they say to you in there," he said. "Anyone who hasn't gone through an armed robbery has no idea what it's like or what you could be feeling."

She chewed on her lower lip. "One of the girls in admin suggested I try Rescue Remedy."

"What's that?"

"A homeopathic medicine for stress."

"Ah, people are full of shit."

"Everyone keeps hanging around my office, staring at me."

"Yeah, and you know why?"

She turned to him; her eyes soft, wide.

He said, "They're hoping you fall apart in front of them. They want to gossip about you, or feel superior, or tell you how to cope even though they've got no idea what they're talking about. Or else they're the type of person who slows down when driving past a traffic accident in case there's something to see, like a dead body with its skull mashed in."

She sighed, frowned. "But what am I supposed to do? I have to go to work."

"That's easy. Keep your head down and do your job. Don't tell them anything. Don't look for sympathy. Most important, let everything they say roll off your back, especially any pinheaded words of advice."

"Okay, I will. Thanks."

"And if you need to talk about anything, talk to me. Night, day, I'm there."

For a second, he thought Cara would either cry or kiss him. Instead, she reached out and grabbed his hand. Then just as suddenly, before he could react, she snatched up her handbag and leapt from the car, slamming the door behind her and dashing across the wet footpath to beat the rain. She shoved through the double doors into reception. He watched as she gave the blonde behind the desk a breezy wave, a big smile, and he nodded to himself in approval. Cara was definitely a woman after his own heart.

The drive to the Melbourne City Police Complex took him about five minutes. He spent the time thinking various thoughts about Cara, like whether she had lower-back dimples, and if so, how much he would enjoy licking at them with the very tip of his tongue. It was only once he was inside the police complex that he remembered to switch on his mobile phone.

There were seven missed messages from his crew.

As soon as the lift doors opened on the ninth floor, he started running. At their desks, Bull, Stevo and Alec were all business, working the landlines, working the computers.

Bull glanced up, stopped pecking at the keyboard with his chunky pointer fingers, and said, "Mick, where the fuck have you been, mate? And what's wrong with your fucking mobile?"

"I missed a job?"

"Yep," Bull said, and recommenced typing.

Mick's heart constricted. "Our boys?"

"Nah, a druggie knock-over."

Relieved, Mick pulled out a chair and sat down. "What's the story?"

"Two bogans hit a bottle shop," Stevo said.

"Ha," Bull cut in, chortling, "that sounds like the start of a joke."

Stevo continued, "A man and a woman, both with handguns. They got away with the contents of a single till, about a grand, and a case of barrel-proof bourbon."

"Definitely worth going to prison for," Alec said, hanging up the landline.

"I keep on telling you, mate," Bull said, "most of our clientele aren't brain surgeons."

Mick reached for one of the notebooks on the desk and started flipping pages. Apparently, the couple was in their fifties and wore matching purple wigs, the nylon type you can pick up at any two-dollar shop. The woman also wore a large-brimmed sunhat.

Mick said, "What kind of fuckwit thinks to put on a sunhat in weather like this?"

"The same kind that doesn't wear a mask." Stevo handed over a stack of printed photographs. "Check out the one where the sheila looks into the camera."

Bull laughed. "Say cheese."

"Nice teeth," Mick said. "That's one of the worst cases of meth-mouth I've seen in a long while. Anyone hurt?"

"No," Alec said. "The girl on the till cooperated. The robbers were in and out in minutes."

"Okay. Where's the sarge?"

"With Chambers," Stevo said, "trying to convince him to put a couple of Dogs onto Brownie tonight. Personally, I don't like his chances. When I spoke to Chambers this morning, he treated me like I'd taken a shit on his desk."

"One day, he'll need a favour from us," Bull said. "And that'll be a sweet fucking day."

Mick said, "All right, regarding our wig-wearing bozos, have we circulated their description to patrols yet?"

"Yep," Stevo said. "If you're looking for something to do, you can chase up forensics if you like. The techies reckon they got a few good footprints."

Mick nodded. He shrugged off his jacket, draped it over the back of a chair, rolled up his sleeves. The job was a good catch. No doubt the crew would have the offenders at week's end, which would boost their clean-up rate by a few percentage points—maybe enough points, if they were lucky, to close the gap with Harlan's crew.

"Hey, Mick," Bull said. "Where the fuck were you, anyway?"

"I told you. Checking a line of enquiry."

"How'd it pan out?"

Mick considered for a moment, then said, "Too early to tell."

Before having lunch with Cara, he had returned to that particular TAB for another word with Dave, as promised. In the laneway, he had punched Dave again, this time in the face, but still got nothing. Dave, catching the blood from a split lip in one hand, had promised to ask around and get the mail regarding the pizza bandits, if it was the last thing he ever did.

Mick swivelled his office chair towards the squad windows. Gazing at the murky clouds, he considered the possibility that Dave might have been telling the truth and had no idea who the pizza bandits were. *Fuck.*

FIVE

Cara shut her office door, sat behind the desk, and began reading through her phone messages.

Golden Sash Real Estate had a new brochure design, and wanted a consultation with trial samples before committing to a print run. Okay, next.

The Fiction Diction Group was threatening to cancel the contract if Premiere Press didn't offer a further discount on stickers and bookmarks. Well, Fiction Diction could go jump; Cara's prices for those tight-arses were already rock bottom. Okay, next.

The print department needed fresh plates for Brief Holdings Ltd, since the dot resolution had worn down. Okay...but not next. Not now.

Dropping the wad of phone messages to her desk, sighing, she gazed at the Van Gogh postcard of 'Starry

Night' pinned to her corkboard. The hypnotic pinwheels of blue, orange and gold pulled her in, set in motion that familiar yearning sensation through her guts.

A million years ago, while still a foster child, Cara had promised herself that as soon as she had squirreled away enough money for airfare, she would visit the Van Gogh Museum in Amsterdam. Of course, Van Gogh's works were scattered in galleries all over the world, and she could never hope to visit every one of them, but the largest collection was in Holland. She had always told herself that visiting Holland, at the very least, was doable.

Ha. Not a chance. Life had been one bill after another, one struggle after another. That's how it is when there's no one looking out for you.

She jiggled the computer mouse to wake the monitor, and checked e-mails: fourteen unread messages. Ah, screw it, she'd read them later. Exiting the program, she turned back towards the Van Gogh 'Starry Night' postcard with its blazing, luminescent sky, and its mysterious dark structure that could be a tree, or perhaps, as she had always believed since stumbling across the picture in an art book during primary school, a glorious witch's castle that struck and curved and twisted itself into organic shapes like magic, like black fire.

Cara sat up in her chair.

God, was she drunk?

As a rule, Cara never drank during the day. She wasn't much of a drinker, full stop. That half-bottle of sauvignon blanc with lunch had smoothed out her edges, made her reflective, almost melancholy. She'd probably had more than half a bottle; Mick had been very attentive, topping up her glass more often than he had topped up his own. The thought of him made her smile.

Until she remembered that he was from Wangaratta.

The coincidence gave her goose flesh. His mention of the town had jolted her, definitely, but she'd recovered so fast that he surely hadn't noticed. That town had been her home for nearly four years. In fact, it was the only place she considered 'home'.

She still dreamed about Wangaratta. Even now.

The social worker drove eight-year-old Cara through the town centre of Wangaratta and out the other side to a weatherboard cottage. A giant palm tree towered over the sparse front lawn. The car stuttered along the concrete driveway and wheezed to a stop. There was an orange VW Beetle parked under a tin-roofed car port. Beyond that, Cara could see a chook-run in the back yard full of hens, each bird pecking and head-bobbing in the hot summer sun.

The social worker turned off the engine, and said, "You mind your manners. A nice first impression makes a difference."

"I'll be good."

Secretly, however, Cara had already determined to be perfect. The couple at the last foster home had liked to whip her legs with the buckle-end of a belt. This punishment had been Cara's fault. She always took too long to vacuum the house, had ironed creases into shirt collars, left streaks on the silverware. Making so many errors every day had exhausted her, carved purple hollows under her eyes. That wouldn't happen this time.

They got out of the vehicle. Cara clutched at the handle of her brown vinyl suitcase with both hands. The social worker knocked on the front door, which opened immediately. They went inside. The entrance hall was tiled, the lounge room carpeted. Shown to an armchair, Cara placed her suitcase next to it, sat down, and kept her eyes on her shoes.

"This is Mr and Mrs Weber," the social worker said. "Now, say hello."

"Hello," Cara said.

"We are happy that you have come to stay with us," said an elderly female voice, a voice that had an unfamiliar accent.

"Both of us are pleased to be meeting with you," said a male voice, similarly elderly and accented.

Curious, she wanted to look up. Instead, she kept staring at her shoes. The social worker gave the Webers a brief rundown of Cara: taken into care at the age of two on account of her alcoholic mother; father unknown; no medical conditions; no mental conditions; no behavioural problems; doesn't wet the bed. Next, the social worker began to detail the financial arrangements, such as foster care benefits being paid fortnightly, the importance of saving receipts if they expected reimbursement for out-of-pocket maintenance expenses. Mrs Weber broke in.

"Little Cara is the twenty-seventh child we have with us," she said. "We understand how it works, thank you."

Cara looked up for the first time. Her new foster parents were old. Mrs Weber, tremendously fat, wore a paisley dress stretched over her curves, her lank hair cut into an unflattering grey helmet. Her husband was stooped, thin, with a meagre white beard that clung to his jaw line.

After the social worker left, Mrs Weber gave Cara milk and a chocolate biscuit.

"Please do not call us by our last name," she said. "I am Oma. He is Opa."

Cara nodded, cramming the biscuit into her mouth.

"Eat the whole packet if you would like," Mrs Weber—Oma—said. "Yet first, please come and see your room. Today, I have made it ready for you."

The room held a single bed with a chequered blanket, a bedside table and lamp, and a poster of a kitten tacked to one wall. A hand-stitched rag doll sat on the chest of drawers.

"This is Gretel," Oma said, picking up the doll and stroking its yellow woollen braids. "You play with her if you like, or not. This is your room. Shut the door any time, is that clear? Leave your suitcase on the bed. I will help you to unpack shortly. Come, meet the hens."

Opa, who had stayed behind in the lounge room, joined them outside for the backyard tour. The chicken coop made Cara afraid. The birds, with their strange gait, their weird sounds, came gibbering over with bobbling heads. Opa squatted down. A few of the birds ran under his outstretched hands, allowing him to stroke their feathers from head to tail. Cara felt an inexplicable thrill.

"Here is Biggie," Opa said. "Here is Whistler. Here is Whitey. The others have no names. They give us eggs anyway."

Next, they showed her the vegetable patch, a square of raised dirt contained within a brace of sleepers, full of fruit-laden tomato plants. Cara reached out to touch one of the tomatoes; a plump, perfect teardrop.

Oma said, "You like food? Good. I like cooking. Please come with us to the herb garden and fruit trees. You like lemons and oranges?"

After lunch, they took her driving about town in the VW. Opa stayed silent at the wheel. Meanwhile, Oma darted her head around this way and that, keeping up a constant stream of commentary, explaining the layout of the main streets, telling Opa to slow down so that she could point out items of interest like parks, monuments or playgrounds. They drove Cara past what would be her primary school, a collection of weatherboard buildings set around a quadrangle, a grassy oval on one side. The sight of the school didn't raise any feelings in her. By now, she had been the New Kid too many times to care.

Upon returning to the Weber house, Cara expected to be shown her chores. Instead, Oma helped her unpack her few belongings, and then revealed the cupboard in the lounge room that was crammed with jigsaw puzzles and board games.

"You play chess?" Oma said. When Cara shook her head, Oma clapped and said, "Good for you, Opa, she is a pupil."

Weeks passed. Cara settled into the household routine. Breakfast, dinner, dessert, bath-time, bed-time, each activity was set to a specific and unvarying schedule. Bed sheets were changed on Mondays; grocery shopping done on Thursdays. Every Sunday morning, Oma cooked pancakes. And every Sunday night was Opa's music night.

Cara looked forward to music night.

While Oma sat in the lounge room to watch television, Opa would retire to the sitting room and play his records—Bach, Handel, Beethoven, Wagner—while smoking a pipe and reading the newspaper. Cara liked to sit in with him. On the bottom shelf of the bookcase were children's titles. Cara would select one to read. Some of the books had illustrations. She would lie on her belly on the rug and flip through the pages, while the music of German composers rolled around the room, and the tobacco smoke made everything smell like wood and cherries.

Above all else, she relished being in a house without other children. In the last house, the other foster child, a boy, had liked to scream and bang his head against the floor, which always drove the foster parents into a frenzy of smacking, yelling and belt-whipping. In the house before that, the two natural children—sweet to her in front of their parents—had enjoyed tormenting her in private, the youngest daughter particularly fond of sticking Cara with thumb tacks.

However, Oma and Opa had three adult sons. On the first Saturday of every month, they would descend on the Weber house for dinner, each bringing his wife and a gaggle of children.

The girls tended to sneer and laugh at Cara. The boys either ignored her with disdain or tried to grab her between the legs. All of the children liked to ask her why she didn't have a family, how come nobody loved her, what had she done that had made her own mother throw her away. Thankfully, 'play time' never lasted long. Oma had been cooking for most of the day so the dinner table always groaned with a huge buffet of sausage, potato, schnitzels, dumplings, fried onions and pickled vegetables that took a couple of hours or more to eat. The relatives spoke too much and too loudly and often at the same time. Oma managed to get a word in. Opa didn't ever try. He used to catch Cara's eye from time to time and wink at her, as if to say, *Don't worry, they'll soon be gone.*

When the relatives had left, Oma would drop into an armchair, cheeks ruddy and sheened with sweat, her fringe stuck to her forehead, and say, "*Gott sei dank* it is over."

Cara helped with the washing up. That always took a long time. Cara didn't mind. Oma would talk about growing up with her parents and five siblings in her hometown of Meissen, or would describe the River Elbe, the old buildings of the town, the castle on the hill with its spires and vaulted Gothic ceilings. Sometimes, Oma would sing traditional songs. Cara learned by heart the words to Oma's favourite nursery rhyme so they could sing it together:

Hoppe hoppe Reiter wenn er fällt, dann schreit er, fällt er in den Teich, find't ihn keiner gleich. Hoppe hoppe Reiter wenn er fällt, dann schreit er, fällt er in den Graben, fressen ihn die Raben. Hoppe hoppe Reiter wenn er fällt, dann schreit er, fällt er in den Sumpf, dann macht der Reiter... Plumps!

A few months before Cara's twelfth birthday, Oma got sick and couldn't get better. She lost weight and stayed in bed a lot of the time. Cara began to fret.

One autumn day at school, Cara was sent to the headmaster's office where the social worker was waiting. A stab of grief lanced Cara's chest. But it wasn't Oma. It was Opa who had died, unexpectedly, from a heart attack while getting a haircut at the barber shop. Cara wasn't prepared for that. She gripped the arms of the chair, a buzzing noise loud in her ears.

"I have your suitcase in the car," the social worker said. "Hurry up and grab your school bag, we have to go."

"Go where? Can't I go home?"

"I thought I'd made myself clear. You aren't staying with the Webers anymore."

The headmaster offered a cordial smile. "Well, Cara, good luck for the future. I hope you enjoyed your time at our school."

The social worker drove Cara through the town centre of Wangaratta and out the other side to the highway. Cara's brown vinyl suitcase was in the front with her, jammed in the foot well. She clutched at its handle with both hands.

"Does Oma know you've taken me?" Cara said.

"You mean Mrs Weber? I doubt it. She collapsed when she heard the news about her husband. They had to take her to hospital."

Cara gritted her teeth to stop the tears from welling. At last, when she could trust herself to speak, she said, "Is Mrs Weber all right?"

"Huh? Oh, I'm sure she'll be fine."

The Italian restaurant was the upmarket kind. Instead of garlic bread, chicken parmigiana, spaghetti bolognaise, the menu featured duck terrine, boned quail, braised ox-cheek pie. Everything sounded delicious. Cara had trouble deciding what to choose; especially since Mick insisted that she order three courses. The argument that she couldn't eat it all didn't matter to him. He'd pointed out that he was paying, and would finish whatever was left on her plate; therefore, sampling three courses of the best Italian food she would ever experience didn't take any skin off her nose. Laughing along with him, she had eventually agreed.

A waiter approached, once again filled their glasses with an expert twirl of the wine bottle, and moved away.

Mick said to her, "See that? Class. I told you this was a nice place."

"It's fabulous."

"Wait'll the food comes out."

The restaurant had an open fireplace, the chunks of wood crackling orange. Mick had taken off his jacket a few minutes ago. His big shoulders were definitely not the illusion of a well-tailored suit. And now that he had his forearms resting along the table edge, she could see against the material of his shirt the meaty bulge of his trapezius muscles, and the width of his upper arms.

Hastily, she looked away. God, perhaps she was drinking too fast. In the days following the robbery, she had drunk more alcohol than in the previous month. Her gaze flitted about the restaurant. Against the far wall stood a group of waiters, every one of them male, middle-aged, and attentively observing the diners.

She said, "Do you think they have a discriminatory policy when it comes to hiring staff? There aren't any young people or women serving the tables."

"Nah, I think it's a family business. Everyone's probably a brother, an uncle, a cousin."

"I suppose." She glanced back at Mick, picked up her glass, took a gulp of wine. "Do you believe in Fate?"

He shrugged. "When it suits me."

"There's something I've been meaning to ask you."

"Okay, go ahead."

"At lunch yesterday, you said you were from Wangaratta."

"Correct."

She took a breath. "As it turns out, I spent a bit of time there too, many years back."

"Yeah?"

"And I'm wondering if I might even remember you."

He considered her for a moment, and then chuckled with a slow shake of his head. "That'd be a small world, now, wouldn't it?"

"It sure would." She momentarily clamped her jaw against the feeling that her teeth would chatter. "When I was in late primary school, there was this group of older boys—just two or three years older than me—that used to shoot birds out of trees."

Mick laughed. "Oh, that's right. Shit. My mate Lyndon had an air rifle."

A spinning sensation began to move about Cara's head. "I don't recognise you," she said. "A few boys had dark blonde hair. Which one were you?"

"The handsome one, of course."

She smiled, despite herself. Then she said, "I can't believe you liked to kill birds."

"Only sparrows. And it wasn't me, it was Lyndon, and he only did it a few times. Mostly, the bunch of us played footy after school."

The group of boys had hung out at the sports oval near her secret retreat: a particular bend along the slow-moving, shallow creek that ran behind the Weber house. While Cara had climbed trees, built cubby-houses out of fallen branches, and tried to construct log bridges across the trickle of water, she had listened to the hoarse voices of those boys on the wind as they had yelled, fought, and cheered. And one of those voices had been Mick's.

She closed her eyes against the bright onslaught of memories, against the vertiginous flood of coincidence, the weight of kismet.

"Are you okay?" Mick said.

"It's nothing. I'm dizzy, that's all. I think I need water."

He ordered it for her immediately. Within seconds, a waiter hurried over with a carafe, pouring her a long glass, the ice tinkling. She drank.

Mick said, "It's very warm in here."

At some point, he had unbuttoned his cuffs and rolled his sleeves to the elbows. His forearms were tanned, thick and corded. Cara shut her eyes again.

"Do you want to leave?" he said. "It's okay with me if that's what you want."

Managing to smile, she said, "Don't worry, I'm being silly. I think I'm still coming to terms with the robbery."

"Which was only three days ago." Mick reached over the table, rubbed his fingers against her wrist. "Take it easy on yourself."

After dinner, he drove her home and parked the unmarked police BMW in the driveway. He turned off the windscreen wipers. The light rain soon obscured the windscreen. As the engine idled, he rested his hand gently on her knee. Cara glanced down. His hand, big-knuckled and workmanlike, wasn't the kind to play a piano or thread a needle, but it would slide ever so easy across her breasts and along her flank, between her legs. The thought of his touch surged her pulse.

She said, "Look, I don't know if I'm ready for this."

"Ready for what? A few meals? Conversation? We don't have to put a label on it."

"Thank you for dinner."

She went to exit the car. Mick grabbed her by the nape of the neck and pulled her close. At first, his kiss was chaste. He smelt earthy, warm, like baked bread. Reaching blindly, she clutched at his shoulder, squeezed hard. The muscles were large and dense without any give in them. Yielding, she parted her lips. He responded. The feel of his tongue made her mouth open wider, allowing his kiss to deepen, making her short of breath. She wanted him. However, when his hand slid up her thigh, she pulled away. Mick did too.

"I'm sorry," he said. "I didn't mean to do that."

Cara couldn't think of a single thing to say. She fled from the car and ran through the drizzle to her front door.

Mick watched her intently. When Cara reached the door, she kept her back to him while she hunted through her bag for house keys. If she hesitated, turned around, if she glanced even once at him, he would switch off the car and go to her. Come on, he thought. *Turn around.* But she didn't. As soon as she disappeared behind the closed door, the porch light went off.

Mick tapped his fingers on the steering wheel for a few seconds, thinking it over. Then he reversed the car out of the driveway, got back onto the main road, and headed east towards home. Friday night traffic on the city-bound Monash Freeway was heavy but moved along at a fair clip. Punt Road was the usual prick. The trip to Richmond took about twenty minutes. Not bad, considering the rain.

Mick turned the car into his street, a court lined with trees, crammed with four- or five-storey apartments. He parked in the basement of his building and took the lift to the second floor. As he crossed the hall, he checked his phone: nothing from the crew. He let himself into the apartment. A light shone into the hall from the lounge room.

He frowned, advancing. "Hello?" he called.

"In here," came a voice.

He went into the lounge room. At the dining table, typing at a laptop, a glass of red on hand, sat Janice. She glanced at him, raising and dropping her lips in a mechanical smile.

"What are you doing home?" Mick said.

"The showing finished early. Someone who was supposed to make a speech didn't turn up because of food poisoning." She gave Mick the once-over. "What about you? Weren't you pulling an all-nighter?"

He walked through to the kitchen, took a beer from the fridge. "It didn't pan out."

"What a shame. I bet you and your buddies were hoping for a good head-kicking."

Returning to the lounge room, he kept quiet, knowing better by now than to answer.

She said, "Get me a refill, would you?"

He picked up the bottle of cab sav and topped up Janice's glass. She took it, sipped, and regarded him with kohl-blackened eyes. Her foundation makeup looked sweaty under the halogen globes.

"Now be a sweetie," she said. "I'm trying to get a head start on this article."

"You want me to go to the other room?"

She nodded. "And no TV or music."

"Okay."

She presented the side of her face. He leaned down and kissed her cheek.

"How was your day?" Mick said.

"Good." Janice began typing again. "What about yours? Did you shoot anybody?"

He didn't reply. She kept her gaze on the laptop, her false fingernails clacking against the keys. It was like he was no longer there.

Mick watched her for a time. Then he walked from the lounge room into the sitting room, making sure to close the door quietly behind him. Loud noises of any kind tended to aggravate his wife, especially when she was working.

SIX

Women in black sat nearby, weeping. Mick approached the hospital bed from behind. Doctors had shaved off most of the man's hair. Snarls of stitches held the tattered scalp together. Mick walked in a slow circle to the man's bedside, trying to acclimatise himself to the horror one glimpse at a time. Trying and failing.

The extent of the injuries raised bile into Mick's throat. The bashing had been so thorough, so brutal, that the man's face had distended to twice its normal size. The eyes were swollen shut, purpled, as huge as duck eggs. Mick leaned in closer. The man lay perfectly still.

"I'm sorry," Mick whispered. "I'm doing everything I can, I swear."

The man's lips, split and scabbed, began to move, slavering bloody spittle. "Mick," he said through his ruined mouth.

"No. Leave me alone. You're dead. I can't help you."

"Mick, wake up, you dumb bastard."

With a start, he opened his eyes. Grinning, Bull let go of Mick's shoulder, gave him a pat to the chops, then sat back on the other cot and lit a smoke.

"I thought I'd have to put a saucepan on your head," Bull said, "and hit it with a spoon."

The remnants of the nightmare fell away. Mick swung his feet to the floor and sat up, rubbing his face. He was in the snooze room at the squad. He had slept fully dressed and his clothes were wrinkled. A whole weekend, and he hadn't managed to see Cara. Then the argument with Janice came back to him in a rush.

Yesterday, Sunday night, they had gone to a dinner party hosted by one of Janice's new friends, a travel writer named Pamela who had a vegan husband and a screw-the-police attitude. Mick hadn't taken the latter too well. At some point, after too many vodkas, he had sneered, "People like you only hate us until you need us. If an armed scumbag broke into your house, raped you in the arse and shot dear old hubby here in the face, who would you call for help? The women from your book club?" Unsurprisingly, the evening had deteriorated fast, very fast. They left soon after. Janice, driving the car, livid, had headed straight to the Melbourne City Police Complex and ordered him to get out. No big deal. It wasn't the first time he had spent the night in the squad room. For just such contingencies, he always had his briefcase packed with toiletries and a change of clothes.

Scrubbing the sleep from his eyes, Mick said, "What time is it?"

"Almost five."

"In the morning?"

"Yep."

Mick pulled a face. "Aw, fuck."

"I know. Come on, we gotta go."

"Where to?"

"A pizza parlour."

Mick's heart almost stopped. He took his hands away from his face. "Our boys?"

Bull nodded, drawing on his smoke. Mick grabbed his shoes, pulling them on without untying the laces. Stevo and Alec were already waiting for them in the elevator hall. As usual, Sergeant Ward was staying behind to coordinate events from his desk. The lift doors opened. The four men stepped inside. Alec pressed the button to take them down to the car park in the basement.

Stevo said, "Not a bad haul this time. It looks like they could've nabbed about nine or ten grand."

"It's got me fucked why these wogs keep so much cash on hand," Bull said.

"They're Italians," Alec said, "not wogs."

"Yeah, whatever, Mario."

"Don't you two ever stop your bullshit?" Mick said. "All right, now what about the car?"

Stevo said, "Not a word."

"Jesus, that's no help."

"But it's the same airline bag," Alec said.

"You sure about that?"

"Completely sure," Bull said. "And they had the same weapons too: shotty and a pistol."

The lift doors opened. They took an unmarked squad car.

Soon, the car was racing along wet and empty Melbourne streets. The moon shining through clouds lit the night in stark, brilliant hues of black and grey. Stevo, who was driving, chose to treat red traffic lights like give way signs, and blew through most of them.

"Our boys went into the restaurant near to closing time, around midnight," Stevo said to Mick, who was sitting in the front passenger seat. "They gave the owner a fractured skull that laid him out cold. About three this morning, he woke up and got on the phone for help. He'd be at the hospital by now."

"No one else was in the shop?" Mick said.

"Nup. The rest of the staff had already finished the shift."

"And no one missed the owner when he didn't come home?"

"Guess not."

Mick nodded. He knew what that was like. Then he said, "This joint is in a strip shopping centre, didn't you say?"

"Yeah, that's right."

"No passers-by noticed anything suspicious?"

Bull leaned forward between the two front seats. "Before they left, our boys must've flipped the sign on the door to 'closed' and turned off the lights. Cheeky fuckers. They're getting smart."

Mick said, "Christ, mate, get your stinking cigarette-breath out of my face, would you? Seriously, you've got to quit those things."

"Aw, bite me, cockhead." Bull leaned back in the seat.

Mick turned to Alec, who was sitting behind Stevo, and said, "What do you reckon?"

"About what?"

"About what the rest of us are talking about."

Alec gave a thin-lipped smile. "I agree with you: his breath stinks."

Bull and Stevo laughed hard. Mick turned towards the windscreen again. The car sped past a brightly lit tram with its sole occupant, apparently asleep, visible only as a tousled head against a window. The sight reminded Mick of how tired and pissed off he was feeling.

He said, "I'm sick of these pricks."

"We don't know yet if it's them," Alec said.

"It's them. They're just giving us the finger."

"Ah, don't worry," Stevo said. "When we catch them, we'll show them exactly what we think of their middle fingers."

"Shit yeah," Bull said. "Now that'll be a party for the photo album."

Mick's hands bunched into fists. Eighteen hold-ups for the pizza bandits in total. Twenty-six victims: seven of them physically injured; four needing to be hospitalised. And every victim, every last one of them, traumatised, emotionally scarred; some broken for all time, to be plagued with a life of anxiety, depression, insomnia, nightmares. Cara came to mind. Would she recover? He didn't know. Suddenly, the overwhelming and savage need to harm the pizza bandits felt strong enough to crack his ribs. He closed his eyes against the bolting of his heart.

"How did you go at the trots on the weekend?" Stevo said, glancing into the rearview mirror. "Did that nag come through for you?"

"Nah," Bull said. "I dropped a fair bit of dough on that one, but never mind. The outing wasn't a total waste, thanks to a sweet little badge bunny I happened to meet."

Laughing, Stevo said, "Oh crap, another one? Did you take this one home, at least?"

"What for? She sucked me off in the car. I'm telling you, I fucking love this badge, I swear to God. It's my never-fail pussy magnet."

"Yeah," Alec said, "but for what kind of woman?"

"Who the fuck cares?" Bull said, incredulous. "I can't believe any man alive would say a stupid thing like that. You're not a poofter, are you, Mario?"

Stevo and Bull laughed together riotously. Alec, however, didn't make a peep. Mick sighed, annoyed. If Alec kept refusing to stand up for himself, this crew and eventually the entire Armed Offence Squad would crush him until he was bawling his eyes out for stress leave and a transfer. The squad couldn't afford a weak link. Not when the crims they were up against could be tougher than railroad iron. Over the years, Mick had seen plenty of cops swagger into the Armed Offence Squad only to whine their way out again a few months later. Alec would be another one.

Bull punched Mick on the shoulder and said, "What happened to you last night? The missus kick you out again?"

Stevo began snickering. "Maybe you should try giving her some."

"Is that right?" Mick said. "I'll give you ladies some in a minute, if you don't shut up."

Bull said, "Hey, pull into that Macca's, I'm starving."

"What time is it?" Alec said.

Mick scowled. "Too early for this shit."

They ordered burgers and coffee. When they at last drove into a parking space outside the Italian restaurant, the pre-dawn sky was flaring a sliver of red on the horizon.

Uniformed officers were waiting for them inside. The premises were divided into two halves: through one door, the sit-down restaurant; through the other, the takeaway section. The pizza bandits had attacked the owner in the restaurant.

The crew walked slowly between the various tables, wordlessly observing every detail. A forensic photographer was snapping away. Mick approached and stepped around the photographer. A chair lay on its back. On the table were the remains of an ordinary meal: a glass with a slick of soft drink in the bottom; a plate with a rind of pizza crust, knife and fork; a discarded serviette. The edge of the serviette was soaking up blood.

Mick moved closer. The camera clicked over and over, the dazzling glare of the flash forcing him to raise a hand to shield his eyes. Gouts of blood spattered the floor and nearby chairs. Against the stucco of the wall, caught in the paint's rough grain by a smudge of dried blood, was a piece of scalp the size of a button, complete with strands of short, black hair.

"Did you get this?" Mick said, pointing.

"Sure," the photographer said.

The owner had been eating a late dinner, Mick realised, when the bandits had busted in here. The poor bastard had been chewing a slice of pizza and drinking his cola after a long day's work. Now his blood and skin were splashed around the very business that he had built up and toiled at week after week; the business that made the money that put food into the mouths of his wife and children; and from this day forward, this business would be the setting for each and every nightmare the poor bastard would ever have.

Mick passed a hand over his face, surprised by the sweat on his forehead. Stevo and Bull were lounging by the counter. The uniformed officers and the photographer had gone.

"Did you hear that?" Bull said to Mick.

"Huh?"

"One of the connies reckons our boys fired a gun."

"From the shotty?"

Stevo said, "From the pistol. I don't know, maybe the connie got it wrong. When I was briefed over the phone, no one mentioned any gunshot injury, just a busted head."

Mick took a step, paused, and steadied himself against a chair. "Is the owner shot?"

"Yeah," Bull said. "Bang! Right through the palm."

"Or so says one of the connies," Stevo added. "I'll believe it when I see it."

"Lose any fingers?" Mick said.

Bull shook his head. "Nah, clean shot. But he'll be using his left for a while."

"If it's true they shot him," Stevo said, "that's another charge we can get them on: grievous bodily harm."

"Not if he doesn't lose a body part, we don't," Bull said.

"It still counts," Stevo argued, "if he ends up disabled. His hand won't be worth shit now. I'm telling you, that's grievous bodily harm."

A bell jangled. Mick spun around. Alec was walking through the front door, the bell over the jamb still tinkling as the door shut on its pneumatic arm.

"The staff at the all-day pharmacy next door didn't hear a thing," Alec said. "One of the women is pretty cut up about the pizza owner."

Stevo shrugged. "Yeah, well, at least he didn't get it in the head."

"She's known him for eight years, apparently. He gives her a free slice of pizza every Friday night: pepperoni and cheese."

"That's probably not all that he gives her, the dirty dog," Bull said.

Mick looked back at the table where the owner had been sitting. Apart from the blood, the scene looked innocent enough. The knife and fork were arranged neatly, side by side on the plate. The serviette, however, lay flung across the table as if dropped in a hurry. The owner must have finished his meal only moments before the assault. He'd put down his cutlery and was dabbing at his mouth with the serviette when the jingling bell signalled the opening of the door.

"What's with him?" he heard Alec say.

"Nothing," Stevo said. "He's probably half-asleep."

Bull slapped Mick on the arm, rounded him up and steered him away from the table.

"Okay," Mick said. "I'm okay."

"Course you are, mate. Now, come on, let's get busy. It's show time."

Cara tapped a knuckle against the open door. "You wanted to see me?"

"Oh yes, come in," Don Reinecke said, half-getting up and gesturing towards the visitor's chair on the other side of his enormous desk. "Take a seat."

She sat down and looked past his shoulder. Behind him was a balcony that couldn't be accessed. Perversely, the floor-to-ceiling window didn't have a doorway. Every time she was in Don's office, she had to wonder whether the architect of the Premiere Press building had made that silly design choice on purpose or by mistake. Since no one could go out on the balcony, it never got cleaned. Cara stared down at the drifts of mouldering leaves decomposing into dirt against the window. How many more years would it take to fill the balcony to the very top of its smoked glass wall? Twenty? Thirty? A hundred?

"Let me know when you're ready to start our meeting."

Cara looked up. Don, grave-faced, had his fingers steepled together.

"I'm sorry," she said. "I was just thinking about something."

"But not your work."

She blushed. Don picked up his reading glasses, balanced them on the end of his nose and peered down at a sheaf of papers on his desk. Cara waited.

"The boss of Fiction Diction called me this morning," he said, "and she's very upset. Do you want to tell me what happened?"

"Nothing happened, really. The admin director rang me on Friday to ask for cheaper stickers and bookmarks. I told him we were already offering them near to cost price."

"So, you told him no."

"Well, I told him that we couldn't discount the items any further."

"In other words," Don said, taking off his glasses, "you told him no."

She gave a smile. "To be honest, I don't see the point in making a loss."

"Oh. You'd rather we let Fiction Diction go."

Goddamn it. Cara fidgeted in her seat. "It's a straightforward case of profit and loss. If we start providing our services at less than cost price, then we'll—"

"I know how to suck eggs, thank you very much. I've been in the industry forty years, at the helm of Premiere Press for eleven. You know what I told the boss of Fiction Diction?"

Cara shook her head.

"That we could offer a further two per cent discount if they upgraded to our Tulip Package. She agreed. You know what she chose? Postcards. And that's where we'll make up the loss on the stickers and bookmarks."

Cara took a breath. "I'm sorry, Don, I figured that we—"

"It's about the clients. Without them, we don't have a business."

"I know, I should have—"

"You're off the deal with Blackbird Books."

She gaped at him, speechless. Don snatched up the papers from his desk, thrust them into a drawer and closed it.

Finally, she said, "But I've got an appointment with them tomorrow."

"Not anymore."

She could feel the tears coming. She said, "Don, I was involved in a hold-up last week."

"And I was very sorry to hear it. But I'm not running a charity. Martin is overseeing the job from now on."

She took a moment to find her voice. "Martin?"

"That's right. Thank you, Cara, that's it for now."

To further dismiss her, Don picked up the handset and began flipping through his desk diary. Cara, face burning, heart pounding, got up and left the room. As soon as she got back to her own office, she closed the door and rang Mick on his mobile. He answered on the second ring.

"Hey, beautiful," he said. "What's up?"

"Come over for dinner tonight," she said.

"I'll be there at eight."

She made roast chicken. Mick cleaned his plate and asked for seconds. As usual, the conversation ran easily. Cara hadn't intended to talk about work, but the bottle of red that Mick had brought along started loosening her up somewhere around the second glass. They were sitting in her lounge room on separate couches, enjoying the last of the wine, when she told Mick about her meeting with Don, relaying the conversation as closely as she could remember.

"What a turd," Mick said.

"But that's not the end of it," she continued. "After lunch, he came into my office and ordered me to take sick leave for the rest of the week. He told me to get my act together. Can you believe that? God, he was pissed off, like he'd been stewing on my mistake the whole morning."

Mick shook his head. "He thinks you should be over the robbery."

"But that's ridiculous."

"Listen, people who haven't been through a trauma don't understand. And you know why? Because they imagine themselves in the same situation and figure they'd be brave about it. That's the truth. People overestimate themselves.

Then something terrible happens to them, and they shit their pants."

Cara laughed.

"Ah, don't worry about it," Mick said. "Life kicks everyone in the head sooner or later. Your boss will get his."

"No, it's not that. It's him giving my account to Martin. For God's sake, how could anyone bear to do business with Martin? He's forever making these little harrumphing noises, like everything is beneath his contempt. Damn, he's irritating. And so is my boss."

Mick put his empty glass on the coffee table and moved to sit next to her. Smiling, resting his arm along the back of the couch, he said, "Want me to do 'em over?"

She giggled. "Both of them?"

"You get a cut-rate for two."

"Oh, wouldn't that be great?" She sat back, nestling her cheek at the crook of his elbow. The red wine had started a pleasant fuzziness in her head. "Do I get to break their legs?"

"Nah, you might get carried away. Better leave it to a professional."

"Like you?"

"Yeah, like me."

Cara sat up. He watched her; his face suddenly unreadable.

At last, she said, "Have you ever broken anybody's legs?"

He shrugged. "I've busted a few skulls in my time."

The scar running from his temple to his jaw reflected in the lamp light as a thin, silver trail. She wanted to trace it with her fingertip, with her lips.

Instead, she said, "Don't you ever get sick of the violence?"

"It's not that bad."

"I don't know how you can stand it."

"It's like anything else. You do a job for long enough, the job becomes second nature."

Sighing, she again leaned back into the crook of his elbow. Mick dropped his other hand to her knee, began to rub gently along her thigh. His touch sent a little shiver through her. Was she drunk? Quite possibly.

"Let me ask you something," she said. "And I've been meaning to ask you for a while."

"Okay, go ahead."

"Do you always devote this much attention to your crime victims?"

"Never before in my life."

His expression was tender, almost sad. Impulsively, she leaned across and kissed him, hard. He embraced her. The kiss went on and on. After a time, he scooped her from the couch and onto his lap, his strength thrilling her, snagging the breath in her throat. She fumbled with his shirt buttons, pulled open the shirt. He wrenched off his tie. At last, she could run her hands across the expanse of his chest, over the thickness of shoulder muscles. The latent power of his body electrified her.

"Let's go to bed," she said.

Without a word, he picked her up and carried her into the bedroom. They stripped, and stretched out together on the mattress, kissing, fondling. She ached for him. His skin felt hot, the brawn of him throwing off heat like a furnace.

"Don't make me wait," she said, pressing closer.

Instead, he parted her thighs and worked on her with his mouth until she was spent and drugged with sensation, and only then did he cover her body with his own.

Their kiss was long and languorous. Strength returned to Cara's limbs. Her legs wrapped around him. He entered her, but only just, holding himself back, moving inside her ever so slowly. Nothing would hurry him. Damn, it was a maddening torment the way he countered the impatient arching of her hips, resisted the pressure of her hands on his buttocks. Oh, dear God, she thought, panting, trembling. This man's lovemaking would kill her.

"Look at me," he murmured.

Cara opened her eyes. Unexpectedly, he was watching her, fascinated. Shit. What kind of foolish, unguarded expressions had already crossed her face? She closed her eyes again, embarrassed. Mick stopped moving.

"No, look at me," he said.

And she did. His lips were apart, his cheeks flushed.

"This is what you want," he said, shifting inside her very slightly. "Tell me."

She nodded, tightening her legs about him as her excitement climbed. He kissed her, gripping her hair in a fist, then drew back to stare at her with feverish intensity.

"Tell me to fuck you," he whispered. "Look at me and say it. Say the words."

A surge of lust flowered in her belly. "Oh, please," she said. "Please fuck me."

With a groan, he thrust deep into her. She clung to him and cried out.

SEVEN

The piercing double-beeps of an incoming text jolted Cara awake.

The milky light that seeped around the curtain edges outlined Mick on the other side of the bed, lying with his back to her. An intoxicating rush of desire quivered along her nerves. She reached out to touch him but he was already flipping back the doona and getting up. Naked, unselfconscious, he grabbed the soft-leather briefcase from the floor, dropped it to the foot of the mattress, and started rummaging through it.

Cara struggled to a sitting position and turned on the lamp. "Was that your phone or mine?"

"Mine."

She glanced at the digital alarm clock: 5.42 a.m. "Oh, come on," she said, "who would send a message at this hour?"

"My crew."

"Seriously? It's not even ten hours since you left work. Don't you guys have a union?"

Instead of answering her, Mick upended the briefcase and emptied its contents across the bed, hunting for the mobile phone like his life depended on it. Cara watched, intrigued.

Apart from work-related items like pens, diary, notepad and shoulder holster, the disparate pile of belongings suggested an itinerant lifestyle—sunscreen lotion, pocketknife, sunglasses, heat rub cream, pair of jocks, shaving kit, socks, woollen gloves, white shirt in a plastic bag, hammer wrench, first aid kit. Mick ransacked through it all until he found the mobile. Only then did he appear to start breathing again.

As Mick pressed buttons on the phone, Cara contemplated the minutiae of his briefcase with interest, in particular the hammer wrench. Why would an Armed Offence Squad detective carry around a tool like that? And then she realised that it wasn't a wrench. She scooched closer, pushed aside a woollen glove with her fingertip, took a better look.

It was a gun.

Not a silver one, not the kind with a cylinder that holds six bullets like a cowboy's revolver, but a black gun, flat and angular, the type that loads with a clip into the handle. The hard, blunt, lethal object contrasted against her pastel doona cover like a spider on a doll's face. The robbery boiled up. The memory became physical, the barrel of Sammy's gun ramming again at her spine. Cara's heart and lungs cramped, shied away and cowered like before, like during the robbery.

"Is that a real gun?" she said.

Mick didn't look up from his phone. "Yep."

"Is it loaded?"

"Wouldn't be much good if it wasn't."

Her voice tightened. "You brought a loaded gun to my house?"

For the first time that morning, Mick looked at her. His hand that held the phone dropped down to his side, the text message forgotten.

"Fuck, I'm sorry," he said.

"Get it out of here."

"No, look; there's nothing to worry about," he said, picking up the gun without fear.

When he sat down next to her on the bed, she lunged away. He didn't try to stop her.

"This is a police issue firearm," he continued. "It's a .40 calibre semi-automatic pistol. It fell out of the holster, that's all. But it's got a safety on it here, see?"

"That's enough, I don't care."

"The pistol can't shoot by itself."

"Just get rid of it."

His arm was around her, his lips kissing her cheek. "Listen to me," he whispered by her ear. "I'm a police officer and I carry a gun and that's the way it is. Okay? I can't help that. It's the only way it's ever going to be." His weight left the bed. "I've got to make a call. I'll be back in a minute."

After a few seconds, she heard his voice murmuring from the kitchen. She sat up. The items from Mick's briefcase were still scattered over the foot of the bed. Except for the gun; that was gone. She pressed her fingertips into her eyelids. Then she lay down, and pushed her face into the pillow.

Mick walked back into the bedroom, saying, "I've got to go."

She turned over. He began pulling on his shirt and trousers. Watching him stretch, bunch and wrestle into his clothes stirred her loins. The jag of lust made her despair. For God's sake, with her emotions back-flipping all over the place, she was out of control; there was no doubt. And sleeping with Mick when she hadn't even known him a week? Jesus. Whether she wanted to or not, she had to see somebody. If she didn't see somebody, a psychologist, a counsellor, she might fall apart completely.

Her gaze roamed over him. "Come back to bed," she said, despite herself.

He shook his head, grinning. "Not today." He found his socks and dragged them on.

"You don't have time for breakfast? I make a mean bowl of cereal."

"I bet you do. Another time." He began loading the items back into his briefcase. "I could drop over tonight and bring takeaway for dinner."

"That'd be nice."

Fully dressed, his briefcase restocked and held in one hand, Mick crossed to the side of the bed and gave her a quick peck on the forehead.

"Hey, wait a second," Cara said, reaching up and folding an arm about his shoulders.

Their kiss was slow and gentle. His free hand found her breast and kneaded it gently. Then he left the room. Cara hoped that he was joking, that he would return to the room and start taking his clothes off again, until she heard the front door open and close. Distantly, from the street, a car started up and drove away. She couldn't help but feel disappointed.

Straightening her arms overhead, she luxuriated in the muscle stiffness from their hours of lovemaking, relished in the soreness of her facial skin from his stubble. Mick had been a passionate, demanding, generous lover.

But he carried a loaded gun.

Wait a second, she thought. *Don't be an idiot.* Every copper carries a loaded gun.

The semi-industrial street had factories on one side and shabby apartment blocks on the other. The couple walked along the footpath on the residential side. The man carried a number of plastic shopping bags. The woman carried one, her other hand clutching a cigarette. Unknown to them, a squad car containing Mick and Alec crawled in their wake. Behind in another squad car were Bull and Stevo.

"Ready?" Alec said into the mobile phone.

"Shit yeah," Bull replied.

Mick gunned the engine, shot the car about five metres ahead of the couple and pulled onto the kerb, braking hard. He and Alec got out of the car and began striding towards the couple. Alarmed, the couple stopped dead. Stevo brought the other car alongside. The man and woman, realising their doom, too scared to move, gaped from one set of coppers to the other.

Smiling, Mick took out his badge. "Armed Offence Squad. We'd like to have a chat about your wig collection."

The crew ferried the man and woman in separate cars to the Melbourne City Police Complex. In the elevator, Bull and Stevo held the man, while Mick held the woman, and Alec held the groceries. With her hands cuffed behind her back, the woman scrubbed her tears and snot along the shoulders of her tatty windcheater. She had been crying non-stop since they put her in the back of the squad car. During the elevator ride, the man kept saying things like, "Are we in trouble? Can't you tell us what this is about?", but other than that, no one spoke. Bull, however, whistled a jaunty tune through his teeth.

They reached the ninth floor and began walking through the squad room. Other Armed Offence Squad detectives came over to hoot and catcall. The man and woman looked about in abject terror.

"Hey, Mick," yelled one of the detectives. "Who did you pay to get a pair of sitters?"

"Piss off," Mick called back, grinning.

Alec dumped the grocery bags on the crew's desks.

"We gotta get that stuff into a freezer," the woman said, hiccupping and sobbing, trying to wrench away from Mick. "Our food's gonna spoil otherwise."

"Aw shit, darlin'," Bull said. "That's the least of your many fucking problems."

The couple was pushed into chairs.

Mick began pawing through the goods in the shopping bags. "Sausage rolls, party pies, oven chips, fish fingers, chocolate biscuits," he said, and shook his head. "Everything you could ever want from the 'beige' food group. How don't you morons have scurvy?"

"Scurvy?" the man said. "But we're not sailors."

Mick, Stevo and Alec cracked up laughing. Bull's confused expression made them laugh even harder. The phone rang, and Bull picked up the handset. "Armed Offence Squad. Yeah, who is it? Hang on." Putting a hand over the mouthpiece, he whispered to Mick, "It's your missus. You out?"

Mick nodded.

Bull said into the phone, "You've just missed him, love. Yeah, no worries, I'll tell him," and he hung up. "Janice says to switch on your mobile and call her back."

Stevo leaned over the desk towards the couple, who quailed in their seats. "This is how dumb you people are," he said. "You knocked over your local bottle shop. Now, why would you do that? Why didn't you go where nobody knows you?"

"How?" the man said. "We don't have a car."

The crew convulsed with laughter again.

"Ah, you couldn't make this shit up," Stevo said, wiping at his eyes.

Sergeant Frank Ward approached and tapped Mick on the arm. "We have to chat for a minute," Ward said. "Let's go somewhere private."

They went to the storeroom.

Ward closed the door, and said, "I heard what happened at the TAB the other day."

Mick didn't answer. Ward frowned and waited.

At last, Mick shrugged. "I don't know what you're talking about."

"Stop trying to bullshit me. Dave Etherington. How you fixed him up in the laneway. I heard what happened."

"Who from?"

"Never mind."

Mick's face hardened.

Ward said, "You want to go up against a police brutality charge? Well, do you? I'm wearing enough shit over these pizza crooks already, and you want to give me more? Now what were you thinking?"

"I was doing what I get paid to do."

"Bash up civilians?"

"Dave's a scumbag, an ex-con. He knows who our pizza bandits are. He has to be persuaded, that's all."

"Then find other means of persuasion."

Mick crossed his arms.

Ward continued, "You broke one of his ribs, are you aware of that? A lawyer would have a fucking field day with that kind of evidence."

"Yeah, but it doesn't matter. Legal Aid wouldn't give a crap, and Dave couldn't afford a real lawyer anyway."

"You admit to bashing him?"

"Like I said, I don't know what you're talking about."

"Yeah, yeah." Ward sighed. "Keep yourself nice. Okay? For me, please. I don't want to have a heart attack until I'm at least fifty, understand?"

Mick flung open the door and stalked to the crew's desks. Bull and Stevo looked up at his approach. So did the arrested couple, faces pale, eyes haunted.

"Where's Alec?" Mick said.

"Having a piss," Bull said.

As Mick stormed across the squad room, through the elevator hall and towards the men's room, a number of possible scenarios flashed through his mind, all of them violent. He shoved open the door of the men's room. Alec, bent over a basin and rinsing his hands under the running tap, straightened and turned around, the startled look on his face bringing a fresh hammering of blood to Mick's temples.

Mick stepped closer. Noiselessly, the door closed behind him.

"Mate," Alec said, showing his palms, "whatever it is, you've got the wrong idea."

Within two strides, Mick was on him, grabbing him by the shirt, ramming knuckles into his throat. Alec didn't resist. Choking off the carotids like this would have Alec unconscious in about thirty seconds—in fact, the intracranial pressure and wooziness must be climbing already—but still the greenhorn did nothing in his own defence. Mick felt like spitting on him. Instead, he shoved him away. Alec stumbled against one of the hand dryers.

"If you want to make it in this squad," Mick said, "you've got to learn how to be a team player. Is that clear?"

The door of the men's room opened. Bull looked at them both. "Everything okay?" he said.

The only sound was the gurgling of water running into the basin. Bull put an arm about Mick's shoulders and steered him out of the men's room and back towards the Armed Offence Squad.

"Don't worry about that prick," Bull whispered. "Little wog boy won't make it in here, all right? Take it easy. He'll be gone soon."

But Mick's heart wouldn't stop clanging around inside his ribcage. He sat at his desk in silence, trying to calm himself, while Stevo and Bull questioned the couple. Alec kept away. If Alec came within swinging distance, Mick wasn't too sure what he would do. When it came time to take the couple to remand, Bull volunteered to accompany Alec in the car. A favour like that deserved a slab of beer, in Mick's book.

Cara had rung around until she found someone who could give her an appointment that morning. The office of psychologist Rob Parkdale was in a room of his two-storey terrace home.

Upon her arrival, Rob had led Cara through the lounge room, up the half-landing staircase and along the hall, revealing at every step a beautifully decorated house: polished boards, framed black-and-white photographs on the walls, fully stocked bookcases, Buddha statues arranged amongst the furniture. The dining table sat twelve. Cara imagined that Rob Parkdale did a lot of entertaining. His guests would be highly educated, worldly, cultured people—unlike her—and the thought had made her, fleetingly, want to turn around and leave.

Now, she was sitting in the office couch under the window. Rob was sitting by the desk on the other side of the room, an older man, bald, with kind blue eyes and a neat, white beard. Without interrupting, he listened to her account of the robbery. She told it quickly, outlining the sequence of events in brief sentences, running out of words in under a minute.

Rob said, "How do you think this experience has affected you?"

Cara glanced at the side table alongside the couch. On it, a full box of tissues and a teddy bear. She shifted around uncomfortably. "Well, in a typical way, I suppose. I'm drinking a lot more than usual. I'm anxious, of course. I can't sleep properly. And then there are the nightmares."

"What are the nightmares about?"

"I'm not sure. About shapes, mostly."

"Of people?"

"Of guns. Shadowy faces. I wake up scared and have to turn on the light." She gestured at the teddy bear. "Do any of your patients actually hold that thing?"

"Some of the younger ones do, yes. And from time to time, some of the older ones too. His name is Marmalade, by the way, if you'd like to give him a hug."

"No thanks." She bit at her lip, gazed around the office, looked at Rob's framed certificates that lined one wall. Rob waited. The silence made her ill at ease. "It wouldn't be that bad if I had my work to keep me busy," she said. "My boss made me take the week off."

"You feel you don't need the time?"

"I want to get on with things."

"Is that how you cope during times of stress? By distracting yourself?"

"It's not about distraction. I'm simply not interested in navel gazing." She pressed her hands together. "You know, I've never been to a psychologist before. I'm not sure what I'm supposed to do."

"Just be yourself. There's no right or wrong."

"Okay." She managed a brief smile. "Will you be able to help me?"

"Yes, I think I can."

Good, Cara thought, only don't ask me about my childhood. If he did ask her, however, she would brush off the question and steer the conversation back to the one and only relevant issue: how to put the robbery behind her as quickly as possible.

It was about an hour after Bull and Alec had left to take the wig-wearing couple to remand. Mick and Stevo were still writing up their reports and finalising paperwork when Sergeant Ward jogged over, his eyes bulging. Loping in his wake was Brian Vaughan, no less, the detective inspector of the Armed Offence Squad, looking equally as animated. The surge of adrenaline hit Mick so hard that he knocked over his chair leaping to his feet.

"Info back from the Dogs," Ward said. "It's a goer on Brownie."

"No shit," Mick said. "What's the deal?"

Vaughan, steel-wool eyebrows jiggling high on his forehead, said, "You're going to give this Brownie an early wake-up call tomorrow morning. Hopefully, he'll still have the gear."

"If we can nab the guns or even the airline bag, that'd be enough," Stevo said.

"Let's get on it," Ward said. "We need floor plans."

"Done," Stevo said, rolling in his chair towards a computer. "I'm onto the council right now."

"What about the warrant?" Mick said.

"Break, enter, search; I'll have it for you by the end of the day," Vaughan said, hurrying to his office.

"For both the house and car, sir, if you can manage it," Stevo called. "You never know."

Without turning around, Vaughan lifted an arm in a wave of acknowledgment, and then disappeared behind the slammed door of his office.

Mick said, "Hey, Sarge, I want to be first through the door."

With a frown and a noisy exhalation, Ward moved away.

"No, listen, I've got to go through first," Mick continued, following the sergeant towards the floor-to-ceiling windows at the rear of the squad room. "I want it more than anyone else."

"You're on the sledgehammer."

"No way, let me do it."

They were clear of other detectives. Ward stopped walking and said, "You're too keyed up for number one slot. No, you take the sledgehammer position and you go in last. Understand?"

Mick slitted his eyes. "Is this how you're going to be? And I'm here four years?"

"Aw, don't get started on shit like that—"

"You're going to shame me in front of the crew? Come on, Sarge, who are you going to put first through the door? Alec?"

"Stop it. That's enough."

"Nobody wants this more than me. Nobody. And I've earned it. Don't tell me I haven't earned it."

Ward sighed. "Let me think about it, okay?"

Mick slapped him on the arm and hurried along the wall, checking the offices. Each one was occupied. Backtracking, Mick walked into the analyst's office without knocking. The analyst looked up from his laptop screen.

"I need to make a phone call," Mick said. "Now."

The analyst offered a stiff, formal smile and ducked from the room. Mick shut the door with a kick, grabbed the handset and dialled. Cara answered on the fourth ring.

"Hey, it's me," he said. "Listen, I can't come over for dinner, I have to do nightshift."

"But aren't you working a day shift right now? It's awful; you put in so many hours."

"Yeah, I know. I can't help that."

"What time will you finish up?"

"I don't know. We're doing a house raid at four tomorrow morning. Maybe I could drop over afterwards."

"What? You're kidding me. Before sunrise?"

"Hey, there's stuff to do back at the squad room. That'll take a few hours. You don't raid a house then go home. Will I drop around, say, mid-morning or lunch time?"

"Yes, please," she said. "God, I can't stop thinking about you."

The tone of her voice was an electric jolt through his gut. Mick closed his eyes for a moment. He pictured the delicate pulse at the base of her throat, her long and slender limbs, those mesmerising little hollows made by her hipbones. He opened his eyes. "Okay, I'll see you," he said. "Be naked when you open the door."

EIGHT

At 3.00 a.m. in the squad room, Mick, Bull, Stevo, Alec and Ward began to suit up. A sprawl of equipment collected from police armoury lay across their desks. Each man checked his own equipment: tactical vest, 128-channel two-way radio, torch, capsicum spray, collapsible baton, taser, pistol, ammunition clips, and shotgun cartridges. Nearby, the rostered nightshift crew watched as intently as hungry men witnessing the consumption of a banquet.

Ward said, "Pay close attention, one last time for luck. Mick, you've got the bedroom first right off the hall. Stevo, you and me will take the master bedroom at the end of the hall. Alec, you check the spare room, laundry, bathroom, dunny. And Bull, you go left to the kitchen and lounge room. Clear?"

"Clear," his men said.

Ward, at about the same time as his crew, shrugged into a ballistics vest and began fastening the clips. "Surveillance tells us Brownie's housemate doesn't carry a weapon. We'll believe otherwise until he's on the floor in cuffs. Okay?"

"Check," Stevo said.

"Don't assume the woman is a bystander," Ward went on. "We get her in cuffs pronto."

"Where are the fucking batteries?" Bull said, raking through the equipment. "I saw them a minute ago."

"Hey, watch it," Alec said. "You're knocking shit onto the floor."

As he donned the tactical vest over the top of his ballistics vest, Ward said, "Don't forget the dog. It should be chained to its kennel in the back yard. If you have to pursue outside, watch out for the dog. We don't know how long its chain is. When we first bust into the house, again, we need to watch out for the dog because tonight could be the night it's kept indoors."

"Stand back while I kick it in the nuts," Bull said.

"If you have to shoot the dog, remember to aim for the body. It's a Rottweiler with a skull of concrete. Okay?"

"I might shoot it anyway," Bull said. "I fucking hate rotties at the best of times."

"Now I know what to get you for Christmas," Stevo said.

"Aw, get stuffed."

"That's enough, stop with the shit," Ward said. "We're going to be careful and we're going to look out for each other, okay? Let's go."

They grabbed the remainder of the equipment and headed towards the elevators.

"Good luck," called out a detective from the nightshift crew.

"Thanks," Ward said. "We'll be back here soon with our catch of scumbags."

Bull added, "And for a slab or two, we'll let you box 'em around the ears."

Everyone laughed at that. Everyone but Mick.

From the underground car park, the crew selected two divisional vans, each with a lockable cage in back. The drive took about three-quarters of an hour.

The suburban street, lit by a waning moon, featured weatherboard and fibro homes, cyclone fencing, front yards of weeds and mud. Like every other house in the street, no lights burned at Brownie's place at four in the morning.

The detectives hustled stealthily up the driveway. They lined the porch in a queue. Bull, against the front door, adjusted his grip on the sledgehammer. He looked back. At the rear, Ward gave a thumbs-up. Bull nodded. With a roll of his massive shoulders, Bull swung the sledgehammer and shattered the lock on the front door with one blow.

The door juddered wide open on its hinges. Stepping back, Bull dropped the sledgehammer between his feet and drew his pistol. The others ran into the house in single file, Mick entering first. Bull ran in last.

"Police, don't move!" the detectives yelled in unison, their torches flashing in the darkness as they ran to their designated areas. "Police, don't move!"

Mick sprinted down the hallway. The white circle of his torchlight jounced madly. Shotgun levelled in one hand, he charged into the first room on the right and snapped on the light switch. In the sudden glare, thrashing at the bed linen, Brownie sat up, bare-chested.

"Who's there?" Brownie said, squinting, his chunky arms flailing at invisible assailants. "What the fuck is going on?"

A woman screamed, loud as a siren. A man yelped. The shouting of Ward and Stevo from the master bedroom went on and on: *police, don't move; show us your hands; get on the floor.* From outside, the deep-throated, hysterical barking of a large dog started up.

Mick lowered the shotgun and aimed it loosely at Brownie's chest tattoo, a necklace comprising a flaming skull flanked by eagle wings stretching from one shoulder to the other.

"Well, if it isn't Detective Thompson," Brownie said, one eye screwed shut against the brightness of the room, the other staring in fear and indignation. "Long time, no see. But I done my time already, remember? I'm not guilty of nothing. You and your boys are off the mark."

The booming clamour of the dog kept sounding, regular as a heartbeat.

"Get out of my bloody house!" screamed the woman, sobbing, from the far end of the hall. "No, you bastard, you let me go. What's happening here?"

"Shut up, Tracy, shut up," cried the man.

Stevo shouted, "Bitch, lie down on the floor or I will break your fucking arm."

Mick slowly approached. Brownie raised his hands.

"Wait," Brownie said. "Aren't you gonna order me to the floor?"

The dog kept barking. The yelling from down the hall hadn't stopped.

"Put your hands behind your back," Stevo was bellowing.

"Do as he says," Ward added. "Stop fighting us."

"Hang on," Brownie said. "Should I lie on the floor now? Is that what you want?"

Mick reached the bedside. Brownie suddenly flung back the sheet. He was naked. Tattoos ranged over his body, a collection of knives, guns, skulls, skeletons, flames, demons. Mick jabbed Brownie once in the cheek with the barrel of the shotgun. The skin split and bled a little.

"Fair enough," Brownie said, holding a palm to his face, and dropping back to the mattress on one elbow. "Go ahead, mate, arrest me any way you like."

The blood stood out against the pallor of Brownie's skin, against the grey of his long, thinning hair, the black of his goatee beard. It shone crimson and glossy under the gleam of the ceiling bulb. There was so much blood over so many different walls, across tables and countertops, takeaway containers, pizza boxes. Chaos, Mick thought. Awful things came to his mind's eye, terrible things: a flurry of wounds jetting blood; a scalp opening in a hypnotic succession of flowers blossoming dark red; a swarm of black stitches roped through flesh.

Mick turned the shotgun around.

"What are you doing?" Brownie said.

The butt of the shotgun slammed against Brownie's head. Brownie let out an agonised screech. Mick threw the shotgun aside and began to hit Brownie, rhythmically, one punch after another, the jolt from each blow travelling up Mick's arms, shivering into the bunched muscles of his torso, trembling down his legs. As Mick's frame continued to absorb the recoil, an intense rush flamed through him, breaking sweat across his lower back, making him heady, drunk.

Alec's voice came from a distance. "Oh shit. Bull, help me! Help me, for God's sake."

They had hold of him, Alec on one side, Bull on the other. They tried to drag him away. He threw off Alec first, then Bull. On the bed lay Brownie, cowering, snivelling. Mick lunged. Hands grabbed him again.

"Thompson!" Ward yelled.

Blinking, Mick looked around. Ward stood in the doorway, shocked, eyes wide. Mick experienced an abrupt, overwhelming exhaustion. He stopped struggling. Bull and Alec held on to him anyway. Behind Ward was Stevo, mouth agape.

"Jesus fucking Christ, mate," Bull whispered.

Mick closed his eyes and tried to catch his breath.

The knocking boomed throughout the house and rattled the front door. Cara hurried over, tingling with anticipation, with excitement. She wore a bathrobe and nothing else. He must have been leaning against the door because as she opened it, Mick barrelled inside, staggering her. She would have fallen had he not grabbed her about the waist. He kissed her cheek soundly, making her laugh.

Clutching him around the neck, she said, "How did the raid go?"

"Fantastic, by the book. The prick's being interviewed right now." Mick was amped, face flushed, pupils dilated, smiling with his teeth clenched. He squeezed her in his arms.

"How did you get away?" she said.

"I told the sarge I had urgent business."

Giggling, Cara said, "Oh, you dirty liar."

"No way," he said, walking her backwards into the bedroom. "You're urgent business."

As he wrenched off his clothes, never taking his gaze from her, she leaned against the wall, heart racing, watching him. No man had ever wanted her this much. It almost frightened her. When Mick was naked, she dropped the bathrobe to the floor. He caught hold of her, his kisses insistent, greedy. Sitting on the bed, he leaned back and pulled her on top of him. His passion fanned hers and she straddled him, taking him inside. He gripped her thighs and dug his fingers into the flesh as if he had to stop her from escaping.

"Oh, you feel good," she murmured by his ear.

Without warning, he became very still. His hands fell away.

Cara hesitated. "Mick?"

She drew back to look at him. His open eyes were flat and empty.

"Are you okay?" she whispered.

He rolled over, flipping her onto her back. Raking fingers along her arms, he grabbed her wrists and, one at a time, pinned them down. His body pressed her into the mattress. She turned her head, smothered by his chest. The tempo of his movements picked up, became driving and savage. Cara struggled to free herself.

"Stop," she said. "Mick, stop it, get off me."

He froze. Then he let go of her wrists, took his weight on his elbows.

"I'm sorry," he said.

"What the hell was that all about?"

"I don't know. I'm not sure what happened."

He went to kiss her. When she averted her face, he dropped his lips to her neck instead. With great patience, he worked along the length of her body; licking, nuzzling, sucking. By the time he put his mouth between her thighs, the feel of his tongue was the only thing that mattered to her anymore.

When they finished their lovemaking, he got out of bed and started dressing.

Cara pulled the sheet up to her chin. "Where are you going?" she said.

"Back to the squad."

"Right now?"

"Yep."

"But you only just got here."

"That's right."

Mick buttoned his shirt, tied his tie, drew on his trousers, took a seat at the edge of the bed to attend to his shoelaces, and never once even glanced at her. Standing up, he began patting along his pockets as if checking for keys.

"What's next?" she said. "Money on the bedside table?"

He turned to her, surprised. "Why would you even say something like that?"

She shrugged. He came over and sat by her.

"I want to stay, but I can't," he said. "I'm not even supposed to be here."

"I know."

"Do you? Listen, my job isn't nine to five. When I'm busy, I'm busy and there's nothing I can do about it. That's the way it is."

Cara sighed, tried to smile. He took one of her hands in both of his and gently kissed it. She noticed that his knuckles were scraped raw.

"If I've been an arsehole, I'm sorry," he said. "I've been awake for over thirty hours and I'm not thinking straight."

She put her arms about his neck. He kissed her and stood up.

"I'll call you later," he said.

"Okay. Try and get some rest."

"Ha," he said, grinning, "maybe when I'm dead. See you, beautiful."

He left the room. The front door opened and closed.

She lay back in bed. There was no reason to feel uneasy. It was the sound of the wind getting on her nerves, nothing else. For a minute or two, she listened to the gusts clawing about the house and scratching the cypress branches against her window. Then she got up and took a shower.

"You used excessive force," Ward said.

Mick crossed his arms. "I didn't have a choice. Brownie was trying to take my weapon."

"That's not how I saw it."

"But that's what happened," Mick said, and indicated Bull and Alec with a tilt of his head. "Ask them. They reached me and Brownie before you did."

The four men were standing in one of the evidence rooms of the Armed Offence Squad. With the door shut, it was crowded in there with the clutter of filing cabinets and open-faced shelves, but every other office had been occupied.

"All right, let's hear it," Ward said.

"Brownie had hold of the shotty," Bull said.

"Alec? Is that what you saw as well?"

"Uh-huh."

Fuming, Ward said, "You two, get out. One of you, take over from Stevo. It's his turn to sleep."

Bull and Alec left the room.

Ward shouldered the door closed. "You're worth ten of anyone else in this squad," he snarled. "Quit screwing up. Okay? Act like a professional."

Mick, stony-faced, said, "I'm always professional."

"Oh, yeah? Then where were you this morning? The other blokes had to carry your can."

"I had business."

"Business? You can't sneak out of here whenever you feel like it. I thought you'd gone to the snooze room. Then I realised you'd taken a car." Ward shook his head, incredulous. "I figured, aw, no worries, he must be out getting coffees because all of us are goddamned tired and needing a break, right? But no, you go missing for over an hour. How come?"

"I told you already."

"Don't shit me. And why do you keep turning off your phone?"

Mick didn't reply.

Ward gave an exasperated wave of his hand, flung open the door, and headed to the elevator hall. Mick left the evidence room for the crew's desks. Before he could get there, Alec intercepted him. The greenhorn held up a wallet: rectangular, tri-fold, black suede, no clasp. Mick stopped and waited.

"What's this?" Alec said.

"You tell me."

"It belongs to a victim from the Benny's job last week: Cara Haynes."

"So?" Mick said.

"I was looking for I.R. sheets and found it in your desk."

The men stared at each other. For an Armed Offence Squad detective, Alec looked too much like a pretty-boy. Who would ever find Alec intimidating? Nobody: that's who. Mick wanted to punch him. Instead, he shrugged.

"Must've fallen out of the evidence box," Mick said. "I'll give it back to her."

"No trouble. I'll do it."

"Suits me."

Mick headed to the interview room and opened the door. Brownie, sitting on the far side of the table, looked up and blanched. Mick grinned in satisfaction.

Lifting both of his hands, still cuffed at the wrists, Brownie pointed at his lumpy, purpled face and said to Mick, "Look what you done, you fucking psycho. I want a lawyer."

"Shut up," Bull said, seated on the other side of the table. "You'll get a lawyer when we say."

"I've answered your questions. When can I get out of here?"

"We'll let you know."

Mick shut the door, leaned against it and said, "How're you going? Being looked after?"

"Come on, mate. Enough's enough. Is this about that fucking supermarket job? You know I didn't do it. Why can't you let bygones be bygones? Aw, fuck. I need something to drink, all right? And a piss."

"There you go, problem solved. Drink your own piss," Bull said.

"Bring your sergeant in here," Brownie said. "Where's Frank Ward?"

"He doesn't do interviews," Bull said.

"Is he coming to do the welfare check on me? Is he?"

"No," Mick said.

"Then who's gonna do the welfare check?"

Bull sat back and laced his hands behind his head. "Let's go over it again. Who's the bloke you sold your Ford Falcon to?"

Brownie's eyes fluttered shut for a moment. "How many times do I have to tell you the same thing? A mate of my sister-in-law, I can't remember his name. Why isn't the camera running? How come you're not taping any of this?"

"Because you're not telling us shit," Bull said. "As soon as you've got something to say, we'll start the interview."

A gentle tapping sounded at the door. Mick moved aside. The door opened.

Alec said, "The sarge says to come out."

"Sure," Bull said, cutting a smile at Brownie. "I need a piss anyway."

"Don't go anywhere, dirtbag," Mick said. "We'll be right back."

Across the squad room, the figure of Ward—hands on hips, face pinched and ashen—stirred a ribbon of dread through Mick's guts. They reached their desks. Alec flung himself into a chair and looked away. Mick knew what it was before Ward had even opened his mouth.

"It's not him," Ward said.

"What?" Bull said, frowning. "Not Brownie? No way."

"I just got confirmation from Phillips. Brownie was in Horsham every day last week visiting his daughter, and got back on Saturday morning."

"That can't be right," Bull said.

"It's confirmed by coppers." Ward glanced around at his men with rheumy eyes. "The bastard got pulled over by a couple of connies and given a speeding fine, late Friday night, coming back from Pimpinio."

"Bloody hell," Bull said. "We got nothing."

Alec looked up. "We can take Brownie on possession charges."

"For a gun and a bag of dope?" Mick said, groping for a seat, landing heavily. "Big fucking deal."

No one spoke for a while.

Finally, Bull said, "Who's going to tell Stevo?"

"Let him sleep," Ward said. "All right, we have to finish up. One of you, go and see if Brownie wants another coffee before we send him on his way."

"You're up, Mario," Bull said. "And while you're in the kitchen, get me a coffee too: white and three."

"Get it yourself."

"I'll pretend I didn't hear that. Come on, Mario, be a good boy. Go grab us chocolate biscuits if there's any left."

Ward said, "You know, I'm surprised Brownie didn't ask for a lawyer."

Bull shrugged. "He probably figured he didn't need one."

Sighing, Ward began putting on his suit jacket. "Well, I'm off to explain this massive cock-up to Vaughan, if I can."

"Aw, jeez," Bull said, groaning, "the Dogs are gonna give us shit for this."

Ward walked off, head down. Mick swivelled in his chair to face the floor-to-ceiling windows. The view was nothing but solid blue sky. At noon, this particular winter's day didn't have a single cloud. Mick scowled at the bright sunshine flooding every inch of the squad room. What a joke. What a sick, infuriating joke.

One of the phones rang. Alec picked it up. "Armed Offence Squad. Yes, who's calling? Okay, just a second." Then he said, "Mick, for you. Cara Haynes."

"Isn't she the sheila from the Benny's Pizza job?" Bull said.

Mick turned in his chair. Alec, the stupid little turd, was staring at him as if trying to gauge his reaction. Mick snatched the handset, pressed the receiver flat to his ear so that Cara's voice wouldn't carry, and said, "What do you want?"

After a moment, Cara stammered, "To talk to you about what happened this morning."

"I'm busy."

"Okay, I understand that, but...when can I speak to you?"

"When I'm not busy. Thanks for calling." He hung up.

Bull gave a low whistle. "That sounded like a lovers' tiff to me. You lucky bastard. Are you slamming this bird, or what?"

"Piss off, mate. Stop thinking with your dick."

Bull laughed. Alec, on the other hand, was regarding Mick with a speculative gaze. Mick closed his eyes and started rubbing at the sudden headache around his temples. Christ, he needed to get drunk.

NINE

It must have been the weather. For a Wednesday night blurring into the wee hours of a Thursday morning, the Pink Peach Men's Club was unusually crowded. Two bars ran the length of two walls, and dozens of chest-high tables crammed the floor between the stages. Mick, Bull and Stevo were pressed up against the centre stage, swaying, yelling, guzzling spirits, jostling the other patrons, while a bottle-blonde wearing sky-high heels and nothing else ground against the pole. Ceiling lights phased on and off in time to the music. The thumping beat of a rap R&B song blared from hidden speakers, and Bull had to shout with every ounce of his strength just so the dancer could hear him.

"I'll give you fifty bucks to suck me off," he bellowed.

Mick and Stevo guffawed. They laughed even harder when she gave Bull an icy glare and a snarled lip.

"I think she likes him," Stevo said, leaning against Mick, sniggering.

"Shit, look at the size of those big plastic titties." Bull leaned over the stage again, cupping a hand around his mouth. "For a titty fuck, I'll give you a hundred."

Mick cracked up, staggered backwards, knocked into something. For a woozy moment, the floor tilted beneath his feet. As he straightened and regained his footing, he realised that a civilian was getting in his face.

"Watch it," the civilian was saying, "you nearly knocked our table over, you idiot."

There were five other men at the civilian's table, young blokes who looked like footy players. Mick felt the soft flick of a little switch. Exhilarated, he threw his glass of vodka to the ground. Stevo grabbed him. Bull showed a police badge to the civilian.

"You want to get busted, cockhead?" Bull said. "You and your faggot mates?"

The civilian shook his head. Stevo and Bull steered Mick back to the centre stage. In the meantime, the bottle-blonde had ascended the pole upside-down, her legs in a twist, her long hair sweeping at the floorboards. As she began rubbing her breasts, Bull put a hand to his mouth.

"Hundred and twenty," he shouted over the din of music. "All right, hundred and fifty, but you cop it in the face."

Mick and Stevo broke out laughing. Suddenly, two giant men appeared amongst them. Blinking slowly, Mick looked them over: both Pacific Islanders, both built like brick shithouses, both looking very pissed off. It was hilarious. The three detectives heehawed again. Bull showed his badge. The bouncers exchanged glances and moved away. Bull and Stevo jeered. Mick closed his eyes. The song had changed. The pumping riff bored into his eardrums, and punched at his heart and lungs like a living thing. Bull still had his arm across Mick's shoulders. They tottered sideways together, lurching against Stevo.

"Aw, look," Stevo yelled, "she's doing the splits."

Mick shoved away. "I gotta go," he shouted.

"What?" Bull said. "Shit, if you take the car, how we gonna get home?"

"Taxi."

"But where are you going, mate?" Bull demanded. "It's after one in the morning."

"I gotta see a man about a dog."

Mick weaved through the tables, steadying himself occasionally against furniture or patrons with an outstretched hand. The green exit sign wavered in his vision.

The banging on the front door jolted Cara awake. Pulse hammering, she sat up in bed, the shadows of her dream falling away, the gun no longer at her ribs. She turned on the lamp. The knocking kept going. She jumped up and pulled on her dressing gown.

At the front door, she said, "Who is it?"

"It's me. Let me in."

"What are you doing here? Do you have any idea what time it is?"

"I have to see you."

She opened the door. On the porch, swaying and grinning stupidly, stood Mick, his tie askew, missing a coat and jacket despite the fog, the needling cold.

"Hey, beautiful," he said.

"Oh my God, how much have you had to drink? You didn't drive here, did you?"

"I'm a copper. I can do what I want."

He stumbled forward into the house, trying to kiss and grope. Cara shoved him away.

"Mick, get off me."

"Huh? What's the matter?"

She walked from the door towards the centre of the lounge room. He followed behind, plucking at her dressing gown.

"Come on, Cara, let's fuck. I want to fuck you."

She spun around. "I want you to leave."

"Leave? What for? I just got here."

His mystified and hurt expression riled her. She put her hands on her hips. Mick's hooded gaze dropped to her chest. For that, she felt like slapping him.

"You're treating me like shit," she said.

"I told you I was sorry."

"No, you didn't."

"Well, I'm saying it now. I'm sorry, okay? For everything. For whatever."

He took a few steps closer. And then it occurred to her, in a chill that trailed along her spine, that she didn't really know this man. Yet here he was in the middle of the night, tall and broad and strong and drunk, advancing, the two of them alone in her house. She tugged her dressing gown closed and drew up to her full height.

She said, "You don't even know why I'm upset, do you?"

The anger in him broke across his face. "Listen, I've been working flat out, around the clock, risking my life. I could get killed."

"What's that got to do with it?"

"You have to make allowances."

"No, I don't."

They regarded each other for a few tense seconds. Cara held firm. Mick's shoulders dropped. He brought a hand to his brow, shaking his head.

"It's the job, that's all. It's hard to switch off." He looked at her again, his smile tender, rueful. "Am I forgiven?"

At last, she said, "I'm tired. I'm going back to bed."

"Want some company?"

In reply, Cara walked across the room and stood by the open front door. Mick's face tightened in shock. Then, with a curt smile, he strode past her and out into the foggy night. Cara shut the door and leaned against it.

Later that morning, Cara sat in Rob Parkdale's office. She held the teddy bear loosely in both hands and fiddled with its ears. The acrylic fur was matted and dense like felt, as if countless fingers had already worked those tabs of material half to death.

"I don't get it," Cara said. "He's under a lot of pressure, but so am I."

"And you're not trained to deal with violence. He is."

"Exactly. Now, what am I going to do?"

Rob propped his chin in one palm, rubbing at the white bristles of his beard as he considered her question. He looked like a kindly grandfather. Cara, in an undisciplined moment, imagined what it might be like to have this psychologist as her actual grandfather, smiling at her with love in his eyes. She dismissed the crazy thought almost as soon as it came to her.

"What is it that you want to do about this policeman?" Rob said. "I mean deep down, in your heart of hearts."

"I don't know. The thing is...he understands me."

"Does he?"

"Yes," she said, putting the teddy bear next to her on the couch. "No one has any idea what I've been through. I can be sitting in a roomful of people and it's like I'm all by myself. With Mick, I don't even have to tell him how I feel. He already knows."

"From a professional point of view, yes."

That took the wind out of her. "You think I should stop seeing him."

"If you don't mind me saying, it sounds like this policeman is compounding your problems, not solving them."

"But who else have I got?"

"Who indeed? Let's explore that thought."

She raked her fingers through her hair. "You know, I'm not sure these sessions are particularly helpful."

After, while driving back home, Cara on impulse took a right turn towards the city. At the next red light, she rang Premiere Press and told Lucy to expect her within half an hour and to set up an emergency meeting with Don.

Within minutes of disconnecting the call, the phone rang again, probably Lucy to confirm the meeting. Touching a button on the steering wheel, Cara answered.

"Listen, I want to say how sorry I am," Mick said.

Cara hung up and switched off her phone.

Just a short while later, it felt good to be back in the Premiere Press building. She waved at Lucy, and took the stairs two at a time. Don's office door was open.

"Hi there," Cara said.

Don looked around from his computer monitor and smiled. "I thought you were supposed to be relaxing on holidays."

"That gets boring. Can I have a minute?"

"You can have as long as you like."

"Thanks." Cara took a seat on the other side of the desk. "How's Martin going on the Blackbird Books account?"

"Well, he kept the Tuesday appointment you'd set up."

"And?"

Don pushed back in his chair to contemplate the ceiling. "And things didn't go exactly according to plan."

"Okay. Let me have a shot."

"I don't want to keep changing horses."

"Come on, we both know that Martin hasn't got the experience for a job this big. And to be honest, no offence intended, his personality can rub people the wrong way." Cara leaned over the desk. "I'm telling you I can get this account. I can *get* it."

"Are you sure you're ready?"

"Yes."

"The robbery was only, what, ten days ago? I don't want to push you into anything."

"I'm the one pushing you, not the other way around. Please."

He slapped his thigh. "Okay. Blackbird Books is yours. But I'm watching you."

"You won't have to." She stood up, relieved. "I'll be back first thing in the morning."

"But it's Friday tomorrow. Why not take the weekend, come in Monday?"

She tried to smile. "No, I'd rather get back to work as soon as possible."

On the drive home, Cara stopped for an early dinner, a seafood curry laksa at a pokey Malaysian restaurant with cheap laminate tables and plastic chairs. Closer towards home, she stopped the car again, this time at a roadside flower vendor to buy a bouquet, a weighty and colourful arrangement of chrysanthemums, gerberas and irises. An expensive treat, but why not? Epiphanies should be celebrated: she had figured out how to get back on an even keel.

All she had to do was take control.

That meant no more drinking, no more talking therapy, no more sitting around feeling weak and pitiful, no more taking shit from Mick or anybody else. Easy done. She would work, stick to her regular routine, keep to herself. And if she stopped thinking about the robbery, stopped building her waking hours around it, the anxiety and nightmares—starved of oxygen—would surely gutter and go out like a smothered fire. Wouldn't they? Yes, she decided, they would. Mental discipline was the requirement here. And after a lifetime of practice, she had that quality in spades, right? Of course, she did.

Feeling the prick of tears, she tightened her grip on the steering wheel and doubled her resolve: mental discipline. From this day forward, the robbery would become nothing but a dusty memory.

By the time Cara pulled into the carport, night was falling. She got out of the sedan, and hugged the bouquet to her chest to shield its petals from the wind. As she crossed the porch, another set of footsteps closed in behind her on the concrete driveway. Her heart gave a panicked squeeze. She whirled around.

"Nice flowers," Mick said, halting at the porch.

She scanned the road. His squad car was parked on the kerb right outside her house, and she hadn't even noticed it. "How long have you been waiting for me?" she said.

He shrugged. "I don't know. About an hour. Can I come in?"

"What for this time?"

"To apologise."

The dim glow from the streetlamp outlined Mick's bulk but not his face. His hands were in his coat pockets, his shoulders hunched. The chill wind bit at Cara's ankles, scrabbled at her nose and ears. Finally, she took keys from her bag.

"All right," she said. "But just for a minute. And only because it's cold."

He followed her inside. She switched on lights, got the space heater going. In the kitchen, she took out a vase, ran water into it, and peeled the cellophane from the bouquet. Rubber bands bound the stems together. Deciding to leave it that way, she dropped the bouquet into the vase. Oh hell. The bright kitchen bulb revealed the flowers as bruised and wilting, the stems running with aphids. Shit. And this whole time, Mick, standing behind her, hadn't spoken a single word. Cara's nerves felt raw.

"Is this crappy treatment going to be a regular thing? Is it?" She turned. Mick looked exhausted, upset. That surprised her. She took a step nearer. "What's the matter?" she said.

"You confuse me." He closed his eyes and shook his head in a helpless, beaten gesture. "I don't know many people like you."

The scar along his cheek appeared almost silver. For a moment, she considered what it must be like to do the kind of brutal work that he did. Then she gently put her hands to his face.

Mick opened his eyes. His irises were a soft, light blue; the blue of robin's eggs.

He seemed to be holding his breath, waiting for a stronger sign.

Cara put her arms about his neck. With a choked sob, Mick clutched at her and buried his face in her hair.

They made love. The previous times they'd slept together, Mick had mentally competed with the unknown lovers in

Cara's past, working hard to out-lick, out-fuck and outlast those spectres by a wide margin, determined to be the best she'd ever had. Not this time. For reasons he didn't quite understand, it was only Cara and nothing else; the softness of her mouth, the feel of her arms and legs wrapping around him, the breathy moans she uttered as he moved inside her. Mick was as gentle as he knew how to be. She responded to him, over and over. When he came, it was a long, sweet release that made him cry out.

He dropped his head to her shoulder, panting. Then he rolled onto his back. Cara pressed her body full-length against him, lying with her head on his chest. It felt good. Closing his eyes, content, he twined his fingers through her hair. His thoughts began see-sawing down towards sleep.

"How did you get this?" Cara said.

Mick opened his eyes. Only then did he realise she was tracing with her fingertips the box cutter scar on his chest, the skin still numb after four years. He never looked at it. The scar was a mangled divot about five centimetres long just back of his nipple, the stab wound that had collapsed his lung.

"I got it the same time I got the scar on my face," he said.

"When you were trying to arrest someone?"

"Yeah, that's right."

"The scars on your back and shoulder too?"

"From the same incident."

"What happened?"

He pulled away from her to sit up against the headboard. Cara scooched to the pillow on the other side of the bed and settled, waiting.

Mick thought of how he had talked about the stabbing to workmates—laughing it off—but didn't want to make the same jokes to Cara. Next, he thought about Janice. Back then, Janice had been his on-again, off-again girlfriend for about a year. When Mick had woken up in intensive care, shocked to find himself still alive, plugged into various beeping machines, it had been Janice holding his hand. In a clawing, sliding panic, Mick had proposed marriage, and Janice—perhaps moved by the dramatic theatrics of the moment, what else could it have been—had accepted.

"Don't you want to tell me?" Cara said.

Mick glanced down. Cara's hair was mussed from his hands, lips swollen and red from his kisses. He closed his eyes against the quivering of his heart. "All right," he said.

He told her what he had never told anyone before.

About how he had watched, incredulous, as jets of his own blood had sprayed across the asphalt of the pub's car park. How, when he had fallen, the sky had leaned over him, bright and brittle as a headache. The shots from Sergeant Ward's gun that had hit Emil in the chest, knocking him this way and that—*pow, pow, pow*—like a cartoon, Emil's hand with the box cutter covered in red gore, Emil tipping backwards like a fallen tree. And the terror, as unconsciousness flooded over Mick's head, that his life was finished at twenty-seven years of age, that he had no idea of what was coming next. Please God, don't let it be oblivion. How he had prayed in the last second of consciousness to be reunited with his mother.

Mick stopped talking.

Cara clambered onto his lap and put her arms about him. He held her, pressing his face into her neck, overcome. Seconds passed. Then a minute, two minutes.

Her breasts against him, her weight across his thighs, her scent, at last, triggered the present moment. Mick's nervous system hit a reset button. The past with its ugliness retreated behind a curtain far away in his mind. The only thing that mattered was his woman straddling him. His blood surged. Cara must have felt him harden because she wriggled closer.

"I want you," she whispered.

Gripping her buttocks, Mick raised his hips from the mattress and entered her, the hot, velvety feel of her body making him suck a breath, grit his teeth. Moaning, she tipped back her head and hung on. Oh Christ, there's nothing more than this, he realised. Nothing more than Cara. Not now, not ever.

TEN

Lunch time, and still no sign of Mick. Alec knew better than to ask the crew any questions. Mick was a golden boy, particularly to Frank Ward, God alone knew why. The misguided hero worship didn't make sense. Alec retrieved his sandwiches from his locker and walked back through the Armed Offence Squad, virtually empty apart from one other crew, most of them out to lunch.

He sat down at his desk. Stevo was screwing around on one of the computers. Ward and Bull were each reading a newspaper, the latter squinting and holding the newspaper almost against his face.

"Hey Bull," Stevo said, "when are you going to admit you need glasses, you dopey shit?"

"There's nothing wrong with my peepers."

"Yeah, it's your brain that needs looking at."

Lighting a smoke, Bull tapped at the newspaper and said, "Check this out. It says here that our pizza boys have grabbed over half a million bucks. Where the fuck did they get that figure?"

"Out of their arses," Stevo said.

"Christ, I dunno. How can they get away with making up this stuff?"

"That's the media for you," Ward said, talking around a mouthful of sausage roll, the only food he ever seemed to eat. "They do whatever they want and they're not accountable to anybody."

"Kind of like us," Bull said, smirking.

Sarge resolutely chewed on his sausage roll, stared at his paper, and didn't reply. Alec unwrapped a packet of sandwiches.

"What've you got there?" Bull said.

"Salad."

"You're not a fucking vego, are you, mate?"

"No." Alec took a few bites. Then he said, "Hey, someone refresh my memory. The customer from the Benny's job, Cara Haynes. Was her wallet part of the evidence?"

"Nah," Stevo said. "Why?"

Alec hesitated. "She lost it and thought we might have it."

"What do we want her wallet for?"

Alec nodded, checked his watch, finished his sandwich and stood up. "I'll be back soon."

"You better be," Ward said, but didn't ask where Alec was going.

The drive took about five minutes. Alec pulled up outside a two-storey, glass-fronted building that had ornate design elements like French balconies and fluted masonry. He parked, went inside. The blonde woman behind the desk gave him an eager, professional smile.

"Welcome to Premiere Press, how can I help you?"

"I'd like to see Cara Haynes," he said, showing his badge.

The receptionist gasped. "Oh my God, is this about the robbery?"

"Please tell her that a detective from the Armed Offence Squad is here to see her."

"Certainly, right away." She pressed a few buttons and said into the headset, "Cara, a detective from the Armed Offence Squad is downstairs."

Within half a minute, Cara Haynes exited from the stairwell in a hurry, wearing a big smile. The flicker of disappointment that passed over her face lasted only a split-second, but Alec figured it meant one thing: she'd been expecting Mick.

He held out his hand, and she took it.

"Detective Constable Alec Castellano," he said.

"Yes, of course, I remember you from the pizzeria. Would you like a coffee?"

"No thanks, I can't stay for long."

"Let's go to my office."

He followed her up the stairs and along the corridor. She wore a burgundy two-piece pants suit, the cut of the material showing off her cinched waist, her pert little behind. Cara Haynes was gorgeous, no doubt about it. How had an ape like Mick Thompson managed to get her into bed? Well, perhaps he hadn't. Perhaps Alec had put two and two together and arrived at horseshit.

They went into an office. She sat down behind the desk. Alec took a wallet out of his pocket and gave it to her.

"Oh, what a relief!" she said, checking through the various compartments. "I thought the robbers might have it. And look, everything's here, even the cash. Damn, I've already cancelled my cards." She laughed, brushed her hair back from her forehead with one hand, her eyes shining. "Where did you find it?"

"At the squad room."

"The squad room? I guess I dropped it while giving my statement."

"Probably. Then there must have been a mix-up, with somebody thinking your wallet was part of the evidence. Sorry about that."

"Don't be. I'd much rather know the police had it than...those men."

"Sure."

Cara stood up. "Well, thanks very much for bringing it over."

"No worries. Actually, my colleague Mick Thompson was going to drop it back for you, but he had to do a few things today with his wife."

"*Wife?*"

The word hit her like a punch. She jolted, her cheeks flushing red then draining of colour. To avoid embarrassing her, Alec pretended not to notice, keeping a neutral expression as if nothing was wrong. She regained a semblance of composure after a moment or two.

Mick Thompson, you low-life son of a bitch, Alec thought.

Casually, as if making polite conversation, he continued, "Janice is a nice lady. Talented as well. She's a journalist for the *Melbourne Metro Weekly*."

"Oh?"

"It must be tough being a detective's wife. The hours are terrible."

Cara nodded, face pinched, her smile nothing more than a flattening of tight lips against teeth. Alec held out his hand. Cara shook it. Her palm was sweaty.

"I won't keep you," he said. "You must be busy."

"Yes. Thanks again for my wallet."

"Don't mention it. I'll see myself out."

Exiting the Premiere Press building, he grabbed his mobile phone and dialled Senior Constable Liz Lansky's number. Liz, one of his closest friends, worked at the Ormond Police Station where Alec had last posted before his assignment to the Armed Offence Squad. She answered within a few rings.

"Hi," he said. "Want a quick coffee?"

By the time he got to the Dirty Chai Café, their regular haunt, Liz Lansky was already waiting for him at a window table. Alec sat down opposite her.

"It's good to see you," he said.

"Ditto. How's squad-life?" Liz shifted her police cap from the table to the windowsill. "After a month on the job, I'm assuming you've fractured at least a dozen jaws by now."

"Very funny. For your information, my jaw-fracture count stands at zero."

"Aw, you'll never make it in the Armed Offence Squad at that rate."

A joke, yes, but a joke that cut too close to home.

"Uh-oh," Liz said. "What's wrong?"

"Mick Thompson is what's wrong." Alec leaned over the table and dropped his voice. "He's banging a victim of a job that we attended last week."

"Ouch."

"Exactly."

"You know," she said, "I always thought he was married."

"He is."

"Did Mick tell you about this affair?"

"No, he's too secretive. I had to go about things in a...devious kind of way."

Liz shrugged. "Talk to your sergeant."

"Frank Ward? I might as well talk to a dead dog as that prick. In the past few days, Mick has beaten the crap out of two suspects, and the sarge couldn't care less. He doesn't ride with us for jobs, doesn't do interviews, doesn't do welfare checks. Can you believe it? And that kind of shit is against regulations."

"Go over his head and tell the inspector. What's his name, Vaughan?"

"That bloke is worse than the sarge. He turns up for his pay cheque." Alec sighed. "The chain of command doesn't exist. Coppers do whatever they want and no one gives a damn."

"Well, well, the rumours about the Loose Cannon Squad turn out to be true again. Not much of a surprise, really."

Alec rubbed at his forehead. "Liz, I'm in a tough spot."

"Is there anyone you could talk to in that place? Anyone at all?"

"I don't know. There's one bloke on my crew, Stevo. He's not too bad. Steve Gardner."

"From Moorooduc CIB?"

"Yeah, that's him. His police work is solid. And I've never seen him slack off."

A waitress came over to take their order. Liz asked for a café latte and a fudge brownie. For the sake of ease, Alec requested the same.

Once the waitress moved away, Alec said, "You know what I can't understand? This victim that Thompson is banging happens to be beautiful, hot, well-spoken; smart in that corporate kind of way. You know what I mean?"

Liz grinned wryly. "Yeah. I've seen the non-bimbo type of woman before."

"Okay, point taken. But why would a woman like that want a mug like Thompson?"

To his surprise, Liz actually laughed.

"What's hilarious?" he demanded.

"Have you ever seen Mick Thompson? Yowza."

Alec sat back in his chair. "For real? The man's got a broken nose."

"So did Marlon Brando."

"Oh, come on, you can't be serious. Mick's an animal."

"Yeah, a well-built one. And he could be the perfect gentleman when he's with your victim, did you ever think of that?" Liz glanced around to make sure no one was eavesdropping. "There's another angle you haven't considered. Your victim's last boyfriend could have been a tee-totalling accountant. She might be using Mick Thompson short-term for a change of pace. Lots of women like to have fun with a bad boy. You follow?"

"Yep," Alec said, tired and beat. "I follow."

"Now you want my advice. Here it is: don't get involved. Against regulations or not, if Mick and this woman want to get it on, it's none of your business. And if it bothers you that Mick likes a bit of the old biffo when he's arresting a crook, look the other way or get out."

Alec regarded her carefully. "Can you hear what you're saying?"

"Oh, stop being the idealist for once. The Armed Offence Squad isn't going to change to suit you. Just transfer. It's no shame when a posting turns out to be a bad fit."

Alec propped his face on one hand. "I want to bust career crims, not jaywalkers."

"And career crims are tough and mean. The coppers who go after them have to be tougher and meaner. Okay? That's why the Armed Offence Squad attracts a certain type of detective. You're obviously not that type." She waved a dismissive hand. "But I'm wasting my breath. You've known my opinion on this from the get-go."

"Yeah, yeah. They'd love me at Missing Persons." He gave a rueful smile. "Is this the part where you say 'I told you so'?"

She laughed. "Do I really need to say it out loud?"

The waitress came over with their order. Alec opened a couple of sugar packets, and was tipping them into his café latte when Liz reached across the table to lay her hand on his arm.

"Don't make trouble," she said. "We work in a very small industry. Pissing off the wrong people could screw up your career."

As soon as Alec Castellano left her office, Cara shut the door and collapsed into her chair. Unbelievably, she was shaking. *Fool.* Hadn't she been cheated a hundred times before? Strung along her whole life by foster families, social workers, people furthering their own interests? Betrayal was a normal, expected part of life. Or at least, it should be by now.

A sob broke from her, which she stifled by holding her breath.

The depth of her grief shocked her. Okay, calm down. This overreaction was simply a hangover from the armed robbery experience, nothing more. She'd known Mick only a few days anyway. Big deal. So what if they'd both lived in Wangaratta? Believing in fate was exactly the kind of superstitious nonsense that lowered one's guard. It served her right for being stupid.

Damn.

She thumbed tears from her lashes. On their first date, lunch at the Little Penguin Hotel, she'd asked him point blank if he was married, that bastard. And then it occurred to her, as her cheeks blushed with shame, that she didn't even know his home address or phone number. Why hadn't that raised a red flag? How could she have been so naive?

Cara swivelled the chair to the computer and Googled 'Janice Thompson journalist'. A string of matches filled the screen. Cara scanned down the list, reading bits and pieces: "Janice Thompson takes you on a journey through the oldest winery in the district of... It's hard to stand out when your bistro is located in prime restaurant territory, writes Janice Thompson... Janice Thompson explores the rich history of olives grown in the unique... Take a look at the story by Janice Thompson in *Melbourne Metro Weekly* about her experiences as a guest sous chef at the prestigious…"

Cara clicked on the 'image' search results and scrutinised the photographs, one at a time. Each showed a confident woman with an attractive face, bleached white teeth, straight hair dyed henna-red and worn to the shoulders. This person was Mick's wife.

His actual *wife*.

The things that he did to Cara in bed, he did to this woman, his wife. The one he loved.

Cara closed the page, feeling nauseated. After a moment, she exited her office, went to the women's toilets, and began washing her hands in the single basin, inspecting her make-up in the mirror. The mascara was fine; the eyeliner might need another application.

The entry door flung open, almost knocking into her.

"Oops, sorry, didn't realise anyone was in here." It was Trish, crowding into the room as the door swung shut. "Hey, is everything okay?"

"Yes."

"You look upset."

"Do I? Well, thanks for your concern, but I'm fine."

Trish touched Cara's elbow, and said, "No, you're not."

Cara felt the pricking of fresh tears. Stay strong and keep your mouth shut, she reminded herself. *There's no point to confiding in people.* "I need to be alone for a while," she said, ripping paper towels from the dispenser, briskly drying her hands. "Thanks anyway."

"You think I'm going leave you to cry by yourself?"

Trish put her arm around Cara's shoulders and gave a squeeze. Cara closed her eyes. God, she felt exhausted, frail, worn down to a nub.

"The man I'm seeing is married," she said in a rush, as the tears ran. "I just found out."

"Oh, you poor thing. What are you going to do?"

"I don't know. I'm supposed to be meeting him for dinner tonight."

"Bugger that. Come to my house instead."

Cara, flustered, couldn't think of anything to say except yes.

Cara took along a bottle of red and a bottle of white. Trish's two-bedroom city apartment was decorated in a jumble of what looked like antiques: plenty of mahogany, rosewood and walnut furniture; old fashioned ladder-backed chairs; brocaded upholstery. Despite owning a music station, Trish instead played vinyl albums on a turntable record player, mostly blues. Soon, the remains of their meal cluttered the dining table. Trish had made beef curry with basmati rice, tasty despite the sultanas, which Cara ordinarily didn't like to eat. Maybe it was the wine, but she was having fun. She sipped at her glass of red and tried to remember the last time she'd had fun like this, but couldn't remember.

"Anyway," Trish was saying, "I don't hear from this guy for about two months, yeah? Then I finally run into him at the same nightclub. You know what he says to me?"

Cara giggled. "What?"

"The same pick-up line he used the first time around. The bastard didn't remember me."

They broke into fresh gales of laughter. Cara's phone rang. She retrieved her handbag from the couch, took out her mobile, and checked the display.

"It's him," she said, stricken.

"Give it here." Trish grabbed the phone, switched it off and handed it back with a grim smile. "Let him sweat."

"But he's probably been waiting at the restaurant nearly forty minutes already."

"Good. Let him wait forever, the arsehole."

Premiere Press's schedule for a Saturday never varied. Lucy manned the reception desk from 9 a.m. to 1 p.m. After she locked up, incoming lines to the switchboard transferred to the print department, located across the lane in the factory directly behind the building. If office staff members needed to remain past 1 p.m., they had to clear it first with Don, and be entrusted with a spare set of keys handed over by Don himself.

Ordinarily, Cara didn't come in on Saturdays. Today, however, she wanted to catch up on work. She parked in her usual undercover space, noting that Trish's sedan was already there. When Cara walked through the back door into reception, Lucy jumped to her feet, her eyes goggling.

"Yes, I know," Cara said, smiling. "I swore blind I'd never work on the weekend, but here I am. Any messages?"

"Good morning," said Mick's voice.

Cara froze. Then she stepped around the planter box of bamboo that screened the visitor's area from the back door. Mick, sitting on the couch, dropped the magazine he was reading onto the table, casually uncrossed his legs, and stood up. He put his hands on his hips.

"What are you doing here?" Cara said.

"I could ask you the same question."

"What do you mean? This is where I work."

He was staring at her with a flat, unreadable gaze. She imagined it was the same look he gave to criminals to scare them, to put them off-balance. Well, *screw him*. Turning to the reception desk, she remarked, "Any messages?"

Lucy, shooting wary glances at Mick, handed Cara a stack of paper slips. "A few people told me your phone wasn't working. Do you need me to get IT to have a look?"

"No, it's okay. I've had it switched off, that's all."

"Uh-huh. Trish told me to tell you to drop into her office when you get here. And the coffee machine's still on the blink, sorry."

The whole time Lucy was speaking to Cara, she was staring at Mick, as if too frightened to look away. It made the hair stand up on Cara's neck. She glanced around at him. He was standing in the same spot as before, motionless, hands on his hips pushing aside his jacket.

"Thanks, Lucy," Cara said, turning towards the stairs. "I'll go out later and buy us coffee."

Mick said, "Aren't you going to invite me up?"

"Fine," she said over her shoulder, and went on ahead. His footsteps sounded on the carpet close behind her. Once they reached her office, Cara put down her handbag and satchel, and began sorting through her messages as if he wasn't even there.

"You were a no-show at dinner last night," he said, and waited. When she didn't answer, he continued, "I rang, but okay, now I know you had your phone turned off. I dropped over to your place a couple of times. You weren't home. Where were you?"

Staying at Trish's, Cara thought. But once again, she said nothing. Seconds passed.

Changing tactics, Mick said, "Great office. Have you got your own secretary?"

She dropped the sheaf of messages to the desk. "I know you're married."

"What?" he said, and smiled.

"Come on. Just be straight with me for once."

"Married?" He shrugged. "What are you talking about?"

She crossed her arms. "You're very savvy about wines and restaurants."

"I take an interest."

"You know, my favourite article was the one about the best cheeses to take on picnics. Very handy. Who would have thought that aged cheddar and Gouda don't need to be refrigerated? I'll be thinking of Janice next time I pack a hamper."

He sighed, and rubbed a hand over his hair for a while, gazing at the floor. Eventually, he said, "Well, it's not like I'm happily married."

"Don't even try it."

"Cara, I really care about you."

"Oh? And you show that by lying to me? Stringing me along? *Using* me?"

He exhaled, hard, and put his hands back on his hips. "Okay, I made a bad call, and I'm sorry. Tell me what to do. How can I make up for it?"

"Are you serious?" She let out a sharp, mocking laugh. "My God, you're unbelievable. Is this the line of bullshit you feed to every girlfriend?"

"Huh? Wait on, I don't have other girlfriends."

"Why don't you wear a wedding ring?"

He gaped at his left hand, shocked, as if noticing for the first time that a ring was missing. "I told you, it's not a happy marriage."

She went to the door and held it open. "Please go."

"I'm sorry. Okay? It's my fault. This whole misunderstanding is my fault. But we're both adults, right? We can work something out. Can't we?"

"Get out."

"No, Cara. No. Things are great with you around."

He reached out and took hold of her hand. She didn't pull away. Despite her resolve, her hand seemed led by its own mind; intertwining fingers with his fingers, palm pressing against palm. She would miss him so much: his voice; his face; his touch; the smell of his skin. She closed her eyes for a moment. Then she wrenched away from his grasp.

"Did you take my wallet?" she said.

After a while, he shook his head.

"You told me you didn't have a wife either."

"Cara," he whispered, moving closer, clutching at her, "I've been more honest with you than anyone else in my life. You've got to believe me."

She slipped away to stand behind her desk. "Our relationship has to be professional from now on."

"What? Like, me copper, you victim? We can't go back to that. I won't."

"Please leave now."

"Don't shut me out."

"Just go. I mean it."

To bluff him, she picked up the phone handset as if preparing to call somebody—building security, perhaps, or the police—and it worked. Mick stepped away, his arms relaxing by his sides. An impassive mask dropped over his face, while his eyes, emptied of emotion, became almost reptilian. He gave a brief nod, turned, and walked out.

Cara groped for the office chair and sat down.

Waiting, waiting, *one-cat-dog, two-cat-dog, three-cat-dog,* breathing slowly and evenly to hush her runaway pulse, Cara sat very still. Then she picked up the phone and dialled Reception.

"Has he gone?" she asked Lucy.

"Yes. Do you want me to lock the doors?"

Taken aback, Cara said, "Lock them? What for?"

"Well, if you think it's okay…"

"Of course, it's okay. Thanks."

Cara hung up and regarded her collection of Van Gogh postcards pinned to the corkboard. 'Irises' drew her gaze. That single, lonely white bloom in a sea of purple petals had always been a heartbreaker, but now it made her vision swim with tears. On impulse, she made a promise to herself: if she got the Blackbird Books account, she wouldn't waste her commission on a house deposit; instead, she would go to Holland to stand in front of Van Gogh's actual paintings, and realise a lifelong dream.

Taking a breath, shaking it off, Cara dialled Trish's extension. "Have you got five minutes? You're not going to believe this. He was just here."

Within seconds, Trish appeared at the office door. She took a seat on the other side of the desk, and said, "Did you tell him where he could shove it?"

"Very clearly."

"And?"

"And he said that his marriage is crap and that he really cares about me."

Trish slapped at the desk. "Ha! The standard defence of the sprung male."

"No, I think he meant it."

"Oh, come on, honey, think about it. What else is he going to say when you've got him on the spot? That he loves his wife?"

Mick visited the track, a strip joint, another strip joint, a bar. Saturday slid away from him in a slewing line of beers and vodka shots. Around midnight, he made it home. He turned the squad car into the driveway. The car didn't take its usual line. In a merry tinkling of plastic, the front right-hand headlight popped against one of the iron posts that flanked the entrance to the basement. Fuck. Mick gunned the vehicle into its regular space, screeched the brakes, parked, got out, and made his way towards the wavering lift doors. So what about the fucking headlight? He'd check out the damage tomorrow.

The apartment was in darkness. He turned on a few lights. When he doffed his shoes, he kicked them and they flew off, thumped into the walls. Pulling at his jacket, yanking at his tie, he stomped into the bedroom.

Janice turned over and sat up. "Mick?"

"Who else would it be?"

The lights from the hall and lounge cut a bright wedge into the room.

Shielding her eyes, Janice said, "I told you yesterday, I've got to cover a champagne breakfast in a hot air balloon. If you're going to snore, do it in the spare room."

"You go in there if you don't like it," he said, staggering, one leg caught in his trousers.

She plumped her pillow and lay down again. Tottering, Mick fell against the bed and slithered to the floor. The room wheeled about his head. He grabbed onto the mattress, clawed to his feet. Janice appeared tranquil, already asleep. This was a ruse she pulled often to aggravate him. Once upright, his remaining trouser leg slipped off. He stalked to the kitchen in his underwear and socks. There were three beer stubbies in the fridge and he opened one of them, taking a long pull on its neck. He dropped into a chair.

Janice called, "And turn off the lights."

He grimaced. See? The bitch wasn't asleep at all.

"Oh, yeah," he muttered to nobody in particular, lifting the beer in a salute to the kitchen blind. "I'll turn them off. Every last fucking one."

ELEVEN

Late Monday morning, a drug addict held up a service station with a dirty syringe. Big deal. In Mick's opinion, any piss-ant case should be handled by the local police station, not the Armed Offence Squad. Attending the scene and interviewing the service station attendant and the dozen other witnesses had taken all day. Now, late afternoon in the squad room, Alec was at the computer keyboard pecking out their joint report while Stevo dictated from a notebook. Mick sat opposite, elbows on the desk, chin propped in his hands, watching them. The hangover from his weekend bender had settled into a dull, queasy throb behind his eyes.

Stevo was saying, "The offender was seen to decamp in a north-westerly direction, whereupon the service station attendant managed to untie—"

"Hang on a second. I'm not a bloody touch-typist."

Stevo flipped pages on the notebook, reading, killing time. Alec tapped at the keyboard for a while. Finally, Stevo said, "What are you up to?"

"*Decamp.*"

"Oh Jesus, even Bull's faster on the keyboard than you. And speak of the devil."

Bull was shambling over from the elevator hall, shirt half-untucked, a cigarette pinched between his thumb and forefinger. "Nope, no biscuits. Not even the plain ones."

"Tell the analyst," Stevo said, then called to a neighbouring crew across the room, "Hey, any of you guys seen Greg? We need biscuits."

"He's on a course today," someone answered.

"Shit." Bull took a seat, flicked cigarette ash to the carpet. "I'm tonguing for those minty chocolate ones, too. How are we going?"

"He can't type for shit," Stevo said.

Chuckling, Alec said, "Okay, swap. I'll read; you type."

Mick shoved away from the desk, stomped through the squad room, and shut himself inside the analyst's office. He snatched up the landline.

Why hadn't she called?

He went to dial her mobile, but checked himself. There was no point jumping to conclusions. Perhaps the flowers hadn't arrived. He rang the florist instead. According to the bloke who answered the phone, the twenty-four red roses had been delivered to Premiere Press just after 10 a.m. Mick hung up. He rubbed at his beard stubble, considering. Perhaps she was out of the office visiting clients. Perhaps she didn't know anything about the roses yet. He called Premiere Press to ask the receptionist if Cara Haynes was available.

"One moment, please," the receptionist said.

Suddenly, he was listening to a ringing tone. It didn't make sense. If the roses had been delivered while Cara was at the office, why hadn't she called?

"Cara Haynes," she said, breaking his chain of thought.

He swallowed. "Did you get the flowers?"

A pause; then she said, "Yes."

He didn't know how to answer that. The hangover intensified, punching at the back of his eyes. He waited for her to keep talking. She didn't. Finally, he mumbled, "Are they red? I told the bloke they had to be red."

"Yes. They're red."

"And there's twenty-four?"

"I don't know. I didn't count them."

"Fair enough." He pinched hard at the bridge of his nose. "Can we have lunch?"

"I don't think it's a good idea."

"Cara, I need to see you."

"What for?"

To stop this pain, he thought. Instead, he said, "We had something going."

"I'm hanging up now."

He jolted upright in the chair. "Wait."

"Goodbye, Mick."

"Can I call you?"

The line went dead. He kept the receiver to his ear for a long time. When he returned the handset to the cradle, he became aware of a loose, disconnected sensation in his head. It made him think of a time on the Murray River when his tinny had broken from its moorings while his back had been turned, stoking the campfire. Leaping into the icy cold water to fetch it had almost stopped his heart. Mick stared unseeing at the phone on the analyst's desk, while in his mind, the bobbing tinny, lapped by rippling waves, smoothly and silently drifted away from him.

He left the analyst's office. Across the squad room, his crew were fooling about at their desks: Bull on his feet, miming out some activity, fresh cigarette dangling from his lips; Alec and Stevo laughing. Mick reached the desks and stopped.

"You missed his best ever impression of a druggie," Stevo said, guffawing. "What a pisser. Hey, Bull, do it again."

Mick seized the nearest desk and tipped it over. Pens, paper, in-trays, telephones flew everywhere. The heavy desk had enough momentum to roll, carrying the castor wheels of a nearby chair through the plasterboard wall. Mick went to grab another desk. Bull and Stevo flanked him, tried to twist his arms behind his back. He broke their hold and lunged away.

Alec, the stupid shit, held out a hand towards him and said, "Whoa there, whoa," as if speaking to a fucking horse.

Mick turned and walked out. Alone, he kept his eyes closed in the elevator ride down to the underground car park. Thankfully, the elevator didn't stop on any other floor. Taking the keys from his pocket, he was approaching one of the squad vehicles, the one with the broken headlight, when a voice behind him shouted, "Mick, wait up. Where are you going?"

Alec jogged over.

Mick opened the driver's side door. Before he could get in, Alec seized an arm and spun him around. The desire to hit Alec flared hard enough to pin Mick's vision for a split second.

"This has got to stop," Alec said.

"I ought to smack your face in."

"What for this time? Cara Haynes?"

Mick froze, dumbfounded. So, it had been Alec to blame. *Alec* who had fucked him up and destroyed his relationship with Cara. Mick felt light-headed by a thundering rush of fury. Gritting his teeth, he threw himself into the car and started the engine. Accelerating, he turned the steering wheel at Alec to make him either jump clear or get run over, depending on the greenhorn's reflexes. He jumped clear. The gate swung open. Mick thumped the car up the driveway and onto the crossover. The sky was metallic grey, hard and cold. He didn't know where he was going, but he had to get there fast. Stamping the pedal, he pushed into the stream of peak-hour traffic on St Kilda Road as car horns sounded all around him.

Alec didn't have any car keys on him, so he couldn't give chase. The BMW tore away out of sight, its back-end twitching and tyres squealing as Mick took a fast corner through the underground car park. Breaking into a jog, Alec hurried to the lift and held his thumb on the button.

When the lift doors opened on the ninth floor, Alec went straight to the tea room, the common area that the Armed Offence Squad shared with the other bureau on the floor, the Rape Squad. And yep, Frank Ward was still in there. This time, he was sitting at a table with his feet up, chatting with Gerard Vandenburg, a detective senior sergeant from the Rape Squad.

"Sarge," Alec said. "A word, please."

Ward turned around. "Need help with the report? Don't worry, I'll be out in a minute. By the way, have you met Gerry?"

"Uh, briefly."

"Gerry, this is Alec Castellano, my newest recruit."

Alec gave a polite smile and held out his hand. Gerard Vandenburg stood up for the handshake. He was a thin, neat man of medium height, middle-aged, wearing a well-cut grey suit and a pencil moustache.

"Pleased to meet you," Vandenburg said.

"Same," Alec said.

"He's only been with us, how long? A month?" Ward said. "And he's already a veteran, aren't you, mate?"

"Yes, sir."

"Tell Gerry how many cases you've had."

"I don't know, exactly. About twenty? Sarge, I need to speak to you."

Ward nodded, slid one foot off the table and kicked out an empty chair.

"In private, if you don't mind," Alec continued.

Vandenburg smiled at them both. "I'll leave you to it."

"See you, Gerry," Ward said. "Don't forget the footy tipping this week." As soon as Vandenburg left the tea room and they were alone, Ward said, "All right, what's up? Make it short, I'm on a break."

Alec sat down. "It's Mick."

"What about him?"

"He's snapped."

"Snapped?" Ward gave an amused snort. "That'll be the day."

"He went berserk and trashed our desks just now. Bull and Stevo had to restrain him."

"Oh, that's Mick letting off steam."

"But you didn't see his eyes."

Ward patted him on the shoulder. "Mate, I understand you're having a rough time settling in, but don't take anything personally, you get me? It's a rocky transition coming into the Armed Offence Squad."

"No, look, that's not it—"

"You and Mick will come to an understanding soon enough. Ask Stevo. When he was fresh to the squad, he used to clash with Mick all the time. It's a question of pecking order, see?" Ward gave a fatherly smile. "Like a bunch of pigeons in a coop."

Alec, irritated, feeling a rise in blood pressure, said, "Mick is banging a victim."

Ward's face dropped. "Which one?"

"Cara Haynes."

"And who's that?"

"One of the victims from the Benny's Pizza job."

"From a couple of weeks ago? The pizza bandits?"

Alec nodded. "He stole her wallet too. If you check the logs, I bet you'll find he's done an unauthorised computer search on her."

Ward stood up, adjusted his trousers at the belt, and paced around the tea room for a while, head down. Alec felt a kind of grim satisfaction. At least he had the slack bastard's attention.

"Okay, I'll deal with it," Ward said, and headed towards the door.

"He's already gone."

Ward spun around. "Gone where?"

"Who knows? He took a squad car and didn't sign it out. Like he always does, right?"

They locked eyes.

Finally, Ward said, on his way out of the tea room, "Calm down. He'll be back."

The warm air hung heavy with garlic. A brass bell jangled behind her as the door closed on its pneumatic hinge. Cara, breathing hard, walked towards the counter. Of course, there wasn't any blood on the counter now. She faltered mid-step. Nearby on a wooden bench sat customers waiting for their orders: a teenage girl fooling with a mobile phone; a man flipping through a tattered magazine with one hand while the other kept hold of a fidgeting toddler. A tinny radio played from the rear doorway to the kitchen. Everything appeared normal.

No, Cara decided. Everything *was* normal in Benny's Pizzeria.

Summoned by the jangling doorbell, an older woman pushed through the PVC strip-curtain hanging over the kitchen door. Her grey hair was combed flat into a short-back-and-sides style, and she had dark, puffy rings under her eyes as if she hadn't slept in a while. Cara thought of the male proprietor, perhaps this woman's husband, and his cheek as it had opened up under the blow of a shotgun butt.

"Miss?" the woman said. "Can I help you?"

Cara approached the counter. "A small supreme pizza with prawns. No olives, please."

"Anything else?"

"No, thank you."

"What about garlic bread?"

Cara shook her head. The woman nodded and retreated through the rear door to the kitchen. Cara turned and leaned against the counter, heart pounding. Beyond the floor-to-ceiling windows, everything seemed ordinary. Cars moved in and out of parking spaces, headlights gleaming in the fading light. Pedestrians mingled back and forth on the footpath. Minutes ticked by. Nothing terrible happened.

She ate the pizza—as much as she could, anyway—at home. To bolster herself, she listened to Beethoven's Pastoral Symphony, relying on the soaring flutes, oboes and clarinets to help her take one bite after another. Even though her appetite evaporated after a single slice, it didn't matter. She had proven a point. As she put the pizza box in the fridge, she made a new resolution: to keep ordering dinner from Benny's, one night a week, for as long as it took until she was able to stand at that counter without shaking.

She could *do* this. And she could do it, as always, by herself.

Without Mick or anybody else.

Mick shambled into the Armed Offence Squad. The early morning sunshine blaring through the windows knifed at his pupils, making him squint. First things first, he'd check for messages then go to the change rooms for a shower. Bull, Stevo and Alec looked around as he neared the desks.

Bull said, "You look shithouse, mate. What've you been doing?"

"Nothing."

"Better have been something," Stevo added. "The sarge has been trying to find you all night. Tell him your phone's busted."

Mick put down his briefcase. "Where is he?"

"Waiting for you in the secretary's office," Bull said. "And I advise you to go in smiling."

What now? Mick cut his eyes at Alec. The dumb shit gazed back, cool as a goddamned cucumber. The secretary's office door was closed. Mick tapped on it once with his knuckles and went in.

Behind the desk, the sarge looked furious. "Sit down," Ward said.

Mick dragged out the visitor's chair and dropped into it.

After a time, Ward continued, "Remember the Orange Pepper Hotel? Four years ago?"

Mick shrugged.

"We were questioning that Baran fucker," Ward continued, "when Emil came out of the dunnies and took off through the pub when he saw us. You followed him into the car park."

Mick laced his hands behind his head, feigning indifference. In his mind's eye, however, Emil was coming at him with the box cutter, lunging again and again, the police badge falling to the ground, the police-issue firearm holstered, blood spraying across the asphalt.

Ward said, "I didn't go after you straight away. Remember why? Because I was too busy putting cuffs on Baran, that's why."

"Forget it," Mick said. "You shot Emil three times in the chest. That ought to be enough."

"Enough? With you a fortnight in hospital? The inspector even made enquiries about funeral arrangements, for God's sake." Ward swiped a hand over his forehead. "You were my recruit, my responsibility. Okay, let me tell you what I've never told you before. That shit haunted me for a long time. Understand?"

"Sure."

"For years."

"Okay. What do you want me to do about it? Start crying?"

"Shut up." Ward leapt from the chair and began pacing the cramped office. "I've let you get away with a crap-load since then. But not anymore."

Mick gave a cold smile. "What's Alec been telling you?"

"Nothing I don't already know. Where do you keep pissing off to lately? You take a squad car and no one knows where you've gone."

"It's business."

"Then why do you ignore your mobile and car radio?"

"I'm busy."

Ward set his teeth. "I'm the senior ranking officer here. Got it?"

"Yep."

"Good. Now where were you last night?"

Sitting in a squad car outside Cara's place, Mick thought. Watching the lights turn off as she got ready for bed, imagining her stretched out on the mattress, asleep and dreaming, naked. Dialling her landline a few times, hanging up before she could answer the call, each time noting the lights as they switched on, one by one, glowing around the edges of the curtained windows as she moved through the house to the phone in the kitchen, the lights switching off again in reverse order as she went back to bed. At various points during his vigil, it kept occurring to him that the lock on her front door could be opened with a penknife.

"Tell me," Ward said, taking a seat again, "for Christ's sake. Where were you last night?"

"Doing a sit-off."

"The whole night?"

"Yeah, the whole night."

"Where?"

Mick didn't answer.

Exasperated, Ward said, "Were you with Cara Haynes?"

"Who?"

"Don't shit me. What do you take me for? Are you rooting this victim or not?"

"No."

"You'd better not be. Why did you have her wallet?"

"I don't know what you're talking about."

They glared at each other.

Ward said, "Something's not right. I want to know what it is."

"It's you trusting a greenhorn over me," Mick said, getting up, grabbing the door handle.

"Fine, I'm done talking anyhow, but don't piss off anywhere. You hear me? Stay in the squad room. Understand?"

Mick slammed the door behind him. Black and red spots swam in his vision as he stormed across the squad room towards Alec, who stood up and tightened his hands into fists. Sweet, Mick thought, his back and shoulder muscles bunching into knots. *Let's sort out this shit once and for all.* But Stevo and Bull skirted the desks to intercept him.

"The sarge," Bull murmured, inclining his head.

Mick glanced around. Ward stood at the open door of the office, paying attention.

Light drizzle misted the windscreen on the drive home. The traffic was heavy, but Cara hardly noticed. Instead, she kept thinking about the meeting she'd just had with the managing director of Blackbird Books, a brisk older woman with a stern manner and hairstyle to match. The woman's severe bob, dyed jet-black, the block fringe a scant centimetre long, screamed *Don't waste my time.* No wonder Martin's sales pitch had bombed. Knowing him, he would have wasted his appointment trying to impress that blunt, laconic woman with his 'droll' sense of humour. Cara, on the other hand, had played it to the point. Not ten minutes into Cara's presentation, the managing director's body language had softened, her style of questions changing from aggressive to interested.

Smiling, Cara turned up the car stereo as Schubert's Allegro Vivace came out of the speakers. She began tapping the steering wheel in time to the jaunty flurry of violins. First thing tomorrow, she would draw up a detailed quote for Blackbird Books. And then she would investigate return airfares to Amsterdam, accommodation packages, and car hire. Van Gogh Museum, she thought, here I come.

She pulled the sedan into the carport, parked and got out. The biting wind sent leaves, grit and debris clawing and skittering along the concrete driveway at her feet. She hurried across the porch, unlocked the front door and opened it.

Hands grabbed her from behind and rushed her inside the house.

Panic flared. Before she had time to struggle, however, she was released with a shove. Momentum staggered her for a couple of steps. She dropped her handbag and satchel and spun around to face the assailant, bracing herself for the balaclava, the twisting grin, the raised stock of a shotgun.

But it was Mick.

"Jesus, that wasn't funny," Cara said, annoyed, even as relief ran through her. "You almost gave me a heart attack."

His car must be parked on the street directly outside her house, she realised. Damn. Once again, she had driven past it and not even noticed.

Mick put an arm behind his back and pushed the door closed. The lock made a loud *click* as it engaged.

"I didn't say you could come in," she said, retrieving her handbag and satchel, dumping them on the console table. "But before you go, let's get something straight. Have you been calling me and hanging up? During the night too? Well, I've had enough. Don't do it again."

She waited for him to speak. Instead, he stood motionless, staring at her with empty eyes. Seconds passed. The wind scraped along the roof tiles, shivered at the windows. A thread of anxiety tightened Cara's chest.

"Okay, you'd better leave," she said. "I mean it."

He took off his coat, slung it across the back of the nearest couch.

"What are you doing?" she said, knowing anyway, knowing in her guts.

He took off his jacket, loosened his tie, and unbuttoned his shirt. She took backwards steps towards the kitchen. Flinging his shirt onto the couch, he came after her. She turned to run. He caught her around the waist.

Lifting her bodily, he carried her down the hall to the bedroom, while her thrashing legs struck furniture and walls in passing. He stripped her like a fed-up parent strips a recalcitrant toddler at bath time: dispassionately, relentlessly, tugging at clothing with one hand while the other held firm to keep her from falling over. When she was naked, he tossed her onto the bed.

She scrambled to get up. He was between her and the doorway. With nowhere to go, she crept back to the bed and covered herself with a pillow. Meanwhile, he unbuckled his belt, doffed his shoes by stepping on their heels.

"Let's talk about this," she said. "I realise you're upset, but this isn't the way forward for us. We can work it out. Just sit down, okay? Sit down and we can talk things over."

He removed his trousers, balled them up and threw them like a missile at the dresser. Jewellery and perfume bottles exploded across the room. Cara flinched, screamed. He lunged at her. Ripping the pillow away, he shoved her back onto the mattress and straddled her chest, crushing the breath from her. She struggled, flailing, as he butted his erection against her closed lips and clenched teeth. Finally, he bored his thumbs into the hinges of her jaw. She yielded. He pushed deep into her mouth. When she tried to pull away, gagging, he took hold of her hair in a fist. No, she thought, this isn't happening. A man who had loved her so tenderly, so attentively, wouldn't do this to her. This was something else, something that didn't make sense.

At last, he released her hair. She wrenched her head to the side, gasping. He responded by sliding down her body, driving her legs apart with his knees.

"Stop," she said. "Mick, please stop."

His face impassive, unmoved, he held his weight on straightened arms. She didn't recognise him anymore. Far above her, looming high up near the ceiling, wavering through the sheen of her tears, he was a malevolent creature, a demon, an implacable force.

"Don't hurt me," she whispered.

He rammed into her. Cara squeezed her eyes shut against the pain. When she opened them again, his face was closer, only centimetres away. He seemed to be studying her with abstract interest, observing her with the dead gaze of a shark. Turning her head, she waited for it to end.

In time, he stopped, withdrew.

Was it over?

Instead of shifting away, he hooked an arm beneath her leg. He bent her knee way up onto her chest, folding her in two. She felt him stabbing blindly at her buttocks, hunting.

"Oh, please," she said, her voice catching in a sob. "Don't. Please don't."

Sharp, burning agony took her breath as he forced his way into her. Mick bared his teeth. Whimpering, she closed her eyes. As the minutes stretched on, the pain wore her down, made her cry. She tried to focus on the storm as it wailed along the roof tiles, tried to ignore the sound of Mick panting and grunting.

TWELVE

Finally, when Mick was done, he moved off her body and got up. As if waking from a nap, he stretched both arms overhead. He wandered around the bedroom to collect his socks, underwear and trousers from the floor.

Cara pulled the sheet over herself.

Without glancing back, he dressed. Next, he sat at the end of the bed, unlaced his shoes, put them on, and laced them again. He left the bedroom. She heard his stream of urine pounding the toilet water, the toilet flushing. After that, faint noises from the lounge room of movement and rustling material suggested that he was putting on his shirt, tie, jacket, and coat. Once, he coughed. The front door opened and closed. A few seconds later, a car door slammed. An engine started up. The sound of the car faded off down the street.

Exhausted, Cara rolled to the edge of the bed. She felt shattered, dropped from a great height. Painfully, she got up. Her work clothes lay in scattered puddles from one corner of the room to the other. She knew enough to leave the items alone. She shuffled to the wardrobe and pulled out jeans, a top, and windcheater.

As she dressed, she had to fight the overwhelming urge to shower. His touch lingered, stinging like sunburn. Everything ached. His musky smell steamed up from her chilled, sweating skin. God, she wanted nothing more than to stand under jets of hot water and soap her entire body, over and over, until the last traces of Mick Thompson had been rinsed away. But showering would destroy physical evidence.

Within minutes of calling the police, two uniformed officers arrived. Inexperienced and awkward, they did little else than sit and wait with her in the kitchen.

Soon, detectives turned up. Both of them wore suits. One detective was male, young, narrow-shouldered, his hair cut so close to the scalp that he appeared bald. The other was a woman, middle-aged, fleshy, her white hair an unkempt halo.

The woman offered a practiced smile. "Cara, is it? Hello, we're from the Rape Squad. I'm Detective Senior Constable Irene O'Brien. This is Detective Constable John Patel."

The ground dropped away. The kitchen disappeared. The night of the robbery rushed back in vertiginous waves. Cara, sitting again at a table in Benny's Pizzeria, looked up at two giant detectives as they introduced themselves. *Don't worry about remembering our names*, Mick said as Alec Castellano stood nearby. *If you forget, I'm happy to remind you.* Can you hear me? John, I think she's shutting down.

"Can you hear me?" Irene O'Brien said again.

"Yes, I can hear you," Cara said, opening her eyes.

Irene O'Brien sat at the table. "Do you know who raped you?"

"Yes. His name is Mick Thompson."

"Good work, Cara. Now we'd like to take you back to the squad so you can tell us exactly what happened. Then we'll drive you to hospital so doctors can check you over and collect a rape kit. Does that sound okay to you?"

"Yes."

"Excellent. Forensic people will have to come in here to gather evidence while we're gone. Do we have your permission for that?"

"Yes."

"Where exactly did the attack take place?" John Patel said, taking out a notepad from his jacket pocket.

"In my bedroom. On my bed."

"Okay. Apart from your bedroom, did the attack occur in any other area?"

For a time, Cara stared at the table. There were crumbs on it from breakfast: a slice of toast with butter and raspberry conserve. Then she said, "Yes. He put some of his clothes on the couch near the front door. When he first grabbed me, it was near the kitchen doorway."

"And this fellow's name is Michael Thompson?" Patel said.

"Mick Thompson, that's right."

Scribbling in his notepad, he continued, "You have an address for this character?"

"No. But he'll be easy to find. He's a detective in the Armed Offence Squad."

Irene O'Brien and John Patel exchanged shocked looks. They recovered just as quickly, their faces setting behind professional masks.

"Thank you, Cara. I know how difficult this must be." Irene O'Brien got up and held out her hand. "Can you come with us now, please? It's time to go to the squad. We'll drive you."

Cara sat in the back seat. Two weeks ago, this very day, Tuesday, detectives had driven her from Benny's Pizzeria along the same route, Toorak Road, to the Melbourne City Police Complex. The nightmare was doubling back on itself.

This time, instead of Alec at the steering wheel, it was Irene O'Brien. Instead of Mick in the front passenger seat—his mysterious, silvery scar running the length of his cheek, his broken-nosed profile—it was John Patel. Cara pressed fingertips into her temples against the oncoming crush of a headache.

And then the real kicker: the Rape Squad happened to be on the same floor as the Armed Offence Squad. Cara ground her teeth. When the bell in the lift pinged at the ninth floor, her heart took off in a gallop against her ribs. The doors opened. Light-headed, she half-expected Mick to be waiting for her. Was he? Acting like bodyguards for a president, O'Brien and Patel hustled her from the lift and shunted her so quickly through the double-doors of the Rape Squad that she didn't even have time to look back.

The Rape Squad was about half the size of the Armed Offence Squad. The interview room featured two vinyl sofas and a houseplant. They gave Cara a coffee and she drank it. Later, they gave her another coffee. In time, she drank that too.

Eventually, Cara said, "How many times do you want me to explain the same story?"

"My apologies," O'Brien said. "But we're just trying to sort out the facts. As they stand, they seem a little muddied."

"Muddied?"

"You admit to having a sexual relationship with Mick Thompson."

"We slept together a couple of times."

"Do you know why he would want to rape you?"

Cara stared at Irene O'Brien's benign, motherly face for a long time.

"I don't know," Cara said. "Ask him."

"We will," Patel said. "But had you argued? Was he drunk or taking drugs?"

"I don't see what difference that makes."

"No difference at all," he went on. "We're only trying to understand what happened."

Cara raked her fingers through her hair. At last, she said, "I found out he was married."

"Married?" O'Brien said.

"Yes. I told him I didn't want to see him again. He started calling me, sent me flowers—"

"Flowers?" O'Brien said. "What kind?"

Cara hesitated. "Two dozen roses."

Patel, taking a quick look at O'Brien, said, "Have you got any obvious injuries to show us? Cuts, bruises, that sort of thing?"

The breath left Cara's body. "You don't believe me."

"Oh, come on, now," Patel said, smiling. "Don't take these questions the wrong way."

"John—" O'Brien began.

"What other way is there? You think I'm calling rape to get back at an ex-boyfriend." Cara stood up. "I want to see your superior."

"He's not due till morning," Patel said.

"Then I'll come back tomorrow."

"Here," Patel said. He leaned across the table, grabbed a business card from the dispenser, and handed it over. "The contact details for our senior sergeant, Gerard Vandenburg."

"I'm sorry if we've upset you," O'Brien said, standing up and heading towards the door. "Would you mind seeing a doctor now? After that, I can drive you home."

When she got back to her rented house, no police were there. The bed sheets were gone. So were the work clothes that Mick had wrenched from her body. However, items from the dresser—jewellery, cosmetics, perfume bottles—were still scattered across the bedroom carpet. She didn't touch them.

Her shower lasted until the hot water ran out, then a few minutes more. There was no need for dinner. She didn't have an appetite. She settled for the night on the couch, under a blanket, watching television until, eyes burning, she fell asleep with the lights on.

She dreamed of Wangaratta. Opa and Oma were picking tomatoes from the vegetable patch. Cara trailed behind carrying the bucket, already heavy in her arms, while her foster parents put more and more ripe fruit into it. Summer: the time of year for kohlrouladen, currywurst, tomatensalat. The morning sun lay warm on the back of Cara's neck.

"*Ach, du liebe Zeit,*" Opa said, shaking his head at the plants, still drooping, still laden.

Oma used the heel of one hand to push back her wet, sweaty fringe. "We shall have to dig them back into the dirt."

Bury the tomatoes? Protectively, Cara hugged the bucket against her skinny chest. Bees and cabbage moths zigzagged ponderously through the air, drowsing under their own weight. Dry lightning flashed beyond the trees.

The following morning, Cara called work and said that she wouldn't be in because of a migraine. Then she called Gerard Vandenburg at the Rape Squad. He listened to her complaint without interruption, and offered an appointment straight away.

"Thank you, I'll be there in fifteen minutes," she said.

"No, don't come here. You might bump into your attacker somewhere in the building. We don't want to risk that. Give me your address. I'll come to you."

Now, he was sitting in her house at the dining table, cradling a mug of coffee, trying to make her understand.

"It doesn't matter if we think a person is guilty of a crime or not," he was saying. "Our job is simply this: to gather enough evidence to present the facts to a court. If there isn't enough evidence, then we can't take a person to court even if we believe that he's guilty. My crew members didn't doubt your word. They were just scouting for legally admissible evidence."

"Like injuries," Cara said.

"Yes, like injuries."

She wrapped her arms about herself. "Obviously, I didn't fight him hard enough."

He sighed, shaking his head. "That's not what I meant."

"Next time I'm raped, I'll be sure to get my jaw broken."

He looked pained. "I know how mercenary it sounds. But like it or not, the legal system favours the accused: innocent until proven guilty. The prosecution has a high burden of proof. As police, we have to gather that proof. Unfortunately, in the course of doing our job, we need to ask the victim a lot of questions that might come across as harsh or unfair."

"You're telling me I shouldn't take it personally?"

"Whenever possible, yes." Vandenburg put down his coffee mug and rested his clasped hands on the table. "If it's any consolation, your reaction is very common. I've worked in Rape Squad for nearly fifteen years, and believe me, most women feel let down or frustrated by the system at various points during an investigation. But, Cara, we're on your side. No matter what happens from here on in, try to remember that."

She said at last, "Do you believe that Mick Thompson raped me?"

"Yes."

"So, what happens now?"

"We interview him to get his side of the story."

"His lies, you mean."

Vandenburg shrugged one shoulder. "Confessions are rare."

"Do you know Mick? Personally?"

"Yes, I do." Vandenburg's gaze didn't waver. "And when it comes to a criminal offence, a police officer is investigated like anyone else. Okay?"

"Okay. When will you interview him?"

"As soon as I get back to the squad room, assuming he's in the building."

Cara's heart gave a panicked lurch. "How do you think he'll take it?"

Vandenburg smiled. "That's my problem, not yours."

On his return to the Rape Squad, Gerard Vandenburg briefed O'Brien and Patel. Afterwards, he went into one of the offices, shut the door, and pulled up a chair at the desk. He called switchboard first to check whether Mick Thompson was in the building. Then he called Frank Ward's extension at the Armed Offence Squad. Ward answered after a few rings.

"Frank?" Vandenburg said. "It's Gerry."

"G'day, mate, how you going? Got your footy tips in yet?"

"Sorry, this is a courtesy call."

"A what?"

"I'm giving you the heads-up. Mick Thompson is accused of rape. I'm looking into it."

After a while, Ward said, "Is this your idea of a joke?"

"No. I'd like to interview him now. Please send him over."

"Send him over?"

"Yes."

"Are you bullshitting me?"

"Send him over, if you wouldn't mind."

Ward hung up. Vandenburg called the extension again.

Finally, Ward answered the phone and said, "Let it go."

"I can't."

"What the fuck's going on here? This is bullshit. Who's the complainant?"

"Come on, Frank. You know better than that. Let me do my job. Please send him over."

"He's not here."

Vandenburg tightened his grip on the handset. "Yes, he is. I've already checked with switchboard. Frank, if you don't send him over, I'll have to ask O'Brien and Patel to come get him." He could hear Ward puffing down the line. Seconds ticked by. "Are you there? Hello?"

"There's no way you'd have the balls to march a couple of your detectives in here."

"Yes, I would."

"With cuffs? You really think the boys in the Armed Offence Squad would let a couple of your pussies come in here with cuffs?"

Vandenburg sucked on his lower lip for a while. "Take it easy."

"Fuck you, Gerry. *You* take it easy."

"Are you sending him over or not?"

Time passed. Ward said, "Keep your shirt on, he'll be there."

The line disconnected. Vandenburg replaced the handset, smoothed his tie, and left the office. O'Brien and Patel looked up as the door opened. They appeared nervous, especially Patel. He was young, early twenties, new, anxious to make his mark as a detective.

"Be ready," Vandenburg said. "Mick Thompson will be here any minute."

Shortly, Mick strolled into the Rape Squad, relaxed and loose-shouldered. By his side stormed Ward, red-faced. They halted just inside the entrance. Rape Squad detectives on different crews stopped and stared. Ward glared back at them. Mick, however, slipped his hands into his pockets, casually put his weight onto one leg, and gazed at a wall. Vandenburg wasn't fooled. For all that studied nonchalance, Mick's eyes glittered with rage.

"Good morning," Vandenburg said, approaching. "Thanks for your cooperation."

"Cut the shit," Ward said. "You and me need to sort this out."

"Let's go into one of the offices. O'Brien, Patel: would you mind showing Mick to the interview area?"

They flanked him. Mick bristled. For a suspended moment, it seemed that something might happen. Nothing did. The air came back into the squad room. O'Brien gestured towards a nearby closed door. Mick nodded curtly. The trio began to move.

Sneering at Vandenburg on the way past, Mick said, "Your cock had better be as big as you think it is."

"I'll let that one go," Vandenburg said, "but only that one."

Vandenburg led Ward into an empty office and shut the door.

"What the hell is going on here?" Ward hissed. "I've got two bandits pulling jobs on pizza parlours all over the suburbs. Sooner or later, a person's going to get killed. If you tie up Mick with stupid charges, you're reducing my manpower on this case by twenty-five per cent."

"I'm sorry, Frank."

Ward flung out his hands in exasperation. "What about the rats from the Professional Standards Division? Are they involved too?"

"Not yet, but that'll depend on what our investigation turns up. Look, if Mick has a case to answer, then yes, we'll contact the Professional Standards Division because we have to contact them. It's procedure, Frank. You know that."

Sighing, Ward rubbed at his forehead. "How about doing me a favour?"

"Stop right there. Don't say anything incriminating."

Ward gave a jeering laugh. "Get off your high bloody horse for once, would you, Gerry? Christ almighty. Can't you cut a mate a bit of slack when he's asking you? Begging you? Drop it now. I need Mick."

Vandenburg shook his head.

Ward's face turned to stone. "No favours for me, no favours for you," he said, wrenching the door open. "I'm going to take your investigation and fuck you with it."

Ward stomped from the office. No doubt he was headed upstairs to try to bring disciplinary action against the Rape Squad for sullying a detective's reputation without sufficient evidence.

Vandenburg plucked at his moustache for a time, thinking it over. He left the office. The island of desks he shared with O'Brien and Patel was located on the far side of the squad room, against the back window. Naturally, O'Brien and Patel weren't there because they were still in with Thompson. Vandenburg expected the interview would go on for a while yet. He went to his desk, took his seat, opened a file, and tried to concentrate.

One of the other Rape Squad sergeants came over. "Congratulations," she said. "I've never seen Ward that pissed off before."

"Me neither."

"But how cool was Mick? Not a care in the world."

"He was faking it."

"You think? Maybe he knows something you don't."

Vandenburg sat back in his chair.

"I've got to be honest, Gerry. I'm glad it's you going up against the Loose Cannon Squad, and not me." She began walking away. "But if you need help, give me a hoy."

"Will do."

The sergeant went back to her desk. Vandenburg gazed out the window. The clouds over the city hung heavy and black with rain. Frank Ward would be upstairs by now, filing the complaint. Sighing, Vandenburg pulled his chair closer to the desk and stared down at the file. His mind wandered. The closed door of the interview room kept drawing his eye. O'Brien was an astute interviewer. How would Thompson be fielding her questions? According to reputation, Thompson was fearless, domineering, cocky—but as a detective, not as a suspect. Vandenburg wanted to go in there, ask a few questions of his own, get a feel for Thompson, but it was too late for an interruption. The change of dynamics could give the man a second wind.

Vandenburg shut the file. He opted to pass the time looking out the window and worrying at his moustache. Then his landline extension rang. It was the secretary for the Assistant Police Commissioner. Vandenburg's stomach gave a small flip-flop. Frank Ward certainly hadn't wasted any time.

"How good is the evidence you've got against Detective Senior Constable Michael Thompson?" the secretary said. "I've got his sergeant here telling me that you don't have any."

"We're still trying to establish whether or not we can prove he committed a crime against the complainant. At the very least, he's guilty of misconduct relating to inappropriate sexual behaviour with her. The complainant is a victim from one of his armed robbery cases."

"Okay, give me the details."

Vandenburg did. The secretary thanked him and hung up. Vandenburg emptied his lungs in a hard rush. About ten minutes later, the door of the interview room opened. Mick sauntered out, head up, hands in pockets, exiting the Rape Squad without looking at anyone or saying a word. Vandenburg waited. O'Brien and Patel left the interview room, looking pensive.

"That was quick," Vandenburg said, as they approached. "Since when does an interview take under half an hour?"

O'Brien dropped into her chair. "He's a tough bastard to interview, that's for sure. He didn't put a foot wrong."

"What's his version of events?" Vandenburg said.

"He's not denying that he had sex with Cara Haynes last night," Patel said, sitting on the edge of a desk, "but he says it was consensual. He reckons she's crying rape for revenge. Apparently, she didn't find out he was married until after they'd slept together."

"Sounds credible," O'Brien said.

"Anything useful on the medical report?" Vandenburg said.

"Not really." Patel consulted his notebook. "Let's see now… 'Semen in the rectum'. Well, there's no point in testing it. He admits that it's his. 'Abrasions to the vulva, vagina and anus consistent with vigorous intercourse'." Patel closed the notebook. "And a small bruise on her left jaw next to the ear, for what it's worth."

"Nothing else?" Vandenburg said.

"Nope."

"We'll canvas the neighbours later today," O'Brien said, "but I doubt we'll turn up witnesses. By her testimony, Cara screamed once. We had stormy weather last night. What are the chances that anyone heard a single scream over the wind? Even so, Mick could argue that Cara screamed in passion."

Vandenburg said, "Let's not race ahead of ourselves. We've got him for misconduct. Thompson has admitted, on the record, to having a sexual relationship with her."

"Only to explain away the forensic evidence." O'Brien shook her head. "Gerry, it's a ruse to sidestep our investigation."

Patel said, "What will happen to him if he's found guilty of misconduct?"

"Next to nothing, that's what. A slap on the wrist. Meanwhile, we get a kick in the arse for dragging his name through mud."

"True," Vandenburg said. "But with a misconduct charge, we can get authorisation to check his file. Let's see if anyone else has made complaints against him. I don't believe that a man can go from law-abiding to law-breaking from a standing start, do you?"

"No way," Patel said, brightening. "There's got to be escalation."

"And on the same ticket, we can get the go-ahead to check his phone and computer logs," O'Brien said, and smiled. "Here's hoping he left us a circumstantial trail."

THIRTEEN

He wanted to punch somebody, anybody. Breathless, his blood pressure surging, Mick walked along the elevator hall and back into the Armed Offence Squad, adrenaline pumping through him so hard that his knees actually felt shaky. Fuck. As he approached, his crew looked around at him. A ruffle of nerves hit his gut. They knew. Ward must have told them. Every one of them knew. He could see it in their faces.

Bull stood up, slapped him on the shoulder as if greeting a long-lost mate, and said, "Mick, you bastard. How'd it go?"

Mick shrugged. "Not bad."

"Aw, don't worry. It'll blow over."

"Yeah," Mick said, and glanced around at the others.

Alec leaned back in his chair, laced his fingers behind his head, and gave him a cold stare. The self-righteous, smug little prick. After years of dedicated service, unpaid overtime, sky-high arrest rate, after putting himself in danger over and over again, Mick gets humiliated by the Rape Squad, treated like a criminal, like scum, and this is how Alec reacts? Like the witch hunt was deserved? Mick's heart slammed about inside his ribcage.

"You got something you want to say to me?" he said, stepping closer, bunching his hands into fists.

Unbelievably, Alec had the balls to smile.

Stevo said, "That's enough. Relax. We're all on the same crew, don't forget."

"It's him that needs reminding, not me," Mick said.

Ward stood up. "Thompson. Let's go."

Ward headed towards an empty office. Mick, after shooting Alec a warning look, followed across the squad room. There were two other crews on call that day. Nobody gawked at him. The word hadn't got out yet. But it wouldn't take long.

They went into the office. Ward shut the door and took a seat on the far side of the desk. Mick sat down opposite. They stared at each other in silence.

"What the fuck is going on with you?" Ward said at last.

Mick shook his head. Sweat began to build up between his shoulder blades, under his arms. He wanted out of there.

He wanted to be on the Murray River, a line in the water, galahs calling overhead from a clear blue sky.

"If it's not one thing, it's something else," Ward continued. "I've had a gutful. You know I went upstairs for you? Yeah, that's right. First, I tried to get you off the hook with Gerry Vandenburg, that fucking stickler, which got me exactly nowhere. Except that he wanted to report me for interference, right? So, then I went upstairs to file a complaint."

"Thanks."

"Thanks? Thanks for what? For looking like a dickhead?"

Mick swallowed. "I don't understand."

"Then let me explain. I told the brass you'd never touched that victim from the Benny's Pizza job, Cara Haynes. That the only contact you'd had with her was of the official kind. Like you told me. Right?"

Mick didn't reply.

Ward's voice raised a notch. "Right? Isn't that what you told me? I asked you if you were rooting her, and you told me no, you weren't. Remember?"

"Yeah."

Ward sneered. "Guess what happened next."

Mick looked down at the desk.

"This is what happened next," Ward went on. "They made a few calls, and what do you know? Turns out you were rooting this sheila all along. Right?"

Mick didn't say anything.

Ward stood up and yelled, "Right?"

Mick showed his palms. "Listen, I was being discreet about it. For her sake."

"For her sake?" Ward sat down. "Not for yours, by any chance? Not so you could avoid disciplinary action for misconduct? Aw, stop pissing in my pocket. You were rooting her."

"Yeah."

"Okay. Now we're getting down to brass tacks. A poor woman feeling emotionally fucked up from going through an armed robbery, upset, defenceless, and you rubbing your hands together and thinking, beauty, I'll be able to get in her pants."

"That's not how it played out."

"No? You fucking arsehole."

Mick recoiled, as if slapped.

Ward continued, "Did you pinch her wallet too?"

"Let's not go over that again."

"No, we need to go over it. We need to go over everything. Did you or did you not pinch her wallet?"

"No."

"Did you run her name through our computer systems?"

Mick hesitated. "No."

"Don't bullshit me. Did you or not?"

"No."

"What about her car registration? Did you check that?"

Mick chewed on his lip. "I can't remember."

"Fuck." Ward got up and paced the office. "The whole lot is going to come out, don't you realise that? Vandenburg's a fucking terrier, he's not going to let go of this thing. Not until it's done and dusted. Understand? Now tell me, for Christ's sake, and tell me the truth. Did you rape that woman last night? Did you?"

Mick clenched his jaw. "I can't believe you'd ask me a thing like that."

"And I can't believe you could be up on a rape charge, but there you go, we're both having a hard time, aren't we?" Ward dropped into his chair. "You know this reflects badly on me."

"No, it doesn't."

"It doesn't? I'm your superior officer. You've done this shit under my command."

"Hang on, there's no proof I've done anything that—"

"No proof?" Ward yelled. "You rooted an armed robbery victim. Gerry Vandenburg can open the whole tin of worms now because of that. Understand? Him and his cronies can dig and dig, and get any amount of dirt they want on you because of that stupid mistake. And then they can turn on me, and say, 'Sergeant Ward, how come your boy was on such a long fucking leash? How come he could waltz in and out as he pleased, take squad cars without signing for them, have affairs with vulnerable women he met while performing his police duties?' And what am I going to say, Mick? What the fuck am I going to say?"

Mick stared down at the desk.

Ward sighed. "You know the worst part? I've got to brief the inspector on this yet. My only hope is that no one's got to Brian Vaughan first. Any thoughts on how I can put a positive spin on this shit storm of yours?"

Mick shook his head.

"If you didn't rape this woman," Ward continued, "then talk to her. Get her to withdraw the complaint if you can. All right? And get yourself prepared for an internal review. For Christ's sake, you shouldn't have rooted her, Mick. You should have kept your cock zipped up, and stuck to doing your job and that's it, nothing else."

Impossible, Mick thought. The night of the Benny's Pizzeria robbery came back. Cara, sitting at one of the tables, had tilted up her heart-shaped face at his approach. Those grey-blue eyes and long dark lashes had started an itch in his belly. Oh Cara, he thought, clenching his fists. Cara, how did everything turn out this way?

"Get out," Ward said.

Mick stood up, opened the door and walked across the squad room towards the locker room, not looking at anybody. He grabbed his gym gear from his locker and descended in the lift to the second floor.

The gym was empty. Mick changed into tracksuit pants and singlet, and cycled on the stationary bike for five minutes to warm up. Numbed, his mind lay blank. He would work his regular routine: a mass-building weights circuit based around squats, dead lifts, straight-leg dead lifts, bench press, military press. As usual, he would add sets for his upper arms and calves, and finish with lower back extensions and crunches to strengthen his core.

He threw himself into the workout, hard. The burning pain in his muscles sandblasted any thoughts from his head. In the mirror, veins stood out in high relief along his chest, shoulders and arms. Grunting, he swung the weights, grimacing. Fuck it all, he was a lion. No matter what shit they threw at him, he was a goddamned lion. Soon, he was running with sweat. The pulse knocked against his ears, the breath rasped in and out of his blazing lungs. Occasionally, he came close to passing out. I'm a lion, he would think, doubled over, gasping.

Harlan, one of the sergeants in the Armed Offence Squad, walked into the gym. Behind him trailed one of his crew members, a bloke named Ainsworth. When they spotted Mick, Harlan and Ainsworth stopped short, frozen.

"G'day," Mick said.

Harlan nodded warily. Ainsworth glanced away.

They know, Mick thought. Word has got out and they know.

He attacked the next set of military presses with a flood of anger and panic, concentrating on raising the barbell from the back of his neck and down again, one-two, one-two, focusing on the breath as it heaved in and out of his open mouth. Harlan and Ainsworth abandoned the gym for the cardio room next door. Mick heard the whirring of treadmills, the pounding of their feet as the men ran and ran.

Cara knew that her psychologist, Rob Parkdale, didn't see clients on Wednesdays, but he made an exception when she told him what had happened.

"Hang up the phone and come right over," Rob had said. "I'll put the kettle on."

Now, she was slumped in the office couch by the window, crying into a handful of tissues, while Rob sat next to her, rubbing her shoulder. Her sobs finally slowed down into little hiccups. She leaned back to catch her breath, then began angrily scrubbing at her face with the tissues.

Rob said, "Tell me what thought just occurred to you."

"The truth."

"Which is?"

"I should have known better."

Rob shook his head. "Don't go blaming yourself for what this policeman fellow did. The choice was his alone. You weren't complicit."

"But I'm normally such a good judge of character." She threw the ball of tissues into the bin. "For God's sake, I've dealt with so many arseholes over the years. How come I didn't recognise Mick as another one?"

"Well, I imagine because he's the duplicitous sort, very practised in hiding his dark side. You may be a good judge of character, but you can't read minds."

Tears welled again in her eyes. "Oh, you know what kills me?"

"What?"

"That this whole thing could have been avoided if I'd turned him down the first time he asked me to lunch."

"You're not clairvoyant either."

"I should have told him no. I should have told him to go jump."

"As I recall from our earlier sessions," Rob said, "you described him as kind and understanding, a person who made you feel safe. And you'd gone through such a terrible experience at that pizza shop. It's only natural you gravitated towards a protective figure. It's not your fault he was presenting a façade."

Cara plucked a fresh tissue from the dispenser and dabbed at her lashes. A sinus headache had started up. Damn this crying. Exhausted, she sat back into the couch. Rob sat back too, and waited in silence. The noises in the room came to Cara's attention: rain sprinkling against the window; a gurgling torrent of water racing along what must be a nearby drainpipe; the murmur of air blowing in through the ducted heating vent. For a few moments, her stilled mind felt almost calm. God, if only she could keep her mind as still as this all the time. How much wine would that take? More than she could hold, probably.

"In my professional experience," Rob said, "victims of assault often blame themselves. Please, Cara, it's very important that you listen to me. You had every right to accept that man's invitation to lunch. You had every right to have a sexual relationship with him. And you had every right to trust him. He was the one who made the wrong choices, not you."

She sniffed, wiped at her face. "I think I need to get away."

"To where?"

"Anywhere. It doesn't matter. I need to pull up stakes and start my life over. And then I'll never have to think about Melbourne or what happened here ever again."

Rob gave a small, surprised laugh. "My goodness, is it even possible to block out memories?"

"If you're determined enough. It's a matter of mental discipline."

"I see. Have you deliberately blocked out memories before?"

"By the hundreds."

"Hundreds? That many?"

She nodded. "Maybe even more."

"Cara, most people enjoy reminiscing."

"Ha. Not me."

"Why ever not?"

She felt a sudden lance of anxiety. Without thinking, she had blundered onto the topic of childhood. Dropping the tissue into the bin, she said, "There's one more thing about Mick."

"Oh? And what's that?"

"Would the police force really put a detective in prison?"

Rob spread his hands. "Why, of course. Just from reading newspapers over the years, I can recall plenty of occasions when police officers have been found guilty of corrupt or unlawful activities and put behind bars. You shouldn't fear a whitewash."

"But if Mick was sent to prison, he'd be side by side with criminals he helped put away."

"And what's wrong with that?"

Cara hesitated. Mick's scars came to mind. She thought of the night he had told her the full story of his stabbing, the same night he'd made love to her so tenderly, so reverently. *Stop*, she thought, and pressed a fist to her mouth against the rising nausea. *Don't think about that night. Don't think about him like that anymore.*

"Cara?" Rob said. "What's wrong with Mick being incarcerated with other criminals?"

She grabbed a fresh tissue, twined it in her fingers, and said, "He wouldn't last five minutes."

"Is that any of your concern?"

"No. I suppose not."

"Do you still care what happens to him?"

She closed her eyes against more tears. The rain pattered. The ducted heating whirred. The paper tissue felt rough in her hands as she tore it to tiny pieces.

"I should go," she said, and looked at the clock on the office wall. "I've been here over an hour already."

"You're welcome to stay for longer. We could make this a double appointment."

But she felt suffocated, claustrophobic. Talking had only made things worse. She reached for her handbag. "Can I give you a credit card?"

"Visa or MasterCard," Rob said with a polished smile. "I'll organise a receipt for you."

Cara drove through the drizzle, the windscreen wipers beating, the operatic swells of Wagner rolling from the car stereo. Focusing on the music and the minutiae of traffic helped to keep her mind vacant.

When she arrived back at her house, she cruised up and down the street to check the parked cars for Mick, holding her breath against the possibility. Every car was empty.

Finally satisfied, she made a three-point turn in a neighbour's crossover and motored into her own driveway. She parked and switched off the engine. Getting out of the car, however, proved to be impossible. Despite herself, she kept looking around, checking her mirrors.

Come on, she thought, as the minutes ticked by. *Show some goddamned backbone.*

At last, she vaulted from the car, sprinted across the porch, jabbed the house key in the lock, and slammed the front door behind her the moment she got inside.

This can't go on, Cara realised, panting. She couldn't live like this. If she didn't get away, and soon, she would have a nervous breakdown.

She went into the kitchen, hoping for wine left over in the fridge. The digital display on the answering machine showed eleven messages. Her heart jolted. She had been gone for less than two hours. Oh, please don't let the messages be from Mick. At the back of the fridge, behind wilting celery and a box of eggs, lay a half-bottle of chardonnay. She poured a glass, drank most of it down, steeled herself, and played the messages.

The first one was from Trish. "You okay, honey? Your mobile's switched off again. I'm worried about you. Give me a call. All right, *ciao*. That's Italian for see you later, don't you know."

Cara smiled. Yes, she would call Trish. But would she tell Trish what Mick had done? Cara took a gulp of wine. Confiding in people didn't come easy. But Cara had just told Rob Parkdale about the rape, hadn't she? A professional who only listens for the money? Then surely, she could tell a friend. Because Trish was a friend, right? Or was Cara deluding herself? Before she could follow this train of thought to any conclusion, the answering machine hissed and bleeped, signalling a blank message. Then it hissed and bleeped again.

Then again. And again. Again.

Incredulous, Cara groped for a kitchen chair and sat down. More hang-up calls from Mick? Who else could it be? Another bleep followed another, and more, on and on. Cara pulled her hair.

Eventually, the answering machine fell quiet. The red digital display that denoted the eleven calls began to flash on and off, ready for her to delete the messages at the push of a button. No, she thought wildly. This was evidence. She would keep these messages and tell Gerard Vandenburg about them. His business card lay face up on the kitchen table nearby. Cara's fingers closed around the handset.

The telephone rang.

She jumped, yelping as if burned. The ringing tone continued. Impulsively, she grabbed the handset, put it to her ear. Silence. A long, dark corridor seemed to yawn before her.

"Hello?" she whispered.

"Cara Haynes?"

It wasn't Mick. The voice was male, deep, roughened by years of cigarette smoking. A voice she didn't recognise.

"Yes?" she said.

"I'm telling you right now to withdraw your statement against Mick Thompson."

"Who is this?"

"If you don't, you're in deep shit."

The call disconnected. For a moment, she felt paralysed. Then she dropped the handset and ran to her bedroom. A small leather suitcase was under the bed. She dragged it out, threw it open on the mattress. Not one more minute, she thought, turning to the wardrobe. She couldn't stay here, alone in this house, for one more minute.

Desperately, she ripped clothing from hangers and grabbed underwear from a chest of drawers, hurling the items at the suitcase. From the bathroom, she snatched up toiletries and threw them on top of the clothes. Hastily, she closed and zipped the suitcase. For all she knew, Mick and this other man, this nameless faceless man, could be coming for her right now.

She grabbed her handbag from the console table. When she wrenched open the front door, the sudden blast of cold air hit her so fast that she flinched, mistaking it for a physical presence, for Mick. She slammed the door and ran for the car. Reversing out of the driveway, she nearly struck a pedestrian walking his dog along the footpath.

Cara gasped, stamping the brake.

Oh Jesus, if the man hadn't dragged on the leash, the animal would be under her wheels.

She wound down her window a crack. "God, I'm sorry," she began to say.

"You stupid bitch!" the pedestrian shouted, leaning down, slamming his open hand against the driver's side window.

Panicked, Cara tramped the accelerator and swung the sedan onto the road.

"You almost killed me, you stupid bitch!" the pedestrian yelled, striding out after her. "Come back here. You come back here, you stupid bitch, you nearly hit my dog."

Cara drove off, hard.

The wind hurled a rattle of hailstones against the windscreen. Cara turned the wipers to high, swiped at tears with her sleeves. Her heart was beating fast enough to burst. She turned onto Toorak Road.

The lunch-time traffic was heavy. She wove in and out of lanes, seeking a clear run. At last, she got one. The road opened out. She sped up to beat a red light. At the bottom of a small dip, the tyres aquaplaned across a sheet of water. For a petrifying moment, the back end of the car came loose before the tyres found grip again. She glanced at the speedometer. Shit, thirty kilometres over the posted limit.

She applied the brake. The car slowed to seventy kilometres an hour, sixty-five, sixty.

The lights ahead turned red. Cara brought the sedan to a full stop. Briefly, she rested her forehead against the steering wheel. Calm down, she demanded. Use your brain. Think. What are you going to do now?

She switched on her mobile phone, thumbed through the list of contacts, and dialled Gerard Vandenburg's extension at the Rape Squad. The call went to an answering machine. Damn. She hung up and dialled his mobile number. This time, he picked up. She felt like crying. Instead, she identified herself, told him about the anonymous man who had just threatened her to drop the rape charge.

"Describe the voice," Vandenburg said.

As she did, the traffic light turned green. Cara drove on.

"I'll find out what I can," Vandenburg said. "Where are you now? At home?"

"No, in my car."

"Heading where?"

She hesitated. Where indeed? She had no idea. The suitcase sat on the back seat. Dead ahead of her on the horizon, about twenty kilometres away at the end of this road, lay the Dandenong Ranges, a set of low-lying mountains blue with eucalyptus trees, the peaks shrouded in fog. Apparently, the area was popular with tourists for its scenic drives, lookouts, restaurants, boutique hotels. She had never been there before. Well, now was as good a time as any.

"Cara?" Vandenburg said. "Are you still there?"

"I'm here."

"Can you tell me where you're headed?"

"Yes, the Dandenong Ranges. I'm booking a room for the night."

FOURTEEN

Alec, stuck with reading the pile of yesterday's tip-sheets for armed robberies, found it hard to concentrate. For a start, where was Mick? He'd been gone from the Armed Offence Squad for a long time, over two hours. And secondly, the information from most of the tip-sheets wasn't worth a toss. Given the opportunity to anonymously call a police hot-line to give up criminals or report suspected criminal behaviour, the average citizen chose to clog the system with crap.

The male caller has a male flatmate who desires rhinoplasty but cannot afford it. The flatmate has purchased a ski mask, gloves and jacket for the purpose of an upcoming ski holiday. However, the caller believes that the flatmate will use the ski mask to commit an armed robbery to pay for the desired rhinoplasty.

Alec dropped the report onto the stack destined for paper recycling.

"Hey, Stevo," he said. "Do you ever get anything worthwhile from tip-sheets?"

"Every now and then." Stevo stopped typing at the keyboard, leaned back in his office chair, and laughed. "You know, this one time, an old biddy rang to say that her cat must have robbed the local fishmongers because he liked fish. I shit you not. She dobbed in a fucking cat."

Alec laughed too. Bull approached, took his seat and lit a cigarette, ignoring them both. The newspaper lay open on the desk in front of him.

"This is a non-smoking building," Alec said, "which means nothing to anybody around here, I know, but shit, that's the tenth durry you've had in ten minutes."

"Aw, piss off, Mario. What do you care?"

"I care about breathing, that's all."

"Having trouble?" Bull held up a pen. "Let me punch some air holes."

"Give it a rest, will you?" Stevo said. "Jeez, you two give everyone the dying shits."

They went back to their tasks. Minutes passed. Alec scanned yet another tip-sheet, but couldn't concentrate. Mick's rape charge again came to mind. Cara Haynes was petite; so petite, in fact, that Alec would be able to carry her with one arm. And Mick outweighed him by five or six kilos. What chance would Cara have had? It didn't bear thinking about.

The female caller owns a hairdressing salon. On a daily basis, four unemployed male youths occupy the bench at the tram stop outside the premises...

Alec, uneasy, rubbed at the back of his neck. He had known Mick was dangerous, had known Mick was having an affair with Cara Haynes. No, more than that, Alec had caused their break-up and had even witnessed first-hand Mick's meltdown right here in this squad room, not twenty-four hours before the rape. Why hadn't Alec put two and two together? He was meant to be a detective, wasn't he?

"By Christ, you boys are going to sit up and pay attention."

Alec looked around. Frank Ward, his cheeks purpled, stood with fists on hips at the far end of the desks. Stevo caught Alec's eye and raised his brow as if to say, *what's the problem?* In reply, Alec could only shrug.

"I just got off the blower from Gerry Vandenburg," Ward said, glaring at them. "Anyone here who might be thinking of hassling Cara Haynes had better forget about it, quick smart, and I mean that most sincerely."

"Hassle her?" Alec said. "In what way?"

"Somebody phoned her up and threatened her," Ward continued. "Told her to withdraw her statement against Mick or else. Now, I won't stand for that. Understand? I'd help Vandenburg decommission our whole fucking squad before I would stand for shit like that."

Indifferently, Bull exhaled a stream of smoke and crushed the butt into the ashtray.

"Understand?" Ward said, louder.

Bull grinned. "No worries. Who'd want to speak to the moll anyway?"

"She's a victim, not a moll," Ward said. "Where's Mick?"

"Dunno. We haven't seen him for a while," Stevo said.

"Oh, hell." Ward turned, lifted his voice to the room. "Hey, anybody seen Thompson?"

Harlan called out from another island of desks. "In the gym."

"Okay, thanks." Ward pointed at Stevo. "Go get him."

"Me? Nah, I'm an hour into cross-checking the system for self-loading rim-fire rifles. I don't want to time out."

"I said go get him."

Stevo propped in his chair. "Come on, Sarge, you want me to time out and start from scratch? Why can't Alec or Bull get him?"

Because we're prejudiced, Alec realised; Bull is for Mick, I'm against. Stevo was the only neutral player left on the crew.

"I told you to go get him!" Ward shouted. "Now move your arse and get him."

Stevo leapt up, shoved his chair so hard into the desk that it rebounded, and stalked away towards the elevator hall. Next, the sarge retreated and shut himself behind the door of an empty office. Alec looked around. The two other crews on call today were staring, shocked, amused. We're falling apart, Alec thought. Falling apart or blowing up, one or the other.

Alec's mobile sounded. He grabbed the phone from his jacket pocket. The text from Liz Lansky read, *Lunch at noon Dirty Chai?*

He texted back, *Yep*, and ignored Bull, instead returning to the pile of tip-sheets.

The female caller has a male schoolmate with long, straight brown hair similar to that of an armed robber in security photographs who wore a Venetian Carnivale mask—

"Mick is the best copper we've got here, in my opinion," Bull said.

Alec glanced up. "That's not much of a recommendation."

"Fuck you. I don't give a shit whether he raped that bitch or not. He's one of us."

Shaking his head in disgust, Alec said, "And you call yourself a copper." He stood up, took his jacket from the back of his chair. "Tell the sarge I've gone for lunch."

At twelve o'clock, the office crowds hadn't yet descended on the Dirty Chai Café. Alec and Liz Lansky were able to grab a booth at the rear, more comfortable and private, and certainly less noisy, than a table near the front.

"I've got incredible news to tell you," Alec said.

"Okay, let's hear it."

She was taking off her police cap, settling herself into the cushions, checking the table for a menu, but Alec couldn't wait.

"You know how Mick Thompson was banging that victim? She's accused him of rape. Apparently, it happened last night."

"Oh yeah? Poor thing. I hope he didn't hurt her too bad."

Alec was taken aback. "That's it? That's your reaction?"

"Yeah, that's my reaction. Why, you want me to do it over?"

"I thought you'd be shocked. I mean, come on, Mick's a police officer."

Liz smiled in that fond, motherly way of hers that always made Alec feel like a dumb little boy who'd done something cute. He didn't like it.

"How many years have you been on the job?" she said.

Shifting uneasily, Alec didn't answer. He knew what was coming.

"About seven?" she went on. "Seven years of dealing with criminals, druggies, losers, scumbags, and there's not a cynical bone in your body. It's very sweet. Look, maybe it's more obvious to women on the force, I don't know, but shit like this happens. We've got our quota of sexual predators like any other profession."

He said, "Okay, it doesn't bother you, fair enough. But it bothers the shit out of me."

"How come?"

"Because I knew that Mick was going off the rails."

"So? You couldn't have stopped him."

Alec gave an irritable shrug. "Fine, I couldn't have stopped him. But I can help the case against him. At least, I want to try."

"Uh-oh, this has career suicide written all over it. Tell me what evidence you've got."

Agitated, he began fiddling with the cutlery, turning the saltshaker, glancing around for a waiter. Liz Lansky in no-bullshit mode was about as comfortable as a cricked neck.

"Come on, let's hear it," she said.

"I'm an eyewitness to Mick bashing two suspects."

"Irrelevant. What else?"

"He stole her wallet."

"You saw him take it? Or did he confess?"

"All right, you've made your point."

"And if you could prove that he took the wallet, what does it establish? That he's a thief, not a rapist. Irrelevant again. What else have you got, mate? Nothing. Not a single piece of evidence that would be worth a damn in court. Agreed?"

"Fine. Let's order lunch."

"If you cross the floor and buddy up with detectives from the Rape Squad," she continued, "what are you going to achieve?"

"Probably nothing. Can we drop it now?"

"No." Liz sighed. "Not until you understand that you can't help on this rape case. And if you try, every detective in the Armed Offence Squad is going to hate your guts. Forget about promotions. Your career there would be over. And forget about transferring. No one wants a copper that turns on his squad."

"Oh, yeah? Says who?"

"Says me. Remember our old boss from years back, Inspector Darrow?"

"What about him?"

"He liked to visit street prostitutes during office hours. In exchange for not arresting them, he'd get freebies."

Despite himself, Alec's jaw fell open. "Darrow? No way. Are you sure?"

"Positive. Actually, I was the one who dobbed him in."

"What? Jesus, you never told me any of this." Alec sat back in the booth. "But hang on a minute. That can't be right. Darrow got promoted to chief inspector, didn't he? And transferred to another branch."

"That's right. Meanwhile, I'm nearly forty, and still a senior connie at a shit-can station. Haven't you ever wondered why?"

Goddamn. Alec gazed at Liz, his good friend of many years, his first-ever superior officer after graduating from the Academy, and he couldn't figure out what was worse: her story, or the fact she hadn't told him before now.

"Everything is so fucked," he said.

She laughed. "Oh, tell me about it."

Mick felt like chucking again. Shit. He was standing in one of the gym's shower stalls, his feet braced wide, arms straight out with palms flat against the wall, head bowed, the hot water blasting a torrent down his back. Every muscle burned, quivered. For two hours, he had lifted heavy without bothering to count reps or sets. Now he was paying for it.

The door of the change room creaked.

"Hey Mick, is that you in the shower?" came Stevo's voice.

"Yeah, it's me."

Footsteps, then Stevo was standing outside the open-faced shower cubicle. Frowning, hands on hips, he looked Mick up and down, and said, "It smells like spew in here."

"I had a hard workout."

"Yeah, I can see that. If you let go of that wall, mate, will you hit the deck?"

"I don't know."

"Ah, lactic acid is such a bitch. You need a protein hit. Tuna or chicken ought to fix you up."

Mick closed his eyes. "What do you want?"

"Sarge told me to come get you. He's ropeable."

"What for this time?"

"Someone rang Cara Haynes and told her to rescind her complaint."

Mick looked up. "Did they threaten her?"

Stevo shrugged.

"Fuck." Mick straightened with effort, turned off the taps, and reached for his towel. "Anyone pointing the finger at me?"

"Not that I know of. Sarge was yelling at Bull mostly, which makes sense. It's the kind of stupid thing Bull would do."

Mick, trembling, sat down on the wooden bench in the cubicle to towel off. After a while, he said, "You haven't asked me."

"Haven't asked you what?"

Mick paused. "Whether or not I raped her."

Stevo leaned against the door jamb and looked away. "It's got nothing to do with me."

Mick dried himself. They passed a couple of minutes talking about weight training. Stevo preferred high-volume workouts that focused on two or three body parts, while Mick liked high-intensity workouts that taxed the whole body. Usually, they could banter for a long time about the pros and cons of each other's approach and get laughs out of it, but not today. Conversation petered out. They lapsed into silence while Mick dressed.

With Stevo by his side, matching him step for step, Mick felt he was being escorted through the building like a civilian. Or a crim. He bristled. They waited in the elevator hall for one of the lifts. Mick couldn't take the silence anymore.

"I suppose Alec is loving this," he said.

Stevo didn't answer. A lift pinged and its doors opened. A couple of blokes from Homicide exited, both of them holding gym bags.

"G'day Keith, Paul," Mick said.

The detectives nodded on their way past, but only at Stevo.

Mick stared after them. "Whatever happened to innocent until proven guilty?"

"Ha, that's pretty funny," Stevo said, "coming from you."

Shaken, Mick didn't know what to say to that, so he said nothing.

In the Armed Offence Squad, it was just Frank Ward and Bull sitting at their desks, which was a relief. Facing Alec, that smug prick, would be more than Mick could take. Ward stood up and crooked a finger.

"What?" Mick said.

"Come with me. Brian Vaughan's been looking for you."

Stevo took a seat. "Good luck, mate."

"You'll be right," Bull added. "Give him heaps."

Mick dropped his gym bag, and followed Ward across the squad room to the detective inspector's office, glancing neither left nor right in case any other coppers felt like snubbing him. His legs were still rubber from the workout, his stomach turning over.

Outside Vaughan's office, Ward gave Mick a stern look as if to say *behave,* and then tapped on the door.

"Come in," Vaughan called.

They did. Ward shut the door behind them. Vaughan gestured towards two chairs set up on the other side of his giant desk. Mick and Ward sat down. Nobody said anything. Mick focused on Vaughan's steel-wool eyebrows.

"A sexual affair with one of your own armed robbery victims," the detective inspector said. "That's your admission?"

Ward leaned forward. "Brian, a man can't help it if a woman has the—"

"Be quiet."

"Yes, sir."

Vaughan, looking back at Mick, said, "You committed a breach of discipline. Let's focus on that. We'll put the rape accusation aside for now, since you haven't been charged."

Mick nodded.

"The Chief Commissioner may want an investigation," Vaughan continued. "I'll try to head that off. My argument will be the importance of squad morale. The brass is very concerned about the pizza bandits. Therefore, I expect a good outcome."

"Thanks," Mick said.

"If I can't swing it and the investigation goes ahead, we'll stall until they run out of steam. Either way, we'll get around it." Vaughan raised his stupendous eyebrows. "But the Rape Squad has your personnel file."

Mick gazed at the floor.

"There was nothing I could do about that. Your confession of misconduct was their green light. Now, I've read over your file and there are problems with it. Especially for you, Frank."

"Me?" Ward said.

"The complaints against Thompson are unsubstantiated. Even still, they show a pattern of behaviour, especially over the past six months. He's got an attitude problem. Anyone paying attention would have spotted that. Frank, don't you conduct performance reviews of your staff?"

"Of course, I do." Ward gave a sly, polite smile. "Don't you read them, sir?"

Vaughan slitted his eyes. "We have to close ranks. I don't want the Professional Standards Division involved."

"Nobody does," Ward said.

"Take the rest of the day off, Thompson."

Mick started. "What?"

"We're dealing with a lot of fallout. Go home. Come back fresh tomorrow."

Mick gripped the armrests of the chair. "I've got work to do."

"You want to argue with me?"

Ward said, "Don't worry, Brian. I'll make sure he leaves as soon as we're done."

"Good," Vaughan said. "And we're done."

The room at the bed-and-breakfast guesthouse held a double bed, television set, chest of drawers, and a free-standing wardrobe. The adjoining en suite was closet-sized. Cara put her suitcase on the mattress. Heavy curtains, pulled aside, revealed a sliding glass door that led to ground-level decking. Beyond lay a grassy expanse, a garden spilling over with low-lying native shrubs and maidenhair ferns, a stand of wattle trees covered in bright yellow blossoms.

"I've never been to the Dandenong Ranges before," Cara said. "How much colder is it compared with the city?"

The owner, an old woman with jowls, her dust-coloured hair wound into a spindly bun, said, "At least five degrees. We're expecting snow tomorrow morning."

"Snow?"

"Four millimetres, according to the weather bureau."

"Is that enough to make a snowman?"

"No, I wouldn't imagine so. Possibly enough for snowballs, if you're that way inclined." Then the owner said, "Are you all right, dear? You look a bit pale. You're not feeling well?"

"I'm fine. A little tired."

"Well, I won't keep you any longer. Here's your key," the owner said, handing it over. "There are more pillows in the wardrobe if you need them."

"Thank you. Do you serve any meals other than breakfast? I'd rather not leave the property if I don't have to."

"Dinner is in the main room at seven sharp. Tonight, it's Irish stew, with apple crumble for dessert." The owner smiled, hesitated. "We don't offer a lunch menu for guests, but if you like, I could make you an omelette."

"That would be great. Are you sure you wouldn't mind?"

"Not at all, dear. Just come to the main room whenever you're ready." The owner left the room, shutting the door quietly behind her.

Cara sat on the bed and stared out at the garden. During the ascent up the side of the mountain, she hadn't dared drive faster than forty kilometres an hour, despite the posted speed limit of sixty. The road, narrow and switch-backed, hemmed in by eucalyptus and giant ferns, twisted around so many sharp bends that Cara hadn't been able to see far ahead. She'd kept expecting something to leap out at her from the fog. At the sign for this guesthouse, the Heathland Chalet Bed-and-Breakfast, she had turned immediately into its gravel driveway. Getting off the road seemed urgent, even though nobody knew where she was and no one had been following her.

Sighing, Cara got up from the bed and went into the en suite. She took the soap from its plastic wrapper and held it to her nose. It smelt like roses. Along the sink were arranged tiny bottles of shampoo, hair conditioner, moisturiser, which was lucky since Cara hadn't brought any from home. She washed and dried her hands, ran her fingers through her tousled hair. There might be a comb in her handbag. While searching through her bag, she noticed her mobile, and switched it on. Two messages from work. Still no word from Gerard Vandenburg. She switched off the phone again, grabbed the comb, and dragged it through her hair.

This overnight stay would be a time-out, a chance to calm down. For now, forget about everything that's happened, she told herself. Use mental discipline. Don't look back. Closing her eyes, she took a long, slow breath in and out: right here, right now. Then she threw the comb into her handbag.

The hall led to the main room. Cara took a seat next to the open fireplace, which had a low fire gently burning. The room was furbished cottage-style, featuring plenty of oak, braided rugs, floral upholstery, embroidered pillows, framed needlework hanging on the walls, potpourri bowls and vases of dried lavender along the windowsills and sideboard. Ordinarily, Cara would have dismissed this kind of decor as mawkishly sentimental and contrived, but the room felt comforting; perhaps, she realised, because she was looking for comfort.

The swing door to the kitchen opened. The owner saw Cara and brightened.

"Hello there," the owner said. "I thought you'd be having a nap. Hungry?"

"Yes. Very."

"I'll fix you an omelette. Ham, cheese and mushroom?"

"That sounds perfect, thank you."

"Won't be a minute," the owner said, and ducked back into the kitchen.

Cara looked around. Next to the fireplace was an open picnic hamper stuffed with magazines. As ever, Cara didn't want to read about celebrities and crash diets. Beneath one of the windows sat a stocked bookcase. She went over to it. The volumes were old, mostly cloth-covered hardbacks with stamped spines and no dust jackets. She knelt down, tipped her head, and scanned the titles. There was nothing she recognised. The volumes smelt like old paper and mould.

"Hi," said a young voice.

She looked around. Standing in the doorway was a boy of about eleven or twelve, red-cheeked and dirty like he'd been running around outside. He was wearing denim jeans and a blue spray jacket but wore only socks on his feet, as if he'd left a muddy pair of shoes on a back step or porch.

"Hi yourself," Cara said. "Are you a guest here too?"

"Nah, my nan and pop own this place. They've got their own house out the back. I'm staying here 'cause Mum's got to work."

"Why aren't you at school today?"

He tore off his spray jacket, revealing a windcheater. "School holidays."

"Oh, is it? I wouldn't know."

"You're not gonna find anything to read in there," he said, poking a thumb towards the bookcase. "It's boring old fart stuff. Pop got them from the op shop. Nan says he picked them like potatoes, without even bothering to check what any of them were. It's to make the bookcase look good."

"I see." With a smile, she crossed the room back to the armchair and sat down. "I'm Cara. What's your name?"

"Ryan. I can lend you a book but you've got to give it back. You like science fiction?"

"Well, I don't know. I haven't read that much of it."

"How about stuff with magic and monsters? You like that?"

The swing door to the kitchen opened; the owner, Nan, said, "Stop bothering the lady."

"I'm not bothering her," Ryan said. "We're talking about books."

"It's fine, really," Cara said.

Nan gave a nod and retreated into the kitchen.

"Thanks for the offer," Cara said, "but I won't be here long enough to read a whole book. I'll be gone first thing in the morning. I need to go to work too."

"Oh, yeah? My mum sells clothes. What do you do?"

"I work in printing. The company I work for makes brochures, business cards, calendars, annual reports, magazines, books; that kind of thing."

The boy screwed up his nose, unimpressed. Cara stifled a grin.

"I'm gonna be a computer programmer when I leave school," he said, dropping the spray jacket onto the nearest armchair, "for an MMORPG company. Know what the letters mean?"

She shook her head.

"Massive Multiplayer Online Role-Playing Game," he said. "It's where the money's at."

"Oh. Does your nan like you playing games on the computer?"

"Nah, she reckons I've gotta be outside. You know what I've been doing just now?"

"What?"

"Helping Pop dig a fishpond. He's still out there, but I've had enough. Nan wants to make a kind of special garden where you can sit around and stare at goldfish all day long. Who'd want to do that?"

Cara shrugged. "Maybe I would. It sounds peaceful."

"Peaceful?" Ryan slung himself onto the sofa. "You know what Pop reckons? If we don't put wire mesh over the pond, birds will come and eat the fish. Who wants to stare into a fishpond with a dirty big old piece of mesh over the top of it? That's what Pop reckons. But you think Nan's gonna listen? No way."

Cara laughed, delighted. The swing door opened. Nan came out with an omelette on a plate.

"Ryan, get off the armchair, you're filthy," she said. To Cara, she added, "Would you like to come with me to the dining table?"

Cara stood up. Ryan began to follow them.

"Not you," Nan said to him. "Go wash your hands for lunch."

Raising his eyes to the ceiling, Ryan spun on his heel and disappeared down the hall. At the dining table in the next room, Nan put the plate on one of the place settings.

Cara, sitting down, said, "Oh, what a great little guy. So chatty and friendly."

"That boy could talk under wet cement. He's like his mother, always running off at the mouth. My Lord, you should hear the two of them together, yap, yap, yap." Nan looked exasperated, pleased and proud at the same time. "It's enough to drive you mad."

Cara didn't see Ryan again after lunch. She waited in the main room by the fire for a long time. When he didn't show, she went back to her room, got her coat and headed outside.

It was cold. The air smelt faintly of wood smoke and eucalyptus. She did up her coat buttons. The back patio had benches and loveseats arranged around a barbecue, which was covered in a sheet of tarpaulin. It looked like it would be very pleasant out here on a summer's evening. Cara stepped off the patio and walked along the brick path that followed the perimeter of the lawn. Beyond, the fog threaded in heavy layers throughout the gum trees.

As far as she could tell, the grounds of the Heathland Chalet featured mostly native plants. She stopped at a fern garden bordered by rocks to admire the cordylines, bird's nest ferns and smaller, more delicate plants that she couldn't identify. Cockatoos wheeled and screeched overhead. Maybe it was time to move back to the country, she mused. She could choose a town, buy a small property, grow a vegetable patch, sit outside after work every night to smell the fresh air and watch as parrots flitted about the trees. Perfect.

An orange tabby cat streaked past on the brick path, startling her. The sound of running feet made her spin around. It was only Ryan. Cara relaxed, smiling, as Ryan slowed down and approached. Right here, right now, she reminded herself. Don't look back.

She said, "Was that your cat, or your nan's?"

"Nan's. The bell's come off his collar again. I'm supposed to put it back on, but do you reckon I can catch him?"

"Oh, he'll come to you at dinner time."

"Yeah, but how many birds is he gonna kill by then? Pop wants to get rid of him, but Nan says over her dead body. Guess what his name is?"

They were walking together by now, Cara on the brick path, Ryan next to her on the grass, his gumboots squelching into the mushy lawn.

"I've no idea," she said. "What about...Tom?"

"If only. Nup, she went and called him 'Bossy Britches', no kidding. It sucks. I call him Boss. You want to see the fishpond we're making?"

"I'd love to."

Behind a hedge of Grevillea shrubs, a beefy old man in a tracksuit was standing knee-deep in a hole, throwing dirt from his shovel. Bossy Britches paced back and forth, looking into the pit with interest. Cara stopped on the brick path.

"How's it going, Pop?" Ryan said, bounding across the grass.

Pop looked around.

"Hello," Cara said, with a small wave. "I'm one of your guests."

"Nice to meet you," Pop said. He wiped the back of his hand across his sweating forehead. "You don't feel like picking up a shovel, do you?"

She laughed. "In these shoes? No thanks."

"I had my little helper for a while, but he's reneged on me."

Ryan thrust his hands at his grandfather, palms facing upwards, and said, "Aw, c'mon, look at these blisters."

"I don't see any."

"The red parts, I mean. See? Any more digging and they'll turn into blisters."

"If you reckon." Pop stabbed the shovel blade into the pit and climbed out. Ambling towards Cara, he said, "I don't know how we can have a koi pond when we've got so many white-faced herons around here."

Cara said, "Ryan was telling me earlier about your idea for a wire cover."

"Yuck, that's gonna look bad," Ryan added.

"Well, you never know," Pop said. "I've been thinking I might sink the mesh down in the water. That way, you won't be able to see it."

"What a good idea," Cara said.

"Only if it works. I'll need to rig up some manner of bracket to keep the mesh in place. Considering the missus wants an irregular-shaped pond, I'm not sure how to go about it. I'll have to see my mate at the hardware store. Now, if the pond was square or rectangular, that'd be a different story."

"Nan says that a square pond would look dumb," Ryan said, squatting on his haunches and patting at the cat.

"And she's right," Pop said, and winked at Cara. "As usual."

Cara smiled. A light misting rain began to float down around them, eddied by the breeze. She pulled the collar of her coat tighter around her.

Pop gestured towards the guesthouse. "You'd better go back. You're not dressed for rain. From the city, are you?"

"That's right."

"Here for long?"

She shook her head. "Not long enough."

FIFTEEN

The fluorescent tube over Gerard Vandenburg's desk was dead. Holding the sheets of paper closer to his face, Vandenburg swivelled his chair towards the floor-to-ceiling window of the Rape Squad to catch the last of the day's natural light.

Thompson's personnel file made interesting reading.

According to the file, Thompson had accrued a whopping fifteen complaints in just four years at the Armed Offence Squad, mainly regarding acts of physical violence such as kicking, punching, choking, or striking with a baton. Since most victims of police violence tended to keep silent, Vandenburg estimated the actual number of assaults to be closer to sixty. Holy Mary. He gave a low whistle and kept reading.

Mitigating factors had allowed Thompson to escape disciplinary action. Firstly, all the complainants had criminal records. Who would trust the word of a crim over that of a copper? Secondly, eyewitness testimony from other Armed Offence Squad detectives backed up Thompson's version of events. Thirdly, the medical evidence had always been inconclusive, usually because the alleged assaults had taken place in private, such as within a complainant's home, meaning any injuries could be explained as 'lawfully inflicted' during a difficult arrest.

Of the fifteen complaints lodged against Thompson, a disproportionately high number—five—had occurred in the last six months. A glance at the general statistics showed that Thompson was an anomaly. The average number of complaints per detective at the Armed Offence Squad was reportedly two per year.

Thompson was the proverbial accident waiting to happen.

How had no one realised? More to the point, Vandenburg thought as he plucked at his moustache, how had Frank Ward not recognised that one of his own crew members was out of control? Vandenburg put down the file, and rubbed his tired face with both hands.

"Anything?" O'Brien said, turning her attention away from the computer monitor.

"Plenty, but nothing that can help us. Thompson is quite the bruiser. I've never seen anything like it. Yet there's not a single complaint from a female in the whole four years he's been with the Armed Offence Squad." Vandenburg picked up the file, and flipped back through the pages. "Years ago, when he was first in uniform, a drunk female resisting arrest alleged that he called her a 'fucking dumb cow' after she spat on him. That's it. Hardly the sign of a rapist-in-the-making."

"Nothing about sexual misconduct?"

Vandenburg dropped the file to the desk. "Not a whisper."

"Well, it could be this is the first time he's ever hooked up with a victim."

"Or else he's covered his tracks every other time."

"True," O'Brien said. "You want to try talking with his crew members about it?"

Vandenburg laughed, straight from the belly.

O'Brien did too. "Okay, you're right. They'd only stonewall us."

"Stonewall?" He laughed harder. "They'd cut off our heads and put them on stakes."

Patel walked into the squad room.

Sobering, Vandenburg glanced at the wall clock. "John, at last. What took you so long? I expected you back here ages ago."

"In peak-hour traffic?" Patel took a seat at the desks. "What do you want to hear first? The bad news or the bad news?"

Vandenburg sighed. "Ah well, damn. We thought it would be this way."

"I went to every neighbour," Patel continued. "Not one of them heard a thing out of the ordinary last night. Nobody noticed that Mick's car was parked on the street. And get this: when I showed his photo around, nobody recognised him. There's no eyewitness evidence that Mick Thompson even visited Cara Haynes in her own home."

"Shit. Don't people look out their windows anymore?" O'Brien said.

"Never mind," Vandenburg said. "We knew the neighbour angle could draw a blank."

"Thompson's phone records aren't looking much better." O'Brien glanced at the computer monitor. "If he called Cara Haynes, he didn't call her from his extension. He could have used other extensions, I suppose, but we don't have authorisation to check the records of every landline in the Armed Offence Squad."

"We might get authorisation if we charge him," Vandenburg said. "Keep looking."

Patel said, "What do you want me to do next, Sarge?"

"Check through his computer history. With luck, he ran unauthorised searches on her."

"Uh, how do I do that?"

"We can trade," O'Brien said. "I'll take computer history. You do phone records."

"But can you show me how to do the history thing?"

"Yeah, no worries."

Vandenburg's extension rang. It was his detective inspector, wanting a final word with him before she left for the day. He replaced the handset, sighed.

"It's getting late," he said. "I understand if you both want to call it a day. I'll be back in a minute. I have to report to the boss."

He stood, walked to the Detective Inspector's office, tapped on the door. This would be more bad news, he thought wearily. Nothing about this Thompson case was anything else.

"It's open," called Howard-Yorke.

Vandenburg went in and shut the door behind him. Sitting at the desk, Detective Inspector Emily Howard-Yorke gestured towards a chair. Vandenburg sat down.

"The Thompson case," she said. "Where is it going?"

"At this stage, nowhere, but we've been working on it for less than twenty-four hours. Evidence might surface."

"And how likely is that?"

"I don't know."

"Okay. Wrap it up as quickly as you can, won't you, Gerry? I've been upstairs in meetings all day because of this. Brian Vaughan's bellyaching about crew morale, and he's got a point. We can't drag it out. Apparently, the Union is starting to make noises already." Howard-Yorke spread her hands and smiled. "If you can't make a charge stick, then drop it. And drop it sooner, rather than later. Fair enough?"

"Yes, of course."

"Good." Howard-Yorke got up, shouldered her handbag and briefcase. "Spargo's crew are having a send-off for Marg tonight. Can you come along for a drink?"

"I'd better not," he said, standing up too. "If I don't get home every once in a while, I'm afraid that my wife might forget what I look like."

"I've got a husband in the same boat." Howard-Yorke paused at the office door. "I'm serious, Gerry. By tomorrow night, either charge Thompson, or drop it with every required apology, upstairs and down. Clear?"

"Yes, ma'am. Very clear."

"Good night."

She walked towards the Rape Squad exit doors. Vandenburg went back to his crew.

"We just got the wind-up," he said. "Please tell me you've found something."

Patel said, "Well, this here looks pretty suss. Monday night heading into Tuesday morning of this week, with the rape on Tuesday evening, mobile phone records state that Mick called Cara's landline at home six times. Four of those calls were after midnight."

"Did she pick up?" Vandenburg said.

"Doesn't look like it. The longest call lasted seven seconds. Long enough to wake her up, I'd guess, or drag her out of bed. Not long enough for her to answer, though. The landline is in her kitchen."

O'Brien smiled. "Evidence of stalking with intent?"

Vandenburg said, "Let's hope so. John, check with Cara Haynes and get corroboration, will you?"

The lounge room was dark. Mick, sprawled in the armchair, took another mouthful of vodka. The room teetered, rocking him gently like a crib. What exactly had he been angry about? Fuck, he couldn't remember. His mouth tasted sickly and tart. He gulped from the glass, closing his eyes. Without warning, Cara swam up into his consciousness.

Hey beautiful, he thought.

He could picture her grey-blue eyes, her dark lashes, the smoothness of her skin, the curve of her waist, as if she were standing naked right there in front of him. She had her arms overhead and her legs apart. His cock stirred despite the booze. How much had he drunk tonight? He couldn't remember that either. Oh Cara, he thought absently, his mind warm and loose, his hand moving to his zipper. Come here, baby, I've got something for you.

A key scraped at the front door. Mick started, froze. The front door opened and Janice walked in, immaculately dressed in trousers and jacket, her makeup perfect. He felt like mussing her exacting hairstyle, but he wasn't sure if he could get out of the chair. Janice switched on the hall light.

"G'day," he said, his tongue partly sticking to the roof of his mouth.

She spotted him, smiled reluctantly, lifelessly, and closed the door. "What are you doing home?" she said. "I thought you were working today."

"Me too."

"What happened?"

"Nothing." Mick dozed a little. The glass slipped from his fingers. A minute or a day passed him by, he couldn't tell which. Eventually, with effort, he lifted an eyelid. Janice was still in front of him, looking annoyed. "What's wrong?" he said. "What the fuck is the matter with you all the time?"

"God, you're such a prick," she said, and stormed from the room.

He fell asleep. The dream ran over him in reds, blues and greens, chaotic memories of fast-flowing rivers and multi-coloured fish, pink flesh, clasping hands and eager mouths that worked at him, getting him hard, getting him right to the fucking edge, and then gun barrels and blood, always the blood. Mick held his breath. He knew what was coming and here it was. The crying women, dressed in black as always, looked up at his approach. No. In the hospital bed, the man's battered scalp, cross-hatched with black stitches, drew Mick's horrified gaze. *No,* Mick said, unable to look away, as he found himself moved, as if on rails, closer to the man's bedside. *No, you're dead, I can't help you.*

"All right, I'm off. I don't know when I'll be home."

With a jolt, Mick woke up. Janice, standing by the front door, was now wearing a long tight dress and heels under a three-quarter length coat, her hair wound on top of her head, her lips scarlet. She held a small red bag.

"Where are you going?" he said.

"Out."

"Out where?"

Janice opened the front door. "If you want anything for dinner, make it your fucking self."

"Hang on, for Christ's sake," Mick said, struggling and failing to get out of the chair. "Who are you going out with? Is it a bloke? Tell me."

She slammed the door behind her.

The Heathland Chalet felt warm and close after the outside chill. Cara removed her coat, draped it over one arm, and wandered into the main room. From the bookcase, she finally selected *The Odyssey of Homer*. She had read it as a child while staying with Oma and Opa. Now, sitting in an armchair by the dying fire, she flipped through the book's dry and yellowing pages that reeked faintly of mildew and searched for the only parts she could remember: the blinding of the Cyclops; and the siren song while Odysseus, tormented, is lashed to the ship's mast.

So many feasts, so much wine, she thought, smiling gently, as her gaze fell across snatches of text. After being taken from the home of Oma and Opa, Cara had often dreamed of Athena materialising to offer advice, guidance, protection. Of course, nothing like that had ever happened. Throughout those many lonely years, nobody had shown the slightest interest. Cara quickly shut her eyes. Right here, right now. Don't look back.

She checked her watch. Perhaps Gerard Vandenburg had called. She went to her room and switched on her phone. There was a message from John Patel. She rang him immediately.

"Thanks for getting back to me," Patel said. "According to phone records, Mick Thompson rang your landline at home, repeatedly, on the Monday night through to the Tuesday morning of this week. Is that correct?"

"Yes. Well, I assume it was him. They were hang-up calls."

"Okay, fine. That's great. Do we have your permission to check your phone records? We're having trouble finding out from our end which landline and mobile numbers Thompson used when he communicated with you."

"My phone records?" she said. "Yes, I suppose you can check them. Do I need to fill out any forms or sign anything?"

"Don't worry. We'll take care of it. Thanks for your cooperation."

"Wait," she said. "Is Gerard Vandenburg there? I'd like to speak to him."

"I'll get him. Stand by."

She sat on the edge of the bed. Her heart was pounding, but she wasn't sure why.

"Hello, Cara. This is Gerard Vandenburg."

"Hi," she said, standing up to pace the room. "Did you find out who rang me?"

"Rang you?"

She bit her lip. "Yes. Don't you remember? The man who called me earlier today. The one who told me to withdraw my statement."

"Oh, that's right. My apologies, Cara. We've been working through a mound of paperwork that it...look, I should've got back to you sooner. However, there's no need for concern. I can assure you that you won't get another call of that nature."

"You can assure me? How?"

"I spoke to the relevant authority. I'm confident the matter has been taken care of."

"Who was it that called me? Do you know?"

After a time, Vandenburg said, "What matters is that the harassment won't continue."

Cara stopped pacing. "You're not going to charge Mick, are you?"

"Our enquiries are ongoing. Please try not to worry. I'll get back to you with an update tomorrow, all right? We're doing our very best, I can promise you that."

"Thank you," she said, and hung up.

The last of the evening light had faded and died. Cara turned on a lamp, crossed the room and closed the heavy curtains. Then she had a shower. She stood under the water for a long time. Afterwards, she lay across the bed and listlessly flipped through *The Odyssey of Homer* until it was seven o'clock and time for dinner.

There were two couples sitting at either end of the dining table: an elderly man and woman who muttered to each other in a foreign language; and two fat, middle-aged women who hardly spoke a word, perhaps inhibited by the strangers in the room. The boy Ryan wasn't there. Earlier, he had mentioned a private house on the property. No doubt that's where he, Nan and Pop would later be having their evening meal, not here among paying guests in the chalet's dining room. Nonetheless, Cara felt disappointed.

Nan served up the Irish stew, followed by the apple crumble. For the duration of dinner, Cara avoided eye contact with the other guests. No one tried to speak to her. As soon as she finished eating, she hurried back to the privacy of her room.

The television had free-to-air channels only, most of them fuzzy. Cara watched a show about amateur cooks pitted against each other, but what the prize was, Cara couldn't figure out. Unwarranted fame, most likely. Bored, she turned off the television and picked up the book. She opened a page at random. The chapter heading was "Scylla and Charybdis". Isn't that life all over, she thought, closing the book and tossing it to the bedside table. Every minute, every one of us caught between a rock and a hard place until the day we die. She wished for wine, but didn't have any. Nor did she have the strength to leave the chalet and drive around the unknown streets of the Dandenong Ranges, in the rain, to search for a bottle shop.

It was barely nine o'clock. Her broken sleep on the couch the night before was overtaking her. She brushed her teeth, took off her clothes and got into bed. The sheets were coarse and burred, the pillow hard, but she fell asleep almost immediately. Most of the night passed in a deep, black and dreamless blur. And then she dreamed about Mick.

She was on her side in bed. He was close behind, naked, hot and hard against her back.

"Let me love you," he whispered.

His hand smoothed back her hair, his lips dropping to her throat. The gentle movements of his tongue made her nerve endings quiver. As she stirred and stretched, waking up, he ran his hand down her flank and slipped his fingers between her thighs.

"Oh, Mick," she said, reaching back to touch him.

Where was he? Confused, Cara turned over and slid a hand across the sheets. He wasn't there. She opened her eyes. Fear stabbed her. This was not her bedroom. Sitting bolt upright, clutching the sheet to her chest, she gaped about the unfamiliar surroundings until, a moment or two later, everything came back in a horrible, sickening rush.

She gave a little sob. Her unconscious mind had betrayed her. That dream belonged to another era, another world. The man she had known and the one who had raped her weren't the same. No, she corrected herself, that's not right. The awful truth? The lover had been the rapist all along.

The digital clock said 5.33 a.m. Breakfast would start in an hour. Cara got out of bed and showered again. Wearing a towel, she opened her suitcase and sorted through the clothing she had haphazardly packed the night before, hoping that she had enough to cobble together an outfit suitable for the office. It was her intent to drive straight to Premiere Press. She didn't feel ready to go back to her rented house just yet. Admittedly, in her haste to flee, she had forgotten to grab her satchel, but there was nothing she could do about that now.

She put on a white shirt and a two-piece pants suit. The items were wrinkled, particularly the shirt, but a quick search around the room didn't turn up an iron. Well, too bad. She would look shabby for the day, and live with it.

During the wait for 6.30 a.m., she packed, then went through her phone messages and made notes on a complimentary *Heathland Chalet* jotter pad she'd found in one of the drawers while hunting for the non-existent iron. She wasted the remaining minutes by flipping through the Odysseus book again. At last, it was time for breakfast. She locked the door behind her.

There was no one in the main room. A fire burned in the grate. The curtains were open. In the faint pre-dawn light, the trees and shrubs beyond were nothing but dark shifting shapes in the breeze. Cara went over to the bookcase, squatted down, and returned the hardback to its empty slot.

"Wow, don't tell me you actually found anything good to read?"

Cara glanced around. Ryan was slumped at the table in the adjoining dining room. His face looked both sleepy and cranky.

Cara stood up and walked over. "You're up before the birds."

"Tell me about it. Nan reckons I've got to help her with breakfast. What for? There's hardly anybody here. Can you believe it? School holidays and I'm kicked out of bed at quarter to six."

"That's rough. What does she want you to do?"

"Put out this junk." His gesture across the table took in the jam and honey jars, the cutlery at each place setting, the wooden serviette holders with their paper napkins.

"Well, you've done a great job."

He gave a proud grin. "Yeah, thanks. What did you end up reading?"

"Homer's tale about Odysseus. You know the one? It's set in ancient Greece. Odysseus is coming home from the Trojan War and gets delayed for about ten years."

"By monsters and gods and stuff?"

"Yes, that's the one."

"But isn't the guy's name Ulysses?"

"Only in Latin. That's what the Romans called him."

"Huh?" Ryan screwed up his nose. "Why give him a different name?"

"I don't know. They did the same with the Greek gods. Jupiter is actually the Roman name for Zeus, and Neptune is Poseidon. There are lots of other examples, but I can't think of them."

Nan came into the dining room. "Ryan, stop bothering our guest."

"I'm not. Jeez, we're talking about books."

"I thought I told you to set up the table. Go get the breakfast menus. And where are the coasters?"

Scowling, Ryan slid off the chair and slouched from the dining room.

Nan turned to Cara and said, "Leaving so early?"

"I've got to go to work. It'll probably take me a couple of hours to drive to South Melbourne from here, with the morning traffic."

"Yes, I wouldn't be surprised." Nan hesitated, and then smiled. "Would you like me to iron your blouse?"

"I'm sorry, what?"

"Packing clothes isn't my forte either. No matter how carefully I fold everything, there's bound to be a thousand creases. It won't take me a minute to run the iron over your blouse."

Cara, momentarily overwhelmed, felt the ache of choked tears rise to her throat. Life can be gentle and kind sometimes too, she thought, like right now and don't you forget it. She wanted to put her arms around the old woman. Instead, she nodded.

Ryan, walking back into the dining room, said, "Which ones are the coasters again? Big ones or little ones?"

"Little ones. Did you get the menus, at least?"

He thrust the laminated cards at Nan with a roll of his eyes. To Cara, he said, "Want to see the snow?"

Nan said, "Oh, what a good idea. It's very pretty outside this morning. Off you go, I'll finish laying the table. Then if you can give me your blouse."

Cara followed the boy through the main room and into the hall. He opened the back door. The freezing air came as a shock. Ryan went out first. She closed the door behind her and turned. The view stopped her breath. The world had become monochrome. In the milky light, the green lawn of yesterday was now a white carpet. Snow lined the dark boughs of every tree. By the garden shed, the water droplets trimming a stand of bare-limbed silver birches gleamed like thousands of fairy lights.

"Pretty cool, huh?" Ryan said, as he jumped from the porch to the lawn.

The heavy crunch that his shoes made against the snow caused her to look down. It wasn't snow exactly, more like hail; countless billions of little ice chips the size of rock salt. Then Cara looked up. The fog moved in swirling veils overhead. It seemed that if she reached out her hand, she could catch a piece by its tail.

"If you ask me," Ryan said, running the back of his hand under his reddening nose, "this is the best time of year for the Dandenong Ranges. Sure, it's cold and whatever, but how awesome does everything look?"

"Completely awesome." Smiling, Cara took a deep breath of chilled air.

SIXTEEN

Gerard Vandenburg held the ceramic teapot up to the urn and began filling it with boiling water. At this early hour, there was no one else in the tea room on the ninth floor and, to his shame, he felt grateful and relieved. Ever since yesterday morning, when word had got out about the rape investigation against Mick Thompson, Vandenburg had sensed a vague menace from detectives of the Armed Offence Squad. Not from all of them, of course. Most ignored him. A few, however, gave the impression that they wanted to belt him, and no one gave this impression more strongly than Bull.

Last night, Vandenburg had been in the tea room, fetching his yoghurt from the refrigerator, when Bull had walked in. Bull, real name Henry Bramich, was a twenty-year veteran of the Armed Offence Squad and, by the looks of it, a thirty-year veteran of hard drinking. As soon as they had locked eyes, Bull had narrowed his. Closing the fridge, Vandenburg had straightened to his full height, painfully aware of his own slight and neat build. It was easy to see how Bull had earned the nickname. The man was unfit and beer-bellied in middle age, yes, but he was still built like a rugby player and carried an awful lot of beef on his frame.

Bull crossed his arms. "What've you got there, mate? Cheese?"

A typical, if uninspired, insult. He was calling Vandenburg a rat for 'ratting out' another police officer. In fact, the Professional Standards Division, the internal police department that investigated misconduct and corruption in the force, was colloquially known as The Rat Squad. The detectives in that department even had the moniker printed on their coffee mugs.

"Big hunk of cheddar, is it, mate?"

"For your information: yoghurt."

Vandenburg went to leave the tea room. Bull moved to block his path.

"Careful you don't choke on it," Bull said. "Accidents happen."

Vandenburg smiled politely. "Henry Bramich, isn't it?"

Bull glowered.

"Listen, Henry, I'm not impressed by childish threats. Neither is Cara Haynes. That's right, I know it was you who called her. Now, Henry, let me be perfectly clear. Unless you want to be reported for harassment and intimidation, get the fuck out of my way."

Looking flummoxed, Bull had stood aside. Vandenburg had marched from the tea room with his shoulders thrown back, even though his knees had wobbled.

Forget the events of last night, Vandenburg told himself. Just make your bloody tea. The ceramic pot was full of boiling water. He put it on the draining board.

Was he a coward? No. You had to be careful, he thought, as he affixed the teapot lid. Despite ninety-nine per cent of the force being aboveboard, that rotten one per cent was enough to see you harmed, professionally or perhaps even physically. There had been plenty of rumours over the years about the Armed Offence Squad, a.k.a. the Loose Cannon Squad. A few of those rumours were nasty enough to make anybody feel wary.

Heavy footsteps sounded on the linoleum behind him. Bracing himself, Vandenburg turned around. It was the newest recruit to the Armed Offence Squad, that tall, athletic boy with the Italian surname.

"Morning, sir," the new recruit said, heading towards the coffee machine.

"Good morning." Vandenburg leaned an elbow on the bench. "Alec, isn't it?"

"That's right, sir. Alec Castellano."

Alec gave a friendly, guileless smile, and then opened a cupboard and hunted through it for a suitable mug. He found one soon enough, and began pushing a couple of selection buttons on the coffee machine.

Vandenburg wandered over. "You're on Frank Ward's crew, aren't you?"

"Yes sir. For about five or six weeks by now."

"And you've got Mick Thompson as a crewmate, isn't that right?"

Alec stopped making coffee, and stared straight ahead at the wall. "Yeah, that's right."

"Perhaps you could do me a favour."

"What sort of favour?"

"I need to ask Mick a couple of questions. Is he in this morning?"

"Yeah, he's in."

"Would you mind telling him to come see me straight away? By straight away, I mean this minute, not when it suits him. In other words, immediately."

"Okay, no problem, I'll tell him."

"No problem? Are you sure?"

"Yes sir." Alec turned to him with a clear, direct gaze. "I'm sure."

Vandenburg nodded, picked up the teapot and left the room.

Sitting at his desk by the window, Vandenburg found that he couldn't concentrate. He kept glancing over at the double doors of the Rape Squad. Minutes passed. Forget it, he thought at last. Go ahead and call Frank Ward with the request. He reached for the handset on his landline. The glass doors of the Rape Squad shoved open. Mick Thompson walked in.

Vandenburg stood up.

Thompson saw him and, frowning, stopped mid-stride to put his hands on his hips. The man's body language said, quite clearly, *what in hell do you want now?* Interestingly, Thompson was alone. Ward hadn't accompanied him this time. Vandenburg hurried over and gestured towards an interview room.

"Thanks for your help," he said, opening the door. "Please take a seat."

Thompson slung himself into a chair. His eyes were bloodshot, his face pouchy, as if he were hungover and needing sleep. Vandenburg took a seat on the other side of the table.

"Haven't you and your buddies got any real work to do?" Thompson said. "You're fucking over the Armed Offence Squad."

"I'm sure it must feel that way to you."

"No, it feels that way to a lot of people."

"Including people from upstairs," Vandenburg said. "Look, I'm well aware of the politicking. You don't have to spell it out for me."

"Don't I? Aw, who cares? Tell me what you want to know. Hurry up, I'm busy. I've got real criminals to catch."

"Fine, I won't keep you. Did you attempt to contact Cara Haynes via your mobile phone on the night of Monday through to Tuesday morning of this week?"

"Yeah, I was trying to return her call."

"And yet you hung up each time before she could answer."

"Only because I thought I'd be disturbing her. Is consideration a crime in your squad?"

"All right, I have another question. Are you aware of the Information Collection Principles that govern every member of the Victorian police force?"

Exhaling through his teeth, Thompson gave a lazy shrug.

Vandenburg took a piece of paper from his jacket pocket, unfolded it, and began reading out loud. "*The first principle is that a police officer is forbidden to collect personal information about anyone, unless the information is collected for a lawful purpose that relates directly to a specific police operation.*" He folded the paper and returned it to his jacket pocket. "You ran unauthorised computer searches on Cara Haynes. First, you checked her for an arrest sheet, which turned up zero. Next, you checked public records, her credit history, driver's licence, and ran her car's registration number, among other searches."

"Yeah?" Thompson said. "So?"

"So, at the very least, you breached a principle, which would require an internal review. Worst case, you performed an illegal search that may constitute a criminal act of stalking. Those are your choices. What do you have to say?"

Thompson's face set into a cold mask. "My computer searches of Cara Haynes were necessary to rule her out as a suspect."

"A suspect?"

"One of our theories about the pizza bandits is that they have a scout inside the target premises who acts like a customer. After assessing the situation, the scout gives the thumbs up or the thumbs down, possibly by secret hand signal through the window or by text message. My enquiries cleared Ms Haynes of suspicion. If my computer searches were tagged as unauthorised, that's my sergeant's fault, not mine. Frank Ward should have put in the requests." The smile, when it came, was mechanical. "Anything else?"

What a crafty bastard. Vandenburg sat back in his chair, speechless.

Thompson stood up. "Thanks for wasting my time. If you want to waste any more, you know where to find me." Flinging open the door with enough force to bounce it off the wall, Thompson left the room.

Sighing, Vandenburg rubbed at his forehead.

"Gerry?"

He looked up. Irene O'Brien was in the doorway. John Patel was behind her. Both were looking at him with questioning, plaintive faces. As a long-serving detective in the Rape Squad, Vandenburg was, unfortunately, very used to losing—most cases were of the he-said-she-said variety, almost impossible to prove beyond a reasonable doubt—but Holy Mary and Joseph, this was his first case against a dirty detective and it hurt to feel it slipping away.

"Thompson found a loophole?" O'Brien said.

Vandenburg nodded. "I think we might be done."

The quote for Blackbird Books ran to five pages. Cara read over it one more time. Satisfied, she attached the document to an e-mail addressed to the company's managing director, the woman with the fierce black bob. There, done. Unexpectedly, Cara found that clicking the 'send' button choked her up. Well, why not? It was a feat to be proud of: living a nightmare for weeks, but still able to put together a killer proposal; a testament to her mental discipline.

She got up from her desk, intending to visit Don's office to tell him in person that she had delivered the quote, when her landline buzzed. She picked up the handset.

"Yes, Lucy?"

"Hi, mate. I've got a detective here to see you."

Cara's heart punched into her throat. "A detective?"

"Yes, a Sergeant Vandenhorn. Huh? Oh, my apologies. Cara, are you there? I mean Sergeant Vandenburg."

"I'll be one second."

Cara hung up and dashed from her office to the offshoot hallway that contained the staircase and single lift. There, the mezzanine overlooked the reception area. Grabbing the railings with both hands and steeling herself, Cara glanced down. To her relief, it really was Gerard Vandenburg. The breath returned to her lungs.

"Good morning," she called, her voice echoing.

The detective looked about. Lucy pointed a long, manicured nail towards the balcony. Following the cue and looking up, Vandenburg spotted Cara and smiled. He held a large brown-paper bag, the type with string handles. Cara didn't like the look of that bag.

"I'll meet you on the first floor," she said.

With a nod, he walked beneath the balcony towards the staircase. She could hear the muffled thud of each of his footfalls on the carpeted steps. When he appeared, she put out her hand and he took it. The expression on his face was resigned, apologetic.

"Have you charged him yet?" she said.

"Let's have this conversation in private."

"Yes, of course. Come to my office."

Once there, she closed the door behind them. He put the paper bag on the desk.

"What did you bring?" she said.

"Your bed sheets and work clothes."

From the night of the rape, she realised. Light-headed, she took her seat. "But won't you need them in court?"

Vandenburg gestured at the visitor's chair on the opposite side of the desk. "May I?"

"Please."

He sat down, clasped his hands together on the desk, chewed at his lip. Meanwhile, Cara's stomach turned over and over in wave after sickening wave.

Vandenburg said, "There isn't an easy way to tell you, so I'll just tell you. We can't build a case against Mick Thompson."

Finally, Cara said, "That's it?"

"Unfortunately, yes."

"He rapes me and I report it and nothing happens?"

Vandenburg looked pained. "Rape can be difficult to prove, especially in cases where it comes down to one person's word against the other."

She felt herself starting to shake. "It's because he's a police officer. His word means more than mine."

"That's not true."

"If he was a plumber or a dentist," she said, her voice rising, "things would be different, wouldn't they?"

"Probably not." He leaned over the desk. "Please understand the job I have to do is very specific in a legal sense. The first step of an investigation is to determine whether a crime has taken place, and if so, the offender's identity. Then a direct link must be made between the crime and the offender. Each step has to consist of evidence that is legally admissible in a court of law. I don't have any leeway. What I believe has happened, what I know has happened, none of that counts. It's about what I can objectively prove. Can you see that?"

"No."

His shoulders dropped. "All right, let me explain it this way: the Australian justice system requires a certain amount of evidence before a case can be brought to court. We simply couldn't get enough evidence to satisfy that requirement. Therefore, we couldn't charge him."

She blinked back angry tears. "In other words, I should have let him break my arm."

"No, for God's sake, no. That's not what I'm saying at all." Visibly agitated, he plucked at his moustache. "I've done everything I can, and I realise it's not enough. The only thing you can do now is put the incident behind you and get on with your life."

"Get on with my life?"

"Yes."

"Are you serious?"

"I'm sorry. Look, I really am."

She shook her head. "How many times have you given this little speech?"

"Cara, please, I'm not happy with this either."

"I don't want your sympathy. I want something done."

"As do I." He got to his feet. "But I can only work within the law. Try lobbying politicians. Once again, I'm very sorry. I can't tell you how sorry I am."

He held out his hand. After a time, she took it.

"I'll see myself out," he said, opening the office door. Then he was gone.

Stupefied, Cara found that she couldn't move, couldn't think. Eventually, she swivelled her chair to face the window. The sky was uncharacteristically blue; a hard, shiny, eye-watering brightness that sliced between buildings, cutting wedges of dark shadow across the street. The cars below shuffled in never-ending lines along the bitumen. Pedestrians criss-crossed the footpaths, back and forth, walking purposefully in their suits or jeans. Everyone was going somewhere, going nowhere, filling in the seconds, minute by minute, year by year, until all the bullshit of a lifetime was over and didn't matter anymore.

Stop it, Cara thought, putting her face in her hands. Right here, right now.

Except that 'right here, right now' meant pain and fear.

Without knowing what she was doing, she got up and put one foot blindly in front of the other, fleeing her office and racing down the central hall. When she reached Trish's office, she burst in without invitation. Trish looked across from her computer monitor, and gasped.

"Oh, Jesus," Trish said, white-faced, standing up and reaching out her arms. "Oh no, Cara, what is it? Oh, tell me what's wrong."

This is bollocks, Alec thought, looking away, feeling uncomfortable. Gerard Vandenburg was standing by the desks of Frank Ward's crew, making an articulate and polite apology, while the detective inspector of the Rape Squad herself, Howard-Yorke, stood close behind him, grim-faced.

"My intent was never to besmirch anybody's reputation," Vandenburg was saying, his unblinking gaze fixed on the floor-to-ceiling windows at the rear of the Armed Offence Squad. "I was called to do my job and obliged to fulfil the requirements of my job without favour."

"Yeah, whatever, cheese-eater," Bull muttered.

"Pipe down," Ward said. "I don't want to miss a single word."

They were lapping it up, particularly Mick, leaning back in a chair with his hands laced behind his head. Wait, in contrast to the others, Stevo's arms were crossed, his mouth set. Alec kept glancing over at him.

"And in conclusion," Vandenburg was saying, "I would like to express my deepest appreciation for the professionalism and cooperation displayed by every member of the Armed Offence Squad, and my regret that my crew had to be pitted temporarily against yours."

"How sweet, now here's my dick," Bull said.

"In particular, I would like to sincerely apologise again to you, Michael Thompson, for any embarrassment and distress that my enquiries may have caused." Vandenburg looked to his inspector, Howard-Yorke, and said, "Is that enough?"

She nodded, and then said to the crew, "Thank you. everyone. Good morning." When she turned and began walking away, Vandenburg followed her.

"Fuckers," Bull said after them. "You dirty cheese-eating fuckers."

Ward called out, "Just so you know, Gerry, I'm not withdrawing my complaint."

Without breaking stride, Vandenburg and Howard-Yorke exited the Armed Offence Squad. The double doors swung shut.

"Arseholes," Bull said, and slapped Mick on the shoulder. "You see, you dumb bastard? See? I told you everything would be all right, didn't I?"

Other detectives came over from different points of the squad room to offer their congratulations, shaking Mick's hand, patting his back. A few seemed awkward or embarrassed. Stevo got up and headed towards the tea room. Alec followed.

Stevo was scowling into the open fridge.

Wandering over to the coffee machine, Alec said, "What did you reckon of that?"

"It's not my business to reckon anything."

"Isn't it?"

"No. And it shouldn't be yours, either."

"Uh-huh. That's how Mick keeps getting away with shit."

Stevo closed the fridge door. "Last time I looked, we're on the same crew." Exiting the tea room empty-handed, he said, "If you want to gossip and bitch about people, join a fucking knitting circle."

Alec sighed. He didn't particularly want a coffee, but he made one anyway, just to delay returning to the squad room. Liz Lansky must be right. The Armed Offence Squad was a bad fit. How could he keep coming to work every day if he didn't respect his sergeant or crew members? Okay, fine, then he'd start looking around, checking out the postings bulletin. The thought of it, however, made him feel depressed, as if he'd failed. Well, he'd failed as an Armed Offence Squad detective, hadn't he? No point in lying to himself about it.

He threw the teaspoon at the sink and headed back out with his coffee. Mick and Sergeant Ward were arguing.

Sitting at the desks, Bull and Stevo were watching with closed faces.

"You want a car?" Ward said. "Then you take Alec."

"But I'll only be half an hour," Mick said.

"I don't give a shit whether you're half a second. You want a car, you take Alec."

"Why not Bull?"

"Because I said so, that's why. Any more questions, Detective Senior Constable?"

"Where are we going?" Alec said, putting the coffee down on his desk.

Ward tossed him a set of car keys, saying, "Mick has a lead on the pizza bandits: an ex-con working in a factory who apparently knows a thing or two."

"Yeah?" Alec raised an eyebrow. "Does this ex-con have a name?"

Mick wheeled on him. "Shut up and give me the keys."

"No way," Ward said. "Alec drives or you're not going anywhere."

They took the elevator down to the car park in silence. Once in the car, besides telling Alec to head north, Mick didn't speak.

Alec sped the car through the streets of South Melbourne. The traffic was light this side of lunch hour. Of course, there would be no ex-con, he brooded. Mick wanted to disappear for a few hours like he always did, and Ward, finally, was catching on, which is why he'd ordered Alec along as babysitter. No doubt Mick would find an excuse to call off the errand—

Mick jolted in the passenger seat. "Pull over!" he shouted.

Alec jammed his foot on the brake. A car horn sounded behind them.

"What is it?" Alec said.

"Pull over now."

Alec flicked the indicator, crawling, looking for a safe place to put the car. They were in the heart of Clarendon Street, a shopping precinct consisting of one- and two-storey buildings stocked with cafés, restaurants, bars, and specialty stores. The paid meter-parking on their side of the road didn't offer a single empty space. Other cars overtook at speed.

Mick, twisted in the seat, craning his head to peer out the rear window, yelled, "Quit looking for a park, dickhead. Just stop the car and let me out."

"What's wrong? What have you seen?"

"Stop the fucking car," Mick said, scrabbling for the door handle.

He flung open the door and swung his legs as if preparing to jump. Alec slammed on the brake. The vehicle lurched to a halt. More horns clamoured. Mick leapt from the car and took off at a gallop, back the way they had come.

"Wait a second!" Alec yelled.

Mick was already gone.

Alec had no choice but to block the whole lane. Putting on the hazard lights, he switched off the ignition, clambered from the car, and pocketed the keys. The passenger-side door hung ajar, but that couldn't be helped. There wasn't time to go back for it. Alec felt for the holstered gun and began to run along the footpath. Pedestrians were stopped and turned in Mick's wake. Up ahead, Mick was barely visible through the crowd as a dark blonde head, a flapping coat jacket.

"Out of the way, police!" Alec shouted.

Alarmed pedestrians scurried to either side of him, a few of them grabbing at hearts, at mouths, peeping out shocked little shrieks.

He was gaining on Mick. Tearing over a side street, Alec held up a hand against oncoming traffic, hoping that the cars would stop. They did. Dodging around a woman pushing a pram, he collided with a businessman stepping out of a newsagency. They landed on the footpath in an untidy sprawl. A few people screamed. For a moment, Alec felt too winded to respond. His knee hurt like crazy. Then he got up. The businessman was looking about, dazed, as if unsure of the surroundings.

"Police," Alec said, grabbing the man, hauling him to his feet. "Are you injured?"

"Huh?"

"Are you hurt?"

"Well, no, I don't think—"

Alec took off. Not far away, Mick was standing with his legs planted wide apart, holding a person—a woman—by the wrist. She was struggling, trying to get free. Realisation hit Alec like cold water even before he saw the terrified face of Cara Haynes.

SEVENTEEN

A burst of adrenaline put greater speed into Alec's sprint.

"Stay away from me," he heard Cara beg. "Leave me alone."

"Never. I'm never going to do that," Mick said.

Pulling up, Alec seized Mick by the arm and swung him around so forcefully that Mick stumbled, lost his footing. He let go of Cara. She fell to the footpath.

Without consideration or planning, Alec hit Mick with everything he had. The right-cross caught Mick on the cheek. Mick's head snapped back. Alec rotated his shoulders, punched again. The right jab landed as Mick was recovering balance. His lip popped and spurted blood.

Alec cocked his fist again. Damn, he could do this all day.

He didn't see Mick's left hook but felt it sure enough, like getting hit by a train.

Every bone, muscle and tendon jarred at the impact. There was no pain. Instead, his brain experienced the blow as a wild distortion of vision. The world flashed bright as a supernova then snuffed out to black, and in that dead space, he decided to relax and take a breather. When his eyesight returned a split-second later, he saw a long, blurred tunnel. At the very end of the tunnel floated Mick's face, contorted into a leering rictus.

What was happening? Still on his feet, he could sense his head and body shifting and rolling and getting jostled about, painlessly, rhythmically.

"Stop it, stop hitting him!" sounded Cara's hysterical voice, cutting through the fog.

Alec understood that Mick must be beating the crap out of him. Raising his arms, he tried to fight back. Whether or not any of his punches landed, he couldn't tell. Then the ground tilted. Consciousness winked out for a moment.

"You really thought you could take me on?" Mick's voice said.

Alec opened his eyes. He found himself lying on the footpath. Mick was squatting nearby. But where was Cara? Alec shifted his weight onto an elbow and glanced around. He couldn't see her. Knots of onlookers stood a few metres away. *Goddamned ambulance-chasers.* A couple of teenagers were holding out their mobile phones as if filming. No doubt their footage would be uploaded to the internet within minutes to entertain countless thousands of ghouls. Alec grimaced. The pain was starting to dial up now; a collection of sharp, gnawing or tender spots across his face and torso.

"You hear me, greenhorn?" Mick was saying. "Hello, anybody home?"

"What? Yeah, I hear you."

"Next time you raise a hand to me, I'll kill you."

Mick reached into Alec's trouser pocket, fished out the car keys, and stepped over him.

"Cara!" Mick shouted, turning this way and that, scanning the street. "Where are you? Come on out. I won't hurt you, I promise. Hey, Cara, it's me. Cara?"

At last, looking disappointed, Mick appeared to give up on her. He began walking in the direction of the squad vehicle. Shocked onlookers peeled back, cowering, giving him the whole footpath. Then he was gone from sight. Exhausted, Alec dropped his forehead to the concrete.

"Oh God, let me help you."

Alec looked around. Cara was kneeling by his side, her face grey, eyes wide enough to show the whites all the way around.

"Where did you come from?" he said.

"I was hiding in the salon. Are you okay?"

"I'm not sure. How bad does it look?"

"Bad."

He nodded. "Can you give me a hand?"

"I'll try."

She stood and heaved on one of his arms. He had to laugh, even though it hurt. A petite woman like Cara didn't have a chance in hell of getting him to his feet. Now what? Perhaps moved by Cara's attempts rather than by Alec's injuries, onlookers at last woke from their collective dream and lifted him upright. His knees wobbled but held.

"If you need a witness, I saw the whole thing," said a slender man with red tips in his hair as he held a towel against Alec's face. The man turned to the onlookers, adding, "Bring him inside. Somebody, call triple-zero."

Cara and the others helped Alec take one step after another, and then sat him into a chair. He was in a hairdressing salon. The mirror gave him a shock. His head was a lumpy, bloodied mess.

The man with the tips seemed to own the place. He turned to a girl who seemed to be his assistant, and said, "Cold wet towels, now. Get a crack on."

The hairdresser and his assistant cleaned Alec's face of blood. Cara sat nearby, weeping a little. In time, the onlookers became bored, or distracted by more pressing matters, and drifted away. Uniformed police turned up. Alec showed them his identification, asked them to forget it; they agreed and left. Next, paramedics arrived. Alec refused to go to hospital. The paramedics taped his cuts, fitted him with a heart monitor and insisted on giving him oxygen through a mask. He put up with that for a few minutes. One of them tried to put a neck brace on him, but he resisted; ditto for the saline drip. When he again refused a ride to hospital, they packed away their equipment and left. By this stage, the hairdresser and his assistant were back servicing their salon customers. Alec and Cara were alone in a corner of the shop.

"Can you tell me what happened?" Alec said.

She nodded. Her nose was red from crying, her eyes ringed with smudged mascara. She took a breath, went to speak, and faltered. Alec grabbed her hand. She squeezed back. He could feel her shaking.

She managed a smile. "It's pretty ironic."

"What is?"

"I should've been at work but Gerard Vandenburg visited me this morning. He's a detective from the Rape Squad."

"Yeah, I know who he is."

"He told me that Mick wouldn't be charged." She took a moment to gather herself. "I felt...stifled. I had to get out, go for a walk. I drove here to window shop."

"What did Mick say?"

"At first, he said *hello*. Can you believe it? Like everything was fine between us. We started arguing and he grabbed me. That's when you showed up." She looked at Alec. "How can I ever thank you?"

"For what? Getting my head smacked in?"

"No, for saving me." Tears filled her eyes. "I thought he was going to drag me to a car."

The fear on her face made Alec contrite. For God's sake, Mick deserved a manners lesson, and Alec had failed to deliver. He set his teeth. Yes, it had been a while since his last fistfight, but there was no excuse for the basic mistakes he'd made. Why hadn't he anticipated a counter attack? Instead of using his left hand to keep hold of Mick, he should have used it to block Mick's punches. And instead of standing there like a stale bottle of piss, he should have employed a bit of footwork to pivot out of Mick's range. Shit. This is the result, he thought, of complacent training. When your regular boxing opponent is a punching bag that hangs from the ceiling, you're not up for a real fight with a human being, especially a hard-arse like Mick Thompson.

"Why don't I drive you to hospital?" Cara said. "Please."

"No thanks. I'd rather a lift to the Police Complex."

The walk back to Cara's parked sedan took about five minutes. Despite her offer of help, Alec limped along without her shoulder to lean on. Pedestrians gawked at him, flabbergasted at his ruined face, recoiling, shooting horrified glances at the woman by his side. Humiliation made Alec feel sick. Christ, was he a man or a mouse? At this stage, *a mouse*, he concluded miserably.

During the drive to the Melbourne City Police Complex, they were silent, each lost in private thoughts. Cara found a park right out front and turned off the engine. Alec didn't move.

"Are you feeling okay?" she said.

"Sure."

But he was wondering how to explain everything to Ward, to the crew, to the other tough men of the Armed Offence Squad. Perhaps Mick had already given a version of events. Perhaps everyone was waiting for Alec to turn up, in order to have a big laugh.

"Do you want me to drive you somewhere else?" she said.

He glanced around. And damn, she was so small, so slightly built, her raw-boned wrists no bigger than a child's, and Mick had brutalised her. Stop with the self-pity, Alec thought, ashamed. What Mick did to him was nothing in comparison.

"Thanks for the lift," he said, and opened the car door.

She got out too and walked around to join him on the footpath.

"You don't have to look after me anymore," he said. "I'm fine."

Her face was pinched. "I'm coming in to tell Gerard Vandenburg what just happened."

"But Mick could be in the building."

"I don't care."

He nodded. "Okay. Then I'll wait until a detective comes to escort you upstairs."

They went into the building together. The reception area was cavernous and high ceilinged, stuffed with potted plants, the giant reception desk located in the middle of the room. As usual, the place thrummed with activity. Uniformed and plain-clothed officers criss-crossed the floor; some passing through various doors in and out of media liaison, administration, or the South Melbourne police station; others coming and going from the elevator hall. About a dozen civilians were clustered at the visitor couches.

Cara stuck close to Alec as they approached the desk. The phones constantly rang, keeping the three desk sergeants on their feet.

"Hey, Grant," Alec said to the nearest desk sergeant. "How're you going?"

Grant looked around, reacted, and leaned over the counter for a better look. "Bugger me. Alec Castellano, is it?"

"Yeah."

"Holy smokes, I almost didn't recognise you." He turned to the other desk sergeants and said, "Look what's happened to Castellano from Armed Offence."

Alec flushed as the trio scrutinised him and asked questions, none of which he bothered to answer. He cut in and said, "Can you buzz Vandenburg for me? Cara Haynes is waiting to see him and it's urgent."

Grant nodded. Alec ushered Cara away from the crowds and towards an empty expanse of wall. Her jaw was clenched. She may be little, he thought in admiration, but she's got a backbone of iron. Time passed. God, his face hurt like fuck. He leaned against the wall with his eyes closed.

"Are you okay?" she said.

He glanced down at her. "Yeah. And you?"

She smiled weakly.

"Here," he said, taking a business card from his jacket pocket. "Call if you ever need me."

The blood drained from her cheeks. Moving in slow motion, she accepted the card.

"What's the matter?" he said.

When she looked up, her eyes were haunted, almost glassy. "Déjà vu."

"Huh?"

"It's déjà vu, but for real." She stared at the business card as if it were a thing of horror.

"I don't follow."

"If I need you, night or day, you'll ride up on a white horse."

He grabbed her elbow. "What the hell are you talking about?"

She flinched, her lips peeling back into a grimace of fear. Realisation struck him.

"Now wait a second," he said, letting go of her, showing his palms. "Relax. History isn't repeating itself, okay? I'm not Mick. I'm not anything like him."

Her gaze seemed to come back into focus. Dazed, she opened her mouth as if to speak, but John Patel from the Rape Squad appeared.

"What happened to you?" he said to Alec.

"Just get her upstairs."

"Whatever, mate." Patel turned to Cara. "Please come this way."

She touched Alec on the arm. "I'm sorry," she said.

"Don't be."

All three of them got the elevator. The ride seemed to take a long time. Cara kept her head bowed. Alec wished for a way to comfort her without scaring her, but couldn't think of what to do. The elevator pinged at the ninth floor. Cara quailed against him as the lift doors opened. Her anxiety was so palpable that he half-expected to see Mick in the hallway too, and clenched his fists. The hallway was empty. They exited the lift. She headed left with Patel.

"Cara," he said.

She turned.

"Call me any time," he continued.

She nodded, ashen. "Night or day. Yes, I know."

Patel took her through the double doors of the Rape Squad. Alec paused, overcome by a mess of feelings he couldn't work out. Forget it, he thought. A jitter of adrenaline rebounded inside his chest as he walked towards the Armed Offence Squad.

Mick would be there, waiting for him.

And then what?

Patel ushered Cara into a room.

"Wait here, please," he said. "Gerry won't be long."

He left and closed the door. Looking about, she recognised the room with its houseplant and vinyl sofas. Patel and O'Brien had questioned her right here the night of the rape.

Déjà vu. *Again.*

For whatever reason, her life was folding back on itself, over and over, in a terrifying loop. With dread, she took out Alec's business card. Its design was identical to Mick's: plain white with navy lettering, blank on the other side. She crammed the card back into her pocket.

No, get a hold of yourself, she reasoned. The explanation was simple. To get the biggest discount from the printer, everybody's business cards would have been printed in bulk at the same time with the same design. It wasn't déjà vu. Okay? Don't look for patterns where they don't exist. Breathe. Stop thinking about the blood on Alec's face. About Mick the demon, baring his teeth. The pizzeria owner's cheek splitting beneath the shotgun butt. Stop thinking about it all, about everything.

The door opened, making her jump.

"My apologies," Vandenburg said, hesitating, closing the door. "I didn't mean to startle you."

"He grabbed me. Threatened me."

"Mick Thompson?" Vandenburg hurried into a seat. "Give me the details."

"After you left my office, I drove to Clarendon Street. Mick confronted me. He said, 'What are you trying to do, destroy my career? Breaking up with me wasn't enough?' He said I could never hide from him, that he only has to press a few buttons and, *bang*, there I'll be on his computer screen. You have to arrest him."

"On what charge?"

"What charge?" Her breath stopped for a moment. "I don't know what charge. You're the police officer, not me. How about assault?"

"Did he punch, slap, kick or bite you? Shake you?"

"What? No. But he grabbed me on the arm."

"Are you bruised?"

She gaped at the white, unblemished skin of her wrist, and couldn't speak.

"Did he say that he would beat you or harm you in any way?"

"No," she said, putting a hand to her forehead. "I can see where this is going."

"It comes down to a question of evidence." Vandenburg made a placating gesture. "But you can always apply for a personal safety intervention order."

"A what?"

"It's a court order to protect you against harm from someone who's not a family member. It covers stalking.

Things like keeping you under surveillance or threatening to trace your movements count as stalking."

Cara gave a hollow laugh. "You want me to stop Mick with a piece of paper?"

"It's proof of wrongdoing. Go to your nearest Magistrate's Court and ask to see the court registrar. They'll get you to fill out an application form."

She gathered her handbag and stood up.

"Take any evidence you've got," he said, "witnesses, e-mails, medical reports, that kind of thing. After you've made your application, if the magistrate agrees that you have a case, the police will notify Mick Thompson with the terms of the order."

She opened the door.

"Wait. If he breaches the terms, he can be charged with a criminal offence." Vandenburg got to his feet. "If he's found guilty, he faces imprisonment or a fine."

"Good to know. Thanks a lot." She left the interview room, spotted Patel sitting at his desk on the other side of the squad room, and called out, "Excuse me, I'm finished here. Please escort me downstairs."

Steeling himself, Alec walked through the double doors of the Armed Offence Squad. If Mick wanted to pick up from where they left off, Alec would be ready. This time, Alec would maintain his guard, move his feet, bend his knees to keep a low centre of gravity, stay on his toes. He took a steadying breath as his crew's desks came into view.

Mick wasn't there.

A jag of relief passed through his body. Wimp, he berated himself.

But the relief didn't last long. Now he would have to explain the beating to his crew. That humiliating thought kickstarted another flood of adrenaline. He neared the desks.

Ward, spotting him first, said, "Oh, Jesus."

Alec stood by the desks and waited for the jokes and jeers to start. Bull and Stevo glanced around. Their faces fell open in shock.

His cheeks burning hot with shame, Alec said, "Where's Mick?"

"Dunno." Ward got to his feet. "He's supposed to be with you. What happened?"

"Mick is what happened."

"*Mick* did this to you?"

"Yeah."

Ward grimaced as if struck by a headache, then turned away to pace around the desks.

Bull roamed his gaze over Alec's face, and said, "You still got all your teeth?"

"Yeah."

"Can you breathe through your nose?"

Alec shrugged. "There's a lot of dried blood."

"The bridge isn't crooked, no black eyes. Does it hurt much?"

"It hurts enough, I guess."

"You haven't got a broken nose." Bull lit a cigarette. "He let you off easy."

"Easy?" Alec said, temper flaring. "You call this easy?"

"You clash with Mick all the time, you little fuck." Bull blew smoke from the side of his mouth. "You never follow his plays. How did you think this would end? Rock paper scissors?"

"Bullshit. I've covered his arse at every turn. What about the raid at Brownie's place? Didn't I keep my mouth shut about what he did?"

"Hey, don't you say another fucking word."

"Enough!" Ward yelled. "Bull, just back off. Alec, come with me."

Alec followed Ward into an empty office and shut the door. They sat down on opposite sides of the desk.

Ward said, "Why did Mick belt your head in?"

"Sure you want to hear it?"

"Don't shit me."

"All right. We were driving through Clarendon Street. Mick told me to pull over. It turns out he'd seen Cara Haynes."

Ward paled. "You're definite it was her?"

"Positive. He confronted her. I went to stop him."

"And did you?"

"I distracted him, but that's about it. While he was busy punching the crap out of me, she managed to get away and hide inside a shop. Mick took my car keys and pissed off."

"How many witnesses? Give me a rough guess."

"I don't know. Maybe dozens. A few people filmed us on their phones. It's probably all over the internet by now."

"Have you got any idea how bad this is? Do you?" Ward stared off at a corner of the room. After a time, he added, "Okay, as a mate, I'm asking you a favour, and it's a big one. Don't make a complaint against Mick."

"What?"

"The Rape Squad is on our case. Professional Standards Division has got us under the microscope. Other things are threatening to boil over, things you don't know about yet. We can't afford any more shit. Don't you see that?"

"No, I don't. You want Mick to get away with acting like a fucking animal? Again?"

"Our crew is copping too much flak as it is."

"Yeah, because of Mick." Alec stood up. "What the hell has he got over you?"

"Watch it. You watch your mouth." Ward got up too. "As your superior officer, I'm ordering you now to keep quiet about the punch-up, end of story."

"You're ordering me?"

"That's right."

"And if I report Mick anyway?"

"Then you're out on your arse."

Alec flung open the door and stalked from the office. Okay, fine, he knew that life wasn't fair, knew that bad things happened to good people every second of every day, but for God's sake, this was unbelievable. How the fuck did Mick keep getting a free pass?

He shoved through the door of the locker room, opened his locker, and shucked his jacket. As he undid his shirt, he saw the bloodstains on it. There was no way those stains would ever come out. Shit. That was a hundred-dollar shirt destined for the bin. He didn't want to look at his jacket or tie. Maybe the drycleaners could do something with them.

He took his spare shirt off the hanger and held it to his nose. After weeks in the locker, the shirt smelt musty, and he flapped it, hard, as if moving it through the air might refresh the fabric. His face and torso hurt. Damn, he should go home. Bowing his head, he contemplated the shirt crumpled in his fists and wondered what he should do next.

"You might have cracked ribs."

Alec looked around. Stevo was standing at the far end of the lockers.

Turning away, Alec began opening the buttons on the spare shirt. "Don't worry about it."

"I'm serious," Stevo said, stepping closer. "Those kinds of bruises are a bad sign."

"Oh, yeah? Well, according to the sarge, the bruises don't exist."

"He wants a cover-up?"

"Doesn't everybody?" Alec shoved his arms into the shirt sleeves. "Mick the golden boy does what he wants. Isn't that the way it goes around here?"

Stevo slumped onto a bench. Alec began buttoning up the shirt.

At last, Stevo said, "Anyway, you should see a doctor. That's what I reckon."

"Whatever."

"Kidney punches are Mick's specialty."

"Yeah, tell me about it."

"I'm not bullshitting. He's probably broken your floaters."

Grabbing Stevo by the collar, Alec said, "You still think we're all on the same crew? You still think we've got to lie for each other, no matter what?"

"Get off me."

Alec let him go and reached for his own jacket. He pulled it on, slammed his locker shut, and headed towards the exit door.

"Tell me something," Stevo said.

Alec spun around. "For Christ's sake, what is it? What?"

"That rape. Do you think he did it?"

"Yeah," Alec said. "There's not a doubt in my mind. He did it, and he'll get away with it."

Alec left the room. At the desks, Ward and Bull were sitting around a computer monitor. They both looked up at Alec's approach.

With a laugh, Bull said, "Hey Mario, check out your performance. It's a pisser."

Oh no. A sinking feeling in his guts, Alec walked over. The monitor showed a video labelled 'Punch-up on Clarendon Street' paused in a blurred flurry. Bull used the mouse to restart the video on the taskbar. With a jolt, Alec watched himself get smashed by Mick's big swing. Revolted, he turned away from the desk, bumping into Stevo who had come up soundlessly behind him.

"You want to see how Mick flattened me?" Alec said. "There it is. Enjoy."

He took a seat, opened one of the manila folders on his desk and tried to concentrate. Bull's incessant chuckling needled at him.

Then Stevo exclaimed, "Wait, shit, go back. Isn't that Cara Haynes? From the Benny's job?"

"Hey, yeah, it is too." Bull stubbed out his cigarette, huffed smoke from the side of his mouth. "I guess Mick was trying to straighten her out."

Stevo said, "Aw fuck, she looks shit-scared."

"Bull, can you delete the video?" Ward said.

"From the internet? Ha, what century are you from? Even if the file was mine, which it isn't, once a video's uploaded, mate, it's there for fucking *ever*."

EIGHTEEN

Mick felt good, floating on the after-effects of vodka and the release of a cheap woman. The elevator opened at the ninth floor. He stumbled out. As he neared their desks, Bull, Stevo and Alec stopped what they were doing to stare at him. Their sombre attention struck him as funny. Grinning, swaying, he stood by the desks and put his hands on his hips. The greenhorn's head was a bruised, cut-up mess. For a second, Mick felt confused. Then he remembered the fight. He'd slugged Alec pretty hard, actually. Harder than necessary. There would be repercussions. Ah well, that couldn't be helped.

Alec got to his feet.

"Why are you shaping up?" Mick said. "You want more?"

"I don't want to get jumped."

"Jumped? That's your trick, not mine. If I start a fight, I do it face to face."

Stevo said, "We don't need any more fighting, that's it."

"Suits me." Mick dropped into his chair. "Where's the sarge?"

"Talking with the inspector," Stevo said. "In fact, they've been talking for a couple of hours now, non-stop."

"Oh, yeah? It's probably about me and the greenhorn."

"You shouldn't have hit him," Stevo said.

Mick laughed. "Gee, Dad, I'll never do it again."

"We're supposed to be a team."

"He didn't give me a choice."

"And you know why?" Bull winked. "Here's my theory: he wants to screw her."

"What?" Mick said.

"Cara Haynes. Alec wants to screw her."

"Get your mind out of the gutter for once," Alec muttered, sitting down, returning his attention to the computer monitor.

Bull chuckled. "Oh, come on, fighting over a sheila? You can't deny it. And you've got those big brown eyes, haven't you? That soulful wog-boy look. Chicks wet their pants for that shit. Right, Mario?"

Alec said, "Piss off."

Mick glared at him. Women had indeed flirted with Alec from time to time. Mick had seen it himself. Would Cara go for a bloke like Alec? Mick had never considered the possibility before. He thought about Cara in bed; how she had responded to his hands, mouth, cock. The memories stirred his blood. He could almost hear her desperate little *ah-ah-ah* noises that always told him when he had brought her to the brink, that it was time to tip her over. He ground his teeth. And now Alec wanted to do all of those things to her? Goddamned *Alec?*

He slammed his palm onto the desk. "You don't touch her."

Alec looked up from the computer monitor. "Huh?"

"You don't go anywhere near Cara."

"I've hardly spoken to her. What the hell is wrong with you?"

"I'll break your fucking face. I'll break you in half."

"Calm down," Stevo said. "Bull was joking."

"That's right, mate. Jeez, it was a lend, that's all. I'm trying to lighten the mood."

Mick stood up. Alec, the dumb shit, got up with his fists clenched even though his face was already mincemeat. Stevo and Bull got to their feet too, flanking Mick.

"You crazy bastard, she's not even your woman," Alec said.

"Not my woman? I've fucked her every which way. That makes her mine."

"Thompson," sounded Ward's voice from across the squad room.

Mick turned around. Ward, standing by the open door of Detective Inspector Vaughan's office, crooked his finger in a *come here* gesture. What now? Mick sighed, dropped his shoulders, and started walking.

"Wish me luck," he said.

"Ah, you won't even need it," Bull said. "They're all piss and wind."

Mick went into the office.

"Give me the car keys," Ward said. "The ones you took from Alec."

Mick complied. Ward pocketed the keys, shut the door, and stood against the wall. Vaughan, sitting behind the desk, was stony-faced, his steel-wool eyebrows hunkered into a frown. No one spoke. Mick shifted his weight from foot to foot. He began to feel uneasy.

"Are you drunk?" Vaughan said.

Mick paused. "No sir."

"Have you been drinking?"

"No."

Vaughan looked at his watch. "It's nearly the end of the shift. Where have you been the entire afternoon?"

"Checking out a line of enquiry."

"Into what case?"

"The pizza bandits."

Vaughan said to Ward, "Is that true?"

"I don't know. I haven't been in contact with Thompson. He had his phone switched off and wouldn't respond to the radio."

It wasn't like Ward to leave him hanging like that. Mick's heart rate nudged higher.

"Thompson, why were you incommunicado?" Vaughan said.

"I was busy."

"Checking out this line of enquiry?"

"That's right."

Vaughan smiled coldly. "You must think I'm a complete fucking moron. Frank, get a breathalyser. I want to check his blood alcohol."

Ward moved towards the door.

Panicked, Mick said, "Sarge, no."

They both looked at him expectantly. Mick exhaled in a rush. What would be the best thing to say right now? Shit, the vodka had dulled his mind, he couldn't think. He must have had at least eight shots, maybe more. Then there were the beer chasers, that glass of red...

"Well?" Vaughan said. "Are we breathalysing you or not?"

"There's no need, sir. Your hunch was correct. I stopped at a pub on the way back here, and had a couple of drinks. I was feeling bad about what happened between me and Alec. I'm sure you've heard about our disagreement."

"More than that, I've seen the footage."

Mick hesitated. "Footage? I don't understand."

"Your assault on Castellano was filmed by a civilian and uploaded to the internet."

"Assault? Now, hang on, I wouldn't call it that—"

"Wouldn't you?"

Mick swallowed. "More like self-defence. Alec hit me first." He pointed at the scab on his split lip. "See?"

"Then you pulverised him in a vicious, sustained attack." Vaughan pursed his mouth. "We've got a lot to get through, Detective Senior Constable. Take a seat. You too, Frank."

They both sat down in the visitor chairs and waited. Vaughan glanced through various papers on his desk, sighing. Mick stared at Ward, who steadfastly ignored him.

Vaughan said, "I hardly know where to start. Frank, do you have a suggestion?"

"We could begin with Rodney Brown."

"Good idea." Vaughan selected a particular sheet of paper and studied it for a while. Then he said, "Thompson, one week ago, you and your crew did a raid on the premises of a certain Rodney Brown, a.k.a. Brownie, on suspicion that he may have been involved in the pizza house robberies."

"Yes, sir."

"You recall the night in question?"

"I do."

"And do you recall assaulting Rodney Brown?"

Mick laughed a little, surprised. "Listen, Brownie had hold of my shotgun. For my personal safety and for the safety of my crew, I had to disarm him and neutralise any further threat. If you read the report, you'll see that Alec and Bull corroborated my version of events."

"You broke the man's nose, two molars and his left eye socket."

"What can I say? He shouldn't have grabbed my weapon."

"This morning, Rodney Brown pressed assault charges against you."

"Yeah?" Mick shrugged. "He's an ex-con. The charges won't stick."

"He also maintains that while in custody, he was denied food, water, toilet breaks, and access to his lawyer, and that no superior officer performed any welfare checks."

"That's not true," Mick said. "We stuck to procedure. Right, Sarge?"

Ward cleared his throat. "I've already informed the Detective Inspector of our lapses regarding how Rodney Brown was questioned on that day."

Despite himself, Mick winced at the misstep.

Vaughan narrowed his eyes. "You're a natural born liar, aren't you, Thompson?"

"No, sir. I was thinking about another interrogation, and got them confused."

"Mick, for the love of Christ," Ward said. "We're way past that shit."

"Mr Brown's lawyer has agreed to drop all charges against the Armed Offence Squad in exchange for you on a silver platter." Smiling, Vaughan placed the sheet of paper onto the desk. "It sounds like a good deal to me."

Wait a minute, was Mick hearing this right? The code was supposed to be inviolate. Every Armed Offence Squad detective was safe behind the united shield of brotherhood, no matter what.

"You're going to give me up?" Mick said, astounded.

"Of course I am," Vaughan said. "You don't leave me any choice. Thompson, you are single-handedly dragging the reputation of my squad through the mud. If you keep this up, the entire squad could be disbanded. Have you forgotten what happened to Major Crime? Frank, tell him about the rest of it."

Dazed, Mick looked around at Ward. "There's more?"

"Plenty more," Ward said. "The rats of the Professional Standards Division want blood."

"But I thought our plan was to stall them."

"On the sexual misconduct charge, yeah, we could've stalled them," Ward said. "We could have run them in circles for months until they lost interest. But now you've gone and given them a fucking bonanza."

"You mean Brownie?" Mick said. "I'm telling you, nobody's going to—"

Ward, counting off on his fingers, said, "Number one: the rape investigation. All right, you haven't been charged, but that kind of shit always sticks. Number two: bashing Alec. Come on, don't piss in my pocket, you bashed him and I know you bashed him. I've seen the footage. Number three: menacing Cara Haynes. Yeah, that's on the footage too. You've got her by the arm and she's terrified."

"I don't know, she must have got the wrong idea about what I—"

"If she got the wrong idea, then I did too. No bullshit, you looked fit to be fucking tied. Now, how long do you think it'll be before Gerry Vandenburg hears about the footage and decides to have a squiz at it? And after watching it, how many seconds do you think will pass before he decides to reopen the rape case?"

"But I was only trying to—"

"And number four: Brownie's assault charges."

"I told you, he grabbed my shotgun."

"So what? This is about excessive force. Don't you get it? One fracture, yeah, everybody could understand that, but five? Five busted bones in his fucking skull? And that's not including his teeth. Jesus, Mick. You see? What did I tell you?" Ward sat back in his chair and shook his head. "A fucking bonanza."

Vaughan made a disdainful tutting sound. "You're a disgrace, Thompson."

Shaking, Mick put a hand over his eyes.

"And don't expect me to back you anymore," Ward continued. "I'm in enough trouble as it is. Guess what? I've got an internal review coming up. Yeah, that's right. I have to explain to the Professional Standards Division how come I've let you run feral. You know what this means? I could get demoted because of you. Demoted."

"I'm sorry," Mick said. "Will they want to interview me too?"

"Interview you? Don't misunderstand what's going on here. You're the one who's the furthest up shit creek, not me. They want your head on a fucking plate. And who can blame them? Tomorrow at precisely twelve noon, you're going before the board for an internal review of your own. If the evidence looks solid, they'll suspend you."

"And the evidence looks solid," Vaughan said. "No question."

"What?" Mick looked from one to the other. Their faces were hard and closed. The air became too thin to breathe. "Suspend me?" he went on. "They can't do that."

Vaughan sniffed. "They can do whatever they damn well please."

"But suspend me? What am I going to do if they suspend me?"

"I don't know," Ward said, throwing up his hands. "Go see a career counsellor."

Mick's heart boomed like a kettledrum. He needed a drink. He wanted out of there. "Is there anything else?" he said, trembling, standing up.

Vaughan's laugh was mirthless. "Good God, I hope not. Fine, get out of my office. And don't hit anybody, is that understood? Try to restrain yourself for once."

Suffocating, Mick left and shut the door behind him, the pulse blatting in his ears. Where to? Across the squad room, he could see Bull, Stevo and Alec at their desks. No, he couldn't re-join them. Not yet, not now. He patted his pockets before remembering that Ward had already taken the car keys. Fuck. The tea room, then? No, Rape Squad detectives might be in there. He couldn't face them either. The gym?

Okay, he decided, stalking towards the elevator hall: the gym.

In the elevator, alone, he travelled down, down, down; his eyes closed and wet, for Christ's sake, his chest heaving. At the gymnasium, he pushed through the swing doors and headed inside. Thankfully, the place was empty. He retreated to the rear of the change room. Sitting down on a wooden bench, he clasped his hands, and dropped his head. A sob lodged in his throat like a chicken bone.

Suspended?

The urge to break something ran over him. Instead, he squeezed his hands together, hard, cracking the knuckles and joints. He took a breath and realised that he was panting as if he'd run a mile. Get a grip, he demanded. Think it through.

After a while, he began to see that Vaughan and Ward must have been exaggerating. There wasn't going to be any suspension. That kind of drastic action wouldn't make sense. The rats from the Professional Standards Division would take one look at Mick's file and realise that he was indispensable in the Armed Offence Squad.

For a start, he had a reputation that made professional crims shit themselves whenever he walked into a room.

Mick smiled. Not two months ago, while out for dinner at a pub, he'd gone to the bar and found himself next to a 'known associate' he'd once questioned. The man had turned white and fled as if the devil had been after him. A reputation like Mick's was gold. It prompted confessions out of fear, turned crims into informants, even occasionally made scumbags think twice before pulling a job. In fact, more than a few crims had reportedly left Melbourne purely because of Mick. How could the Professional Standards Division ignore the power and prestige his name brought to the Armed Offence Squad? They couldn't. Simple.

Not only that, he put in more hours than anybody else, most of the overtime unpaid. And he always volunteered for the roles no one wanted—the dangerous arrests, the boring sit-offs, the visits to inform family members that a loved one had come to serious harm at the hands of robbers—he was the one always stepping forward when everyone else busied themselves looking the other way. That was dedication.

Mick swiped at his eyes with the heels of both hands. So the witch hunt was at noon tomorrow? Okay, he'd be ready. Stashed away at home were letters and thank-you cards from robbery victims expressing their gratitude for his help, single-mindedness, understanding, compassion. He would bring a few of those notes, maybe the whole shoebox, and dump them in front of the rats. Here, he'd say, for your fucking edification. And after reading for thirty seconds, the rats would appreciate the gravity of their mistake. They would apologise and let him go.

It couldn't turn out any other way. It just couldn't.

By now, Mick's heart rate had slowed. Sitting back, leaning against the wall, he felt almost calm. Once the farce of tomorrow's internal review was over, he would confront his enemies and sort them out, one by one. Exactly how he would sort them out, he didn't know yet, but trusted people had betrayed him, and it hurt. Every double-cross was a physical pain, a knife to the guts.

"Mummy, what's wrong with that man's face?"

Simultaneously, Alec and Liz Lansky looked around. It was dusk. They were standing outside on Liz's porch at her suburban home. Peeking through the open front door was one of Liz's daughters, the older one that Alec figured must be about six by now. He offered what he hoped looked like a friendly smile before turning his back. She didn't need to see his injuries. That's why he'd insisted that Liz talk to him outside.

"Chloe, what do think you're doing, spying on me?" Liz said. "Didn't I tell you I was working? Go back inside. What's Daddy doing?"

"Trying to make Annabelle eat her peas."

"Then you go help him."

"How?" the girl said, whining. "If she doesn't like 'em, I can't make her."

"Tell her you'll share Polly."

"Polly? But she's *my* doll."

"I know, but you're a big girl, aren't you? Tell your sister if she eats two more spoonsful of peas, you'll let her brush Polly's hair. Okay? Just until bath time. You know that Mummy can't get anything done without your help around here. Please?"

"Aw, okay."

"Good girl. Please shut the door."

"I'm shutting it. Bye, Mister Man."

The latch clicked as the door closed. Alec turned back around. Liz was smiling at him with one side of her mouth, as if embarrassed.

"Sorry about that," she said, with a shrug. "Kids."

"I'm the one who's sorry. I shouldn't have come."

"Are you joking? Who else could you talk to about this stuff? I'm like your mother." She stepped closer, her face drawn and strained in the half-dark. "That's why you've got to leave this one alone. Okay? For me."

"What about Mick? Somebody's got to stop him."

"And why does that somebody have to be you? Why not his sergeant or inspector? Why not the Rape Squad? The Professional Standards Division? Lots of people have the authority to put the brakes on him without suffering any repercussions."

"I told you, nobody's doing anything."

"Not yet. Things are probably still in motion. Please, if your sergeant has ordered you not to report the assault, then don't bloody report it, okay? And if you do, you'll only aggravate Mick." She grabbed Alec's arm. "And look what he's done to you already."

Alec pulled away. "He caught me by surprise."

"Bullshit."

"So, he's a better fighter than me. Is that what you want to hear?"

"I don't want you getting in any more trouble."

"Hey, I'm not an idiot. I don't want to lose my job. But at the same time, why did I become a copper if I'm not going to stand up and do the right thing? Fuck, I just don't know."

Alec's mobile rang. With an apologetic glance at Liz, he took it from his pocket. Surprisingly, the caller was Cara Haynes. He never thought he'd hear from her again after her weird reaction to his business card, yet here she was on the other end of his phone with her soft, clear voice. He would recognise that voice anywhere.

"Cara, are you okay?"

"No, not really," she said. "Look, I have a favour to ask."

"Sure, what is it?"

"I'd rather ask you in person. Can you meet with me? There's this bar in South Yarra."

Alec paused. "Give me the address."

She did. He knew the place. He promised to meet her there in half an hour, and hung up.

Liz skewed an eye at him. "If that was Cara Haynes, you'd better be careful. Mick is bound to be the jealous type."

"Yeah, he already thinks I'm sniffing around."

"Play it safe with her."

"Oh, come on." Alec tried to laugh. "I'm a professional."

The drive took twenty minutes. The meeting place Cara had nominated, located in Chapel Street, was more of a licensed café than a bar, featuring red leather booths, polished wood, jazz played at a gentle volume, and an older crowd. Alec opened the door. He spotted Cara straight away but she didn't see him. She was sitting in a corner booth, staring into an empty wineglass, still wearing her work clothes, the skirt hitched up across her thighs, her legs crossed at the knee, high heels.

Approaching her table, he said, "Would you like another drink?"

She glanced up and smiled. "Yes, thanks. The house Riesling."

He nodded and went to the bar. As he waited for the bartender to fill the order, Alec wondered how Mick would react if he were to walk past the window and see Alec here with Cara, one on one. It would be a bad reaction, no doubt. The thought made Alec feel smug.

Back at the table with the wine and beer, he sat down opposite Cara. He sipped his drink, self-conscious, as she studied his face.

"Does it hurt much?" she said at last.

"A little, yeah."

"Did you see a doctor?"

He shook his head.

"Why not? Something could be broken."

It shamed him, this talk of the beating, as if Mick were standing nearby and laughing. Alec said, "Forget about that. How did you go with Gerry Vandenburg?"

"I told him how Mick had confronted me, threatened me. It didn't matter. Gerard had me out of his office so fast I didn't even have chance to tell him what Mick had done to you."

"Your rape case is still closed?"

She nodded. "Gerard told me to apply for an intervention order."

"That's the best he could do? What a joke."

"I know. I felt the same way at first, but then I got back to the office and Googled it. An intervention order would cover harassment, stalking, assault, sexual assault. If Mick came near me again, I could have him arrested."

"I guess it's worth a try."

"Anything's better than nothing. I can't keep living this way."

She picked up her glass with trembling fingers and took a long drink, looking away from him across the room as she fought to maintain composure. He wanted to reassure her, to lay his hand on hers.

Instead, he said, "How are you holding up?"

"Not that great." She gave a wan smile. "I can't eat, can't sleep. I'm too scared to be at home overnight in case he knocks on the door."

"Do you live alone?"

"Yes."

"Can't you stay with relatives? Just for a while until this situation blows over?"

"That's not possible."

"How come? Are they interstate?"

"To be honest, I want to get out of Melbourne. Coming here was a big mistake."

Tapping his fingers restlessly on the tabletop, he said, "Look, do you mind if I ask you a personal question?"

"If it's too personal, I won't answer it."

"Okay, that's fair."

Then he hesitated, embarrassed. She sat back in the booth and stared at him fixedly, as if holding her breath. He almost didn't want to ask anymore.

Finally, he said, "Why did you get involved with Mick?"

She dropped her eyes. Then she took hold of her drink by the stem and turned it around and around on the tabletop, watching the Riesling as it tilted and lapped inside the glass. Time passed. Alec didn't think she was going to answer.

Eventually, she said, "After the armed robbery, I was frightened. He made me feel safe." She looked up. "Don't worry, I'm aware of the irony. But he was different in the beginning. Considerate, protective. Kind."

Shit, Mick Thompson? Really? Alec didn't argue with her. "What happened?" he said.

"I don't know. He did a raid on a house, and he wasn't the same after that."

The raid on Brownie's place, Alec thought. Now why would that be significant to Mick? Musing, Alec took a sip of beer. In the morning when he got back to the squad room, he would investigate the details and background of that particular raid. He didn't know what to look for, but maybe he'd find something anyway. Cara broke into his reverie.

"I asked you here because I'm hoping you can do me a favour," she said.

"Name it."

"It's about this intervention order. I need help to convince a magistrate. Since Mick's a police officer, the court is more likely to believe him than me. Would you be my witness? The court will listen to you."

Stumped, Alec bit at a thumbnail.

She continued, "You don't have to come with me, if that's what you're worried about. A written statement would be enough. A couple of paragraphs, not much. Would you do it?" She leaned across the table, her face suddenly earnest, desperate. "Please. Help me if you can, for God's sake."

"Okay, now here's the thing..." And he didn't know what to say.

She withdrew. "I understand."

"No, look... Cara, I want to help."

"Then what's stopping you?"

"My sergeant. He's ordered that I don't report Mick for assaulting me. The Armed Offence Squad is in hot water, and we're supposed to be closing ranks. Sarge isn't going to like it if I testify against Mick on your behalf. It could mean my job."

"I see." Cara stood, gathered her handbag and coat. "I'm sorry for wasting your time."

"Hang on a minute."

"No, it's fine. Thanks for meeting with me. I really do appreciate it."

Alec got up and blocked her path. She drew back, studying him with her sombre eyes, her grey-blue irises the colour of storm clouds heavy with rain.

"Don't go," he said at last.

"Why not?"

"I've been thinking I might report Mick anyway."

She regarded Alec as if weighing him up. He waited. She sat down again. He did too.

"What about your job?" she said.

"If I have to cover for arseholes like Mick Thompson, I don't want it."

Momentarily, Alec felt irritated, aggrieved. Life wasn't fair, and here was another perfect example: Mick had been this woman's lover. Mick knew everything about her naked body and how it looked, felt, tasted; knew whether she preferred it lying on her back or up on all fours. What words had she whispered to him in bed? What had she begged him to do to her when the last of her self-control was gone?

Mick didn't deserve a woman like Cara. That bastard didn't deserve a goddamned thing.

"Okay, I'll be your witness," Alec said, in a rush.

"Are you sure?" Cara said. "I don't want you to get fired."

"Don't worry." He smiled despite the pain in his face. "I know what I'm doing."

The motel's cabins were arranged in a horseshoe around a gravelled parking area. Cara pulled the sedan into the space outside her cabin and cut the engine. The night was moonless. The glow of the motel's floodlights showed two other vehicles, neither of them likely to belong to Mick: a station wagon; and a ute with a tradesman's lockbox in the open tray. Don't get paranoid, she thought, exiting her car. Mick had no way of knowing she was here. Even so, her heart trip-hammered until she was inside the cabin with the door locked.

She had booked this place earlier that day, straight after leaving work. The room had a double bed, wardrobe, two armchairs arranged around a table, a cabinet with a television on top. Despite the place being clean and well-maintained, the anonymous blandness struck her as depressing. She missed her house, her belongings.

But until this situation with Mick ended, she had resolved to stay at a different motel every twenty-four hours. Instead of making advance bookings via internet or phone, she would drive and pick a place at random. Payment would be cash only, no credit cards. On Clarendon Street this morning, while holding her wrist in an unbreakable grip, Mick had said that he could use the police computer systems to find her anywhere in the country. Just let him try to locate her now.

Enough, she told herself. Don't think about it anymore.

Too late.

She tried and failed to block the memory of Mick's assault on Alec. It came back in a torrent: the strength of Mick's body; the punches he had unleashed without mercy; and most harrowing of all, his face, angry at first, more terrifying still when he'd started to grin. She shut her eyes against a swell of panic.

Right here, right now.

She grabbed a water glass from the en suite, and opened the chardonnay she had bought at a drive-through bottle shop after her meeting with Alec. She poured a tall drink, sat on the bed, and took off her shoes.

Thank God the meeting had gone well. With Alec on her side—one of the members of Mick's crew, no less—a magistrate was sure to authorise an intervention order.

Hopefully, Alec would provide his statement tomorrow: Friday. Or perhaps Monday at the latest. Then again, if he was busy, he may not get back to her for weeks. Or ever. He'd been worried about job security; maybe he'd already changed his mind.

No, she thought, Alec promised he would help. She had to believe him.

Tomorrow morning, she would ring and ask Gerard Vandenburg, Irene O'Brien and John Patel for their statements. How long would they take to get around to her request, she wondered, assuming they agreed? It would probably depend on their workload. She took a gulp of chardonnay. What if they were swamped with cases more 'legitimate' than hers?

More importantly, could input from the Rape Squad hinder her application? She didn't know. Vandenburg had dropped the case against Mick for lack of evidence. How might that influence a magistrate? The magistrate would be making deliberations based on the exact same evidence, or lack thereof.

Cara's hands were shaking again. She took another drink.

Stop trying to predict the future, she demanded. Stop trying to mind-read. One step at a time.

At least getting a copy of her medical report should be a straightforward task. But since she hadn't incurred any obvious injuries, the report may not be much value either. It may even weaken her application. That possibility had to be considered too.

Cara leapt up to pace the room.

The most stupid thing about this whole, convoluted nightmare? That it had started with pizza. The very idea struck her as ludicrous. She even managed to croak out a laugh. All of this...*shit*...because of a small pizza supreme, no olives, added prawns.

The robbery came back. She held her breath against it, too late again.

Here was the jangle of the bell over the door, the grimace of terror on the owner's face, the pistol barrel dug into her spine, the cheekbone splitting under the shotgun butt. *Get down on the fucking ground. I swear on my daughter's head, I have no safe. Don't worry about remembering our names. If you forget, I'm happy to remind you.*

Weakly, Cara dragged out one of the motel's armchairs and slumped into it.

If only Alec had taken the lead that night, and not Mick. If only Alec had interviewed her at the Armed Offence Squad, driven her home, checked through the rooms of her house.

Then a terrible thought came to her, one that brought on a wave of self-loathing: would she have slept with Alec instead? Was she really that lonely and damaged?

NINETEEN

Start of the shift, early Friday morning, and typically, Mick was nowhere to be found. Ward was behind closed doors in conference with Vaughan. Bull, still in the tea room, was probably raiding the biscuit tin again. Alec read through the information on Rodney Brown one more time, and glanced at Stevo.

"You busy?" Alec said.

"No more than usual."

"I've been checking out Brownie's file. He looked good for a supermarket robbery about six months ago, didn't he?"

"Yeah, that's right." Stevo turned from the computer monitor. "But we couldn't make anything stick."

"What happened?"

Stevo tipped his head, squinting one eye as if dredging his memory. "The joint was one of these little stores, you know, run by an independent. Late night trading, a female staff member on one till, the male boss on the other, no customers, nothing happening, and two robbers came in with a shotgun each. They pinched about eight or ten grand, I think."

Alec nodded. "Anyone get hurt?"

"Yeah, the boss: Arash Kazemi. He carked it."

"Died at the scene?"

"A couple of weeks later. He tried to play hero. One of the robbers smashed his skull in for it. The whole time he was in hospital, he never woke up, not even once. After he died, Homicide took over. Typical of those lazy pricks, the case went cold. If it's not a bloke killing his ex, they wouldn't have a fucking clue." Stevo shook his head. "That poor bastard. His wife and daughters didn't leave his bedside."

Alec closed the manila folder. "That must have been a pretty rough case."

"One of the worst I've ever done. Not the absolute worst, but up there."

"How did Mick take it?"

Stevo frowned. "Why? Are you trying to dig up shit?"

"I'm just trying to get the back story to the pizza bandits."

"Look, I know you've got it in for him, and I don't blame you. He punched you up. I'd be the same. But let me tell you something about Mick that might come as a surprise: he visited that bloke in hospital every day."

"Yeah?"

"Yeah. He got close to the family too. The missus used to say he was the spitting image of her dead son. You know she asked him to be a pallbearer?"

"That's quite an honour."

"He had to take time off after that." Stevo swivelled his chair back towards the computer monitor. "There you go. Mick Thompson isn't quite the heartless bastard you reckon he is."

Alec sat back, mulling it over. Finally, he said, "I wonder why the case bothered him so much."

Stevo shrugged. "Who knows? Life bothers people in different ways."

Vandenburg said, "Which one of you wants to serve a couple of subpoenas today?"

Patel volunteered with a raised forefinger.

"Are you for real?" O'Brien laughed. "Admit it, John. You don't want to take the deejay's statement. Well, me neither."

Patel said, "That's got nothing to do with it. You did the subpoenas last week."

"Let's not waste any time on this, I'll deliver them myself." Vandenburg made a note on his jotter pad. "Next order of business. Irene, have we made any progress on locating the outstanding witness from the Boronia case?"

She didn't answer. Vandenburg looked up. O'Brien was gaping open-mouthed at something behind his back. He turned in his chair. Walking across the Rape Squad towards their island of desks was Alec Castellano, his face bruised and welted, his eyebrows cut. Vandenburg dropped his pen.

"Good Lord," he said. "Were you in a fight?"

Alec nodded. "Yesterday morning."

"How's the other guy look?" O'Brien said. "Worse than you, I hope."

Alec offered a lopsided smile. "As a matter of fact, Mick Thompson looks fine."

Vandenburg stood up fast enough to clatter his chair against one of the neighbouring desks. "Let's talk in private."

"Lead the way, sir."

Once they were inside one of the offices, Vandenburg shut the door. They both sat down. Vandenburg hardly knew where to start, which question to ask first out of so many, but then Alec began talking.

"I've agreed to be a witness in Cara's application for an intervention order," he said. "When Mick confronted her yesterday, I was the one who stopped him. Or at least, kept him occupied while she got away. Search YouTube for 'Punch-up on Clarendon Street'. A few ghouls filmed the fight and uploaded it."

"Holy Mary and Joseph." Vandenburg plucked at his moustache. "Thompson is suspended?"

Alec shook his head. "Sarge ordered me not to make a report."

"But that's against regulations."

"Everything that happens on my crew is against regulations. Why do you think I'm here?"

"I don't know why. Perhaps you'd better tell me."

Alec sat forward in his chair. "I want to stitch up Mick. I want him out of the force for good, and doing time if I can swing it. Reopen Cara's rape case and I'll be a signed witness. I'm prepared to testify against him if you can get the case into court."

Vandenburg nodded. "Once I have a look at the video footage, I'll let you know."

"Okay. Now, you realise Mick's got his preliminary interview with the Rats today?"

"Yes, at twelve noon."

"I want to make a statement to them first."

Vandenburg felt a thrill: perhaps all was not lost. "All right, I'd like to go with you. Whatever you say could help my case too. Let me arrange a time." He picked up the landline and spoke to one of the officers at the Professional Standards Division. When he hung up, he said to Alec, "We've got an appointment in half an hour."

Alec checked his watch. "No worries."

"Meet me by the elevators a couple of minutes beforehand."

"Thanks, sir. Guess I'd better get back before Sarge wonders where I am."

They both stood up.

At the office door, Vandenburg said, "I'm assuming you know what you're doing. And how this course of action might affect your career."

"I know."

"Do you? Thompson is dangerous, there's no doubt, and I admire your courage, this stand you're taking. But how many bridges will you burn over this?"

Alec offered a resigned grin. "Probably all of them." Then he left the office, crossed the squad room, pushed through the double-doors and was gone.

Vandenburg rushed over to his crew. O'Brien and Patel were wide-eyed and expectant.

"Well?" O'Brien said. "Come on, spill it."

"Our case against Mick Thompson might be the proverbial phoenix."

"Huh?" Patel said. "What does that mean?"

"That you should read more books." Vandenburg pointed at the computer monitor. "Irene, search YouTube for a video called 'Punch-up on Clarendon Street' or similar, and tell me what you think. I'm getting a pot of Earl Grey."

Vandenburg hurried towards the tea room. Having Castellano onside could make the critical difference. What secrets would he be able to reveal about Thompson? More than that: about the corrupt culture of the Armed Offence Squad? Just how high was this whole shebang going to stink? All the way to heaven, God willing, Vandenburg thought with a gritted smile. He couldn't wait for the next half-hour to pass.

At the door of the tea room, he pulled up.

Frank Ward, looking around from the coffee machine and spotting Vandenburg, sniffed and hawked as if preparing to spit. Vandenburg walked cautiously into the room. Only a week ago, Frank had been a friendly workmate. That seemed difficult to believe right now.

"Hello, Frank. How are you?"

"Fuck off."

Vandenburg laughed politely. "Always the gentleman."

"You and your fancy talk. Go shove it in your arse." Ward flung open the refrigerator door and snatched out a carton of milk.

"Look," Vandenburg said, "here's a word of advice that you don't deserve but I'll say it anyway. Professionally speaking, you need to distance yourself from Mick Thompson."

"I couldn't give a crap what you reckon about Mick or anything else. Understand?"

Ward stalked to the bench and slopped milk into his coffee mug. The man was a cheerless sight: his business shirt caught in the folds of love handles, the material pulling tight over a growing paunch. Back in the day, when he had played football, Ward had been all muscle.

Vandenburg said, "Come on, Frank. We went through the Academy together."

"So?"

"So, we've known each other more than twenty-five years. Doesn't that count?"

"Not for shit. I hate my ex-wife too, and I've known her for thirty."

"All right, forget it." Irritably, Vandenburg took a teapot from the cupboard, reached for the tin of loose tea leaves, and hesitated. He had to try again, if only for old times' sake. "Frank, it's too late to start your career over from scratch."

"What's your point?"

"That Thompson has gone rogue. There's no denying it. At the very least, he's bound to get suspended. Perhaps dismissed, even jailed. Do you really want to back his play? Are you prepared to lose everything because of him?"

Ward let out a long, tired sigh. He put the carton back in the fridge, then returned to the bench and stared morosely into the coffee mug.

"Gerry?" Ward said at last.

"Yes, mate?"

"Mind your own fucking business."

The furniture was arranged to maximise intimidation. Mick knew the tactic. They used it in the Armed Offence Squad. The sweat prickled along his hairline anyway.

At one end of the room, under a wall of flags and official insignias, was a straight line of tables that seated five officers from the Professional Standards Division. Each table had a floor-length wooden skirt that served to both conceal the lower body of every officer, and present an unbroken phalanx.

In the middle of the room, marooned on an empty patch of carpet about two metres square, sat Mick in a chair. To maximise the feeling of exposure, his chair didn't come with a desk or table that he could use as a physical barrier. There were no armrests, and no controls to adjust the back tilt or seat height. Not only that, his chair was comparatively much lower to the ground, subtly suggesting that the officers were looming over him. Clever, he thought.

He glanced around, noting other devices designed to rattle an interviewee's composure: the high temperature, bright lighting, absence of wall clocks, lack of windows. The furniture arrangement meant that the only door was located behind him where he couldn't see it.

All in all, very effective. But this wasn't his first rodeo.

The body language he chose to display suggested relaxation: crossed legs with the ankle of one leg propped on the knee of the other; one hand resting on a thigh, the other arm hung over the back of the chair; his shoulders angled slightly to one side in a slouch, his head tilted to the other side in compensation. To the officers, he would appear casual, calm, as if waiting for a bus and not in any particular hurry for it. As for his face, he presented a polite and mildly interested expression.

Arseholes.

Time continued to pass. The officers were still flipping through their notes, occasionally conferring by way of pointing at each other's pages rather than talking. Extended periods of silence: another standard interrogation tactic. How green did they think he was?

"Ah, excuse me, please," sounded Ward's voice.

Mick twisted around in his chair to glare at Ward, who was seated behind him next to the closed door. *Shut the hell up*, Mick wanted to say, but had to say it instead with his eyes. However, Ward stared back as if unseeing; his entire, balding head a flushed, sweating shine of anxiety. Goddamn it. Mick turned to face the front again.

"Yes, what's the problem, Detective Senior Sergeant Ward?" said one officer, a middle-aged man with jug ears and a prominent Adam's apple.

"Can we get water? It's pretty muggy in here."

That's on purpose, Mick thought bitterly, to make you ask for a drink and get rejected.

The officer said, "We won't be too much longer. Do you mind waiting?"

"No, that's fine," Ward said.

Hadn't they used the exact same tactic on interviewees countless times in the Armed Offence Squad? Fuck. Mick ground his teeth.

"Is everything okay, Detective Senior Constable Thompson?"

He looked up. The bitch who seemed to be running this farce, a brunette named Zoe Manousakis, was regarding him with arched eyebrows.

"Everything's fine," he said, and gave what he hoped was a breezy grin.

"You're not thirsty too?"

"No, ma'am. Only I'm starting to wonder how come we're wasting time."

She tapped her pen against the table and glanced around at the other officers.

"I thought the purpose of this meeting was clear," she said. Reading from her notes, she went on, "To recap, Detective Senior Constable Thompson, the purpose of this review today is to assess your suitability for duty. We're looking at your pattern of behaviour, at the complaints made against you, at your breaches of discipline, and we're conducting a series of interviews with both police officers and civilians. That takes time. Make sense to you?"

"Yes, ma'am."

She continued, "On the strength of this preliminary review, the board will advise by Monday if you have a case to answer, and if so, the board will schedule an official disciplinary investigation." She put the page she was reading back onto the table. "Is that clear?"

"Yes, ma'am."

"You don't need me to explain it again?"

Mick crossed his legs the other way, jiggled his foot. "No, ma'am."

"Excellent, let's move on," she said, and shuffled through the other papers on her table before settling on a particular sheet. "Now, one more time. We'd like to go over the details of the house raid that your crew carried out on Mr Rodney Brown."

What the fuck for? Mick wanted to stand up and leave, but instead, forced himself to sit as nonchalantly as possible. His shirt collar was starting to itch. The damned tie felt too tight.

"As you know," she said, "we've already spoken to the other officers involved in the raid. You were assigned to the master bedroom, is that correct?"

"Yes, ma'am."

"As you ran in, announcing 'Police, don't move', where was Mr Brown at that point?"

"Like I said before, sitting up in bed. Listen, no matter how many different ways you get me to tell it, my story's not going to change."

"Okay, we appreciate your patience. We understand our questions may seem repetitive to you." She offered a patronising smile. "According to you, he grabbed your shotgun. You must have been on top of him."

"I was next to the bed."

No one spoke for a time. Mick could feel the sweat building up in his armpits.

A fat man wearing glasses said, "After you pulled the shotgun from his hands, you struck him with the weapon. Is that correct?"

"Yes, sir."

"Twice."

"No, just once."

The fat man took off his glasses. "Not according to the hospital report."

Mick shrugged. "It could have been twice."

"And then you started beating him with..." The fat man put his glasses back on, consulted a piece of paper, and concluded, "...your fists."

Mick didn't answer. The panel shuffled papers. Ward began clearing his throat repeatedly, a strained and nervous sound. Mick refused to look back. At last, Ward stopped hacking and spluttering. The silence stretched on. Mick uncrossed his legs. One heel started to tap against the carpet.

"We've received evidence contrary to your statement," Zoe Manousakis said. "One of the detectives involved told us you went berserk during the raid and assaulted Mr Brown without provocation."

"Who said that? Did Alec Castellano tell you that?"

Ward began, "Excuse me, but if I could put in my two bob's worth at this point—"

"Please be quiet unless directly questioned," the man with the jug ears said. "Thompson, who is Mr Kazemi?"

Mick's chest constricted as if his diaphragm had set into a plate of concrete. In his mind's eye, he saw the women in black, weeping; the hospital bed; the shaved portions of Mr Kazemi's tattered, ruined scalp held together with black stitches. He'd dreamt that scene so many times that he couldn't be sure anymore if the details were real or imagined. *I'm sorry, I'm doing everything I can, I swear*—had he actually said those words to Mr Kazemi? To the man's wife and daughters? He didn't know that either.

"Thompson? Do you want me to repeat the question?"

"No." Mick swiped at his dry lips with the back of one hand. "Mr Kazemi was a victim of an armed robbery that occurred about six months ago at a supermarket. He was the owner and manager. One of the robbers assaulted Mr Kazemi, pistol-whipping him with the butt of a shotgun."

Jug Ears pointed a pen at Mick. "In other words, Mr Kazemi was assaulted in the same way that you assaulted Mr Brown."

"Incorrect." Mick fidgeted in his chair, feeling breathless. He continued, "And Mr Kazemi died from his injuries. I don't see how you can draw any parallels."

To stop his heel from tapping, Mick crossed his legs at the ankles and tucked his feet under the chair. Accidentally, he kicked the shoebox of thank-you letters from his armed robbery victims, which was sitting, untouched and ignored, on the floor beneath him. It was almost too humiliating to bear. He'd told the officers about the letters at the start of the interview, but they hadn't given a flying shit. He wanted to grab each fucker by the throat and cram wads of cards and notepaper into their mouths until they choked.

"Let's move on," Jug Ears said. "Who is David Etherington?"

"An informant of the Armed Offence Squad."

"Two weeks ago, did you assault this informant in a laneway alongside a Brooklyn betting agency?"

A pulse started up inside Mick's skull, thudding at the roof of his mouth.

Zoe Manousakis said, "You broke one of Mr Etherington's ribs."

"Please tell us how that could have happened," Fat Man added.

Mick placed his feet flat on the floor and gripped his knees hard with both hands, knowing how his posture must look, but unable to stop himself, to help himself.

"Detective Senior Constable?" Zoe Manousakis said. "Do you need a break?"

"No." He tried to smile, his lips quivering. He stopped smiling and laced his hands behind his head. "Listen, Alec Castellano is lying. Whatever bullshit he told you about what happened that day between me and Dave outside the TAB, he's lying. Alec has it in for me, you see? He's jealous of my relationship with Cara Haynes. He wants her for himself."

"Cara Haynes?" Zoe Manousakis sat bolt upright. "The woman you're accused of raping?"

As if on cue, the five officers sat up in their chairs and looked around at each other, incredulous. Oh Jesus, thought Mick, head spinning.

Oh, Jesus fucking Christ.

On the way back to the Armed Offence Squad, along every corridor and during the ride in the lift, Ward kept up a constant, agitated chatter. Mick felt too shell-shocked to pay attention. Every now and then, however, a phrase would break through—*bloody inquisition, we'll get the Union on board, the cheek of those bastards*—but mostly, Ward's yabber ran over Mick like white noise, like rain on a roof. Mick had the shoebox clutched at his stomach. The cardboard felt smooth and dry. He thought about lying down, about going to sleep for a long time.

The only crew in the Armed Offence Squad was their own; a small mercy. They neared the desks. Bull noticed them first.

Standing up, glancing at his watch, Bull said, "You've been gone over two and a half hours. What the fuck happened in there?"

Stevo looked around. Alec, however, remained glued to the computer monitor and kept tapping at the keyboard, ignoring their approach. Mick put the shoebox on the desk. Then he stared at the side of Alec's head, thinking a few things over.

"You want to know what happened?" Ward said, flinging off his jacket, loosening his tie. "I'll tell you what happened. We got rooted up the arse, that's what happened."

"Fucking rats," Bull said.

"They're biased. And if they hang Mick, they'll hang me too. You blokes will be next, and then the whole bloody squad after that. Understand? We need to contact the Union, pronto. We've only got until Monday before the pricks make a decision, and without the Union onside, we already know what it's going to be, the dirty bastards."

From behind, Mick put an arm around Alec's neck and tipped him from the chair to the floor. He used his full body weight to pin Alec face down. As forcefully as he could, Mick closed the elbow of the arm he had locked around Alec's throat. Simultaneously, he leaned into the back of Alec's skull with the other forearm. The combined pull-push action of opposing forces would soon yield interesting results. Mick closed his eyes. Making a range of choking noises, Alec bucked and struggled beneath him.

The crew got them apart, but it took some doing.

First, they wasted time trying to overpower him. They should have known that attempting to pry open his arms couldn't possibly work. Mick's adherence to four-weekly weight training sessions should have told them that. Using strict form, he could curl fifty kilos with a straight barbell for set after perfect set.

Next, the crew tried to lift him bodily away. That did nothing to loosen his grip. Alec just got throttled at a different angle.

They kicked at his sides. Well, he wouldn't take that personally. Ditto the hair-pulling and eye-gouging. You can't blame people for their actions when they're desperate, he thought. He tightened his grip and hung on.

In the end, a simple pressure-point tactic did the trick.

It must have been Stevo, always a big fan of that Ju-jitsu kind of stuff. No matter who you were or how tough you figured on being, the intense pain of a thumb pressed into the mandibular angle behind the jaw couldn't be ignored.

Mick let go of Alec and rolled away.

After a while, Mick sat up.

They had Alec propped in a chair, Bull on one side of him, Ward and Stevo on the other, all three holding him upright while he coughed, his face grey beneath the cuts and bruises. One of the landlines rang. No one reacted. The phone stopped ringing.

"Can you breathe okay?" Stevo was saying.

Alec nodded.

"You want me to get a first aid officer?" Stevo continued.

Alec shook his head.

Ward spun around. "Mick, if you touch him one more time, so help me God, I'll file your dismissal papers myself. Understand? I'll hammer your nut-sack to the wall."

Huffing and puffing, Ward looked like he was getting ready for a heart attack. Meanwhile, the colour had come back into Alec's face. Mick got to his feet and took a seat at his desk. There were a few phone messages. He picked up the papers and began sorting through them.

"And as for you, you little shit," Ward said.

Mick looked up. Ward had a finger pointed at Alec. Mick put down the stack of messages and sat back in his chair.

"Who, *me*?" Alec said in a creaky rasp. "I didn't do anything. He attacked me."

"Didn't do anything?" Ward made a snorting noise. "Not in here, maybe, but you've done plenty for the Rat Squad. How else did they know about Dave Etherington? And you were their eyewitness for Mick beating the crap out of Brownie, weren't you? Huh? And the bullshit about Cara Haynes's wallet getting pinched, I suppose they got that from you as well."

Bull put his hands on his hips. "He's a cheese-eater?"

"Hang on a minute," Stevo said. "We need to calm down."

"And why dob on Mick for the punch-up? You hit him first anyway. You had it coming. And I expressly told you not to report him. I told you things were in the balance for us, I ordered you to keep your mouth shut."

"Aw, that's it, cheese-eater," Bull said, and grabbed Alec's collar.

"Step back," Stevo said. "Now."

"That's right." Ward angrily flapped his arms about as if breast-stroking through water. "Everybody, get away from him."

They did.

Ward took time to catch his breath. His eyes were wild, hectic.

Finally, he said, "You're on your own now, Alec. You're finished in this squad. And I'm going to do everything in my power to make sure you never get another posting anywhere in the force across the whole of bloody Australia. Got it? Fucking traitor."

Alec lifted his head from his chest to glance at Mick. They locked eyes. Mick smiled.

Ward dropped into his chair. "Okay, chop chop, let's contact the Union rep."

TWENTY

T he dojo was in a strip shopping centre about a twenty-minute drive from Premiere Press. Located on the second floor above a gift shop, it was only accessible via an exterior flight of wooden stairs. Cara felt nervous as she took the steps. Gratefully, she looked around and smiled at Trish, who had not only suggested self-defence training but offered to join Cara for each lesson. Cara had then spent the next hour at work chasing up a suitable teacher. When she'd spoken to the owner of this particular dojo, a man named Ethan, she had told him that she needed to protect herself against an ex-lover. Like he'd heard this scenario a thousand times, Ethan wasn't shocked. Instead, he had asked her to hang around after class for under-the-table help if she wanted it. Of course, she had said yes.

Now, however, as she neared the top of the stairs and the dojo door, she felt increasingly anxious. Ethan was not only a black belt in karate, but a mixed martial arts competitor. She'd seen pay-per-view ads on television for those horrible cage bouts. God, why on earth would she put her trust in Ethan? He was a man trained in violence who could mete out extreme physical harm, even death. His 'under-the-table help' could only be offering to beat up Mick for money. Shit. More than that, what terror could a man like Ethan inflict on a woman if he felt like it? And wasn't her life already doubling back on itself, over and over? This decision could be an invitation for more trouble. Cara hesitated at the door, her mouth drying out.

"You okay?" Trish said.

"Yes. Thanks again for coming with me."

"Oh, it'll be great fun," Trish said, opening the door and ushering Cara through.

She had never been inside a martial arts school before. The front door opened immediately into the training room, which was a large, empty space. Cara had expected to see equipment. Blue crash-mats covered the floor. Lining the windowsills were dozens of trophies, some of them almost as tall as a person. The windows didn't have any curtains. It was night. Anyone looking in from the street would be able to see inside. No, that wasn't true, Cara corrected herself;

we're on the second floor, we're too high up. Even still, she decided that she would stand on the opposite side of the room to the windows. Her heart was beating fast. Calm down, she thought.

Eight other women were already there, gathered in groups or sitting at the row of plastic chairs that lined one wall. Most of the women were middle-aged or older, talking and laughing. A couple of teenagers stood close together by the toilets, thumbing through their mobiles in companionable silence. Cara gave Trish another grateful smile.

From behind a high desk, a man stood up and walked out onto the mats. Barefoot, he wore a loose-fitting karate uniform, black instead of white, the shirt belted at the waist. That must be Ethan. He was pale, stocky, perhaps in his twenties, with pierced ears, acne scars about his chin, and masses of blonde hair gelled into a dozen or more peaked tufts. Well, he didn't look mean at all, Cara decided, and forced herself to relax. In fact, he seemed pleasant enough. A person who might give up his seat for you on a train.

Spotting her and Trish, he walked over. "I'm Ethan. Which one of you ladies is Cara?"

"Me," Cara said, putting out her hand.

He took it. "Pleased to meet you. That makes you Trish?"

"Yeah, hello."

"Glad you could both make it tonight." He shook Trish's hand too. Then he said, "I already mentioned this over the phone, but my beginner class has been running for a few weeks now. To be fair to my existing students, I'll only do a quick recap of the moves we've covered, but don't worry. I'll give you ladies extra instruction during the practice sessions, okay?"

"Okay," Cara said.

He stared into her eyes without blinking. "And you're right to hang around afterwards?"

Cara paused. Taking a breath, she finally nodded.

Ethan smiled, and headed towards one end of the room, clapping his hands together.

"What did he mean?" Trish said.

Flustered, Cara said, "Nothing."

"All right, ladies," Ethan announced, his voice raised and booming. "Let's get started."

The other women hurried to take their places on the crash-mats. Cara and Trish ended up towards the back.

Ethan waved at them to come closer. "Take a spot up here. Don't be shy, I won't bite."

The women tittered, some more than others. Cara glanced around as she and Trish took their new positions at the head of the class. Two old women standing next to each other were ogling Ethan, their faces a lecherous twinset. Revolted, frightened, Cara suddenly wanted to go home. Wherever that might be, she thought with a start. Oma and Opa's place was long gone.

"Remember the chicken beak from last time?" Ethan said.

He lifted one hand, his fingers and thumb pressed together as if he were trying to pick up a pinch of dust. The rest of the class made the same gesture.

"That's right. One of the best strikes against an assailant's eyeball is the chicken beak. Peck, peck, peck," he said, jabbing his hand at the air to punctuate each word, "like a chicken pecking at grains."

Cara raised her hand and did the same motion. She glanced around at Trish, who was laughing and 'pecking' along with the other women. Cara focused on Ethan. For the duration of the one-hour class, he seemed to be making a lot of eye contact with her. Or was she imagining things? His instruction flooded over her in dizzying detail—spear-hand strike, palm-heel strike, knife-hand chop, knuckle-fist punch, hammer fist, roundhouse fist, elbow strike, stamp kick, head butt, and on and on, the vulnerable points on the body including the sinuses, throat, collar bone, top of foot—until she felt giddy.

The class was over. Ethan approached and took her by the arm.

"Could you wait for me outside?" Cara said to Trish, not waiting for a reply.

Ethan led Cara into an office. The room smelt organically warm, a musky combination of liniment and male sweat. As Ethan moved to close the door, Cara spotted the two lewd women looking at her enviously, whispering and hissing at each other, their eyes slitted. The door latch clicked shut. Cara's heart skipped a few beats.

"How did you go?" Ethan said, sitting down on the edge of the desk.

"Good, thanks."

She stood awkwardly by the door. The room was tiny, crowded by the chipboard desk, a chair, a filing cabinet. On one of the walls hung a giant poster, a photograph of a man with blood running freely down his face, brows split, eyes puffed shut, a blue mouthguard still clamped between his teeth, the large-type caption beneath the picture proclaiming in capital letters, 'Stay tough'.

Cara grabbed the door handle. "I've made a mistake. I should go."

"Hang on a second." Ethan leaned back, opened a desk drawer, and took out a slim aerosol can. He held it up and said, "Know what this is?"

She shook her head.

"Capsicum spray, known as mace or pepper spray. Heard of it?"

She nodded. He held it out. She took the can, gingerly, as if it could explode in her hand.

He continued, "It's against the law in Victoria to buy, possess, carry or use capsicum spray. To get around the rules, I buy online from Western Australia. Occasionally, I sell to clients. Not for the money. You know why?"

"No," she whispered. "Why?"

"Because men beat up their women every day. In my book, an unfair advantage for the lady is the only fair way to go." He smiled. "Ten bucks. And don't show the spray to anybody. You could get in a heap of trouble."

Cara scrutinised the can. It was about the size of a mouth freshener spray, the packaging black with white lettering, the prominent warning label stating in bold red capitals: *keep out of reach of children; this product may irritate eyes.*

"All right," she said. "Let me get my wallet."

Ethan stood up. "This will make him cough, choke, go blind for a while, puke. The effects last about half an hour. Hey, but you've got to be careful. Give him a tiny squirt, and then run. Otherwise, the spray is going to get you too."

The bike path was deserted early Saturday morning. The chilly temperature probably had something to do with that. Not even three degrees when Alec pulled into the car park and set up his mountain bike. Normally, he wouldn't be out at this time either, but sleep had been elusive. Finding out that he'd soon be losing his job had hit hard. Watching the crew fuss over Mick had hit even harder. Wincing, Alec clipped on his helmet and mounted the saddle. Every movement aggravated his various aches and pains, but to forgo his Saturday-morning ride would be to concede yet another thing to Mick. Fuck that.

As the bike path meandered alongside the creek, Alec stopped pedalling and slowed down to watch the creeping fog roll up from the banks. An animal skittered across the water and rustled into grass. Perhaps a duck, maybe a cormorant. Whatever, Alec didn't know much about birds. In fact, he didn't know much about anything besides police work.

The whole shit-storm washed over him again.

Christ, how could Ward take sides with Mick, after everything that the bastard had done? And why was Alec the bad guy, when he'd acted like any decent copper would? No matter how many times Alec ground over the details—last night in bed or right now on the bike path—the situation didn't make sense.

Around a bend in the path, he spotted a jogger. Alec rang his bell and took a wide berth. The jogger raised his hand in acknowledgement as Alec rode by. The path cut away from the creek and began its slow, gentle climb through stands of gum trees. From far off, a dog barked. Another dog yelped in answer. Half a kilometre away ran the length of back fencing that separated the housing estate from the reserve, the succession of red or black roofs visible over the capping, some roofs with satellite dishes, evaporative air conditioners or solar panels; a few with all three.

Alec took the water bottle from its cradle and took a sip. Maybe he would appeal his dismissal. If Mick could turn to the Union for protection, then so could Alec. Well, why not? Ward had only filed the dismissal papers. The dismissal hadn't yet been approved. There was still time to save his job—if he wanted it. And that was the next thing to consider. Did he even want to keep working alongside those pricks?

The best person to talk to about this was, of course, Liz Lansky, but—out of cowardice, probably, or embarrassment—he hadn't yet told her what had happened. He just couldn't face her angry, exasperated *I told you so* routine. Still, who else would understand? He made a mental note to call her tonight regardless, whether he felt like it or not. Come Monday morning, he'd need an action plan. He couldn't afford to be unemployed.

He grimaced. Unemployed? Fuck. Despair and resentment flared up again.

His mobile rang. Don't let it be Mick, he thought. Or worse, the sarge. Alec steered to one side of the path, braked, and dug his phone from the backpack. Unexpectedly, the caller was Gerard Vandenburg.

"Did I get you out of bed?" Vandenburg said.

"No, sir. I'm riding my bike."

"Enjoying the fresh air? Very good. You put me to shame. I must try to exercise more often. It's been an awfully long time since I last rode a bicycle. I've got a ten-speed buried in the garage, unless my wife has thrown it out, of course. She accuses me of hoarding."

Alec hesitated. "Are you all right, sir?"

"Yes, sorry to be blathering. I'm a little excited about recent events. We need to meet up straight away. Where are you?"

Alec told him. They figured out that, with Alec cycling and Vandenburg driving, the best meeting point would be the car park alongside a particular railway station. When Alec hung up, he cycled at top speed and got there first.

Vandenburg turned up about ten minutes later. He pulled his Suzuki sedan into a space and cut the engine. Alec headed to the driver's side door and opened it.

"Morning," Vandenburg said, hopping out. "Thanks for meeting with me."

They shook hands.

Alec said, "With respect, sir, don't keep me in suspense."

"Fine. I'm reopening the rape case against Thompson."

It took everything Alec had not to whoop in triumph. Restraining himself, grinning and shaking his head, he eventually said, "Christ, that's fantastic."

"A jury will take one look at that footage from Clarendon Street and deliver a guilty verdict, I'd bet my bottom dollar. There's no doubt the DPP will give me the green light. Are you still willing to testify?"

"I sure am. Have you told Cara?"

"Not yet. To be on the safe side, I thought I'd better wait until I get confirmation from the DPP. When I'm about to formally charge Thompson, then I'll let her know." Vandenburg leaned against the car and studied Alec's face. "The bruising has gone down."

Reflexively, Alec touched at an eyebrow. "Yeah, it's getting better."

"What happened to your throat?"

It hadn't seemed so bad last night but Alec knew how his throat looked today after gaping at it this morning in the mirror: an angry, thick line of red, blue and purple contusions running from ear to ear. A business collar could hide the bulk of it, but right now he was wearing a singlet. He sighed. Was there no end to the humiliation?

"Mick attacked me yesterday after figuring out I'd testified against him to the Professional Standards Division."

Vandenburg nodded. "Sadly, that doesn't surprise me."

Alec turned away and studied the sky. The foggy clouds were starting to lift. He wondered how to extricate himself from this meeting without seeming rude.

"I'm starting to cool down," he said. "If there's nothing else, I'd better get going."

Vandenburg said, "I heard around the traps that Frank Ward submitted dismissal papers against you last night."

"That's right. Come next week, I guess I'm out of a job."

"What are you going to do?"

"I don't know. I haven't thought that far ahead. I might appeal to the Union. Maybe I'll try for a posting back in uniform, I'm not sure yet."

"Uniform? Wouldn't that be a backwards step?"

Alec shrugged, kicked at the gravel underfoot. "I suppose."

"Have you ever considered a career in sex crimes?"

Alec looked around. Vandenburg was smiling the kind of smile that a father might give to his kid on Christmas Day when handing over a puppy.

"Sex crimes?" Alec said. "You mean a posting in Rape Squad?"

"The victims are adult only, minimum eighteen years of age. Sex crimes against children are managed by another department entirely. Usually, there's no crossover. I can think of only a couple of cases where the two squads needed to work together, it's that rare. Most of our victims are women; a few are men. About fifty rapes are reported every week. As you can imagine, we get very few cases to court, and our conviction rate hovers at about sixty per cent, which can be very frustrating. That's the number one challenge of the job, I think. Persevering even though the odds are against you. It's not for everybody."

Bowing his head, Alec put his hands on his hips and walked around his bike for a while. The cleats on his shoes clicked against the bitumen.

"I don't know anything about sexual assault victims or offenders," he said.

"And I wouldn't expect you to. You'd have to undergo training. But are you interested? I would assign you to my own crew. You would be working alongside me, O'Brien and Patel."

"But why?" Alec said. "Didn't you get the memo? I'm a cheese-eater."

"No. You're an officer with integrity who refuses to look the other way."

Alec stopped walking and regarded Vandenburg. The man's reputation was that of the proverbial squeaky-clean copper. He did everything, absolutely everything, by the book. Ward often mocked Vandenburg for being a stickler. *He doesn't even cheat on his fucking taxes*, Ward liked to say. If Alec joined the Rape Squad, there would be no leeway for favours, no turning a blind eye, none of that *just this once* kind of bullshit that was rife in the Armed Offence Squad. Alec put out his hand, which Vandenburg heartily shook.

"I'll start the paperwork Monday morning," Vandenburg said.

Grinning, Alec thought about the icing on this particular cake: that he'd be going up against Mick when the rape charge was reinstated, and helping to send that bastard to jail where he belonged.

"Hey, wake up."

That voice wouldn't quit, kept buzzing in his ears like a mosquito.

"I know you can hear me," the voice went on. "Come on, stop pretending."

Mick rolled over, scrubbed at his face with the palm of one hand, and looked about. Ow, fuck. Moving his eyes had been a big mistake. His eyeballs were wired directly to his skull and stomach, triggering pain in one and nausea in the other.

"Get up."

"Janice?" he said. "Is that you?"

"Yes, it's me. Get out of bed and clean the lounge room. It looks like a fucking sty."

"What happened? Did we have people over?"

"How am I supposed to know what you got up to yesterday? I wasn't here. I've just got back from Daylesford. From the looks of it, you were drinking the whole day and night. Were you?"

Good question. He couldn't remember. Yesterday after a few beers, he'd decided to sit in front of the television and watch the qualifying for the Silverstone Grand Prix. Once he'd got a nice buzz going, he'd opened a bottle of vodka. He ran out of orange juice and began using cola as a mixer. After that, his memory went blank.

Mick opened his eyes again, gently this time, to avoid aggravating the headache. Janice was standing by the bed with her hands on her hips, looking so radiantly well and sober that he immediately felt worse.

Pushing his head into the pillow, he muttered, "Let me sleep."

In reply, she ripped the blankets from him.

"Hey," he said, "there's no need to be shitty." Glancing down, he realised that he had gone to bed fully dressed, shoes and all. He didn't remember that either. "Is it Monday already?" he said. "Do I have to go to work?"

"It's Sunday afternoon."

Janice stomped to the curtains and flung them open. Sunlight lanced his eyes and cleaved an axe-pain through the middle of his head.

"I'm not getting up," he said.

"Yes, you are. You hear me? You're getting up and cleaning that fucking lounge room."

She stormed out. He could hear her clattering and banging around in the kitchen. It sounded like she was making herself a coffee. Perhaps she would make him one as well. Grunting, he sat up and swung his legs out of bed. The queasy feeling slopped from one side of his guts to the other. Shit, he could taste onions. The thought of food, any kind of food, made him want to retch. Coffee was probably a bad idea too.

It took him a while to get out of bed, but he managed it. His appearance in the bathroom mirror came as a shock. Unshaven, puffy-faced, his eyes swollen and bloodshot, he'd aged ten years overnight. He glanced at his watch: 3.18 p.m. On the toilet floor, he found the television remote and picked it up.

He shuffled into the lounge room. The coffee table looked like a bin had been emptied over it. Dozens of beer cans, a dead bottle of vodka, half a bottle of cola, empty packets of biscuits, chips, chocolate. Most of the mess was on the table. Some of it was scattered around on the floor. What was that in a ceramic bowl, leftover ice cream?

"Here," Janice said, handing him a large plastic bag. She returned to the kitchen.

Leaning over hurt his head, so he had to squat down to collect the rubbish. On the couch underneath Saturday's newspaper, he discovered a takeaway pizza box with one slice of Hawaiian still inside. At what point had he ordered pizza? Hopefully, he'd had it home-delivered. As soon as he was feeling better, he'd go down to the garage and check the car for dents.

When the debris was cleared away, he wiped the coffee table with a damp rag, swept the floor, and then reported back to Janice, who was sitting at the breakfast nook with a cup of coffee, staring out the window. There was a folded piece of paper on the bench near her elbow. She seemed a lot calmer.

"Done," he said.

"Okay." She handed him the paper. "Have a look at this."

"What is it?"

"The terms of our separation. I wrote it at the hotel last night after dinner."

"Separation?" he said. "What do you mean: separation?"

She got up and pushed past him. He opened the paper, scanning the lines of her neat handwriting:

To Mick,

I am filing for divorce. Our legal fees will be substantially less if we can agree on the division of assets ourselves rather than fight each other through the courts. My suggested terms and conditions of separation are set out as follows:

a) Effective immediately, you are to move out of our apartment and find alternative lodgings.

b) I will offer complete, accurate and fair disclosure of my financial affairs, and expect you to do the same.

c) We will agree to pay our own personal debts, such as credit cards, and not hold each other responsible.

d) Neither of us will incur any further debt that may result in joint liability.

e) I will keep the apartment and its entire contents, apart from your personal belongings such as clothes, sporting equipment and DVDs…

There was more, much more, but he couldn't go on. He screwed the paper into a ball, stuffed it into his pocket and hurried through the apartment.

"Janice," he called. "Where are you?"

He found her in the bedroom, unpacking her suitcase from the Daylesford business trip. Momentarily, she stopped what she was doing to give him a cold, distant look.

"You want to get divorced?" Mick dug his fingertips into his temples. If only this headache would piss off, he'd be able to think straight. "Is it my drinking? Listen, I know I drink more than I should but I have to unwind from the job."

"Unwinding from the job is how you live your entire life. Let me spell it out: piss-ups; boys' nights; strippers; girlie bars." Janice threw the hairdryer she was holding back into the suitcase and turned to glare at him. "Prostitutes."

Mick didn't know what to say. She turned her back again and snatched at clothing from the suitcase, grouping items into different piles on the bed. Slowly, carefully, he approached. Everything that he did, every word that he spoke, his entire demeanour from here on in, was critical.

"Baby, I'm only letting off steam," he said. "None of it means anything."

"Is that right?"

"I swear to you. I swear on my mother's grave."

Janice gave the kind of braying, mocking laugh that told him that he'd just made the fatal mistake, had walked into the trap that she'd been setting out for him all along.

She said, "What about your girlfriend, Cara? Is she meaningless too?"

Stunned, he felt his stomach drop. He'd been so discreet, and yet, Janice had known? This new situation needed careful handling, but he couldn't think of how to answer. Janice shoved past him. He followed her into the laundry and watched her load the washing machine, measure out and pour the laundry detergent.

At last, he said, "How did you find out this stuff?"

"I'm a writer. I hang out with other writers. One of my colleagues is a court reporter who hangs out with coppers from your building every day. You think coppers don't gossip? You're up on disciplinary charges for shagging a little slut named Cara." Janice slammed the washing machine lid, jabbed a couple of buttons. "I'm fed up with talking. Read over the terms of our separation. They're pretty straightforward."

She slipped past him and headed back into the bedroom. Mick could feel the pulse banging behind his eyes, within his solar plexus. He took the crumpled paper from his pocket and opened it out:

f) The money in our joint bank account shall be equally divided, and the account closed down.

g) You are to be removed as a beneficiary from my life insurance and will...

He folded the paper, over and over, smaller and smaller, until his fingers strained to crush the sheet one last time into the size of a matchbox. After holding up the compact wad for scrutiny, he tossed it to the laundry floor.

Janice was kneeling in front of the open wardrobe, reverently putting high heels into their designated spots on the shoe rack. Yeah, that was one of the things he'd always hated about Janice: her tiresome bullshit about shoes. He approached, very quietly, padding on the carpet. She didn't turn around. She didn't know he was there. A spot on the back of her head drew his attention.

Standing up, she went to the empty suitcase on the bed, shut the lid, and started to close the zipper. Mick sat on the mattress. Then he picked up her toilet bag and squeezed it with both hands, kneading at the angular shapes inside.

"Watch it, you'll break something," she said, snatching the bag off him.

"Sorry."

Janice put the toilet bag on the bed and returned her attention to zipping the suitcase. A lock of hair fell from her ponytail. Mick thought about smoothing the tress behind her ear, then kissing her, and, if he could manage it, making love. No, he realised straight away, that was beyond him. In fact, everything was beyond him.

"This is shit timing," he said.

"I can't help that."

"But there are things going on I haven't told you about."

She gave a derisive snort. "Ha. What an understatement."

"About work, I mean. Stuff has happened. I might get suspended. Don't leave me."

"You left me first."

"Huh?"

Sighing, Janice shoved the suitcase aside to sit next to him on the bed. "The job has changed you," she continued, her voice tired and flat. "I don't know you anymore."

"I don't know myself." He clutched at her hand. "Listen, Janice, things aren't making much sense at the moment. I'm in a bad way, I'm messed up. Please don't do this to me."

"You did it to yourself." She pulled her hand free and stood. "I used to believe you were a tough guy, but it's a front, isn't it, Mick? You're only tough when you've got a gun in your hand."

She grabbed the toilet bag and left the room. He didn't have the strength to follow.

TWENTY-ONE

Cara read the first line of the e-mail, gasped, and couldn't read on. Covering her mouth with her hands, laughing in relief, she sat back in the office chair. This is the result when you set your mind to a goal and refuse to waver, she thought, as feelings of pride and vindication bubbled up. This is the reward when you don't let the terrible things in life beat you down.

Blackbird Books had agreed to sign their business to Premiere Press.

She sat forward to read the e-mail twice over in its entirety. To her satisfaction, she noticed that the managing director had cc'd Don Reinecke, who should be bursting into Cara's office any minute now.

And to think he had doubted Cara, had tried to give the account to Martin.

But Cara would be gracious about that. She'd never mention it to Don. To Martin either. Bottom line, she was too professional to indulge in egotistical point-scoring. She started giggling again. Ah, who was she kidding? She wouldn't mention it solely because there was no need. Everyone in the company would be talking about this score for weeks. Blackbird Books wanted to sign over their contracts for the whole lot, including the print run for the unpublished novel that had already been sold as a mini-series to a commercial television network. Cara's commission on that alone could be worth thousands.

Thousands.

Damn, winning for a change felt wonderful. Feeling wonderful for a change, rather than afraid, was even better. She got up to lean her arms on the windowsill, admiring the world as it went by.

"You're my clever, clever girl."

Cara glanced around. Don was at the open doorway of her office, beaming, his arms held wide to invite her embrace. She went over and—what the hell—hugged him, just briefly. Then she went back behind her desk and dropped into her chair. Don leaned against the door jamb, grinning like a proud parent.

"How are you going to spend your commission?" he said.

"Oh, I'll think of a way."

"You're the star of my show, Cara, do you realise? Any time I need to chase down a difficult client, I'll come to you."

"Great! I look forward to it."

"And look forward to lunch," he said, giving her a salute. "I'm taking everybody, Lucy too. We'll shut the office for the afternoon, let the phones ring off the hook while we celebrate. What do you say?"

"Fabulous."

"Be ready at one." He dashed along the central hallway, calling back over his shoulder, "I'm off to spread the good news."

Cara took a deep breath. Tears were crowding her lashes, her heart racing. She got up from the desk, approached the corkboard and took down the Van Gogh postcard of 'The Café Terrace at Night'. Even in this crappy reproduction, the gold of the building's fascia, awning and patio shone luminously, bursting with energy, spirit, hope. Overcome, she kissed the postcard, and went to slip it into her handbag.

She pulled up short.

Nestled alongside her wallet was the capsicum spray, looking as innocuous as a pocket-sized can of hair product. She'd never owned an illegal weapon before. Staring at the can, she imagined training its stream of liquid fire into Mick's face.

Then she tucked the postcard into her handbag and closed the zip.

"Well done, honey, I knew you could do it," Trish said, walking in and taking a seat on the visitor's chair. "I'm envious, but who wouldn't be? That's a good contract. Don is beside himself, by the way, the funny thing. And you should see Martin. He reckons he's going home because of earache. What a sook."

Before Cara could reply, the landline rang. It was Lucy on reception, no doubt calling to offer congratulations. Cara pressed the speaker-phone button for Trish's benefit, and said, "Hi, Lucy, are you ready for a posh lunch?"

"I know, gee, I can't believe Mr Reinecke is closing the place so I can come too. Isn't it great? That's not why I'm calling. You've got a visitor. He doesn't have an appointment, but there's a policeman here to see you."

Cara's heart stopped for moment. "A policeman?"

"Yes, Detective Constable Alec Castellano."

Exhaling, Cara said, "I'll be right down." Then she disconnected the call.

Trish's eyes bugged. "Isn't he from Clarendon Street, the man who saved you from Mick?" She jumped up. "Stay there, I'll get him."

"What?"

"Oh, come on, I want to check him out."

"Wait. Trish, wait a second."

But Trish was gone in a whirl of trailing skirt fabric and red hair. Oh shit. Cara sat back in her seat. Then, impulsively, she tidied her desk by scooping notepads, pens and mail into the top drawer and closing it. Seconds passed. Trish's voice floated up from the nearby stairwell, followed by a male laugh. Cara felt a jitter of apprehension. Stop being stupid, she thought. There was no reason for nerves.

Trish led Alec to the door of Cara's office, saying, "Well, here you are."

"I appreciate the escort," he said.

"Any time. See you later."

Now the office held just Cara and Alec. His facial bruises had faded into soft yellow and green marks, barely visible against his olive skin.

"I should have called first," he said. "I hope I'm not interrupting."

"No, of course not. Please take a seat."

He did. They smiled at each other. The assault on Clarendon Street flashed through Cara's mind. That Alec had taken a beating for her seized her tongue. She wasn't used to people giving a single, solitary damn. What was she meant to say?

"For you," he said, holding out an envelope. "My statement for your intervention order."

She took the envelope, delighted. "Thanks, but you didn't have to deliver this in person. You could have faxed or e-mailed it."

"Not from the Armed Offence Squad, I couldn't."

Sobering, she put the envelope on the desk and regarded him. "I didn't mean to sound flippant. You're taking a big risk. Does your sergeant realise that you're helping me?"

"Yeah."

"Is he mad?"

Alec hesitated. Finally, he said, "Don't worry about it. Have you heard from Gerry Vandenburg today?"

"Yes, first thing this morning, he sent over the statements for my intervention order. I'm still waiting for a copy of the medical report. They said it could take up to five working days."

"Uh-huh. Did Vandenburg say anything else to you?"

Cara paused, wary, studying Alec's expression for clues. "Not really. Why?"

"No reason."

"Is something going on?"

"Everything's fine. Trust me." His face was calm, solemn. "Do you want to meet for a drink later?"

She felt herself blush. "What for?"

"I don't know. To talk. We had a drink together the other night, didn't we?"

"But we had business to discuss. That's the only reason I asked to meet with you."

"All right. You've got my business card. Give me a buzz if you want."

He smiled the kind of smile that reached his eyes and lit them up. They were the same shade of brown as dark chocolate, she noticed. He stood, extended a hand. She clasped it. His palm was large, warm. Then he left.

Cara wasn't sure what to do, what to think. After a while, she went to the window. Alec appeared on the footpath below. He strode to the kerb, his head turning left and right as he judged the traffic. Then he struck out, jogging across the road with a loose and easy gait towards a parked car. His athletic grace suggested that he might be a runner. Sprint, however, not marathon; his build was too big for any kind of long-distance running.

"He's a real cutie."

Cara looked around.

Trish walked into the office and took a seat. "Why didn't you tell me?" she continued. "Wow, he's got some bedroom eyes on him."

Cara laughed. "I've got his number if you want to call him."

"And waste my time? It's you he wants."

"Me?" Cara sat down and stared at the floor. "That's ridiculous. I don't even know him."

"Yeah, you do. He saved you from Mick. If that doesn't tell you what kind of person he is, I don't know what will."

The afternoon ticked by in rounds of witness interviews. Three blokes in baseball caps, wearing scarves over their faces, armed with machetes, had knocked over an Asian-fusion restaurant at lunchtime, taking not just the proceeds of the till, but the wallets and purses of every customer, numbering thirty-four at the time. It would no doubt be a sizeable haul of banknotes. Upon entering the establishment nearly five hours ago, Mick had noticed the hand-written sign by the counter that read 'Cash only: no EFTPOS'.

The customers and most of the staff were gone; processed and sent on their way. The forensic technicians had packed up and left. As usual, the Armed Offence Squad was the last to leave. Mick took a can of cola from the fridge, momentarily wished for vodka, and resumed his seat at one of the laminate tables. Three things were bothering him. None of them had anything to do with the robbery.

Number one: Ward had not only come along to the crime scene, but had taken charge.

Number two: Under Ward's direction, Mick and Alec had been relegated to back-up roles. Mick had never before been treated like an assistant at the scene of an armed robbery. He didn't like it, not one little bit.

Number three: the thing that was bothering him the most, Alec's upbeat attitude.

Alec was sitting on the other side of the restaurant flipping through a newspaper. Cautiously, Mick looked about for the others. Ward and Stevo were still behind the serving counter consulting with the owners, standing well out of hearing range towards the back of the kitchen. Bull was nowhere to be seen, perhaps in the can, or outside having a smoke.

Mick sauntered across the room and stopped next to Alec's table. Alec put his finger on a line of print in the newspaper, as if to keep his place, and looked up.

"What's going on?" Mick said.

"Nothing much. Just the sports pages."

"Don't bullshit me. How come you're so fucking happy?"

Alec shrugged. "I woke up in a good mood."

"A bloke about to lose his job doesn't wake up in a good mood."

"And you should know."

Mick clenched his teeth. "I'm not losing my job."

"Aren't you? Okay. No worries."

And then, grinning, the little shithead turned back to the newspaper as if he were safe, as if he had nothing to fear. Mick grabbed the newspaper and swept the sheets to the floor. That did the trick. Alec stood up. They were nose to nose. He had Alec's full attention now.

"Tell me what's going on," Mick said, "before I beat it out of you."

"The next time you try, I'll shoot."

"Yeah?"

"Yeah. I'll put a bullet right in your guts."

"That'd be the only way you could ever win against me."

Alec laughed. "Oh mate, I've won already. You just don't know it yet."

What the fuck was he talking about? Mick clutched at the lapels of Alec's jacket. Alec shoved him away. Mick staggered, regained his balance, lifted his fists.

"Opposite sides of the room," Ward yelled, running between them and flapping his hands. "I told you to sit at opposite sides of the room, didn't I? Christ almighty, I've got to watch you bastards every minute like a couple of little kids. Now give it a rest."

They resumed their seats and glared at each other.

The front door opened and Bull came in, bringing with him a raft of cigarette smoke. Beaming, he said, "I got witnesses for the getaway vehicle, a refrigerated food van, 'Sea Dragon Freight'. Boys, we've got ourselves a walk-up start."

Mick should have felt good, but he didn't. He felt ill.

The crew returned to the squad room to continue working the case.

There was no message from the Union rep. That was odd. During their meeting on Friday, the rep hadn't expressed a whole lot of confidence, but had promised to do his best anyway. Why hadn't he called? Fuck. Rubbing at his eyes, Mick tried to concentrate.

He was supposed to be cross-checking the weapons of today's robbery against the computer database—a job usually undertaken by the goddamned analyst—but his mind wouldn't focus. The past four years kept washing over him, certain details coming back, like the Gatling gun he had personally confiscated during a raid on a gang that had robbed an armoured van of almost half a million dollars...the padlock he had snipped on the door of a hired self-storage room, revealing nine hundred top-of-the-line sewing machines and overlockers stolen on the roadside along with the semi-trailer truck...the bag of rent money ripped off at gunpoint from a real estate agent and recovered in a bus locker, the bag heavy not with coins but with tightly-rolled wads of paper money that resembled miniature hay bales, more than a hundred rolled wads that had amounted to approximately—

"Mick. Come here."

He opened his eyes. Ward stood in an office doorway, waving him closer.

Mick walked over, his heart floundering about inside his chest like a wounded thing. Ward pointed Mick at a chair and closed the office door.

"Okay, that's it," Ward said, sitting down, looking grey and old. "The word came back from upstairs. I'm sorry, mate. You're suspended, as of this second."

The world slowed and stopped. Mick gazed around at the office, stunned. A forgotten DVD lay on the desk, an action movie with plumes of fire and black lettering on the cover. Mick stared at it, unable to think. He felt an abstract kind of amazement that his lungs were still able to work.

"You okay?" Ward said.

"No. How long are they suspending me for?"

"Until things are smoothed out. You'll be on full pay. Maybe you can take a holiday."

Mick snorted. "A holiday?"

"Why not? Your wife might like time away. This kind of nasty shit is rough on a missus too. Don't forget about Janice."

"Yeah, that's right," Mick said with a long sigh. "Janice."

"Look, no matter what, getting out of Melbourne for a while is a good idea." Ward put his hand on Mick's shoulder. "The rape charge has got a second wind."

Mick leaned forward to put his face in his hands.

"Aw, Jesus," Ward said. "Now, don't cry."

But Mick wasn't crying. He never cried in front of other men, not ever—not even as a child when his mother had passed away—and he wasn't about to start. His old man had taught him from an early age, with his belt and the back of his hand, exactly how to be a man and it didn't involve crying in front of other men, that's for sure. However, there were no words Mick could find to explain any of that.

Ward continued, "Look, once this crap blows over, you'll be reinstated."

"In the Armed Offence Squad?" Mick lifted his head. "Don't bother trying to explain. I know the deal. With my suspension, I'm worth shit."

"You could always teach at the Academy."

"The Academy? Fuck that."

"At least you're still on the force."

"I'd rather eat shit and die."

"Hey, I'm in the same boat, remember?" Ward said, stung. "We're both screwed. I'm telling you, the Academy won't be so bad. I'll probably end up teaching there myself." He sighed. "All right, I need you to hand over your stuff."

"Now?"

"Sorry, mate."

"Let me see out the shift. Just give me that much, okay?" Ward hesitated.

"Come on, Sarge," Mick continued. "Please."

Against regulations, Ward agreed.

Mick sat with the crew for a time, numb, their conversations running over the top of him. Then he slipped into the locker room and collected his briefcase and gym tote. Car keys were in his pocket already. He took an unmarked sedan.

At 5 p.m., traffic was already thick on St. Kilda Road. Fat, woolly clouds hung so close to the ground that Mick fancied he could touch them if he wound down his window and stuck out an arm. He headed straight home.

In his apartment building, the rising lift made its regular whining, whistling clamour, as if a tormented creature was trapped within the mechanism. For once, Mick didn't mind. Since it would be one of the last times he'd ever hear this particular lift, he listened intently, committing the racket to memory, to heart. In life, when something happened for the last time, the loss was only clear in retrospect. Mick felt privileged. This sliver of prescience was a gift.

Using keys, he opened his front door. Laughter came from the lounge room. Putting down his briefcase in the entrance hall, he wandered towards the voices.

Janice looked at him, her face flushed. Sitting opposite her at the dining table was a man perhaps in his late thirties: handsome, goatee beard, blonde curly hair worn short with sideburns. Janice and the man each had a laptop open in front of them.

"This is Tristan, our theatre critic," Janice said, eyes shining. "Mick, I take it your day is done. Grab a drink. We're talking about the six elements of Aristotle's drama theory, and how they might apply to character-driven plays, especially the experimental kind."

Tristan sniggered.

Giggling, Janice said, "Do you think my soon-to-be ex understood a word of that?"

"Oh, darling, you can be a cruel bitch. I love it."

They stared at Mick like he was a fool, a joke. A half-bottle of red sat on the table between them, an empty bottle alongside.

Showing his teeth, Mick approached. "Is this your boyfriend?"

"Are you kidding?" Janice said. "Is he my what?"

"Boyfriend. The man you want instead of me."

Janice and Tristan glanced at each other and burst into gales of fresh laughter. Mick raised the gun. They didn't notice at first. By the time they noticed, it was too late.

"Tristan likes men," Janice said. "Oh, what do you think you're doing?"

"I'm not sure," Mick replied.

The gun went off. The noise was deafening. A whirl of blood and brains spackled the white wall. With a frozen, startled expression and a dark purple hole above one of her manicured eyebrows, Janice dropped from the chair and spilled across the floor like a glass of water. She didn't move. It occurred to Mick that she must have been shot in the face.

Surprised, Mick watched as his finger tightened on the trigger again and again, until the magazine was empty and Janice was full of holes. He gradually became aware of Tristan, who was screaming a long and shrill note over and over, like a parrot. Mick went back to his briefcase in the entrance hall. After swapping out the empty magazine for a fresh one, he left the apartment.

TWENTY-TWO

Vandenburg walked across the Armed Offence Squad. When he reached the desks belonging to Alec's crew, he said, "Good afternoon. I'm here to arrest Thompson for the rape of Cara Haynes. Where is he?"

Alec regarded Stevo, who shrugged.

"We don't know, sir," Alec said. "You'll have to ask Sergeant Ward. He's in with the Detective Inspector at the moment."

"Thank you," Vandenburg said, and headed towards Vaughan's office on the other side of the squad room.

Stevo crossed his arms. "Mick won't like getting arrested."

"Who cares if he likes it or not?"

"Yeah, but Vandenburg is such a little bloke, is what I mean."

"Well, if Mick resists arrest, I'll step in to help."

Stevo sighed. "Yeah, me too. We'll need all hands on deck for that job."

Vandenburg came out of the office trailing Ward and Detective Inspector Vaughan. They approached the desks.

"Neither of you has seen Thompson?" Vaughan said.

"Not for about an hour," Alec said. "He could be down in the gym."

Ward, sweating, uneasy, glanced about. "Where's Bull?"

"In the tea room," Stevo said. "You want me to check if he knows Mick's whereabouts?"

Ward nodded. Stevo came back with Bull, who hadn't seen Mick either.

"He's probably pissed off with one of the cars," Bull said. "You know how he is."

Vandenburg put his hands on his hips. "No one knows where he's gone? I don't like it. We should try to get onto Cara Haynes."

"Do you think he'd go see her?" Alec said.

"I don't know what the devil this man would do. Has anyone got her contact details?"

Alec did, and rang Premiere Press first. Cara had already left for the day. Next, he rang her mobile and got voicemail. He didn't leave any messages.

"I've got her home number in my file," Vandenburg said, turning away. "I'll let you know if I reach her. In the meantime, please do me a favour and find Thompson."

As was her habit now when returning to her house, Cara drove in slow laps up and down the street, checking for unfamiliar sedans that could be unmarked police vehicles. Satisfied, she pulled into the driveway and parked in the carport.

Once inside the house, she locked the front door and switched on the lights. Everything was in its place. The house was as cold as a meat locker. She thought about turning on the space heater—the temperature in here must be less than ten degrees—but decided against it. Fifteen minutes, tops, and she'd be gone. She took her suitcase into the bedroom, and kicked off her shoes.

First things first, she dumped the dirty washing into the laundry hamper. She would have to run a load tomorrow or the next day. Back in the bedroom, opening the wardrobe doors, she paused to consider her clothes. Hypothetically speaking, if she were to call Alec Castellano and say yes to that drink he'd suggested, what would she wear?

That depended on the venue. Assuming she wouldn't know where they were going, the safest option was a dress. Perhaps the woollen stripe or the one with mint-coloured lace. Hang on, black trousers might be better, teamed with the swing jacket or maybe the camel-coloured trench. No, that didn't seem right either. A skirt? But they were business-cut.

Frowning, she slid coat hanger after coat hanger along the rail, searching. The problem was that she didn't go out much. Usually when she socialised, it was straight after work, which meant she wore the same outfit she'd chosen for the office that particular day. Then again, she wouldn't be calling Alec anyway, so this speculation about outfits was a moot point...

But if Alec had rung to see if she'd changed her mind about meeting up with him, it would be rude not to call back. And besides, she should thank him for his statement, which was very detailed at two pages in length.

She went to the entrance hall where her handbag sat on the console table. She took out her mobile, remembered that it was still switched off, and thumbed the button. The familiar start-up graphics wended across the screen. The knock on the door came as a jolting shock. She dropped the phone to the console table, snatched the capsicum spray from her bag.

"Who is it?" she said, her heart banging into her throat.

"Gerard Vandenburg."

"Oh, Gerard," she said with a small laugh of relief. "Give me a second."

Cara put the spray on the console table next to her phone. As she turned the lock, she realised her mistake. The door shoved open, staggering her backwards. Despite all of her care, her diligence, he'd got her using a simple lie.

Mick stepped inside the house.

He took a deep, satisfied sigh. With his coat, briefcase and big smile, he looked like a husband coming home from work. Keeping his eyes on her, he reached one arm behind his back and pushed the door closed. Déjà vu. Life was doubling back on itself again. A buzzing sensation started up in Cara's head. The lock clicked. The sound stopped her breath. Mick stared at her intently for a long time, as if committing her face to memory.

"You've been hard to catch at home lately," he said, putting his briefcase down, taking off his coat. "Where have you been?"

She didn't answer. Mick slung his coat over the back of the nearest couch. The capsicum spray on the console table was too far away for her to reach. He stepped closer. She stepped back. Her legs were shaking.

"Every night, you're not here," he went on. "Where are you? Tell me. With another bloke? You're fucking someone else already, isn't that right?"

"No."

Mick slapped her with enough force to rattle her teeth.

"Is it Alec?" he said, his mouth pinched.

"What? No, I'm not seeing anybody, I swear."

She realised the backhander was coming, saw the swing of his arm moving towards her, but she didn't feel the blow. Instead, she opened her eyes and found herself lying on the carpet while trinkets from the bookcase landed around her—framed postcards, a scented candle, unshelved paperbacks—as if the bookcase were tipping over. She looked around. The bookcase, rocking back and forth, slowed and stopped. She understood that she had fallen against it, and ended up on the floor.

Her back hurt. The pain across her face made her eyes water.

Mick's shoes moved into her line of sight. He fitted his hands under her arms, lifted her as easily as if she were a child, and hugged her close. One of Ethan's self-defence instructions came to mind: if your attacker is up against you, spear your fingers into his throat. At the time, it had seemed plausible. But now, crushed in Mick's grip, dwarfed by him, she recognised that she could strike at him all goddamned day and it wouldn't make any difference.

One of his hands moved through her hair, made a fist, turned her head. He put his lips and tongue on her exposed throat. He tightened his other arm about her waist as if intending to snap her in half. She couldn't breathe.

"Oh God, I've missed you," he whispered. "I've missed you, baby."

Alec gaped at Stevo, Bull, Ward, Detective Inspector Vaughan, each man white-faced, stunned. So too Vandenburg and his subordinates, Patel and O'Brien, who had rushed into the Armed Offence Squad as soon as they'd heard. Alec supposed that his own face held the exact same look of stupefaction.

Christ, it was hard to believe. Even for Mick.

But they'd got the news straight from Homicide Squad; it had to be legitimate. The attending senior sergeant had sent digital pictures of the crime scene, corpse, and the shell-shocked witness, a man named Tristan Bradley, a writer for the same newspaper as the late Janice Thompson.

Bull lit a cigarette with trembling hands. Exhaling a plume of smoke, he muttered, "I knew Mick was a bit twitchy, but fucking hell."

Vandenburg recovered first. "All right, let's get cracking. We have two priorities: locate Thompson and secure Cara Haynes. Find out which car he took, and get an all-points bulletin on the licence plate."

"Got it," Stevo said, taking a seat, reaching for the landline.

"We don't know where she is at present, but let's send a couple of divvy vans to Cara's home address anyway. Make sure there's one sergeant apiece, no double-ups of constables. And no sirens, either. If he's there, we don't want to spook him."

Bull nodded and picked up a handset.

"He's armed," Vaughan said, hurrying towards his office. "I'll line up the SOGgies."

"Good idea. And if we're going after Thompson ourselves, we'll probably need vests." Vandenburg turned around. "Irene, John, would you mind rustling up protective equipment?"

They took off.

"Now, Frank, you're the closest thing Thompson has to an authority figure. See if you can raise him on the phone or radio."

Ward, his eyes glazed, kept his head down as if he hadn't heard.

"Frank!" Vandenburg shouted.

Ward looked up.

Vandenburg went on, "If you get hold of Thompson, don't tip our hand. Tell him anything but the truth. Tell him there's been another armed robbery, and you need him to come in. Can you do that?"

Ashen, Ward nodded and wandered off.

"I've got to find Cara," Alec said, standing up, opening his desk drawer and taking out the shoulder holster with its sheathed .40 calibre semi-automatic.

"Hold your horses," Vandenburg said. "We don't know where she is. Let's not waste time driving to the wrong location. I'll try her numbers one more time. Get the schematics of her rental property sent over from the real estate agent."

Excited, breathing hard, Mick squeezed Cara around the waist, licking and mauling from one side of her throat to the other. He walked her backwards, and pushed her against the wall.

The landline rang, loud and shrill.

Mick reacted, raising his head, holding his breath, alert. His grip on her loosened.

The answering machine picked up the call, announcing: "You've reached Cara Haynes. I can't come to the phone at the moment. Please leave a message and I'll get back to you."

The answering machine beeped.

"This is Gerry Vandenburg. Cara, I've been leaving messages for you everywhere. Look, it's imperative that you leave the house immediately. All right? This is very important. Leave the house and call me from a public place, like a pub, anywhere. I'll explain later."

The call disconnected. Cara felt faint. The scariest thing about life was the way catastrophe turned on the smallest thing, the most insignificant detail, and here it was again. If she'd left her mobile switched on after leaving work, she could have received one of Vandenburg's warnings in time, bypassed home, and driven instead to a safe place.

"Where are your house keys?" Mick said.

When she didn't answer, he shook her.

"In my handbag," she said. "On the console table."

He strode over, still holding her about the waist. Cara's stockinged feet, up on tiptoes and barely touching the ground, fumbled over the carpet, knocked against his shoes as he took each step. Please don't let him see the capsicum spray, she thought. Please.

Mick used his free hand to upend her handbag and scatter its contents. He began rifling through the items. Cara was right next to the capsicum spray but unable to reach for it. Her arms were locked within Mick's one-armed bear hug.

Picking up the key ring, he said, "Which does your deadlocks?"

"The purple one."

He rotated the key in the front door lock, and then tested the lock to make sure that it would no longer turn from the inside. Dragging her with him, he continued on through the kitchen and deadlocked the back door too. Now Cara couldn't get out. He pocketed the keys and let her go. Reeling, she stumbled, almost fell. He ripped the landline out of the wall socket and threw it into the kitchen sink, exploding dishes and glasses. Cara shrieked.

Grabbing her by the hair, he led her into the lounge room and swung her into one of the couches. He shrugged off his jacket, loosened his tie. There was blood over the front of his white shirt in a v-shape, finely misted, as if puffed from an aerosol container. Along the rim of his right cuff were larger flecks. Cara's teeth began to chatter.

Mick dropped heavily into the other couch and noticed the bloodstains.

"Aw, shit," he said, annoyed, scraping at his cuff with a fingernail.

Then he froze. After a moment, the tension in his face softened, his lips turned down. Cara's breath seized. God almighty, was he about to cry? With a moan, he slumped back in the couch and put his hands to his face.

"My wife's dead," he murmured.

Cara's mouth dried out. "Dead?"

"Yep." He dropped his hands. "I drove here in her car, a shitty hatchback roller-skate. By the way, I saw you do your little recce up and down the street before you pulled into your driveway. What were you looking for? Me in a BMW squad car?"

She nodded, exhausted.

"Ha," he said. "Fooled you."

"Yes, you did. What happened to your wife?"

"She got shot."

Cara brought a cushion up to her chin, hugged it. "By you?"

"To be honest, I'm not sure. I can't really remember. But I was the only one with a gun, so yeah, it must have been me." He clenched his jaw. "Fuck going to jail, though. No way."

"What will you do? Go on the run?"

"Nope. Fuck that too."

Meaning what? Cara's heart flittered in panic.

"Maybe it was an accident," she said, trying to placate him. "If you explain that you made a mistake, I'm sure you won't get into trouble."

"Nah, I really did want her dead."

"Do you want me dead too?"

"Yeah, but not yet." He smiled. "Right now, I wouldn't mind a beer."

Stricken, she couldn't move. He waited a few moments, staring at her, and then he raised his eyebrows expectantly, peevishly.

"Hey, are you deaf? I asked for a beer. Or vodka, if you've got it."

Her legs were almost too weak to bear her weight. Cara stumbled to the kitchen, leaning against the wall, holding to the backs of dining chairs. At the refrigerator, she hesitated. Crossing instead to the knife block on the bench, she drew out the biggest one, the carving knife. The handle felt solid and hefty. She returned to the lounge room.

He had his back to her, combing through her music collection, dropping each CD to the carpet once he'd glanced at the cover. She stole up behind him.

"You got anything other than this classical shit?" he called, and turned around.

She stopped, perhaps a metre away from him. His face opened out in surprise. Then he laughed, straight from the belly, the type of fond, amused laugh that a parent might give when a much-loved child does something adorable. Cara's resolve faltered.

Mick gestured at the knife. "How long do you reckon before I get that away from you?"

She raised the knife as if to stab him. The blade shimmied from side to side in her trembling hand. Seconds passed. Mick's grinning face slackened, turned to stone. Her hand shook even harder. Finally, in resignation, she lowered the knife.

"That's better." Mick turned to the CD rack. "Don't forget my drink."

She got it for him. They resumed their places on the respective couches. Mick opened the beer and took a long swallow, never taking his gaze from her. His eyes were dead and glassy, doll's eyes. Staring into them was like staring into the abyss.

From the console table directly behind her, Cara's mobile phone rang.

Galvanised, she leapt over the back of the couch, fleet as a deer. Mick scrabbled to put his drink on the coffee table, vaulting from his seat. She reached the phone first and answered it.

"I'm at home!" she screamed. "Help me!"

He pulled the phone from her grasp and pitched it across the room. The phone hit the wall. By the time he spun around, Cara had hold of the capsicum spray and was fumbling with the lid. He punched her. She bounced off the front door and spilled to the carpet.

The sluggish, hot flow trickling through her nostrils must be blood, she realised. The side of her face was numb. Mick lifted her head by a fistful of hair. He was down on one knee, pressing the can against her cheek.

"You were going to use this shit on me, weren't you?" he said.

"Please, stop."

"Do you want to try it? Do you? You want to try this shit?"

"No. Let me go. Please, let me go."

After a moment, he seemed to regain his composure. He released his grip on her hair. She rolled onto her back. Straightening, he pocketed the capsicum spray and picked up his briefcase. Cara felt a giddy buoyancy of spirits. He must be leaving. Perhaps her terror and the blood on her face had moved him at last, had brought him to his senses.

"Okay, beautiful," he said. "Let's fuck."

Hoisting her by an elbow, picking up his briefcase, he dragged her into the bedroom. Her suitcase was sitting on the foot of the bed and he glared at it for a while before kicking it to the floor.

"Every one of you bitches is the fucking same," he said, shoving her on to the mattress. "Always ready to walk out. Let me show you what happens to bitches when they walk out."

"Don't hurt me," she said. "I'll do whatever you want."

"That's right, you will."

Mick dropped his briefcase, removed his tie, unbuttoned his shirt. Red spatters covered his chest from where his wife's blood had soaked through the material. He threw the shirt aside. His eyes were empty, the dilated pupils like black holes.

"Take your clothes off," he said.

She began to cry.

From the lounge room, Cara's mobile phone trilled.

"What the fuck?" he said. "I thought I broke that fucking thing."

He stormed out of the room. Cara leapt from the bed, grabbed Mick's briefcase, and upended its contents over the mattress, searching frantically. Woollen gloves, shaving kit, sunglasses. Where was it? She could hear Mick in the lounge room, grunting and snarling, the phone ringing on and on. There was a tinkling noise. The ringing stopped. A rhythmic pounding started up, the noise thundering through the house, shaking the foundations. He must be stomping the remains of the mobile phone beneath his heel, over and over.

Cara found the gun.

It was heavier than it looked. The stippled pattern on the handle was rubberised, sticking the gun against her palm. Whether or not the gun was loaded, she couldn't tell. She flipped it from side to side, checking for anything that might look familiar, anything that might tell her how the hell to use this thing. Nothing popped out at her. Oh God, every part of the gun looked the same: matt and black.

Mick appeared in the doorway.

For a second, his face registered shock. Cara drew away on her knees, shifting towards the top of the bed. When she was pressed up against the wall, as far away from him as she could get, she pointed the gun at arm's length.

"Don't come any closer," she said.

Shaking his head with a half-smile, as if she'd made one joke too many and he was getting a little tired of her shenanigans, he put his fists on his hips. "What are you going to do with that?" he said. "Throw it at me?"

Cara brought the gun back for a quick inspection. There was a recessed button located next to the trigger guard. Tentatively, she put her thumb on it.

"You don't want to press that," Mick said, taking a step into the room. "If you do, the magazine drops out."

"What does that mean?"

"You've lost your bullets."

"How do I know you're not lying?"

He shrugged. "Try it and see."

Panting, light-headed, Cara twisted the gun about and scanned it, trying her best to keep her eyes on Mick at the same time. He had gained ground, however, now standing by the foot of the bed.

"Get back," she said, shaking, pointing the gun at him again.

"Or you'll do what?"

He took another step. As he neared the bedside, she squirmed backwards on her knees. Beneath the angular barrel of the gun, high up on the handle, was a black lever. It was in the 'up' position. She used her thumb to press it down. Mick halted. The taut look on his face told her she was on the right track.

"You know you can't point a weapon at a copper and get away with it," he said. "Drop the pistol and I won't hurt you. Okay? Do we have a deal?"

Wincing, she pulled the trigger.

Nothing happened. She gasped, sobbed, gaped at the damn gun.

He held out his hand. "See? Come on. Don't make me take it off you."

The back section of the barrel carried a pattern of wavy serrations as if to improve purchase. Cara pinched at the serrations with her free hand and pulled hard. The roof of the barrel slid back. The weapon made a snapping sound. At the same time, beneath her palm against the handle, she felt the telegraphed energy of a hidden mechanism clacking inside the gun. It must be loaded this time, ready to fire.

"Get on the floor," she said. "Face down. I mean it."

Mick bared his teeth. "Now I'm really going to hurt you."

He lunged.

She pulled the trigger.

The explosive boom, the orange flame, the convulsive kick of the gun as if a live thing were trying to leap from her hands; these sudden and unexpected things closed her eyes involuntarily. When she opened them again, Mick was gone.

Panic streaked through her body.

"Where are you?" she screamed.

Flattening herself against the wall, she swung the gun at arm's length. How had he moved out of sight so fast? At any second, he would jump from his hiding place like a jack-in-the-box. She held her breath and strained her ears.

Not one sound from within the house.

She clambered from the bed. Creeping on stockinged feet, she exited the bedroom and paused in the doorway. The hall was empty. The portion of lounge room she could see was empty too. Using the muzzle of the gun, she pushed open the door of the spare room. Empty. She worked her way through the house. Mick wasn't anywhere. How could that be? The house was quiet.

"You're not going to frighten me, are you?" she called.

Then an outlandish possibility came to mind. She returned to her bedroom. There he was on the far side of the bed near the window, sprawled across the floor on his back with one hand flung over his head and the other resting on his chest, the fingers curled into a relaxed posture, as if he were dozing.

"Mick? Are you all right?"

She approached in a wide circle, pointing the gun. One of his eyes was half-open, the hooded lid showing a sliver of iris, the light blue of a robin's egg. Cara put a hand to her mouth. Was he looking at her? Seconds passed. No, he wasn't looking at her. He wasn't looking at anything. Next to the hand on his chest was a neat, bloodied hole.

"Oh, God," she whispered. "Mick, did I kill you?"

No answer. He didn't appear to be breathing. Perhaps he was dead, she considered, or else playing possum. Either way, she had to get out. But she needed the house keys.

The house keys were in his pocket.

She nudged him with her toes. His body rocked and lay still, the half-open eye riveted on infinity. Kneeling down, trembling, waiting for him to spring to life, aiming the gun at his cheek, Cara searched his pockets. When her fingers closed on the key ring, she ran to the front door, turned the purple key in the lock and flung the door open, stumbling outside.

What the hell was going on?

Vehicles were everywhere. Red and blue flashing lights filled the street. Men dressed like soldiers lined the front lawn. Shotguns aimed, they hurried towards her, ready to shoot. Quailing, Cara staggered back. Gerard Vandenburg's face came into focus.

"Give me the gun," he said, twisting her arm, taking the weapon. "Where's Thompson?"

"I shot him."

"Where is he?"

"In my bedroom. I think I've killed him."

"Is anyone else in the house?"

"No."

"Does he have other weapons apart from this one?"

"I don't think so."

"He's in the master bedroom," Vandenburg called out, "alone, likely unarmed. Wounded or deceased."

Vandenburg and the men dressed like soldiers ran past her into the house. Cara gazed at the sky. A mass of clouds was whisking along on an unfelt breeze. The stars bore down, cold and hard, the points of a million needles making her dizzy, spinning the earth beneath her feet. Blackness rolled in.

"Can you walk?" Alec said.

She opened her eyes. Alec was holding her shoulders. His grasp, she realised, was the only thing keeping her upright. Could she walk? Probably not. Her legs had lost their bones. She tried to answer him but her throat had closed.

"It's okay," Alec said. "I've got you."

His arm went around her back. He bent down, hooked his other arm behind her knees, and picked her up. The swing of her body through space momentarily disoriented her. Afraid, she clutched at him.

"What's going on?" she said.

"You're safe. Everything's all right. You're safe now."

Alec carried her across the lawn towards the waiting ambulance.

DEBORAH SHELDON

DEBORAH SHELDON is a multi-award-winning author and anthology editor from Melbourne, Australia. She writes poems, short stories, novellas and novels across the darker spectrum of horror, crime and noir. Her award-nominated titles include the novels *Cretaceous Canyon*, *Body Farm Z*, *Contrition*, and *Devil Dragon*; the novella *Thylacines*; and collections *Figments and Fragments: Dark Stories*, and *Liminal Spaces: Horror Stories*. Her latest title is the novella *Redhead Town*.

Deb's collection *Perfect Little Stitches and Other Stories* won the Australian Shadows 'Best Collected Work' Award, was shortlisted for an Aurealis Award, and long-listed for a Bram Stoker. Her short fiction has been widely published, shortlisted for numerous Australian Shadows and Aurealis Awards, translated, and included in various 'best of' anthologies. Deb has won the Australian Shadows 'Best Edited Work' Award twice: for *Midnight Echo 14*, and for the anthology she conceived and edited *Spawn: Weird Horror Tales About Pregnancy, Birth and Babies*. Her anthology *Killer Creatures Down Under: Horror Stories with Bite* is currently shortlisted for the Australian Shadows 'Best Anthology' Award. Forthcoming in 2024 is *Spawn 2: More Weird Tales About Pregnancy, Birth and Babies*. As senior editor at IFWG Publishing, she specialises in horror anthologies of her own design.

Other credits include feature articles for magazines, non-fiction books (Reed Books, Random House), TV scripts such as *NEIGHBOURS*, stage plays, and awards for both script editing and medical writing.

Visit Deb at deborahsheldon.wordpress.com

If you are a fan of horror stories and tales,
you'll want to follow Undertaker Books.

We're bringing you stories to take to your grave.

SIGN UP FOR OUR NEWSLETTER ONLINE